THE S  REY

THE SHIFTING PRICE
OF PREY

Spellcrackers.com

SUZANNE MCLEOD

The right of Suzanne McLeod to be identified as the author
of this work has been asserted by her in accordance with
the Copyright, Designs and Patents Act 1988.

First published in Great Britain in 2012 by Gollancz
An imprint of the Orion Publishing Group
Orion House, 5 Upper St Martin's Lane,
London WC2H 9EA

An Hachette UK Company

A CIP catalogue record for this book
is available from the British Library

ISBN 978 0 575 09840 4

3 5 7 9 10 8 6 4 2

Typeset by Deltatype Ltd, Birkenhead, Merseyside

Printed in Great Britain by
CPI Group (UK) Ltd, Croydon CRO 4YY

The Orion Publishing Group's policy is to use papers
that are natural, renewable and recyclable products and
made from wood grown in sustainable forests. The logging
and manufacturing processes are expected to conform to
the environmental regulations of the country of origin.

www.spellcrackers.com
www.orionbooks.co.uk

For Mum and Dad
With Love

Chapter One

The garden fairy was as desiccated as a dead frog squashed by a passing car and left to dry in the summer sun. Its claw-tipped appendages, stringy arms and legs, big bulbous eyes and wide slash of a mouth made it look even more amphibian-like. With its large gossamer wings folded down its back, it wasn't much bigger than a frog either, so there was plenty of room in the plastic sandwich box that served as its makeshift coffin.

Though, as I adjusted the angle of the lamp and bent over the marble-topped desk to peer closer, I noted, of course, that 'it' wasn't correct. Judging by the lack of neck-frill, and the corkscrew-shaped penis pointing down past the fairy's knees— 'it' was a 'he'.

And 'he' was a perfect example of why September – mating season for garden fairies – is called the screaming month.

Except this was the middle of June.

Hatching time, not mating time.

The fairy's death was a freak of nature— if I was to believe my 'client', Mr Lampy.

'More like a freaking scam,' I muttered, hoping my co-worker was digging up some much needed dirt during his sneaky look round, because so far, when it came to the dead garden fairy, Mr Lampy was looking annoyingly squeaky clean.

Regrettably the same couldn't be said for his house.

I shot a disgusted glance around me. The large high-ceilinged room was home to a mismatched collection of

1

wooden junk-shop furniture that was hosting enough multi-coloured fungi to devour a dead forest. The whole ground floor of the house was the same. Considering the Victorian terrace was in fashionable Primrose Hill, London's celebrity-studded urban village, and had to be worth a good couple of million, it made for an unlikely combination. Of course, Mr Lampy was ancient so he'd probably been here longer than the house, or even the village, itself. Once a gnome's settled their manor, it takes a lot to uproot them.

Not to mention that Primrose Hill (the actual park) has always been a major breeding site for garden fairies, and still was, judging by the occupants of the other eight sandwich-box coffins stacked to my left. The small creatures have long been valued by those with green fingers – like gnomes – as nature's magical helper. While the fairies are alive and zipping.

Dead, they have another use, one that is illegal without a licence.

My job was to issue the licence, but only if the fairy's death was natural, not induced.

I picked up the padded kitchen tongs next to the box and carefully turned the fairy over, the acid-free tissue paper beneath him rustling as I did. Despite looking like sun-dried roadkill, there were no obvious injuries to his little body. I reached out to gently lift his chin—

A low growl stopped me.

I squinted left into the unblinking, warning glare of the large ginger cat sitting to attention on the desk, the tip of its tail twitching over its front paws. The cat was close enough that I could see a tiny reflection of my angular features in its dark oval pupils. I glared back, my own catlike sidhe pupils no doubt mimicking the animal's in the dimly lit room. Not that my glare fazed the huge ginger tom one bit. But then my maternal grandmother is a sidhe queen – something I'd learned only recently. I was still coming to terms with it since my queenly grandmother liked me a whole lot less than the cat appeared to – so maybe the cat's unconcern was apt.

'I'm wearing gloves, puss.' I waggled my latex-covered fingers in front of its disapproving face. 'I know better than to contaminate the merchandise, scam or not.'

It continued to give me the evil-feline stare, and I sighed. Why the hell I was talking to a cat anyway? It wasn't like it could answer back; it was just one of the gnome's trained gun-dogs, or rather gun-cats, used to retrieve dead fairies like the one in front of me before male-member shrinkage rendered it worthless.

Awareness prickled down my spine and I turned, expecting to find the gnome doing a lecherous eyeball of my arse from the doorway.

But the large room was devoid of life …

If, that is, you discounted the other dozen or so cats that made up the gnome's clowder of fairy-finding felines, and the floor-to-ceiling shelves full of variously sized plastic boxes and glass tanks that held the gnome's stock. Not all of which was as lifeless as the fairy in front of me and some of which had their own creepy eyeballs.

I opened the metaphysical part of me that *sees* the magic, and *looked*, repeating the check I'd done on arrival. But the only active spells were the Buffer spell in the tiny crystal stuck to my phone and the mega-strength Knock-back Wards buzzing like electrified bars over the room's tall sash windows. With all his stock, it wasn't a surprise the gnome took security seriously.

I shrugged the 'watching eyes' feeling off, blaming it on the creepsville house and returned my attention to the dead fairy. I angled the light and this time ignored the cat's growl as I lifted the fairy's little chin. Sure enough his throat had been slit; a long slash from ear to ear. A wound that would have killed him instantly at the height of his frenzied fairy ecstasy.

3

The noisy slap-slap of bare feet on wooden boards signalled the gnome's imminent return. I pulled off the surgical gloves with a snap, tucked them into my jacket pocket, and sat down quickly on the overstuffed guest chair.

'Refreshments, Ms Taylor,' the gnome said as he bustled into the room. He rounded the desk and placed a tea tray covered in a lace-edged cloth next to the fairy's plastic coffin.

I stifled a shudder. Small yellow-green things speared through with cocktail sticks had been stuck hedgehog-like into a tin-foiled potato; they were still writhing. The sickly sweet smell steaming from the cup and saucer wasn't any more appetising. Only the opaque lumps of what looked like unpolished quartz seemed vaguely edible.

'Mead-soaked slugs. Nettle tea with lavender blossom honey, and raw sugar crystals.' The wrinkles in the gnome's round face deepened as he beamed, nearly blinding me with the brilliance of his ultra-white human dentures.

Vodka, bacon sandwiches and liquorice torpedoes are more my snack of choice, but even if he'd offered those I wouldn't have trusted them. I'd only agreed to his 'refreshments' so I could examine the fairy without having the gnome's beady little eyes crawling all over me. He'd spent the whole time since I'd arrived addressing my chest – and not just because it was on a level with his face. Nor because I have much to address; I'm slender, verging on skinny. And this not being my first visit, I'd deliberately covered up, buttoning my shirt to the neck and wearing the jacket of my business suit, despite it being too warm in the summer weather. Irritatingly, it hadn't stopped him ogling. Or copping a feel of my butt as he'd ushered me in (which got him a swift elbow to the temple; annoyingly it only made his ogling more enthusiastic). So the idea of checking out the dead fairy while he watched was way too icky.

'Thank you, Mr Lampy,' I said politely, since even if he was currently suspect he had paid the Spellcrackers.com fee up

4

front so was, until proved otherwise, a client, though not one I wanted any of my staff subjected to. 'But the glass of water I asked for would've been fine.'

'Ah, but I know this is what you fairies like, Ms Taylor.' He pushed the plate towards me, the edges of the mustard-coloured lichen mapping his bald pate crinkling with encouragement.

'I'm sidhe fae, Mr Lampy,' I said, more sharply and less patiently than I had the first three times I'd corrected him. 'Sidhe fae are not related to garden fairies.' Something you'd think a gnome, one of the Others should know. 'We have more genes in common with an ordinary human than a chimpanzee does. While garden fairies are more closely related to insects and amphibians.'

'Of course they are.' He gave me a sly wink and tapped the sandwich box. 'But these little beauties can tap into the magic, much as you yourself can, unlike even the most extraordinary of humans.' He clasped his fat little hands and rested them on his shirt-straining pot belly. 'It's what makes them so desirable.'

Ugh. Dried garden fairy parts – smoked, snorted, imbibed or injected – are the equivalent of magical Viagra, and not just in the obvious, sexual way, but in the boosting-your-magical-abilities way. The resulting power spike is said to be a hundred times better than sugar (the standard way to amp up magic), a phenomenon discovered in 1835 by Jacob Sabine, a prominent Victorian naturalist and wizard. By the end of the nineteenth century, garden fairies had gone from being as common as dragonflies to near extinction, only to be saved by Sclalter's Intervention, the Parliamentary Bill passed in 1902 which now protected them.

I'd fine-combed the legal stuff, hoping for something to nail the gnome with.

Unfortunately, the gnome was an accredited conservationist and therefore an authorised dealer. He was allowed to trade as a way to independently fund his fairy preservation work. Once licensed, the fairy would be worth around a grand. Given its rarity for this time of year, the gnome could probably charge three, maybe five times that. Add in that the Carnival Fantastique was in town, and ten times probably wasn't beyond the realms of the gnome's greedy calculations. Which was a hell of a monetary incentive to find a way to fast-track nature. The only thing stopping him coining it in was me.

Anyone would think he'd be more politic about things. But that's gnomes for you.

'It's very early in the year for the fairies to be ... active,' I said, opting for euphemistic vagueness.

The gnome hit me with another denture-filled leer. 'But you've examined the body haven't you, Ms Taylor? So you can confirm that his death was part of normal mating and entirely unassisted.'

It was— if you ignored the fact that the male fairy's near decapitation had been assisted by the female fairy's neck-frill stiffening during fertilisation. Black widows have nothing on garden fairies.

'I'll agree it looks like it,' I said. 'But that doesn't stop it being much earlier.'

'I think it's a side-effect of global warming.' The gnome's eyes behind his glasses watered, as he gave me his version of an innocent look.

Global warming, my arse. 'I see.'

Of course, there was always the other, illegally assisted alternative. That somewhere, the gnome had a hothouse dialled up to tropical, and had used it to accelerate the fairy's life cycle, then trapped him in an airtight box with a rubber frog and a handful of foxglove flowers a.k.a. fairy catnip. As soon as the excited, albeit confused, fairy lost consciousness, the gnome had slit the fairy's throat and left him to dry out with a sachet of silicate crystals. That was the modern way: the

Victorians used to use live frogs and rack the comatose fairies in small oak-lined smoking bins.

Trouble was, as the Victorians had discovered, garden fairies are almost impossible to breed in captivity. They need natural light. Which means glass. And they zip. Zipping into glass at the fairy equivalent of fifty miles an hour is like bugs hitting a car window. They splat.

The only time captive breeding had succeeded on any scale was when the Victorians had relocated Crystal Palace to Sydenham Park. An accident had placed it right on top of the local fairy hatching ground. So if the gnome did have a hothouse, it would have to be at least the size of a football field. Something that huge was hard to hide, even with magic. But my gut said the gnome was up to something. And I was determined to prove it. Only every time I'd moved out of his 'office' during my last inspection, he'd stuck to me like some of his nasty lichen, so now I was back, with my invisible-to-the-gnome co-worker in tow.

I unpacked my kit – measuring callipers, scalpels, pestle and mortar, ultra-violet light, magnifying glass and various potions and test spells I needed to complete the extensive tests prior to granting the licences – carefully lining up the items on the marble-top table under the gnome's eager, creepy gaze.

Ugh. Last thing I wanted was him rubbernecking my every move for the next couple of hours.

'This is going to take some time,' I said firmly as I placed the last, most important item on the table: a packet containing the manmade crystals I'd superglue to each fairy's head (the least valuable part), each crystal holding the actual Licence spell. The crystals were clear just now, but would glow viridian green once activated. 'And I prefer to work undisturbed, Mr Lampy. I find there's less chance of contamination or error that way.' I paused, baring my teeth in a wide smile; he might not be a goblin, but he'd recognise the threat. 'I'd hate to have to resample anything because I was distracted.' In other words: *leave me alone or I'll chop large expensive chunks off your stock.*

The gnome got the message. 'Of course, Ms Taylor. I'll be in the kitchen if you need me.'

I needed him like a vamp needed a suntan! He scuttled away and I settled down to work until my co-worker reappeared. Hopefully with something incriminating that would spell bad news for the nasty gnome.

Chapter Two

Thirty minutes later a familiar brush against my senses had me looking over my shoulder again to see a clear crystal appear on the room's threshold. The crystal started to glow with the pink blush of dawn and the heady scent of peat and whisky shimmered through the room, sending desire shuddering through my body. I braced my hands on the desk, let the power ride me to the soft edge of pleasure, then bit back a frustrated cry as the spell set, leaving me wanting.

The cause wasn't the spell: it was a simple Privacy one. Anyone could buy five of them from the Witches' Market in Covent Garden for under a tenner. No, my reaction was down to the person who'd activated it. Tavish, the kelpie, defacto *àrd-cheann* – Top Dog, or in Tavish's case, Top Water Horse – of London's fae, and my co-worker/employee … when the inclination took him.

It didn't matter what spells Tavish set; if I was near it was like getting blasted with magical pheromones. The longer we worked together, the more potent it got. I'd learned the hard way not to block it, as all that did was make my frustration worse. Not that he was doing it deliberately: in fact, when I'd brought it up, he'd looked dismayed then concluded it must be a side-effect (caused by my usual random reactions to magic) of the protective Chastity spell he'd *tagged* me with three months ago (he'd removed the Chastity spell soon after, once the threat was gone) and should fade in time.

Only the 'side-effect' wasn't fading.

The second time I'd mentioned it he'd proposed we 'swim in his lake' and sort it out that way. But rather than his idea being one of his usual semi-serious suggestions we have sex, he'd been obviously reluctant.

Which confused the hell out of me.

Until it clicked that while Tavish had never missed an opportunity to sic me with his kelpie power and I'd often found myself gazing at him like a Charm-struck human, he'd always had an ulterior motive for hitting on me; the infertility curse afflicting London's lesser fae. The fae had expected me to have a curse-breaking baby and, Tavish, as *àrd-cheann*, had been number one prospective daddy. But Tavish had only volunteered as 'daddy' to protect me from the rest of them. Something I was grateful for despite my annoyance at being kept in the dark about his whole take on the curse situation.

Of course, I didn't need his protection any more, not since the true reason for the fae's infertility had become common knowledge during the Tower of London Abductions case three months ago (codenamed ToLA by the police); their lack of fertility wasn't due to a curse, but rather their fertility had been stolen. And, thanks in part to Tavish's Machiavellian plotting, I'd recovered it.

Which was when Tavish had stopped hitting on me.

His reluctance hurt. Though, with the curse hanging around like an impatient Grim Reaper bent on eradicating London's fae, I could understand why he'd faked fancying me. And it wasn't as if I wanted us to be an item: Tavish is hot, and there's a definite chemistry between us, at least on my side, but all my heart truly felt for him was friendship.

Of course, there was another reason why Tavish's ardour might have cooled ... stabbing him in the gut with a five-foot bull's horn, and leaving him to the Morrígan's tender ministrations probably hadn't endeared me to him.

But whatever the reason I was no longer on his 'SILF' list, I didn't want to complicate things for either of us by 'swimming in his lake', so I'd kept my confusion to myself and pretended the inconvenient and frustrating 'side-effect' had faded, in the hope that it actually would.

I blinked as Tavish suddenly appeared on the other side of the desk, shedding the Invisibility spell he'd been wearing, then did a double take. When he'd gone invisible and piggybacked after me into the gnome's house, he'd been sporting his usual Sam-Spade-pinstriped-suit-and-Fedora work outfit. Now he was poured into a black unitard, pewter-coloured cobwebs decorating the super-tight Lyrca covering every part of him, including his head, hands and feet. He should've looked ridiculous in the costume; instead it left nothing to my libido's imagination and he looked ... disturbingly jumpable— *Down, girl!* Briefly I closed my eyes. How the hell had he even got himself into it, not to mention—

'Tavish, why are you dressed up as a bad-ass Spider-Man?'

He stripped his hood off and the lacy gills either side of his neck snapped open like black fans. He shook out his green-black dreads; they writhed around his shoulders as if objecting to being contained, beads flashing from cobweb pewter to a clear sun-drenched turquoise.

'Och, doll,' he said, giving me his shark's grin, serrated teeth white against the green-black of his skin. 'The fancy dress shop dinna have a Cat-Man costume, so what else should I be wearing to be all sneaky and stealthy?'

Having him 'work' with/for me was like employing a two-year-old sometimes; still, most of my clients loved his 'eccentricities'. I shot him an exasperated look. 'You were invisible. It didn't matter what you wore.'

'Maybe. But where's the fun in that? And look.' Tavish lifted his hand and shot a stream of magic at the high ceiling. It expanded into thin filaments, attached, and then with a leap

11

he was above me, crouched upside down on the ceiling, giving me an excellent view of his, *oh-so-gorgeous arse.*

Crap! Either I was as bad as the dirty-minded gnome, or Tavish's magical pheromones were hitting a new high. I was going to have to find a way of getting rid of the damn side-effect, and soon. I dragged my attention back to the dead fairy then decided that staring at his appendage probably wasn't the ideal way to cool down my libido.

I fished a bottle of water out of my backpack, took a long drink. Spidey impersonation aside, at least now Tavish had finished his search I'd find out if he'd dug up any incriminating evidence on Mr Lecherous Lampy.

'Any luck?' I asked, sitting down.

'Nae a glint, doll,' he said, disappointing me. He dropped silently down, lifted the gnome's heavy throne-style chair as if it weighed nothing, set it next to mine and slumped into it. His long, angled features took on a despondent air. ''Tis near like an untouched tomb upstairs, all inch-thick dust and empty, echoey rooms. Gnomes don't care too much for air twixt them and their earth.'

The huge ginger tom growled, subjecting Tavish to the same evil-feline stare it had me. Either it didn't like Tavish talking about its master, or maybe a giant Spider-Man looked like a tasty banquet. Tavish snorted, baring his teeth at it. The cat decided its paws needed cleaning.

I huffed. Figured Tavish would be more intimidating than me. 'So if there's nothing to be found, what's next to investigate?'

His gills closed as if in defeat. ''Tis the nature of others to die.' He plucked a slowly wriggling slug off the silver-foiled potato, held it up. 'All of them live too short a life: slugs, garden fairies, humans, even the lesser fae.' He dropped the slug into the tea then raised his eyes to mine; his were now a solid murky grey. 'You're nae but a youngster, doll, but you'll discover it soon enough. They're nae like us, the rest all *fade* too easily.

His words seeped into my heart like acid trickling through half-healed cracks. My friend Grace had died. She'd sacrificed herself to save me. I missed her ... and every day suffered the loss and pain and anger that she was gone too soon. Tavish's eyes carried the same suffering. I'd never seen him like this.

It pushed my worries about the gnome away and I reached out, grasping his hand. 'Who did you lose?'

He blew out a soft sigh. 'Och, 'tis nothing, doll. 'Tis maudlin, I am, for nae other reason than the wee dead mannie here, taken afore his time.'

I shook my head. 'It's more than that.'

He looked down at our joined fingers then nodded as if he'd come to a decision. 'We're nae any closer to finding the way to release the fae's fertility.'

Trepidation fluttered in my stomach. When I'd recovered the fae's stolen fertility it was trapped inside a sapphire pendant. I'd given the pendant to my friend Sylvia, a dryad, for safekeeping, and now she and Ricou, her naiad partner, were expecting the first full-blood fae in eighty years. They were ecstatic.

The rest of the lesser fae not so much.

Oh, they were overjoyed for the coming baby (though some weren't happy about its mix), but with the fae's fertility still trapped in the pendant no one else could conceive without wearing the thing and, being a cautious lot, no one expected Sylvia to take the pendant off until after her baby was born. The practicalities of the situation were awkward. Much more terrifying was the threat the pendant could be lost or stolen again, condemning them all to die.

Tavish squeezed my hand, expression intense. 'You're the key to sorting it all, doll, you ken you always have been.'

Yeah, and didn't I know it. It was my sidhe queen

grandmother, Clíona, who'd laid the original curse – *that they should also know the grief in her heart* – on London's fae eighty-odd years ago, in revenge for the fae not protecting her mortal son from the vampires. Later, in a fit of remorse, Clíona had secretly 'borrowed' the fae's fertility (evidently her feelings of remorse only went so far) in an attempt to break the curse by having another child. My mother.

Long story short. My mother's birth didn't break the curse, and as a result of Clíona's continuing 'attempts' to 'put things right' without dropping herself in the shit big-time, the pendant with the fae's fertility was lost. It was found just long enough to enable my conception, and then stolen.

Now, thanks in part to my family connection with it, I'd recovered the pendant.

It should have been the happy ending everyone wanted. Trouble was the pendant carried only half of the spell trapping the fertility and before the fertility could be released, the other half still had to be found. Until it was, Clíona's original curse was just on hold, not broken. All the fae had to go on was a riddle from the Morrígan:

That which was taken, must be recovered.
That which is lost, must be found.
That which is sundered, must be joined.

Half-arsed as it was, the riddle wasn't hard to work out: the fertility had been taken, and was now recovered. The rest of the trap was lost, we had to find it and join the two halves together then, hey presto, the fae's fertility would be restored. Except no one knew what the other half of the trap was, never mind *where* it was. Just once it would be great if the goddess-in-the-know had handed over specifics like a picture, or maybe even a map with a big red X marking the spot. But the Morrígan obviously hadn't been feeling that helpful. So Tavish and the rest of London's fae had been searching, magically and mundanely, to find it. So far all they'd found was a big fat nothing.

Of course the sensible thing would be to ask Clíona what they were looking for. Only sense doesn't come into it when all the parties involved have been refusing even to acknowledge each other for more than half a century. I'd have asked her myself if not for the fact I was 'an abominable stain on her royal sidhe bloodline' and she was determined to be rid of me. That she hadn't succeeded in killing me off yet was due in no small part to Tavish. Something else I owed him for.

I frowned at him. 'Thought you said you'd had some foretelling that if I helped search I could screw things up; that the fae's fertility could end up trapped or lost permanently, and if that happened the curse would never be broken?'

'Aye, I did.'

'What's changed then?' I asked.

'Nae a thing, doll.'

'So why now?'

'We're running out of ideas.' Frustration turned his beads black.

'So you're prepared to risk me helping, even though it could all go wrong?'

'Aye, but only in a small way. One I dinna think will cause any harm.'

I took a swig of water as dread settled like iron chains over my shoulders. I didn't want to get sucked back into it all again. But if I was honest, the fae's fertility problems weren't something I could or even should turn my back on. It was my family who'd started the whole 'stolen fertility' ball rolling, way back when. And I wasn't the one hurting in all this. The fae were. And as Tavish said, I was the key. If he needed my help, however small—

'Okay,' I told him briskly. 'What do you want me to do?'

Chapter Three

'**N**ae much, doll,' Tavish said, the relief flooding his eyes making me glad I'd said yes. 'Just give me some honest answers.'

It sounded too easy. 'Sure. When do you want to talk?'

'Now, of course.'

I looked at the ginger tom sitting on the desk, and at all the other cats in the cluttered room; sleeping, washing, or watching us like we were a play put on for their amusement. 'What about the gnome?'

'Och, he's nae thinking of interrupting you. I've seen to that.'

I sent out my own Spidey senses … the gnome's presence, from the direction of the kitchen, pinged against my inner radar. He was fast asleep, no doubt Tavish-induced. Plus, with the Privacy spell in operation, it wasn't like the gnome would be an issue even if he did wake up. And now Tavish had made the decision to ask for my help, I could see he was impatient to get on with it.

'Fire away, then,' I said.

''Twill be better with Compulsion?' He gave me a cautious look. 'If you agree?'

He'd asked, which made all the difference. I nodded and held my hand out. He traced a finger along my lifeline, the greyness in his eyes bleeding away until they were silver, shimmering with intensity. 'So, doll, who or what is it you want?'

The Compulsion pricked me and my mouth answered without hesitation. 'Spellcrackers. I want to keep it.'

Surprise stung me. Spellcrackers was my company now. Sort of. My boss stint was temporary and I was going to have to give it up. Something I'd thought I was okay with. Until now.

'So, you're wanting to stay the boss of Spellcrackers' – he gave me a probing look – 'where's that leave Finn?'

Finn.

My friend. My ex-boss. My—

Bone-deep hurt and angry disillusionment threatened to explode out of me. I shoved it back down, slammed it back in its box. I didn't know what else Finn was.

Three months ago I thought I did. I thought, along with being friends and working together, we were finally going to be more to each other. We'd been heading that way ever since we'd met, more than a year ago, despite everything keeping us apart.

Then I'd found the fae's stolen fertility.

And we should've had our chance.

But Finn's teenage daughter, Nicky, was one of the victims of the ToLA case, an awful consequence of which was that she was pregnant. Finn had, of course, gone with Nicky to the Fair Lands to be with her until her baby was safely born.

He'd asked me to go with him. I'd reluctantly said no.

Part of me, the part that wanted Finn and damn everything else, *had* desperately regretted that no. But I knew it had been the right thing to do. He needed to be there for Nicky without me. We needed that breathing space. And after all Finn's declarations about not wanting me just for my curse-breaking abilities, that my vamp genes didn't matter despite him hating vamps with a vengeance, I needed to be sure he'd wanted me for me. Without that time apart, a tiny bit of me would always wonder if Finn and I were really meant to be.

Now I knew.

Two letters, then nothing. No messages, no excuses, just nothing— He'd cut me off. Something that had sliced my heart into tiny pieces. And, now I'd stuck it back together, Finn was someone I'd promised myself not to even think about, let alone waste any more tears over ...

A quiet warning snort from Tavish made me look down.

I loosened my grip on the half-full plastic bottle I'd almost crushed. It popped back into shape with a sharp cracking sound. My mouth twisted down as I tried to give him a wry smile. I took a breath and locked my hurt, anger and all thoughts of a certain fickle satyr away.

'You know I haven't heard from him,' I said, my tone flat.

Tavish's expression sharpened. 'So, when he returns, you'll be giving Spellcrackers back?'

I didn't want to, but— 'Of course, it belongs to him and the satyr herd.'

'I ken the herd elders are already asking for it. You nae think of just giving it up?'

The herd elders weren't so much asking as demanding I do exactly that.

Their point: it was their money invested in the company and they'd only signed it over to me as a sweetener to get me to make little curse-breaking baby satyrs with Finn. Now their fertility was found, albeit still trapped, I wasn't needed, and they wanted their investment back. Immediately. Only my gut told me that if I gave Spellcrackers up now Finn would lose out too. So I'd give Spellcrackers back to him, and only him. What he did then was his choice. I might be hurt and angry, and hugely pissed off at his fickleness but that didn't mean I was ready to stitch him up. Or that I was stupid.

I picked at the broken tab on my water bottle. 'It's pretty convenient that Finn stops communicating right at the time the herd starts putting pressure on me.'

'Aye. That it is.'

Good to know I wasn't the only one with suspicions. Not that my suspicions meant the cut-me-off-without-an-explanation satyr's silence was forgivable.

'But is being the boss at Spellcrackers truly what your heart wants above all else, doll?'

Tavish's quiet question diverted my thoughts back to the matter at hand. Spellcrackers was just a company, after all; and yeah, financially I needed to work, preferably doing something I loved and was good at, but it wasn't like I wouldn't have my old job back when I gave up the reins ... except I wouldn't be the one calling the shots any more. *That*, I realised, was what I truly wanted.

'No, not Spellcrackers as such,' I clarified. 'But what it represents. I want to be the one in control of my life. No other people making decisions for me or thinking they can force me into doing what they want.' Which really, after everything, wasn't so much of a surprise. 'I want to make my own choices, on my own terms.'

Tavish was silent for a long moment, then something shifted in the depths of his eyes like a fish sliding beneath shadowed waters. ''Tis a big ask, doll.'

Impossible more like. 'Yeah.' I lifted one shoulder in a shrug. 'But what does what I want have to do with releasing the fae's fertility?'

'Told you, doll,' Tavish said briskly. 'You're the key, but you're nae wanting to find the spell, so the magic's nae keen on helping.'

I considered that. 'So, if I decide I want it, the magic will help me find it?'

He shook his head. ''Tis nae quite that simple. The magic's a tricky mistress. You know that.'

I did. Magic wasn't something you could talk or reason

19

with, yet it still had a mind of its own. Sometimes, when I'd needed it, it had helped me in the past.

'She likes you,' Tavish said softly.

'She?'

'The magic.'

'Why are you calling it "she"?' I asked, puzzled. 'Isn't it more like a natural … force or something?'

He smiled, turquoise eyes dancing. 'We all come from The Mother, and she was the first to come from the magic. So what else would the magic be? But now's nae the time for debating, doll. We want to find the spell, you want to keep Spellcrackers and be your own boss. Help me and I'll help you, with that anyways.'

'Tavish,' I said, more than a little insulted. 'I don't need to be bribed.'

'Och, I ken, but a little incentive never harms a body, now does it?'

'Fine, I'm not going to say no.' I shot him a grateful smile. Having him go to bat for me with the satyrs staking their claim was a bonus. 'What do you want me to do?'

'Ask the one who knows.' He flicked his fingers and a pack of cards, larger than normal playing size, appeared on the desk in front of me.

'Tarot cards?' I asked.

'Aye.'

Curiosity flickered. I hadn't known he did readings.

'Pick them up and hold them in your left hand, doll.' I slid the water bottle on to the table and did as he said. No magic tingled; the cards felt like ordinary card, and oddly both sides were plain white. He took hold of my right hand, lacing our fingers together. 'Don't let go, nae for anything?' he warned. I nodded, and his gills fanned wide either side of his throat, his eyes turning the deep cobalt blue of a midnight sea. Magic, needle-sharp, pierced me, twisting a storm of desire at my core. I gasped, squirmed on the chair before I could stop. Again he didn't seem to notice. I clutched at the cards, ignoring the feelings. The need would pass. It always did.

'Shuffle,' he ordered, Compulsion fuelled his voice.

'I can't one-handed—' But even as I spoke, my fingers did an expert shuffle.

'Toss them in the air.'

My hand threw the cards. The light in the room dimmed as they fountained up high like a mushroom cloud, before tumbling like glistening snowflakes on a winter's night. I winced, expecting them to clatter on to the desk, dreading the damage they could do to the fragile fairy body in its sandwich-box coffin, but they dissipated, melting like the snowflakes they'd mimicked, fading away into the ether ... Soon only five remained. They snapped into a line, hovering in front of me. Still blank.

I looked at Tavish. 'What now?'

He picked up one of my scalpels, held it out to me, his hand shaking. 'They need to be fed.'

'Blood?'

'Aye, doll. Blood for your question answered. Usual terms.' Sweat beaded on his forehead.

I frowned. 'What's the matter?'

'Feed 'em,' he urged, shoulders bowing as if with pain.

O-*kay*. I pressed my left index finger against the scalpel. The edge sliced the tip, dark viscous blood welled, scenting the air with honey and copper, and I readied for the pain but it didn't come. Odd.

'Quick,' he whispered.

I took a steadying breath. 'I offer my blood solely in exchange for the answer to my questions. No harm to me or mine,' I said and touched the first card.

A tiny tongue licked at my finger— Startled, I jerked my hand back, or would've without Tavish's Compulsion holding me in place. The tongue licked some more, tickling, then I felt a little mouth press against the cut, lips sealing around it. It started sucking my blood down, hard and fast enough that I could feel the draw on my heart. I shot an anxious look at Tavish. He was hunched in his chair, the cobalt colour leaching from his eyes, leaving them pale and cloudy, his dreads turning dry and brittle, their beads clear as glass. Then a bead shattered, the pieces hitting the floor with a soft ping. Uneasy, I tried yanking my hand from the card. I couldn't.

'What the hell's happening, Tavish?'

'Channelling.'

'Channelling what? Something in the cards?'

He grunted.

I took it as a yes. And judging by the way his hand gripped mine, whatever it was, it was powerful. What the hell was in the cards if they could do this to him? And why hadn't he told me what to expect? Unless this wasn't it?

'Harder,' he muttered. 'Harder than I thought to stop you.'

'Stop *me*? But I'm not doing anything!'

More beads shattered. He crumpled forwards, his head dropping to his knees, his hand a death-grip on mine. 'The card? Is it changing?'

I dragged my attention back to the card. Thick gold mist topped it like a tiny thundercloud, and on the front the dark bruised red of my blood coloured the card from the bottom up, as if it were litmus paper drawing it up. Which in a way it seemed it was, as there was still a thin white strip at the top.

'Tell me when.' Tavish's words were a hoarse whisper.

The strip turned pink …

Brighter red …

Then the dark bruised colour of the rest of the card.

Suddenly the mouth released my finger with an audible satisfied sigh.

I cut a troubled glance at Tavish. 'It's let go—'

He toppled out of the chair, his hand slipping from mine, and curled into a foetal ball under the desk.

I flung myself to my knees, grabbed his head; his face was lined and shrunken like an old man's.

Weakly, he pushed at me. 'Talk to the card, doll,' he ground out harshly, 'afore she leaves.'

She? But a stab of Compulsion had my body pulling back into the chair, my eyes fixing on the bloodstained card and my mouth said, 'Tell me how to find that which is lost, and how to join that which is sundered, to release the fae's fertility from the trap and restore their fertility back to them as it was before it was taken.'

The tarot card vibrated. The blood swirled away in wisps of reddish smoke until I could make out a picture. A dark-haired, hawk-nosed male in his thirties, dressed in a purple toga, his head wreathed with a crown of golden laurels, lounged on an ornate throne. He held a silver-bladed dagger in one hand, and behind him a large golden eagle perched on a staff-like pillar. The Emperor.

The Emperor on the card laughed; a loud arrogant sound that filled the large room. I started. The ginger tom leaped from the desk, its fur bottle-brush stiff, and at my feet Tavish whimpered. On the card a huge, fanged snake slithered up the staff and hissed at the golden eagle. The bird flapped its wings angrily and launched itself out into the room, soaring up to the ceiling.

I repeated my question.

The Emperor laughed again, pointed his silver dagger out of the card at me and bellowed, 'He knows! He will tell you! For a price!'

Of course he would. 'Who's *he*?' my mouth demanded.

'He is I!'

'Who are you?'

The Emperor gave another booming laugh. 'I am the Emperor!'

Great. Was it a tarot card or a pantomime villain? Next he'd be shouting, 'He's behind you!' I gritted my teeth. *Specific questions, Gen.* 'What's the name you were given at your birth?'

'My father named me—'

An angry screech drowned his words as the golden eagle dived back into the card. The card exploded in a splatter of crimson as if a bullet had hit dead centre. Droplets of blood expanded out in a starburst of brilliant red light, their blinding afterimage searing my retinas.

Crap. Crapcrap*crap*.

No way in hell was that supposed to happen … I rubbed at my eyes, crouched and desperately stretched out to Tavish under the desk. Who knew what harm the explosion of magic had caused him? I patted around but couldn't feel him. Finally, as my vision returned I realised the only things under the desk were me, the ginger tom and some disgusting toadstools sprouting from the mouldy rug.

Tavish was gone.

A soft snorting noise made me turn. In the centre of the room, making the place seem small, stood a kelpie horse. The kelpie's green-black coat was rough over hard, ropy muscles, its tangled mane glinted with dull gold beads, its black-lace gills fanned wide to either side of its arched, serpentine neck, and its eyes flickered with golden light.

Damn. Tavish's wylde side had come out to play. Perfect.

Chapter Four

I crawled out and stood with my back against the desk, cautious. I trusted Tavish, but he wasn't the one in control of the kelpie. It was as if taking his waterhorse shape stripped away his couple of millennia's worth of civilisation and left him as he must have been when he first came into being in the Shining Times: something feral and predatory, birthed from magic. Good news was: we weren't near the river so the kelpie wasn't likely to Charm me to ride it into the depths. Bad news: Tavish wasn't exactly easy to communicate with in this form.

'Um, you okay?' I asked.

The kelpie shuddered as if shedding water; its usual signal to changing shape. Its eyes flashed black, then back to the odd gold light. It shook again, pawed the scratched wooden floorboards with one camel-toed hoof and flicked its tail over its flanks as if dislodging irritating flies, then shot me a wild, white-rimmed look.

'Guess that means no,' I muttered, glancing round the room in case a helpful solution jumped out at me. The window was still buzzing with Knock-back Wards, the gnome's cats were milling in a furry tide in front of the interior door, obviously wanting away from the kelpie but trapped by the spells on the threshold—

The kelpie half-reared up, ears flat against its skull, and wheeled towards the door. The cats scattered, scrambling onto shelves or under furniture. The kelpie dipped its head, snatched

25

up the spell crystal from the threshold with a disgusted snort and thudded out and away.

I stared after it for a long moment, expecting Tavish to return in his human form or to hear the gnome's surprised shout on discovering a kelpie horse rampaging round his house.

After a few minutes' silence the ginger tom peered from beneath the fungi-covered sofa, its eyes wary, then it clawed its way out, stood with its tail up. It hissed at me as if to ask, 'Scary horse-thing gone?'

I sent my senses out. The gnome was still fast asleep but there was no ping telling me Tavish/kelpie horse was anywhere near.

'Yep, looks like the scary horse-thing has gone,' I muttered, wondering how a waterhorse without opposable thumbs had bypassed the doors and Wards.

Frustration slumped my shoulders. Figured something would go wrong. No matter what I did with magic it always seemed to mess up, even with something as supposedly simple as a tarot reading. Still, maybe the rest of the cards would be more informative … I turned back to the desk.

The tarot cards were gone.

Three hours later, I called it quits. While I'd waited for the tarot cards to reappear or Tavish to contact me, I'd got on with the investigation. I'd finished all the tests on the dead fairies – all of them were apparently dead from natural causes – checked out the gnome's creepy stock, and had a good snoop round the house. And found no clues in the 'incriminating' department.

I called Tavish. Same as the last however many times, his phone went straight to voicemail. Presumably, he was working off whatever was bugging him with a swim in the River Thames. I added another message to my earlier ones saying I was packing up, the tarot cards were still gone, and to call me.

I wasn't sure what to take from the Emperor card. Tarot wasn't my strong suit (bad pun aside), but as any self-analysis was a non-starter – this was about the fae's fertility after all – I went with a literal interpretation.

The card had said: 'He knows! He will tell you! For a price!' And then, 'He is the Emperor!'

The Emperor, whoever he was, would do a deal for the info. Simple. Of course, whatever he wanted in exchange wasn't likely to be simple at all. But I was doing the cart-before-the-horse thing. First I had to find him. Which would be so much easier if I knew who he was. Only, thanks to the eagle (or whatever the cards were channelling) cutting the reading short, I had no name, other than he called or thought of himself as the Emperor. Of course, that could be down to the tarot card's standard depiction, so could be something or nothing.

But I did have a couple of clues.

The first was that, instead of the usual sceptre, the Emperor held a silver dagger. What that signified was anyone's guess.

The second clue was more enlightening. The golden eagle had been perched on a snake-entwined staff. I'd recognised it: it was the Rod of Asclepius.

Asclepius was the Greek god of healing. According to myth, the goddess Athena, his aunt, gave him a gift of Gorgon's blood to help him in his work. Only he didn't just use it to heal the sick, he started bringing them back after they'd died too, thereby giving them what turned out to be a new bloodsucking immortal life. Hence all new vamps 'Accept the Gift' when they leave their human mortality behind. Turned out creating a new species was a fatal life-choice for Asclepius, though, since Zeus, his überdivine granddad, wasn't too impressed by his grandkid overstepping his healing remit. He struck Asclepius dead with a thunderbolt. Then Apollo, Asclepius's dad, got equally pissed off and decided to dispose of his son's creations, whenever they stepped into his light, by burning them to a crisp. Which is why vamps don't do storms or suntans.

And why the Rod of Asclepius on the tarot card had to mean the Emperor was a vamp.

'So I'm looking for a vamp with delusions of majesty,' I muttered, which left the suspect pool wide open. Though since I couldn't imagine how some unknown vamp would have the answer to releasing and restoring the fae's trapped fertility, the 'Emperor' would more than likely have some connection to London's fae, and/or to me. Which narrowed the suspects down considerably. In fact, to the one vamp who did the whole royal thing *ad nauseum*. The psychotic, sadistic, murdering sucker I was supposed to marry when I was fourteen. The Autarch.

Panic rose up to close my throat. I forced it back down and told myself I was jumping to conclusions. I'd never known the Autarch to be called 'Emperor'; he was always called a prince. And just because I thought I knew all the vamps in London, didn't mean I did. There was probably some other vamp I'd never heard of who was the Emperor. *Yeah, you just keep telling yourself that, Gen.* I stifled the scared voice in my head. I needed more info before I let the possibility that I might finally have to face my own personal blood-sucker nightmare, turn me back into that terrified teenager who'd run away. And the quickest way to get that info was to talk to the vamp in the know.

Malik al-Khan. London's Oligarch and my 'owner/protector' ... according to the vamps' icky 'property' database, anyway. What our relationship actually was ... was complicated and confusing, and needed working out. Not just between us, but in my own head. And in my heart—

I halted my thoughts before they strayed any further into that particular emotional minefield. This wasn't the time or place. Still, I couldn't quite stop the eager leap of anticipation at having a reason to contact Malik ... I snagged my phone, and, getting his voicemail, left a brief message for him to call me. That done, I put my phone away. As I took a steadying breath, noticed the ginger tom was crouched on the edge of the desk, hackles raised, gaze fixed on the window.

Peering round the edge of the sash window was a dark-haired figure, tall and broad enough to be male, his face in shadow.

For a moment my panic-induced paranoia screamed, *the Autarch*, then my sensible, prosaic head took over: the watcher was more likely to be a poacher casing the gnome's joint for his magical valuables.

The male jerked out of sight, and I rushed to the window.

The house's small front garden had once been a grassed square with shrubs around the outside, but the plants were now choked and overgrown, the grass knee-high with weeds. But, despite the jungle, there really was nowhere for anyone to hide. And other than one of the gnome's cats disappearing into the bushes, the garden was empty. As was the road in both directions as far as I could see, and the open grassy space of the Primrose Hill park opposite.

Crap. I'd missed him—

A human couldn't disappear that fast.

I sent my Spidey senses searching for any Others nearby, but all I picked up was the gnome at the back of the house ... I closed my eyes and concentrated ... *There*, distant enough that they had to be a good few houses away, the ping of a vamp—

Fuck. Maybe my first guess had been right, and the peeping tom/poacher *was* the Autarch.

Except, even with the sunset starting to paint the sky red and orange, it was still too bright and therefore too dangerous for any vamp to be out – Apollo's crispy critter look is never a healthy choice for a sucker – so the vamp was probably just a local waking up. Although, my paranoia reminded me, while I'd never heard of any vamp having the ability to walk around during the day, that didn't necessarily mean it wasn't possible. And a daywalking Autarch had starred in not a few of my nightmares over the years.

I shuddered at that scarily uncomfortable thought and gave the empty garden a last once over, mentally filing 'Autarch is stalker is Emperor' for later discussion with Malik. We were going to have a lot to talk about.

I packed my stuff up and woke the sleeping gnome (eventually, though it took a cast-iron frying pan bouncing off his head; I'd be lying if I said I didn't find that satisfying) with the bad news that he'd have to wait a couple more days for his dead garden fairy licences (despite the lack of evidence, I'd decided to play it safe), and that he might have a poacher problem. Which, since something had punched out the cat flap in his back door – *the kelpie? Could he shapeshift that small?* – had the gnome shoving me out of his house in frenzied alarm so he could fix it and reinforce his Wards.

Outside, I perched on the gnome's low garden wall. As I waited for my lift, thoughts of trapped fertility, tarot cards, disappearing kelpies, peeping toms and daywalking Autarchs circled my mind like the gnome's anxious cats. My shoulders started to itch with the feeling I was being watched. I smoothed my thumb over the emerald ring on my right hand, and the large square-cut gem, guarded by baguette-cut rubies, warmed with a tingle of magic. The ring's mediaeval gold setting was ugly and heavy, but that was its only downside. I took a quick scan, double-checking the road was still empty (not wanting to panic any bystanders), and clenched my fist.

A ball of green dragonfire erupted from the ring, and a sword sprang into my palm. A Roman gladius. Just over two feet in length, its two-edged blade a mix of steel and silver tapering to a sharp point. The sword was made for cutting, slashing or stabbing. And on the blade was an engraving of a dragon crouching along with the sword's name: Ascalon. The sword was blessed and bespelled and would cleave through anyone, other than an innocent, killing them instantly.

Ascalon had been a present, of sorts, from an old flame a couple of months ago; he'd taught me to use it as a teenager, and since he'd given it to me, his current girlfriend – a fencing teacher and fitness instructor – had insisted on sparring with me thrice weekly (read beating me into the ground) to bring my sword-skills back up to scratch. Not that I minded; the sword was more than useful, and it came in the super-handy, concealed carry-size.

I lifted the sword in a warning salute to whatever/whoever was causing my 'being-watched' itch (be it just my paranoia or something more) then let the sword slip back into the ring, loving the fact I finally had a weapon I could take anywhere, and unlike the flick-knife I once carried, one that wouldn't get me into trouble with human law. Even better, the ring came with its own See-Me-Not spell and would only work for me.

Maybe I should show the gnome the sword, next time he grabbed my arse.

Yeah, that would make him keep his filthy hands to himself. I grinned and let my paranoia relax slightly, breathing in the scent of a night-blooming jasmine and admiring the view of London's skyline, its lights sparkling against the darkening sky. A warm summer breeze lifted the sweaty hair at my nape and brought me the faint sounds of bells, whistles and the rhythmic clank of machinery mixed with excited shouts and screams: the 24/7 fairground was in full money-making swing at the nearby Carnival Fantastique in Regent's Park.

Rumour has it the Carnival, which descends on London every year in the week leading up to the Summer Solstice, was given the Regent's Park pitch in the early eighteen hundreds after some shenanigans between the Prince Regent and the then Carnival Ringmaster, a triton (said to be immortalised in the fountain in Queen Mary's Garden). Which may be true. But despite its initial colourful royal patronage, now the Carnival has to apply to the Department for Culture, Media and Sport for all the relevant exhibition permits exactly like any other temporary show. Something I knew about in more detail than I ever wanted, since Spellcrackers (thanks to the company's Witches' Council associations) had won the contract to provide magical security for the Carnival. Tedious permit details aside, it was a solid high-profile contract and good for business.

The throaty roar of a motorbike drowned out my musings along with the Carnival's distant noise.

The bike rode up the centre of the quiet road like a modern-day knight on a mechanical charger, and rolled to a showy stop in front of me. The tall, lean rider, dressed in black bike leathers and heavy boots despite the summer heat, silenced the engine, kicked the stand down with casual skill and turned a black-helmeted head my way, face a pale blur behind the dark smoke of the visor.

My lift had arrived.

Chapter Five

I raised my hand in greeting. The bike rider dipped her head and removed her helmet in one smooth continuous movement. Lifting her gaze to mine, she hit me with a stunning smile and whisked her swathe of shining blonde hair round in a practised flip worthy of any hair product advert.

Katie: part-time Spellcrackers receptionist (and my occasional taxi service), soon to be full-time student dancer, and the nearest thing to a kid sister I have.

I grinned at her. 'Ten out of ten for the hair whip, Katie. All you need now is to get someone to pay you to do it.'

'Well, funny you should mention that ...' She did another expert flip and stretched out her arms, excitement glinting in her eyes. 'Ta da! You are now looking at L'Oréal's newest hair model!'

'Really?'

'Reallyreallyreally!'

'Woot!' I held my hand up for a high five, and she slapped my palm with her leather gauntlet. 'Go you!'

'Yeah! Go me!' She beamed and punched her fist in the air. 'Finally!'

'That's brilliant, Katie.' I hugged her, breathing in the scent of leather, hot metal and the citrusy perfume she always wore as her arms tightened around me. She'd been hoping for this for so long. 'So what's the job?' I said as we broke apart.

'I'm to be in the background of an ad with about ten others, so there's no face work. It's only a couple of days. But it's a start. And the pay's good for a chunk of college fees, but then' – she gave me a mischievous grin that made her look about nine years old – 'I'm worth it!'

I groaned and rolled my eyes at her. 'Plea-*se*. You're killing me.'

She stuck her tongue out. 'Wait till you hear my other news.'

By the way she was almost bouncing, I didn't need to hear, I could guess. Marc, the boy – no, not boy, man, since he was my age: twenty-five – who'd been seriously flirting with her for the last few weeks (at her other part-time job in the Rosy Lea café), had finally asked her out. Marc was the first guy she'd been interested in after her last 'date' turned out to be a vamp's human blood-slave. The vamp had kidnapped Katie to blackmail me into taking his blood-bond. Katie hadn't been hurt, but I'd promised myself I'd never let anything bad happen to her again. I couldn't change the fact that her confidence and trust in herself and others had taken a beating, though, so Marc asking her out was momentous.

Especially as he'd spent so long getting to this point, which had taken Katie from agonising over whether to say yes to wondering what was wrong. Katie's mum, Paula, thought it showed he'd picked up on Katie's nervousness. But for me, it smacked too much of manipulation and had me uneasy. Of course, anything to do with Katie pushes my Red Alert button. But still, just because I might be rabidly over-protective, and over-reacting, didn't mean Marc wasn't someone to watch. Damn it, I *so* wanted to wrap Katie up in the proverbial cotton wool, but I hate it when people try to do that to me.

I pasted a teasing smile on my face. 'You won the lottery?'

This time she rolled her eyes at me. 'Gen-*ny*!'

'Kat-*ie*!'

She crossed her arms with a disgusted glare.

I laughed. 'C'mon then. Out with the details.'

'First night at the Royal Opera House for *La Sylphide*.'

Marc was good; I couldn't have chosen better for Katie myself. I clamped my mouth shut before my paranoia made me say something I'd regret.

'And no,' she said, her glare turning determined, 'I'm not bringing him into the office so you can give him the once-over.'

Then again, I didn't really need to say anything. Katie knew me.

'Look, I've got it under control,' she carried on earnestly. 'I'm meeting him there. I'll book a Gold Goblin taxi home. I won't go anywhere else with him, or get into any strange cars, go down any dark alleys, or drink or eat anything that's been out of my sight.' She leaned forwards and hooked her blue heart-shaped pendant out from under her jacket. It carried a mega Personal Protection Ward and Tracker spell that had cost me near enough six months' wages, even with Tavish doing the *casting* for free. She dangled it before me. 'I'll be wearing this as usual. I know what I'm doing. Marc's a nice guy. Trust me? Please?'

'I do trust you,' I said. *Just not him.*

'It's a first date, Genny,' she warned. 'I don't want to get all heavy about things and scare him off.'

If he likes you, then it won't. But again I didn't say it. If I didn't trust her judgement, then how could she? And really, the vamp kidnap thing had been my fault, not hers. She'd done nothing wrong. She didn't deserve to have her every date interrogated, magically or otherwise, because I felt guilty. What she deserved was to have an awesome night out with a guy she liked.

'*La Sylphide* is a' – romantic, tragic tale of impossible love; not *my* choice for a first date, but hey, Katie would adore it – 'wonderful ballet,' I said, happy for her, my smile only a tiny bit forced. 'You'll love it.'

She grinned and clapped her hands. 'I know! So exciting.'

35

I grinned back then changed the subject. 'So how's things back at the office?'

Her expression turned businesslike. 'All under control. Rotas are done and agreed for the Carnival. I've got a couple of interviews lined up for the vacancy, and we're all caught up on the non-Carnival jobs.'

Katie wasn't our summer receptionist/office manager because she's my sort of kid sister. She's also Ms Super Organised. I was going to miss her come the start of college.

'So all I've got you down for tomorrow, so far, is Harrods,' she finished.

I nodded. Harrods were having problems in their lingerie changing rooms. Their Magic Mirror spells kept mutating and instead of coming up with the appropriate recommendations, they were spouting subtle put-downs that meant customers were walking without buying. Obviously, store management were *not* happy. It was Spellcrackers' top contract and, once the Magic Mirror problem was sorted would be a good steady earner.

'Okay,' I said. 'Anything else come in for tonight?'

'You're free as a—' Katie's eyes rounded with alarm as she pointed at the park. 'Look, Genny!'

I looked. And saw nothing. 'What?'

'There! In those bushes!' She waved frantically at a dark clump about fifty metres away. 'He was naked. '

I raced alongside the iron railings enclosing the park, through the entrance and ran towards the bushes, clenching my hand around my ring and releasing Ascalon. 'Naked' said the male was probably some lowlife pervert so he wouldn't warrant a killing blow, but as a scare tactic the sword would make him think twice next time he got the urge to get his junk out. And if he was more than just a lowlife, like, say a peeping tom Autarch, then I was way happier being armed and dangerous.

I slowed as I neared the spot, sending my Spidey senses out. No one. Naked or otherwise. I'm fast, part due to my sidhe blood and part because I run daily, so I should've got some sort of ping back. So either he'd disappeared into thin air – possible, but I couldn't sense any magic either – or he was fast enough to sprint out of range. Which could only mean a vamp. I scowled, ignoring the way my pulse was pounding harder than it should for a short run and debated whether it was worth poking about in the bushes. Katie shouted again.

'There! Down by the trees.'

I spun towards the wooded area a couple of hundred metres away ... No naked male, but a brief glimpse of a dark shape moving low and merging into the deeper gloom. My inner radar pinged: 'human' and 'animal'. I started running then stopped as my senses zeroed in on the path coming from the far side of the wooded area. A man was walking his dog. His shoulders were stooped under his beige-coloured shirt and trousers, and the dog – a yellow Labrador – padded slowly on age-stiffened legs. Even without being close enough to see the man's face clearly, it was obvious he was old. No way was he the flasher. Neither he nor his dog could move fast enough to get over there from the bushes.

I ran to the trees and did a swift check round. Had I seen something, or was my imagination on overdrive? Whatever, there was no hint of vamp, or of magic. Letting Ascalon slide back into the ring, I jogged over to the man and his dog, said a brief hello, and confirmed he was as old and human as he appeared and hadn't seen a flasher making a fast exit. Then I sprinted back to the bushes, poked around and again found nothing. Rolling my shoulders to get rid of the tension, I jogged back to Katie.

'Did you see him?' she asked, expression worried.

Crap. Katie really didn't need to hear I thought her flasher might be a vamp stalking me; it would knock her confidence way down. 'Sorry, no. Probably scared him off with the sword.'

She frowned at me. 'He was weird.'

I snorted. 'I think sick is the word you want.'

'No. He was naked, but he wasn't trying to, y'know, flash. It was more as if he was spying and he sort of fell over.'

I pursed my lips. 'He fell over?'

'Maybe not fell over exactly, but sort of crumpled downwards.'

'Okay, that is weird. But he's gone now,' I said, aiming for reassuring. 'So he can't have been hurt.'

She hugged her helmet, still anxious. 'Maybe. Did you see the animal under the trees? It was weird too. Dog-like, but not. And big.'

I gave her a considering look. Maybe my imagination wasn't on overdrive. A big dog might account for the dark shape I thought I'd seen. 'I didn't get a clear look, Katie. Sorry.'

She gave an almost imperceptible shudder. 'Do you think the animal was something to do with the Carnival? They've got some odd exhibits. Maybe one of them escaped? The man could've been looking for it?'

I hadn't thought of that, but then my paranoia was stuck on vampire. Whereas Katie's was stuck on finding an explanation that wasn't scary. 'Could be,' I said, and dug out my phone and called Carnival security, more to reassure Katie than anything.

The duty manager hadn't had any escapees reported, so he took my rather sparse details, asked if I was sure they were animals and not some sort of fae, then thanked me and said he'd check it out. He also suggested I phone the zoo. I did. And got almost the same response, albeit with the guarantee that they took security very seriously, and would have known if any animal had escaped. They would, of course, look into it.

'Nothing, but they'll let me know,' I told Katie as I came off the phone. 'I think we should tell the police about the flasher.'

Which the naked male was, whatever else he might be, and as such needed to be reported. 'Can you describe him?'

She twisted the strap of her helmet, chewed her lip, frowning at the bushes. 'Dark, wavy hair. Pale-skinned. Tall-ish … I think.'

'And definitely naked,' I prompted.

'Yes, but I didn't see anything, y'know, important, just enough that I could tell he didn't have clothes on.'

I gave her a comforting hug, and phoned the police.

An hour later, we waved them goodbye. They'd taken our statements and I'd managed to let them know, without Katie hearing, my suspicion the flasher might be a vamp. They'd said it wasn't unusual to get flasher reports from the park and they'd do a more thorough check during daylight. Then they wrapped the bushes up in enough blue and white tape that it looked like the vegetation had been a victim of an over-excited troupe of maypole dancers. The coppers' parting shot had been to ask if we wanted a police liaison officer to contact us to arrange some counselling.

'Counselling,' Katie muttered miserably once we were on our own again. 'We don't have to, do we? It wasn't like I even saw anything.'

I hugged her again. 'It's only if you think you need it, hon.'

'Yeah, well I don't. I had enough counselling last year.'

When the vamp kidnapped her. She didn't say it, but she didn't have to. That counselling hadn't been fun, but it had helped, which was what mattered. 'Hey.' I gave her shoulders another consoling squeeze. 'Wanna hit the Rosy Lea for coffee and a fry-up?'

She eyed me dubiously from under her lashes. 'You don't do coffee and I don't do fry-ups.'

I grinned. 'Semantics.'

She huffed and handed me her spare helmet. 'You gonna tell Mum about tonight?'

'Do you want me to?'

She heaved a sigh. 'No. I'll tell her. She's gonna freak out, though.'

Yep, Paula would. But in a good way. Then again, what mother wouldn't? She was as protective as I was about Katie, apart from when it came to Katie's new boyfriend, Marc. But before I could say anything, a bird-like warbling sounded. Katie started, grabbed for her phone. She frowned then shot me a bemused look. 'You're never gonna believe this, Genny! Someone's pulled a "Harry Potter" in Leicester Square!'

'A what?'

'A "Harry Potter". At least that's what they're calling it on Twitter. Tavish's bots picked it up. Look!' She held her phone out.

The display showed a video clip of the Empire's façade. The huge poster over the cinema's entrance advertised *Conan the Barbarian*. On the poster, a half-naked, muscled-up Conan was looming high above the battling hordes, actually swinging his sword at his legion of attackers. As the video clip played, Conan's adversaries stopped attacking and traipsed off into the wings as if taking a tea break. Conan looked around in satisfaction, hoisted his sword over his shoulder and followed, leaving the poster advertising nothing more than an out-of-focus vista of an empty, rocky plain.

I looked at Katie. 'That is a poster, isn't it? Not some new vid-screen the cinema's using?'

'Definitely a poster.' She tapped her screen. 'And it's definitely a prank of some kind; there're already apologies and reassurances on twitter that it'll be fixed soon.' She gave me an expectant glance.

'You're right,' I said, answering her unspoken question. 'It sounds like an ideal job for Spellcrackers, if we can—'

Katie's phone gave another bird-like warble at the same time my phone beeped with a text – from Leandra, the witch who monitored our night phones.

Big problems in Leicester Square! Six jobs already and more coming in. You available?

Leandra had sent the text to every witch on Spellcrackers' books. I raised my brows at Katie. 'Jobs, plural?'

'Yep. The rest of the posters are the same. Well, according to Twitter, anyway. Going by the ton of tweets, it looks like it might even be trending soon.'

'Going by the tweets,' I corrected, 'it looks like we're in for a busy night.'

Chapter Six

Conan the Barbarian twirled his sword like a cheerleader's baton, pointed it out at the cheering crowds forty feet below in Leicester Square, then did a slow bump and grind as he shot me a salacious wink.

'Bet you don't do that in the film,' I muttered, ignoring the whoops, whistles and calls for 'more'.

I used the controls on the hydraulic lift basket I was standing in to nudge myself closer to the top of the film poster, then *focused* on the splatter of muddy-coloured oil paint that was the 'Harry Potter' spell. How the hell the magical vandal had got it this high was a mystery – one the police were responsible for unravelling – all I had to unravel was the spell.

Which was proving easier said than done.

'Okay, let's try this again,' I murmured, crunching three liquorice torpedoes to boost my magic, and touching the cleaned mascara brush I held to the paint. Carefully, I teased out a fat orange stripe from the muddy mess, then another of indigo, followed by pink, green, and five shades of yellow, until I had all the stripes separated out into a seemingly random colour wheel. Mentally crossing my fingers, I checked the poster. Conan scowled, hefted his sword like he meant business and froze. I compared it to the A4 copy the cinema manager had given me, and blew out a relieved sigh. They matched. Finally, I'd hit on the right combination. After two long hours.

The time was within the budget, but I'd hoped to nail it in

less. Of course, *cracking* the 'Harry Potter' spell would've taken a couple of seconds, but *cracking* a spell also cracks whatever it's attached to, and shredded posters and damaged buildings were a definite no.

I'd tried *absorbing* the spell, but all that had done was turn the poster white. Luckily I'd managed to spit the spell back out unchanged before the magic had mutated, though I was still suffering the nasty side-effects: mouth dry with the bitter taste of juniper berries, and six, so far, desperate trips to the cinema's facilities. Even that hadn't killed my constant urge to pee. The idea of setting a Privacy spell and making use of the spell-dumping bucket as a handy potty was my newest fantasy. *Absorbing* magic can sometimes bring out its 'mischievous' side.

Mischievous magic aside, now I'd managed to reverse-tweak the spell to get the poster back to normal, all I needed to do was suck it up and dump it in the potty – sorry, bucket – with our new Spellcrackers spell remover, a.k.a. the common turkey baster: the kitchen implement with a hundred and one uses, according to Leandra when she'd suggested it. (Unnerved by the slightly manic glint in her eye at the time, I'd refrained from asking what the other ninety-eight were.)

A sudden gust of warm wind hit and I grabbed the metal hopper's handrail as it gave a stomach-dropping shudder. Heights don't usually bother me, but something about being forty-odd feet up, in a three-foot-wide metal basket, suspended on a seemingly fragile-looking arm cantilevered up and out from the back of a small lorry, brought on an unexpected attack of vertigo.

Dizzy, I slumped down and tried not to think about water, potties or how far away the ground was. I took a few deep breaths, willing the dizziness to pass, then switched my phone on (leaving it on when dealing with unknown magic is a sure-fire way of *cracking* the Buffer spell) and texted the rest of the team with the 'reverse tweak'. Now I'd figured out the colour combo, removing the 'Harry Potter' spell from the other fifty-odd posters (who knew there were *so* many posters in Leicester Square?) would be as easy as, well, sucking up gravy.

I checked my messages— and found one from Malik, his clipped, ice-cold tone almost willing me not to phone back.

I took a breath and brought his number up, the nerves in my stomach not made any better by my constant need to relieve myself. And the minefield of thoughts I'd sidestepped earlier, when I'd decided Malik was the obvious choice for info, opened up in front of me. If I was honest, things weren't just complicated and confusing between us, they were downright awkward. And it was all my fault.

I should never have blackmailed him.

Oh, it had seemed a great idea at the time. He'd started ordering me around, right in the middle of the ToLA case, and as he'd had my freely offered blood, I had no choice but to do as he said. His orders were all meant to protect me, and the one chance I had of recovering the stolen fae's fertility. Later, when I'd discovered that, I'd forgiven him. But at the time I'd felt betrayed, mad as hell, and had been determined to stop him from ever abusing his power over me again. Plus, I had a plan to rescue the victims with his help, and knew the only way to get it was to force him.

So I'd come up with the clichéd 'in the event of my death' letter, left with the police, except I didn't actually have to die for the letter to do its stuff; I only had to give the nod to Hugh – (acting) Detective Inspector Hugh Munro – and the full force of English justice would fall on Malik like the bricks of the High Court collapsing atop him.

Not that I thought Malik cared so much for himself. It was more that if what he'd done became public knowledge, it would break the ancient Live and Let Live Tenets between the vamps and the witches, and set them at each other's throats. If the witches and the vamps went to war, then no one was going to come out a winner. Least of all the vamps. That, Malik did care about, hence the awkwardness.

And the reason I'd only seen the beautiful vamp once since the end of the ToLA case three months ago.

Not that I'd realised anything was different at first. In fact, I'd sort of fantasised that after he'd helped me, and healed me after the – literal – dust from the ToLA case had settled, things between us would … move on … and that the heart-thudding attraction I'd always felt (and had a wishful idea wasn't just on my side) might develop into more. Though quite how 'more' would work out, his being a vamp and my running Spellcrackers, a witch company – and with a certain satyr I'd promised myself not to think about in the picture – was a problem my fantasies didn't have an answer for. I wasn't too proud of myself for wanting to have my relationship cake and eat it when it came to the satyr – I – wasn't – thinking – about and Malik.

So despite my fantasies, or rather because of them, I'd reluctantly told myself it was better to stick to being 'just good friends' with Malik.

Then I'd called him to thank him. Malik had been distant and formal as if there'd never been anything between us, and my 'just good friends' idea was slapped back in my face. Though after my shock dissipated it hit me that, as far as he knew, I was still prepared to carry out my blackmail threat, so in order to protect the vamp/witch status quo, he was doing exactly what I'd demanded: leaving me alone.

Hoping to ease into sorting things out, I'd come up with a minor problem with Darius, my ex-fang-pet, and asked to meet. The meeting hadn't gone quite as planned – an under-statement if ever there was one – and I'd been left with the impression that the last thing Malik wanted was any sort of relationship with me.

Now, if nothing else, this Emperor/Autarch stuff counted as a good opener to clear the air.

I chewed my lip, worked out a polite greeting in my head and called.

He answered on the second ring. 'Genevieve.'

My heart did a stupid excited leap at hearing his not-quite-English accent, even if his tone was the same clipped, ice-cold one as his message. Then, as the metal bucket shuddered in another gust of wind, my carefully prepared words disappeared and I blurted, 'Do you know a vamp called the Emperor?'

'Why?'

The part of me that didn't need to pee relaxed at his sharp question. If he'd given me an unequivocal 'no', I'd have hit a dead end on all fronts. But his question was almost an acknowledgement.

Keeping it business-like and brief, I told him about Tavish wanting my help, the Emperor tarot card with the Rod of Asclepius, the peeping tom and the faint ping I'd got off a nearby vamp. I finished with the million-pound question that had been bugging me: 'Can the Autarch go outside in daylight, if he was in the shade of nearby trees or something? Is he the Emperor?'

There was a brief silence. 'Where are you now, Genevieve?'

He hadn't denied it was possible. My heart leaped again, with fear this time, and thanks to my magically irritated bladder I nearly wet myself. Crap. I swallowed, clenched my inner muscles tighter and said, 'Leicester Square, I'm dealing with the problems here.'

'What problems?'

'A prank spell on the movie posters. It's been all over the news. They're calling it a "Harry Potter",' I finished wryly.

There was a brief burst of noise as if a TV had been switched on, then it was gone. 'Ah, I see.' Malik's voice held a thin thread of amusement. 'Do you plan to be there for some time?'

'Probably another hour.'

'I would prefer to discuss this situation in person. I would like to meet you there, if you agree?'

He wanted to talk face to face— relief, and not a little hope, filled me despite his formal tone. 'Of course I agree, Malik. I wouldn't have called you if I didn't want your help.'

'You require my help?' The words seemed to whisper out of the phone and slide like ice down my spine. Goosebumps pricked my skin with uneasy anticipation, and I shivered.

'Yes.'

'Good. I will see you shortly.' The phone went dead.

I stared at it. Had I heard a note of eagerness beneath his coldness, or was it just my imagination? And if so, what did it mean? I shook my head. No use biting off trouble before the gorgeous vamp arrived. Time enough for all sorts of things then, including biting. If the Autarch was about, I wanted Malik on my side. Whatever it took. And if the Autarch wasn't, I still needed his help to find and do a deal with the Emperor.

I looked up at the scowling Conan, decided it would only take minutes to finish up and dug the turkey baster out of my backpack. I crunched another liquorice torpedo, and activated the glyphs (drawn on the plastic with Leandra's silver sharpie) with a quick touch of my will. Time to suck up the 'Harry Potter' spell and then I really, *really* needed to pee.

Fifty minutes later, feet thankfully back on solid ground, I was dealing with the 'Harry Potter' spell tagged to a poster for *Kiss Kiss Bang Bang*. Val Kilmer and Robert Downey Jr were playing Russian roulette and hamming it up whenever they bought it. After another desperate visit to the cinema's facilities, along with the drastic measure of drinking a pint of salt water followed by the expected stomach-emptying results, I'd knocked my magical bladder problems on the head. I didn't do the salt emetic often, but it was either that or a full cleansing ritual followed by a salt bath, something I didn't have time for. Not with Malik due to appear shortly.

'Miss?'

I carefully sucked up the spell's last daub of paint then plunged my turkey baster into the bucket of salt water at my feet before turning to the owner of the soft, hesitant voice.

A Gatherer goblin, small at about two foot six, was waiting a deferential distance away, entertaining himself by hopping from one foot to the other to make the lights in his trainers flash red and green (much to the delight of a group of snap-happy Japanese tourists who'd previously been pointing their cameras my way). The goblin wore the standard issue navy boilersuit of a worker goblin, with the goblin queen's logo embroidered in gold on its right chest pocket. On the left chest pocket was a large enamel badge, its design enhanced by tiny silver sequins. A similar badge was pinned to the front of the goblin's peaked cap, which was doing a good job of flattening the tinsel-silver curls of the goblin's massive Afro.

'Hi,' I said.

The goblin looked up and I noticed another badge under his chin; it said his name was Obadiah. Obadiah ran his knobbly finger down his long ski-slope nose in the respectful goblin greeting and gave me a tight-lipped smile. He closed the distance between us, careful to make his trainers flash (goblins always attack in the dark; showing the shiny is a flag of truce), the silver-lamé satchel slung across his body reflecting the bright lights in Leicester Square. He took something that glinted from the satchel and offered it to me.

'For you, miss. From Mr al-Khan.'

'Thank you, Obadiah.' I returned his greeting and the tight-lipped smile, and took the glinting thing. It was a silver-coloured electronic hotel keycard. The logo on it was the same as the one on Obadiah's badges (minus the silver sequins) and on the hotel occupying one corner of Leicester Square.

Obadiah tapped the plastic keycard with a silver-painted claw. 'Penthouse. Miss take lift.'

I dropped the keycard into my pocket and glanced at the hotel's seven floors thinking I was hardly likely to take the stairs. And more importantly why was Malik using a goblin to play messenger? But as my paranoia twitched, Obadiah held out his hand again and said, 'For our blood, now lost.'

Dangling from his knobbly fingers was a long-stemmed rose, leaves stripped, thorns blood-red and sharp, petals a rich dark crimson.

The meaning of the flower bled into my mind. A rose for Rosa – the only vamp Malik had ever offered the Gift to. The only vamp to survive the curse of his blood and not turn into a mindless, shambling revenant maddened by bloodlust.

Though Rosa not turning into a revenant was pretty much irrelevant, as she'd been off-her-head nuts before becoming a vamp, and sadly the lifestyle change only added to her issues. Something I knew only too well, since I'd unwittingly borrowed Rosa's body (until she died the true death during the demon attack last Hallowe'en) after buying what I thought was a Vamp Disguise spell. The 'spell' had blipped a couple of times, merging my consciousness with Rosa's and leaving me with fragments of her memories. Those memories were enough to tell me that Malik had given Rosa the Gift out of guilt, but not why he felt guilty. They also told me he'd loved her, and she him … as much as she could love anyone, damaged as she was. The crimson rose was a secret tryst signal between them.

Rage and jealously ignited like wildfire that he would use *our* secret sign with another. I snarled at the goblin, baring my teeth. He threw the rose at me, backing off quickly, stamping his feet hard as he disappeared into the crowd.

Then the emotions were gone, leaving me with nausea roiling in my gut. I pressed my lips together and slowly unclenched my fists, remorse at frightening the goblin warring with fear that Rosa's memories, and the emotions they aroused, had … *What? Influenced me? Possessed me?*

Crap. No way did I need this. I had enough of my own bad memories without hers surfacing. And no way did I need Malik to help them resurface, whether intentionally or not.

I grabbed the rose, squeezing the stem until the thorns punctured my palm. The brief pain twisted magic low inside me, and the honey smell of my blood mixed with the dark spice scent of Malik's as the spell the flower carried activated. The rose shed its petals into the ether leaving me holding a platinum ring set with a black crescent-shaped gemstone: Malik's ring.

Except his ring was attached to my bracelet. Wasn't it?

With a thought I revealed the bracelet hidden beneath the rose-shaped bruises encircling my left wrist – Malik's mark; signifying that I was his blood-property and giving me protection from other vamps. The bracelet popped out of my body, its various spells glowing red and gold, with a clattering of charms: the plain gold cross to protect me from the demon (the one that had attacked last Hallowe'en); the cracked gold egg that had trapped the sorcerer's soul I'd eaten during the attack and which had stopped the sorcerer from turning the tables and possessing me (The Mother goddess had later hooked the soul out of me and sent it on its way, thankfully); the inch-long obsidian scimitar to cut my connection to Rosa (a precaution in case she wasn't quite as dead as Malik believed); and the tiny platinum ring that, apart from its current size, was a twin to the one I held.

So if Malik's ring was still attached, whose ring was I holding now?

It came to me in a swirl of angry disbelief: Rosa's.

He'd given me Rosa's ring. Which, whoever's emotions I was channelling, hers or mine, was all sorts of wrong.

I let the bracelet sink back into my skin, texted the rest

of the Spellcrackers team that I was going into the hotel to sort a problem, and went to beard the infuriating vamp in his penthouse.

Chapter Seven

I expected the penthouse to be the ubiquitous luxury hotel suite. Instead it was a smallish function room, albeit still luxurious with varnished woods, brown-on-beige décor, and art large enough to be a talking point but bland enough not to offend.

The room had a post-party feel: the huge art-deco-style lights recessed into the sloping ceiling were dimmed to almost nothing, chairs were stacked along one wall, and the four tables in the room – all of them round and each large enough to hold at least a full coven of thirteen witches (though I doubted the hotel ever seated thirteen, even witches; some superstitions just won't die) – were draped in white cloths, holding only a domed centrepiece of rose heads— the same dark crimson colour as the one Malik had sent with the ring.

Malik was at the far end, looking out of the windows that stretched from one side of the room to the other. I vaguely registered the lit-up pods of the London Eye, glowing deep blue against the night sky, as I strode towards him, Rosa's ring clenched in my fist.

I slowed as I neared. His hair had grown. It had been buzz-cut last time I'd seen him, now it was pulled back and bound in a queue that cut a silky black line down his white shirt to his shoulder blades.

Briefly I wondered how he'd got it to grow that long in the last couple of months, then any curiosity was eclipsed by fury.

'I am not Rosa!' I yelled. 'I don't want her fucking ring or her magic flowers!' I threw the ring at his head. It missed, chinking loudly off the window—

He snatched it out of the air. And turned.

Shock stripped away my anger. He was beautiful, his face all perfect lines and angles, his part-Asian heritage shaping his black eyes, but his forehead was marked. Branded. With delta, the fourth letter of the Greek alphabet, in the lower case: δ. The brand was delicate rather than disfiguring, and gave him an almost mystical air. I *looked*: it emanated with low-level power and some sort of Veiling spell. I forced my *sight* past the Veil, and the brand turned from matt black to a pulsing painful red.

My stomach heaved. 'Why haven't you healed it?' I demanded.

'Genevieve.' His eyes darkened with grim mockery. 'The correct greeting of blood-property to their master should carry more reverence. An offer of the throat is ideal, a wrist acceptable, a deferential falling to your knees the bare minimum.'

An image flashed in my mind of me on my knees before him; what I was doing took deference to a whole other level. Lust spiralled within me like a tornado and slick heat bloomed between my thighs.

I dropped my backpack to the floor with an incensed thud. 'I am *not* your blood-property, Malik.'

He moved faster than I could track and was behind me, one steel-hard arm clamping my arms and chest, trapping me against him, his other hand thrust in my hair, yanking my head back to expose my throat.

I yelped in shock before snapping my mouth shut. My heart pounded, flooding adrenalin through my veins, urging me to flight or fight. Instead I froze, my childhood training kicking in: struggling over-excites vamps, and over-excited vamps, even one as normally übercontrolled as Malik, are more likely to forget whatever *fucking infuriating game they're playing* and tear your throat out.

'You are my blood, Genevieve.' His breath seared along my pulse. 'As such there are expectations on both of us.'

My mind stuttered as his words penetrated. Had I missed something: like maybe we weren't alone? I pinged my inner radar. But all I could sense was Malik ...

His dark spice scent wove around me like smoke, his lips cool against my skin, a certain part of him pressing hard against my arse. Damn, it wasn't just the blood-sucker in him that was excited. Though to be honest, blood and sex are two sides of the same coin with vamps.

'You didn't expect anything before.' I kept my voice quiet and calm.

'Before you had not admitted yourself such,' he said. 'In writing.'

It took me a couple of seconds, then ... Crap. I had. Last Hallowe'en. As part of my 'blackmail', I'd given another letter to the witches. It had been the carrot to go with my stick. That letter gave Malik dispensation for any unspecified crimes he may or may not have committed (so long as he had Hugh's agreement) against any witch, past, present and future, in ex-change for his property – a.k.a. me/my blood – used in a spell. My 'admission' seemed to have changed something. Leaving me vulnerable. My pulse sped faster.

'I'm sorry,' I said, keeping my annoyance at myself out of my voice. 'In hindsight that was a stupid idea.' For me, anyway.

He didn't react. Not an indrawn breath or a muscle moved. He'd shut down. His lungs not working, his heart not beat-ing. Which was a sign, hopefully, that he was getting himself under control. I had an urge to swallow. I stifled it. Waiting. Hardly breathing myself. Then after a long drawn-out silence, I opened my mouth to apologise again.

'Shh.' He stopped me. 'I am not fully myself. I need—' He broke off. 'It may aid me if you would calm your pulse. I find my thirst for you is greater than I anticipated.'

At the self-disgust in his voice, a suspicion slithered into my mind like one of Asclepius' snakes. Maybe this wasn't his game, but someone else's. Like the Autarch's. He had to be the one who'd branded Malik; no one else would have the power.

Angry resolve, rather than the usual panic, filled me. I concentrated on counting, slowing my pulse.

What felt like aeons later, Malik's grip on my hair lessened, allowing me to lower my chin a few millimetres, and ease the painfully stretched tendons in my neck. My gaze caught on our reflection in the windows in front of us. Malik was fully vamped out— pupils flaring red with flame, lips drawn back in a silent snarl, canines and needle-thin venom fangs white and sharp. The brand on his forehead now pulsed dirty silver in my sight.

My stunned eyes met his grim ones in the glass. 'It's doing something to you. If I remove the spell, will it stop it?'

'It marks me as his. As the Ancient Greeks used to mark their slaves.'

Bastard Autarch. 'You're not Greek,' I said flatly. 'And neither is he. And I don't get how that's even relevant.'

'You are right. We are not Greek. But the symbol is understood by those who need to see it. I am Oligarch, but all know that I took the position without his knowledge or permission. He has asserted his authority. It is necessary to maintain the status quo.'

Great. This was some sort of political vamp crap. 'So keep the brand,' I said. 'What about the spell?'

'The spell?'

'Vamps can't see magic. So what's the point?'

His hand spasmed, tightening his hold on my hair. 'It is for his personal entertainment.'

Sadistic psycho. 'What's it doing to you?'

He was silent, a dark weight at my back.

'C'mon, Malik. It's doing something, or he's doing

something through it. You're not usually so volatile.'

'Volatile?' He yanked my head back again. 'Volatile is for the undisciplined, Genevieve.'

'If you keep doing that,' I croaked, 'you're going to break my neck. I'd be happier not wearing a brace for however long it takes to heal.'

'My apologies.' His voice was contrite.

'Okay,' I said slowly, trying to think of an out. 'So we've both said we're sorry. How about you let me go and we'll talk about it?'

'I find myself unable to do that. It is taking all of my … discipline to hold you like this and not feed.'

Right. Well, maybe taking my blood would help. After all, what was a drink between friends? And Malik *was* my friend, despite the current stand-off. 'So feed,' I said.

'No. I am too … volatile.'

Underneath his attempt at dry amusement, I could taste his fear, like bitter aloes mixed with rancid blood. Fear of losing control, and of hurting me. Not that I wanted either of those things to happen either, but hey, the other options – standing here until inevitably the sun came up or his disciplined restraint gave way – weren't cutting it either.

'Look,' I said, frustration making me sharp, 'I haven't donated yet so I've got plenty of blood.' My usual donation was a pint into a blood-bag; a daily necessity thanks to the 3V infection turbo-boosting my red cell production. But hey, Malik could probably take a good three, even four pints before things got too iffy. 'If you get too carried away then you can heal me. And, I'm not human, remember. There's no way you can pass your curse on to me, if that's worrying you.'

'It is a tempting offer, Genevieve. Thank you. But no.'

Stubborn vamp. Sometimes his phobia about his curse made him even more paranoid than me. 'So what's the plan, then?'

'The plan?'

'Yes. The plan to get out of this.'

There was a long silence. 'I find it impossible to marshal my thoughts.' The confusion in his voice was raw, as if he'd suddenly woken in a frightening place. 'I do not have any plan.'

I'd have sighed, if his arm around me had let me take a deep breath. Not working out what needed to happen next wasn't like him. Had to be an effect of whatever the Autarch's spell was doing to mess with Malik's mind.

Well, I had an easy way to sort that, whether he wanted me to or not. Except I'd left my turkey baster down in the square; not that I thought Malik, or rather the Autarch controlling Malik, would let me take the turkey baster to his forehead. I choked back the slightly hysterical laughter at the image that thought conjured.

Next option was *absorbing* the spell; definitely not a good idea with who knew what side-effects the magic would sic me with. Much better to get rid of the spell totally, which meant I'd have to *crack* it. Preferably not while it was on Malik. He'd heal the smashed-watermelon effect it would have on his skull, but I needed to talk to him tonight, not in three or five or however many weeks' time. So I needed to *call* the spell off of him and *tag* it to something else first. Something I could destroy without too much damage.

I stared up at the painted ceiling and visualised what the room contained. There wasn't much to choose from. Windows, pillars, paintings, stacked chairs, tables and ... *Got it!*

I *focused* on the spell. Or at least I tried to, but the damn thing kept slipping away from me as if I was trying to hold water in a sieve. I needed to physically touch it.

'Um, any chance we can change positions here?' I asked. 'Like, face each other?'

'Why?'

'This isn't exactly comfortable.'

'I do not think a change of position is wise.'

Because he wanted to sink his fangs into me. And going by the way a certain part of his body was still pressing into my back, he wanted to sink something else into me too … Which might be enough to distract him from the bloodsucking bit.

Recalling the image he'd flashed in my mind of me on my knees before him, I closed my eyes, took a moment to get my thoughts in order, then, hoping the visual communication went two ways, started sending mental pictures.

A shudder travelled through him. 'What are you doing, Genevieve?'

Giving you ideas, hopefully.

His arm around me loosened slightly.

Yes! I sent more images to his mind—

His hand plunged into the V of my shirt, yanking it open violently enough that I saw a button hit the ceiling above us. He shoved my shirt aside, roughly cupping my lace-covered breasts. I moaned loudly, pushing back and wiggling encouragingly against his thick length. He growled, driving his hips into me as he ripped away my bra, knuckles grazing my nipples. They tightened in response, then I bit back a scream as he pulled on one, rolling the sensitive point between his demanding fingers, the pain/pleasure arrowing straight to my core. Liquid heat filled me making me wish that this was for real.

Reluctantly, I reminded myself it wasn't. This wasn't about my fantasies, but about distracting Malik to get at that spell.

As his hand continued to map my body, making me yearn for more, I forced aside the distraction, letting my magic rise as I sent more images. He obliged, feverishly tearing the zipper on my trousers, shoving them down my hips so they pooled around my ankles. I kicked them off, thankful they were loose and as the golden glow of my power surrounded us, I slowly reached up to grasp his queue—

He ripped off my briefs, jerking me off my feet, his firm hold on my hair the only thing keeping me upright. Heart thudding, I sent another picture, praying this would work like the others as I tugged persuasively on his queue. Finally, he released me and I almost sagged with relief as he slid gracefully down to fall to his knees before me. I looked at him gazing up at me and my heart stuttered. The flames in his pupils were feathered with gold. I'd almost caught him in my Glamour.

My plan had worked better than I'd believed possible.

For a second I revelled in his worship ... then, half-regretful, I blocked it.

Now for the next part.

I bent, using his queue to tug his head back and slapped my hand over the brand on his forehead. The magic in the spell felt slippery, like soft jelly. I grabbed it, panicking as it threatened to ooze out of my fingers. I gave it a small experimental pull; the body of the spell lifted away from Malik, but a forest of thin trailing threads – *tentacles?* – was still embedded inside his brain.

Eww, the thing was like some sort of horrible jellyfish.

Then some of the legs pulled out of him on their own, flicking round to sting my wrist. Intense pain shot up my arm and my hand jerked open. The spell disengaged, burrowing back inside Malik's skull and disappearing. A pained grunt escaped his mouth, red flames eclipsing the gold in his pupils. He snarled, lips peeling away from his fangs as he readied to strike.

Crap. I was losing him.

I clasped his face, digging my fingers into his temples, frantically pouring my magic into him as I shouted more images into his mind. He growled low in his throat; the flames in his eyes flickered red, gold, red and then disappeared totally as his pupils, irises and whites all turned a brilliant gold. I stared transfixed as bloody tears ran down his face, and power rose around us like a red-gold mist. I bent lower, needing to place my lips on his, to drink down all that power, to take it into myself until it filled the hollow place inside me. But before our mouths touched, his cool hands touched my hips, slid up to my waist and, as he stood, he lifted me up—

And I flew back through the air to land with a jarring thud on the nearest table.

The pain and the heavy perfume of the roses next to my face brought me back to my senses. I stared at the ceiling, trembling as I pushed away the horrific thought that I'd been ready to consume Malik's … *what? Power? Soul?* And gave thanks that he at least was still following the script of images I'd shoved into his head.

Hands manacled my ankles.

Now to get rid of that torturous spell.

I looked at him. He stood at the table edge staring adoringly at me from golden orbs.

He'd lost his shirt. I gaped. Not so much at his broad shoulders, or his lean, hard chest with its silky triangle of black hair, but …

I pushed myself up on my elbows.

It wasn't just his shirt that was gone. All his clothes were gone. He was naked … Gorgeous … My eyes followed the silky black hair that shaded a line down his washboard stomach, all his muscles crisply defined beneath beautiful taut skin … skin that glowed a soft silver as if he'd somehow consumed the moon. I looked lower … all of him was—

Oh my gods! That wasn't in the script!

He pulled me slowly towards him, his hands gliding like rough satin up my legs. My pulse turned erratic and instinctively I clutched at the tablecloth. But it and I slid unresistingly across the table until I was half lying, knees bent, legs dangling and Malik standing between them.

'Well, Genevieve.' He grinned: a feral, fanged slash. 'This is how you wanted me, was it not?'

Chapter Eight

'**U**m, sort of,' I said, sitting up, bemused that he was talking and sounding like himself. He was trapped in my Glamour; he should be my willing, adoring slave, waiting for my every whim. So why wasn't he?

'Sort of?' He raised an elegant brow. 'Maybe you would prefer me like this.' His grip on my knees tightened as he jerked me towards him. I yelped, surprised, clutching at his shoulders as his hands clamped high on my thighs, holding me teetering on the table's edge. 'Is this close enough, Genevieve?'

I looked down; there was only a breath of air between us. My skin flushed, need and anticipation coiling tight inside me as the urge to wrap my legs around him and feel him thrust deep flashed in me like lightning; it had been too long since I'd last lost myself to pleasure. And this wasn't some venom junkie; a stranger I'd picked up in Rosa's body to satisfy my cravings, only to leave me with a bitter taste in my mouth … This was Malik.

A feeling hotter and sweeter than mere lust trembled inside me. I'd wanted him since I'd first seen him and that want had strengthened, shifting into something indefinable as my initial fear and distrust had dissipated. All it would take was one of us to move, and then—

I swallowed and raised my eyes to his. They were still gold with my Glamour … He might seem like he wasn't my slave, but I wasn't about to trust that, not when Glamouring anyone was akin to force. Shame mixed with yearning rolled through me.

This. Was. *Not*. Real.

'I think that's close enough,' I said, though my voice held uncertainty instead of the dryness I'd been aiming for.

His mouth quirked. 'Are you sure?'

'Yes,' I said, this time more firmly. 'What I'm not sure about is how come you seem yourself again.'

His thumbs traced circles over my inner thighs, sparking desperate desire. 'Ah, you wonder why haven't I succumbed to your magic?'

Succumb! Gods, I *so* wanted to succumb, *so* wanted to pull him to me, to close that infinitesimal gap between us. 'Yes.'

'I told you once before, Genevieve, your magic is not powerful enough to hold one such as I, not even weakened as I am with this.' He dipped his head to indicate the spell on his forehead. 'But your magic does appear to be strong enough to keep it at bay. It is allowing me some respite from the need to fight it.' He lowered his voice. 'As does inducing me to taste the delights of your body.'

I inadvertently dug my fingers into the cool skin of his shoulders as an image filled my mind: we weren't talking euphemisms here. I batted the thoughts away before they shattered my resolve. I was the one supposed to be doing the distracting, not him. And my distraction was working, even if it had been a rough, roller-coaster ride. And even if the ride had ended before the big finalé. Which was for the best, I told myself firmly, determinedly keeping my eyes on his face and ignoring both the frustration itching through my veins, and how tantalisingly close he was, almost brushing against me.

'Right,' I said, adopting a businesslike air. 'If you hold still, I'll have a look at the spell and see how to remove it.' I lifted my hand only to have him catch my wrist.

'I do not think that is wise,' he said, mimicking my brisk tone. 'Magic has an adverse effect on you.'

'If I absorb it, yes,' I agreed. 'But I'm not going to do that.'

'What are you going to do?'

His slightly too casual question rang a warning bell in me. He appeared fully in control, but I didn't know enough about the spell to trust it truly wasn't still influencing him, albeit less than before. I decided to sidestep, and satisfy my curiosity at the same time. 'First, I think you need to tell me why you're shining.'

'You are the one that is shining, Genevieve. Like the desert sun at noon.'

Despite his playful tone, a faint echo of sadness twisted in me. Did he miss the sun? I pushed the thought away. 'I know I'm shining,' I said. 'I'm concerned about why you are. Is it something to do with the spell?'

'The risk is too great for you to remove the spell.'

Okay, so he wasn't going to answer. And whether his silvery moonlight glow was connected or not didn't really matter. Time to bait a hook, see what I could catch. 'I've got something that takes all the risk out.' I grinned. 'A magical turkey baster.' Not that I could magic it up here from Leicester Square, but hey, he wasn't to know that.

Emotion flickered in his eyes, eagerness, desperation, or both, though with my magic colouring them gold, it was hard to tell. 'Do you have it in your bag?'

'Well, it's not stuck behind my ear, is it?' I said, giving him an arch look.

Pain contorted Malik's face. He dropped my arm and made a slashing gesture at my backpack. It lifted itself from where I'd dumped it and smashed into the wall at the far end of the room with a resounding crash.

Well, that confirmed my suspicions that Malik had some sort of kinetic power. And – I shot my crushed backpack and its scattered contents a resigned look – that confirmed my other suspicion. Malik wasn't fully in control of Malik.

'Genevieve. I order you—'

I grabbed his cock and squeezed. It had the desired effect.

He stopped speaking, a heavy groan of need cutting off whatever order he, or the Autarch using Malik as his mouthpiece, had been about to give me.

'I knew there was a reason you got naked,' I muttered, slapping my other hand on his forehead. This time when I seized the Jellyfish spell I was ready for its stingers, gritting my teeth as the pain arced though my body. Only my own determination and Malik's hands clamped around my thighs held me in place. I panted through the pain, working my fingers into the jellyfish, caging the mass tightly in my hand. Another groan came from Malik, this one less needy, more agonised. I glanced down at the hand holding him ...

Oops. Looked like I was going to have to do the adult equivalent of the kids' trick of patting my head while tracing circles on my stomach, otherwise this was *so* not going to be any fun for him.

Not that fun was what this was about.

I *focused* on his forehead, slowly tugging the jellyfish, taking care none of its stinging tentacles snapped and were left behind. The things were vicious, alternatively attacking my arm or trying to reattach to Malik through the brand. The jellyfish pulsed against my palm, and horror washed through me as I realised it wasn't the normal magical spell construct but was a living organism the spell had been *tagged* to. Ugh. It had been inside Malik's brain, constantly stinging and no doubt feeding off him. No wonder he couldn't think. I swallowed back bile. The sadistic Autarch really had it coming for this.

The jellyfish finally pulled free with a disgusting sucking sound. I released Malik, threw myself back on the table and plunged the jellyfish into the flower arrangement, using my will to *tag* it to the roses. I yanked my hand back, *focused* on the magic at the Jellyfish spell's heart, and *cracked* it.

The roses exploded in a blinding flash, petals raining down like bloody confetti. Crimson seared my retinas, burned inside my skull and down my arm. I had a moment to think ... *that's not right* ... before red-hot flames roared up and consumed me.

'Genevieve.' Malik's voice pulled me from the fire I was twisting in. I opened my eyes. His were only inches away. For a long moment I wondered why I was on my back with Malik almost lying on top of me, his hands clasping my head as if he meant to kiss me. It was an intriguing position, and one part of me wanted to take advantage of— if it weren't for the gleeful little devils sticking my arm and skull with their hell-hot pitchforks.

'Do you remember what happened, Genevieve?'

'Yep,' I whispered past the pain. Pain that, I now realised, came from having parts of the spell, thanks to the jellyfish's venom, inside me when I'd destroyed it. Damn magic, always ready to sting you – literally this time. Good job I was hard to kill. 'Jellyfish stung me. Infected me with spell. *Cracked* it. Hurts. Happens.'

Exasperation and concern warred on his face. 'What hurts?'

'Arm. Head,' I muttered.

A soothing chill emanated from his hands as his power cooled my blood. Not quite a healing but enough to banish the pain and spread a welcome peace through my body. I noted his pupils were back to their normal obsidian black, no hint of gold or red. I smiled, relieved, and as exhaustion swept over me, let myself drift away. Nothing appealed more than sinking into that coolness and sleeping for at least a month.

Ice seared my veins as he dialled his power level up, instantly shocking me awake. 'What the hell was that for?' I muttered.

'You were losing consciousness again.'

'Yeah, well,' I said grumpily. 'I've had a busy night. Let me sleep.'

65

'You can sleep once I know the spell is gone, Genevieve. Not before.'

'Stop worrying. I blasted it and now you're good to go.'

'Yes. I am fine.' He braced his hands either side of my head, raising himself up. I thought about pushing him totally off me, and getting up, then decided moving was too much effort; I might as well lie here while we chatted. 'But it is you I'm concerned for. The jellyfish is parasitic. It has been living inside me for the last three months, feeding off my blood. It stung you. I want to ensure that you are not infected by its poison or any remnant of the spell, or my curse.'

I sighed and forced myself to *focus*. The brand on his forehead was a healed scar, nothing more. He was clear of the spell. I scanned round. Shredded rose petals, tiny chunks of glass, bits of something green which had me frowning until I realised it had to be the florists' foam stuff the roses had been stuck in, and specks of translucent jelly littered the table and no doubt the floor nearby. It was all free of any magic. As I was.

'Everything's clear,' I said, turning my attention back to Malik. 'They could add salt when they do the clean-up if they want, but the spell's dead. There're just the physical remains left.' Bits of which peppered his pale skin— which was no longer glowing. Because the spell was gone? I ditched that thought as I belatedly remembered I'd been naked. I looked down. I was draped in something white … Malik's shirt. And judging by the sticky itchy feeling of my skin, I hadn't escaped being speckled by sticky spell debris either. Even as I wished for a shower, and wondered how long I'd been unconscious, frustration sifted in me as I saw I wasn't the only one who was no longer naked.

'You dressed,' I said, stating the obvious as I eyed his trouser-clad legs where they straddled my hips.

'The situation was not conducive to remaining unclothed,

Genevieve. Nor had I anticipated that your desires would result in such emphatic handling.' One corner of his mouth lifted. 'I fear you have unmanned me.'

Unmanned him? I raised my brows, suddenly feeling much more alert. 'Is that some archaic euphemism for what happened when I grabbed you?'

Amusement sparked his eyes. 'It was ... unexpected.'

'It was meant to be, buddy.' I poked him in the chest. 'I was trying to distract you.'

'And you succeeded. In that, and in removing the spell.' He smiled, his amusement tempered with gratitude and something that was balm to my heart: respect. 'It was well done, Genevieve. Thank you.'

'You're welcome,' I said, happily appeased. 'Anyway, it's not like you were being particularly gentle either.'

'My apologies.' Remorse replaced his amusement. 'I would not have destroyed your clothes nor marked you if I could have avoided it.'

I frowned. 'Marked me?'

He touched my chest gently where his shirt covered me. I peeked under it. For a moment, I thought the red marks scattered over my breasts and stomach were a dusting of finger-sized rose petals ... then I realised the marks were like the bruises encircling my left wrist. Vampire property marks.

'They can be removed,' Malik said quietly, answering the question I was too stunned to think of, never mind ask. 'I did not intend them, nor did I mean to cause you harm, but the force of the images you sent me was difficult to counter. If we should find ourselves in a similar situation, the equivalent of a whisper instead of a shout would be sufficient.'

I let the shirt drop as I processed it all. The marks weren't permanent, he'd been out of his mind with the spell, and I'd chosen that particular way of distracting him, so ... 'There's nothing to apologise for.'

'Yes, there is. I should not have proposed we meet, not when I knew Bastien would take the opportunity to use me to cause you injury.'

Yep. Bastien, the Autarch, was never happier than when indulging his vicious side. The usual terror flashed in me. I squashed it.

'But I was disturbed by your mention of this Emperor on the tarot card,' Malik carried on.

The tarot cards. Right. The reason I was here. 'So it's not just the card, there is a vamp called the Emperor? '

'I know of one who goes by that title—'

'He's not the Autarch then?' I interrupted.

'No, they are not the same, Genevieve.'

'Good,' I said, relieved, then as surprise lit his eyes, I added, 'The Emperor can't be as bad as the Autarch …' His brows drew together and I sighed. 'Okay, stupid assumption. I take it he is as bad?'

'If the Emperor is the one I know, he is not as … impulsive as Bastien.'

'Bastien is not impulsive,' I snapped. 'He's homicidally violent, sadistic and psychotic.'

'As the Emperor can be, in more considered ways.'

Figured. 'Sounds like he'll be just as much fun to deal with then,' I said drily.

'If it is him,' Malik said, 'then we should prepare. But first I would like to see the image you saw on the tarot card.' He touched my temple. 'If you would allow me to access your memory, of course, Genevieve.'

He'd put me in a trance once by holding my hand. Apparently, the relaxed state helps you remember details only noticed by your subconscious. It had been like having a conversation through glass: I could see, but not hear. I'd asked him not to do it again without my permission and that hadn't stopped him, not until now. Seemed he was finally getting the 'do not treat me like blood-property' message, despite the Jellyfish spell and the extra vamp marks. Maybe we were moving on at last.

I smiled, waggling my hands. 'Sure. Hit me with your best vamp hypno-mojo.'

He glanced at my hands and then shook his head. 'I propose a different method.'

I gave him a narrowed look. 'And what method would that be?'

Chapter Nine

'**Y**ou've had some dealings with Declan,' Malik said, 'the head of the Red Shamrock blood-family, have you not?'

I frowned at his seeming change of subject, then realised what he was suggesting. Red Shamrock vamps could influence mood by evoking a person's emotions from memories; it was why their Irish pub, the *Tir na n'Og*, was as successful as it was. Punters always experienced the best *craic* ever, thanks to the vamps trawling their minds for happy memories and bringing the associated feelings to the surface.

But Declan, the blood-family's head vamp, could do more. He could share or even steal memories. I'd seen him do it once with Fiona, his seneschal and human partner. They'd kissed. It hadn't been a quick peck on the cheek either. Well, that explained why Malik was watching me like he expected me to pitch a fit. Either he was worried about the memory bit, the kissing bit, or both. Easier to go with the kissing, which after what we'd just nearly done ...

I looked up at him. 'We're talking about a kiss?'

'If you have no objection.'

I showed him my finger and thumb, almost touching. 'Malik, we were this close to doing a lot more than just kissing right on this very table. Why would I object?'

'Our actions were dictated by magic,' he said stiffly. 'They were not consensual.'

Oh. Was he still worried I was about to cry the-big-bad-vamp-enslaved-me, or something?

'Well, yeah,' I said slowly, wanting to reassure him I was okay with things. After all, it had been my idea, sort of. 'I know we didn't exactly start out planning to have sex with each other, but it's not like it's never been a possibility.' Hell, I'd practically laid myself out on my bed for him at one point during the ToLA case to persuade him to help me. Not that he'd taken me up on my offer, thanks to his pact with Tavish about protecting me. At least, not in real life. In my fantasies, however … I felt slight heat rise in my cheeks as I carried on, 'And as I told you when we last had this discussion, I'm perfectly willing if you …' I trailed off. He looked like I was asking him to inhale garlic.

'You may be willing, Genevieve. I am not.'

Hurt and rejection stung me more painfully than the jellyfish had. Looked like I'd really got my attraction wires crossed somewhere along the way. Maybe his refusal last time hadn't just been because of his deal with Tavish. Though if his body language was anything to go by, he wanted me as much as I wanted him. He was either lying to me or to himself. Well, fuck that.

'Are you saying that you *don't* want to have sex with me?' I snapped out. 'Because, spell or no, that's not the impression I've got.'

His black eyes turned opaque and unreadable. '*Le Théâtre du Grand-Guignol* is performing scenes from *Scars of Dracula* all this week, Genevieve. I would be honoured if you would attend as my guest, and after the show, it would be my pleasure if you would join me for refreshments.'

I stared at him speechless. *Le Théâtre du Grand-Guignol* was in the Blue Heart. He wanted me to go to a vamp show in a vamp club. Then join him for *refreshments* … Was this some sort of weird sucker crap? Something to do with showing off his property? My mind stuttered between annoyed disbelief and bewilderment—

Unless, was he asking me on a *date*?

A heady lightness filled me, only to deflate like a pricked balloon. Hell, even if it was a date, why ask me to go somewhere I couldn't be seen? I might not need the Witches' Council's protection any more, but I was the boss of Spellcrackers: it's a witch company, and I needed my witch employees. If I started publicly hanging out with vamps when I was off-duty, the Council would forbid them to work for me. No employees. No Spellcrackers. Malik knew that—

'Genevieve?'

I shot him a narrow look. 'Are you asking me on a date?'

'I believe that is the current term, yes.' Amusement twitched his mouth.

I blinked. He thought this was funny? It was more like inviting a starving woman to a banquet then telling her she couldn't eat. 'Then why invite me to a vamp club? You know I won't visit one unless it's on witch-authorised business.'

His amusement died; replaced by ... *regret*? *Sorrow*? 'That you even think to ask that question, Genevieve, is the reason I ask.'

Damn. Now he was doing the cryptic thing. I hate that. 'I'm asking because I want to know the answer, Malik. So explain it to me.'

'It is not only yourself you hurt,' he said softly, 'when you deny who you are and refuse to embrace your true heritage.' Then he was gone, leaving me frowning up at the ceiling. I sat up to see him lift a shirt from the table nearest the door and slip it on.

What the— 'You're leaving?' I said, stupidly, as that was obviously what he was doing.

'There are clothes here to replace the ones I damaged.' He indicated a suit carrier on the table.

When the hell had he organised them? Not to mention why was he running off in the middle of ... *asking me on a date*?

And how the hell had we got here from his asking permission to kiss me to check out my memories of the tarot card? Damn it! I was missing something here, something important, only I couldn't work out what past the confused whirl in my mind. And judging by the way he was leaving— Crap. Had left! He wasn't prepared to stick around long enough for me to sort things out.

I scrambled off the table and ran to the door. The corridor outside was empty.

Fuck. 'Malik?' I called, hoping he'd come back. 'What about the Emperor?'

I will look into it. His voice sounded distant in my head. *If you wish to accept my invitation, leave a message with my answering service.* Then there was nothing but silence.

Angry and confused, I grabbed the suit carrier and headed for the en suite restroom to find myself surrounded by more bland beige luxury: marble sinks topped with well-lit mirrors that flattered, expensive toiletries that smelled of lilies, and towels rolled and tucked into wicker baskets. The replacement clothes – black trousers, silky cream T-shirt and a dark lilac linen jacket that wasn't a colour I'd have chosen, but looked surprisingly great with my hair – were from a local 24/7 chain store. Whoever Malik had got to shop for me had good taste. Briefly I wondered who, and if they'd seen me unconscious and naked on the table ... which was kind of creepy ... then decided that wasn't worth worrying about. There was underwear too. The cream lace would look good against my honey-coloured skin, or it would have if not for the rose-coloured bruises marking me.

He'd said they weren't permanent. Not that I cared one way or the other right now. I yanked the labels off the underwear. Damn it! The beautiful vamp had reached whole new levels of annoying. He'd told me he wasn't willing. Then asked me on a date. To a vamp club. Then spouted some cryptic crap about hurting myself, and him, by denying who I was and not embracing my heritage.

Only I wasn't denying anything. Everyone knew my father was a vamp, but I was sidhe like my mother. And while I might want to embrace Malik, no way was I going to rock the boat by going on a public date with him, not when I didn't know what the hell he was playing at. And not when he was making iffy comments about knowing what my answers to his questions would be. Almost as if the irritating vamp was testing me ... I tugged on the briefs, following that thought ... As if he wasn't willing to have sex with me unless I made some sort of grand gesture or declaration that he meant something to me.

Damn. Didn't he know that he did? Hell, I'd already forgiven the idiotic vamp for doing his mind-meld on my memories, for ordering me about as if I were a blood-slave, and for killing me more than once – not that I'm masochistic, and the circumstances were extenuating; I'd even asked him to, that last time – but hey, how much more of a declaration did he want? *A date. In public. In a place you wouldn't normally go. For no other reason than to be with him.* And my knee-jerk reaction had been: *no way.* Crap. I'd failed his test. He was right. Why the hell should he want sex or anything else with me when I wouldn't even be seen with him in public?

I jerked the bra's straps to adjust them, and slipped it on.

Except, by that same standard Malik was wrong too.

If he was going to play stupid games with me, instead of talking things through, then why the hell should *I* want sex or anything more with *him*?

Only I did want more. My heart thudded erratically as the trembling, indefinable emotion I felt for Malik crystallised into something steady and tangible in my heart.

'So I should probably go on this date and sort things out,'

I told my reflection, then scowled as my mind threw a huge curve ball at me.

The Autarch.

The psychotic prick had been pulling Malik's strings with the Jellyfish spell, trying to stop me removing it. And then there was Malik's answers about the Emperor. Or rather his non-answers, seeing as he'd started prevaricating as soon as I'd mentioned the tarot card. How far could I trust that whatever game Malik was playing was down to him and not the Autarch?

And if it was the Autarch speaking through Malik's mouth, then the Blue Heart date scenario made more sense. It was vamp territory, I'd be more vulnerable, and so would Malik. Damn. I needed to talk to him; without the Autarch's interference. I touched the rose-shaped bruises on my wrist that hid my bracelet; I could use Malik's ring and contact him through the Dreamscape: that might work. And the best place to do that was— well, not here; it wasn't safe.

Last time we'd met in the Dreamscape, he'd used Tower Bridge as a backdrop, but really it could be any place we were both familiar with, like oh, say, my bedroom? After all, I couldn't get much safer than my own bed ... My pulse raced as my Malik fantasies roared back to life, fuelled by our recent near miss. We'd been a breath away from sex. Lust and longing twisted low inside me. And, boy, was I missing sex after nearly a year of no touch but my own. Sighing, I traced the bruises on my breasts, following them down my body to the last mark, which disappeared beneath the lacy briefs, remembering the glorious feel of his hands on me—

Sudden excruciating arousal made my legs buckle. I fell to my knees and, desperate for release, shoved a hand into my briefs. As soon as I touched myself, an orgasm rocked through me, more pain than pleasure. Panting, I collapsed against the mirror. My reflection stared back at me with molten-copper eyes wide with shock. Magic wreathed me in a swirling golden haze, and Malik's marks suddenly gleamed like blood-tinted silver pennies.

The mark on my wrist had never done that – I looked – was still not doing that. Arousal flamed through me again, making me feel I'd perish in agony if I didn't come. This time it took much more than a touch to get me off as I crumpled over on the floor, forehead on the cold marble, arse in the air, my fingers working feverishly, unable to stop – *what the fuck was wrong with me?* – until finally the orgasm ripped through me as if the pain/pleasure were trying to tear me apart. I screamed my release, the sound reverberating like a banshee's screech in the small room.

The door slammed open.

A vamp stood framed in the doorway, his platinum hair hanging loose around his shoulders, his hooded blue eyes cold as they scanned the room. He was dressed in jeans and a T-shirt with a picture of a tongue-lolling Irish wolfhound's head on it: an outfit that would've seemed odd if you didn't know him.

I did. He was Maxim Fyodor Zakharin a.k.a. Mad Max. My uncle on my sidhe mother's side; or distant cousin on my vamp father's side. Neither of the relationships were ones I wanted to acknowledge, even without the icky overtones of incest. Not that the family relationship, or the incest, stopped there; Mad Max had taken both further by having a fling with his niece, my half-sister Brigitta, who I'd never even known existed until I'd learned she'd been killed by the vamps. I say fling, but it was more than that, seeing as they'd had a kid together, Ana.

But even without the close family connections, there was no way I trusted Mad Max. He was the Autarch's pet vamp. He was a crazy sonofabitch who hardly cared for himself, much less anyone else; I'd seen him cheerfully stake his own father on a whim. And he was the vamp who'd kidnapped Katie last year. As relatives and vamps go, Mad Max was the last one anyone would want to see, even if they weren't huddled half-naked on the floor, fighting a compulsion to pleasure themselves again.

A compulsion my gut told me was magical.

Somebody – *the provider of the underwear?* – must've sicced me with some sort of sex spell.

But despite that, and the soreness between my legs telling me I'd been more than rough in my desperation, I still throbbed with arousal. I wanted. Needed. But my gut also told me another attempt at release was likely to drive me as crazy as Mad Max, and quite possibly render parts of me raw and bloody. What I wanted, *needed,* was something more.

Mad Max stopped scanning and his gaze settled on me. For a moment he stared as if I were some strange specimen he'd never seen before, then he sniffed. A grin broke his face, flashing all four of his fangs. 'Paddling the pink canoe, are you, Cousin? Good for you. But a bit of rumpy pumpy's much more fun than flying solo. Want some company?'

Not in a million years, and *Touch me and I'll stake you* vied as answers in my head, but the Compulsion riding me had other ideas. It wasn't too impressed with the faint reddish glow emanating from him, but it decided it was better than nothing, so even as part of me recoiled in horrified disbelief, I flung my magic at him. It snaked out, twisting round his limbs like thick golden vines, and my mouth growled, 'Yes, I want company.'

He barked a laugh, his eyes flashing from white to gold like manic warning lights. 'It'll be my pleasure, Cousin!' And he stepped towards me, his stance familiar in a way I realised way too late to counter, as he shifted his weight, swung his leg in a fast roundhouse kick and his boot connected with my temple.

The world exploded into the proverbial Milky Way of spinning stars—

And I plunged into darkness.

Chapter Ten

The world swam back into head-pounding, dimly lit focus. I still throbbed with arousal. Not as desperately as before, but more like banked embers that would burst into flame at the slightest breath of air. But the Compulsion nagged at me. On autopilot I tried to touch myself, only—

I was tied down. On a bed. Spreadeagled like I was a star in some tacky bondage video.

Panic roared up. I struggled, my screams muffled by the fabric gagging my mouth.

'Good-oh, Cousin, nice to see you're awake.' Mad Max loomed over me, eyes burning white fire, and slapped something wet and warm over my thighs and between my legs.

Enforced calm relaxed my body, muscles going limp as cooked noodles. My panic retreated deep inside, where it clawed and spat like a caged tiger; the pounding in my head diminished and everything around me took on a recognisable shape and form.

I was in a hotel room, going by what I could see out of my oddly swollen eyes and the trickle of light coming from behind the wall of drawn curtains. The light's sodium hue told me it was still night. As did the red electronic clock on the plasma TV opposite, which also told me I'd been here for a good hour.

On the plasma a large St Bernard was lolloping after a blonde standard poodle. The St Bernard was wearing a bow tie, and streaming from the poodle's collar was something white and lacy ... *a bridal veil*? The sight was so surreal I stared until

Mad Max grunted and pointed the remote. The TV flicked off.

In its place, spent magic drifted like dust motes, and the place smelled of herbs, treacle and something vinegary. The same fabric – *ripped sheets?* – that gagged me was tied around my wrists and ankles, with knots that tightened as I gave an experimental tug. Silver banded my head— silver that stopped me using magic. Not that I had any, other than my Glamour. Which had obviously been so successful – *not!* – at trapping Mad Max earlier.

I gave myself a quick mental once-over: as well as the silver burning my head, my skin itched from dried sweat, my body felt like a horde of Beater goblins had introduced me to their baseball bats, and the rawness in my throat suggested I'd been practising sword swallowing. The only part of me that didn't hurt, or throb, was between my legs … numbed by whatever the warm wet thing was.

Which would've been a whole new worry, if not for the enforced calm.

Mad Max leaned over, poked my cheek. I glared up at him, wanting to knock his hands away.

'Bleeding hell, love, you're a hard nut to crack,' he drawled. 'I've met mountain trolls who break easier than you.'

I was going to kill the sonofabitch.

The white fire in his eyes faded. He settled into the chair next to the bed, crossed his arms over his bare chest, and stretched out long pale legs with an exaggerated sigh. All he was wearing was a pair of red boxers decorated with black coffins.

It hit home that all *I* was wearing was the cream bra. I couldn't feel the briefs, but I couldn't tell if that was because I was numb, or they weren't there.

I lifted my head, straining to look. The wet warm thing moulded to me like a thick second skin was made of nubby towelling. It was pink-tinged, dotted with bits of green leaf and the magic in it glinted like the tiny chunks of glass of a smashed car windscreen. Did our mutual state of undress mean he'd had sex with me? After all, I'd been offering it to him on a plate – or the Sex-compulsion spell had. The panic and rage inside me threw itself against its cage, but the calm kept it contained.

I jerked my chin at him and tried to spit the gag out.

He got the message. 'Start screaming,' he warned, 'and it goes straight back in.'

I nodded, and he pulled it out.

'Why—' I coughed, licked my lips, which were split and tasted of my own dried blood, and started again. 'Why the hell am I tied up?'

'Just keeping you out of my pants, love. Much as I enjoy a bit of the rough stuff when it comes to foreplay, you're a tad too forceful for my liking.' He spread his arms wide. Long bloody furrows ran down his chest and stomach, disappearing into his red boxers, as if some rabid animal had attacked him; only a hazy memory told me the rabid animal had been me. I almost apologised, but he added, 'Of course, as a bit of slap and tickle was all that was on the cards, I have to confess I did rather let my frustration get the better of me when it came to subduing you. But y'know, Cousin, what goes around, comes around.'

The swollen eyes, split lip and various other pains made sense now.

I'd attacked him once – he'd been hurting my friends – and had beaten his face almost to a pulp almost with a backpack full of bricks. He'd obviously decided to return the favour.

'Bastard,' I spat out.

'Payback's a bitch! Oh, no, wait! This time payback's a dog!' He chuckled then growled menacingly exactly like a dog, which was eerily apt since his other form was an Irish wolfhound. Like the picture on the T-shirt he was no longer wearing.

'Why aren't you dressed?'

'Just being practical, Cousin.' He pointed at my bottom half. 'That's a wet towel and I've got a bath full of Poultice potion.'

Practical? Him?

'But I 'spect you're asking 'cause you're wondering if I took you up on your offer to do the old in and out together,' Mad Max continued cheerfully

I gritted my teeth. 'Yes.'

'Enticing as making the beast with two backs with you might be, a few too many interested parties would get a tad upset about it. My loopy fruitcake of a sister with her part-time goddess gig, for one – or two, depending which way you look at it.'

I wasn't sure that his sister, a.k.a. my mother, Angel, would even notice, though she had spied on me magically in the past, but why was anyone's guess. She wasn't just loopy, but seemed to have the mental age of a five-year-old, so I doubted she even knew I was her daughter. Hell, I hadn't even known she was my mother until I'd met her for only the second time three months ago. Until then I'd believed my mother died at my birth— all of which was something my head, never mind my heart, was still coming to terms with.

And as for Angel's goddess hitch-hiker, The Mother, well no way could I predict how she'd feel; it wasn't like she'd been overly concerned about me in the past other than to dump me with a problem she couldn't be bothered to solve herself. Though Mad Max knew them better, so if he thought they'd be 'a tad upset', I was happy to go along with him. On that, anyway.

'Then there's the Turk' – he gave a dramatic shudder – 'I'd have to be insane and suicidal to get on the wrong side of the great and powerful Malik al-Khan. Oh, and let's not forget His Royal Brattiness—'

'The Autarch's not coming here!' I interrupted as a spurt of panic overcame the spell's calm.

Mad Max waved a dismissive hand. 'Oh, don't get your knickers in a twist, Cousin. It isn't worth sticking my head above the parapet to tell him about your little problems. He enjoys eviscerating the messengers too much.' He cocked a finger and mimed shooting himself in the head. 'So, unluckily for you, Cousin, you're doomed never to know the magnificence that is my love wand.'

Relief flooded through me. Not that his self-serving restraint was going to stop me removing his love wand and shoving it, along with the rest of him, where the sun *did* shine, given half a chance.

'Now, of course, you're probably also wondering why we're having ourselves a little bondage party here.' He flashed a fang-filled grin. 'I must admit I was too, for a while, since it's unheard of for me to be so altruistic. But then I convinced myself that having everyone find out I've got more than one crazy relative was going to reflect particularly badly on me.'

And they say chivalry is dead.

'So I magnanimously opted to save you from beating around your own bush until some poor unsuspecting human stumbled into your Glamour.'

The suspicious part of me wondered exactly how and why he'd been oh, so conveniently on hand to *save* me, but that thought was eclipsed by the horror of what could have happened. Humans can't survive full-on sex with a sidhe outside of the Fair Lands. If a human had found me, I'd probably have fucked them to death.

'I'm sure you can think of a suitable way to thank me later, Cousin,' Mad Max said, a smug smirk on his face. 'But I can't always be waiting around to clear up your nasty little messes, so this lesson is by way of a heads up.' He leaned forward in the chair. 'So, listen carefully.'

I snorted. 'It's not like I've got any choice.'

'Good-oh!' He wagged an admonishing finger at me. 'Living like a nun while shacking up with a Fertility spell isn't the best lifestyle choice for a sidhe fae.'

I wasn't shacking up with a Fertility spell, exactly. I was living with Sylvia, my friend who was pregnant. And Sylvia was wearing the sapphire pendant with the fae's trapped fertility that had made that pregnancy possible. She and her partner, Ricou, had moved in with me after the ToLA case, due to their families arguing about where they should live; my flat was apparently nominated neutral territory. I hadn't been too thrilled having new flatmates to begin with, but it had turned out to be fun, though evidently the fertility magic in the pendant had been having its own fun without any of us knowing— if I was to believe Mad Max.

'Are you saying the pendant is' – I eyed him mistrustfully – 'spreading its magic around, or something?'

'Leaking is the word you're looking for,' Mad Max said cheerfully. 'Which means denial isn't just a river in Egypt; for you, love, it's a cracked dam leading to a flood of impromptu orgies every time you feel a tad frisky. Sticking your finger in the hole, however enthusiastically, isn't going to do a damn thing.' He gave a barking laugh then poked me in the side. 'Dam and damn. Get it, Cousin?'

I got it. Along with a jagged pain that said: cracked ribs. Sonofabitch had really gone for it with his payback.

I also got what he was going on about: the stupid sidhe sex myth, the one where the humans all think we're gagging for it at the drop of a hat thanks to the ancient fertility rites once held to replenish the land and encourage its future fecundity, and the salacious tales about the rites being huge free-for-all orgies. Tales I'd been told were the product of humans prurient imaginations, since the rites, usually held during the main equinoxes – *like the Summer Solstice we were fast approaching*

– had always been well orchestrated, rigidly controlled and only for those specifically chosen participants who'd carefully prepared … by purposely abstaining from intercourse in the months leading up to the rite …

Like I'd been abstaining!

Shit! How could I have been such an idiot? I'd been obliviously setting myself up for my own personal fertility rite. And the Glamour I'd hit Malik with, along with the frustration of *oh, so near* sex, had flipped some sort of switch inside me. Only by the time it had, Malik was gone. Hence my desperate self-pleasuring (which really hadn't been any pleasure at all) until Mad Max had turned up and the fertility magic blazing hot within me had decided it wanted a piece of him. Even though the thought of jumping *his* bones, blood relationship aside, was enough to make me want to throw up, it seemed being male had been enough for the magic to go, 'Screw the crazy sonofabitch!'

Maybe I should thank him for tying me up instead? Nah. Never gonna happen. I was pretty sure he'd gone for overkill, and even if he hadn't, he was enjoying the pseudo BDSM way too much.

I glared at him. 'What's the spell in the towel for?'

'Oh, just a little magic poultice I cooked up to help you.'

'Since when do vamps do magic?'

'You forget, Cousin,' he admonished, 'that my mother is a sidhe queen. Clíona might have chosen to make me human and mortal, but I'm still a wizard by birth. Becoming a vamp didn't change that.'

I frowned, suspicious. Was he kidding me? Though now I thought about it, he would be a wizard, as the son of a sidhe and a human (as his dad had been, when Mad Max was – nauseatingly – conceived). And I'd never known any vamp who'd been anything other than a straight human before they'd Accepted the Gift – unsurprisingly, given the whole ancient

84

Live and Let Live Tenets between the witches, wizards and vamps: the last thing they did was socialise. So a wizard keeping his magic after being given the Gift could be possible …

'Though Mommie Dearest didn't actually teach me anything. That was down to your sister, Brigitta.' He gave me a cat-that's-got-the-canary smile.

Half-sister, I mentally corrected him, though you couldn't tell by looking at Brigitta's picture. We could've been twins, if she hadn't been born forty-odd years before me. Even though I'd thought of her earlier when Mad Max had first appeared, his mentioning her again, and the fact she'd taught him magic, raised a mix of grief and anger that I'd never known her, along with the usual frustrated envy that she obviously hadn't lacked anything in the magical ability department. Unlike me. But then Brigitta's father had been the fossegrim, a lesser fae, while my father had been a vamp. For a moment I almost asked Mad Max whether he knew if our having different fathers was the reason why I couldn't do magic, then I nixed that idea. No way was I going to discuss the ins and outs of anything with *him*. Instead, I scowled and said again, 'What's the spell in the towel do?'

'Stops you wanting to polish the peanut, Cousin. What else?'

Ah. 'Okay,' I said slowly, 'it's worked. So you can untie me.'

His smile widened, blue eyes lighting with unholy delight. 'Oh, I don't think so, love. No gain without pain, isn't that what they say?'

He whipped the wet towel away. A cloud of dust motes floated up, the calm feeling vanished, and the painful arousal throbbed back to even more agonising life than before. The shock pulled a scream from deep inside me; but before it could escape, he stuffed the wad of sheet back in my mouth. I bucked and writhed, desperate to get free, to kill him, or myself, whatever would bring me release—

His fist slammed into my jaw.

'Oh, and next time, Cousin,' I heard him say as I slid into unconsciousness, 'just fuck the Turk. It'll sort you out, put the great Malik al-Khan out of his misery, and save the rest of us the hassle of his bleeding melodramas.'

I woke to the sun streaming round the curtain edges. The clock told me it was not long past dawn. The crazy sonofabitch was gone. No way would he stick around after the sun had risen, not when he'd have dropped into a vamp's daytime sleep – a sort of hibernation mode that looked very much like being dead. And if I had my way, next time we met the vicious sonofabitch wouldn't just look dead *he'd be dead*. I was going to make sure of it; the mad vamp had left me *still tied to the damn bed*.

He'd also left me draped with the towel, which was now a sludgy mess dripping cold water adding to the existing wet spot beneath me. Ugh. On the positive front, that part of me felt fine. And I was no longer gagged, verbally or magically; the silver headband was gone. The rest of me felt fragile, in a beaten-unconscious sort of way. Unsurprisingly, since Mad Max had roused me a couple more times, whipped off the towel, cheerfully watched as my frantic struggles demonstrated that the spell hadn't done whatever it was supposed to yet, and enthusiastically knocked my lights out again.

I was going to enjoy killing him. Slowly.

Once I got free.

I debated shouting for help. Unfortunately any 'rescue' would come with embarrassment. There was no way this wouldn't end up in the scandal rags. I'd have to live with headlines like SIDHE IN KINKY SEX ROMP until something more salacious came along. Not to mention the risk of YouTube.

I shuddered. Maybe I should just wait. After all, Mad Max couldn't leave me here like this …

Just as I was thinking the sonofabitch might be crazy enough to do exactly that, a tentative knock sounded on the door.

I froze.

My phone rang, the ringtone coming from the short corridor outside the bathroom. As it went to voicemail the door clicked open. I braced myself, pulse racing, wondering if they were friend or foe.

The door clicked shut.

Chapter Eleven

A figure moved slowly into the room, tall, dressed in black leathers, hair pulled back in a sleek blonde ponytail, phone in one hand, half-a-dozen bags in the other.

Katie. I almost cried with thankfulness.

'Genny?' She stopped, shock rounding her eyes.

'I'm fine,' I said, forcing a rueful tone into my voice. 'Practical joke that went a bit far.'

'Your face is all beat up,' she whispered, horrified. 'Shall I phone for an ambulance?'

'No.' I sighed. 'I doubt it's as bad as it looks.' Not that I knew how I looked, but— 'Don't suppose you could untie me, hon?'

'Oh my gosh, of course.' She dropped the bags, and rushed to me, tugged at the knots, then resorted to nail scissors to cut me free. Never had I been so grateful for the girlie contents of Katie's huge designer handbag.

As she snipped away freeing my wrists, I gave her a short, highly edited version of the night's events. I'd had a problem with my magic, a 'friend' had helped me, and to stop me hurting myself or anyone else they'd had to tie me up. I hadn't been too happy about it, which was where my injuries had come from. Only the 'friend' had a crazy sense of humour, and hadn't untied me when they'd left. None of which was a lie; something I physically can't do.

'Frigging frenemy, you mean, leaving you like this,' she growled when I'd finished. 'They need a taste of their own medicine.'

'Already with you,' I muttered, as she started work on my ankles. I sat up carefully, mindful of the cracked ribs and the aching stiffness in my shoulders. Not to mention my head and face which felt tight and swollen, like my skin was about to burst like a rotten plum. Crap, the mad sucker had really done a number on me. I'd heal, and way quicker than a human, but quicker wasn't instant. How the hell was I supposed to work like this?

My gaze fell on a glass on the desk. It was full of dark red-brownish liquid.

Suddenly hopeful, I asked Katie to get it for me.

The glass had one of the hotel's cardboard hygiene-covers on it. Scrawled across it, in what looked like blood, was: 'Drink Me! ☺'

'Is it another joke?' she asked.

'Better not be.' I took the cover off and sniffed. Sour apples tinged with copper. Definitely Mad Max's blood. I knew it had healing properties, almost on a par with Malik's blood, having been injured once before (also Mad Max's fault, albeit indirectly) and healed by his blood. I looked for a catch but couldn't think of one, mainly because I regularly gave my donated blood to Mad Max's faeling grandkid, Freya, my whatever-number-removed cousin (since she's only eight, it's easier to call her my 'niece').

Thanks to Freya's mixed-up genetics (vamp/sidhe/fae/human), she's ended up with a vamp's need for blood along with the more usual need for solid food in order to survive. With Ana (Freya's mum and Mad Max's daughter) pregnant, I'd stepped in as Freya's blood donor instead. Mad Max knew that and, despite his seeming lack of family values, I could probably stake my life on his never doing anything to harm Freya.

Plus it was like the crazy sonofabitch to leave me a way to heal the damage. After all, he'd enjoyed watching me suffer through bouts of painful arousal, while at the same time making a spell to rid me of it ... or so he'd said.

I put the blood down. No way was I drinking it unless the spell had worked. I explained briefly to Katie, then before her worried eyes, slowly peeled the sludgy towel away.

Once it was gone I waited for the agonising throb to start up. It didn't. Relieved, I let out the breath I'd been holding. I was okay. Mad Max had been telling me the truth about the spell. Another thought struck me.

I looked up at Katie. 'How did you know I was here?'

'I got a text from you. The keycard was left in an envelope at reception.'

Mad Max was evidently Mr Organised.

I sighed. It was either drink his blood or send Katie out for an expensive, and not so quick, healing spell from the Witches' Market.

I couldn't afford to show up anywhere looking like a victim of domestic abuse. Even without the embarrassment it would cause my clients, all it would take was one paparazzo and my battered face would be splashed across the front pages.

Decision made I picked up the glass and slugged the sour-tasting blood down. My stomach clenched as it hit, then I grunted as it spread through my body like battery acid, burning me from the inside out.

'Okay, that's just ... gross.' Katie's quiet mutter made me look at her.

'What?'

'Your face,' she said, quickly dropping her gaze back to the sheet she was cutting. 'It's moving like there's something running around under your skin.'

Nice! 'It doesn't feel too good either,' I mumbled around what felt like a mouthful of tiny crab apples. Not to mention my rippling skin was making me nauseous, or maybe that was

Mad Max's blood. I started picking at the sheet round my right ankle, hoping I wasn't going to puke.

Katie cleared her throat, the sound nervous, then keeping her gaze fixed on her scissors, said, 'Did anyone get back to you about last night? The Carnival or the police?'

Inwardly I cursed myself. Of course she'd be worried about the flasher, whereas I'd totally forgotten about it. Some friend I was. 'I don't know,' I said. 'I haven't had chance to check my messages.'

Katie jumped up and retrieved my backpack. Fishing out my phone she checked, then looked up disappointed. 'Nothing.'

'I'll call a bit later and ask,' I said, hoping I'd get some sort of answer that would reassure her.

She gave a small nod. 'Thanks.'

'I'm pretty sure it's nothing to worry about. The police said they'd had reports of flashers in the park before, so it was just really bad luck we were there. It's horrible, but there's nothing personal in it.'

'Yeah, I know. I talked to Mum about it last night. But then when I went over it in my head I realised I'd seen something else.'

Had she seen a vamp? Worry pricked goosebumps on my arms. 'Something else?'

'Yeah.' She stopped snipping and fixed me with an odd expression, half excited, half anxious. 'Remember I said the man sort of collapsed, and then I saw that weird animal? Well, I think, instead of the man looking for the animal, I think they're the same. I think the man turned into the animal.'

I stared at her. 'You think he was a shapeshifter?'

'Yes!' She leaned forward. 'Is it possible?'

Hmm. I hadn't seen the naked man, or vamp as I'd thought he was. I hadn't seen any weird animal. All I'd seen was an odd shadow of movement, and even that might have been my imagination. And the only pings I'd got on my inner radar had been the old man and his dog, who, when I mentioned them to the police, had confirmed the man was a local, and kosher …

Except, what if the male had been a vamp, and had turned into an animal. It was possible and it would explain how he had vanished so fast, and why my Spidey senses hadn't pinged him. After all, Mad Max turned into an Irish wolfhound, and when he did I couldn't tell he wasn't anything other than the dog he seemed. Not to mention if someone *was* spying on me, Mad Max was the obvious candidate.

Only Katie had said the man in the park was dark-haired. Mad Max was blond. But the Autarch was dark-haired, and he'd given Mad Max the gift. Vamp powers ran through the bloodlines, so it was possible that the Autarch could turn into some sort of animal. Plus, I'd asked Malik if the Autarch could go out in daylight if he stayed in the shade and he'd never answered my question. Just told me the Autarch wasn't the Emperor. Crap. Maybe my paranoia was spot on and the Autarch had been spying on me last night.

'I looked up shapeshifters,' Katie said, interrupting my worrying thoughts. 'Did you know the only non-fae shape-shifters are werewolves? There used to be other animal/human-shifters but they were all hunted to extinction.'

I blinked at her, surprised. 'You think it was a werewolf last night?'

'Well, they exist, so it's possible, isn't it?'

'Yeah,' I said slowly. Possible didn't mean probable. 'I suppose so. There aren't any werewolves in Britain, though.'

'Not living here, no,' Katie agreed, dipping her head so her ponytail fell to hide her face, then went on to tell me were-wolves had been hunted to extinction in Britain sometime in the 1700s, as had real wolves which was around the same time the rest of the world's therianthropes or wereshifters had been killed off. However, werewolves – lycanthropes – had managed to escape total extinction when they were given 'full human rights' status in Russia by Empress Anna Ivanovna, who used them as part of her security police force. Apparently, there were only about hundred packs left worldwide, which amounted to just under a thousand lycans in total, the majority of those were in Russia. As usual, Katie's research was thorough and gave more detail than I wanted or probably needed to know.

'It also said that once they get the scent of a virgin,' Katie finished, 'they hunt them down so they can Change them.' She stopped cutting, scissors poised above my foot. 'I'm still a virgin, Genny.'

Well, your mother will be pleased to hear that! Not that I'd thought any different. But I'd heard the hitch in Katie's voice. She was worried some imaginary werewolf was going to come looking for her. I knew it wouldn't happen.

'That's just an old wives' tale,' I said, trying to reassure her. 'Far as I remember, new werewolves get recruited from long-serving members of the military or police. I'm pretty sure they're all volunteers, and I doubt any of them are virgins. You know Wikipedia isn't always right, don't you, Katie?'

She snorted and jabbed the tiny scissors back into the knotted sheet hard enough to make me flinch. 'I didn't get this from Wikipedia, but from the witch archives in the British Library.'

'They're password protected,' I said, wondering how the hell she'd got access.

'Tavish gave me one.'

Crap. 'Tavish has a lot to answer for,' I muttered. I wasn't surprised he'd hacked the archives, just that he'd given Katie the password.

'So do werewolves hunt virgins?'

I sighed. 'Told you, it's an old myth, and even if it were true, I doubt the male was close enough to you for it to be a problem.'

'Genny! I know you told that policeman something last night, that you didn't tell me.'

93

Damn. Sometimes Katie was too observant for her own good. I picked at the knot I was working on for a moment, then sighed; if she was going to worry about something, it might as well be the truth. 'I think the male you saw was a vamp who was following me. One that can shapechange. Only I won't know for sure until I get some answers. When I do, I'll let you know. And I'll make sure that you're not in any danger this time.' Whatever I have to do. 'Okay?'

She stayed quiet for a long moment, head down, blonde hair covering her face. 'A vampire?' She glanced up, a mix of anger and fear flashing in her grey eyes, just as I felt the skin of my face twitching like it had popcorn jumping beneath it. She grimaced and looked down again. 'Okay. Actually that's less worrying than thinking he was a werewolf.'

I blinked. 'Really?'

'Yeah. I know you're sort of half vamp, and I know they're not all bad. And I know you can deal with the bad ones anyway.'

What was I supposed to say to that? It was good she had confidence in me, but I wasn't sure I could live up to it. Only if I said that, it might only make her anxious again.

'And I've got these.' She grabbed her huge designer bag and upended it on the bed between us. In amongst the make-up, hair products, glossy mag and other girlie stuff were half-a-dozen bulbs of garlic, three tubes of minced garlic paste, one of chilli paste and a bag of red chillies, the tiny super-hot ones, and a thin bundle of what looked like brass chopsticks.

She'd got her very own vamp-repelling kit. Eating the garlic and chilli wouldn't put them off, but the paste smeared on skin would stop them biting; charred lips are a quick, easy way to kill a vamp's appetite.

She waved the chopsticks. 'Tavish says one of these in the heart will paralyse a vamp. He said I'd probably never need to use it, just wave it around to get their attention and remind them to behave.' She leaned forwards and hooked her heart-shaped pendant from inside her top. 'He also added some spells to this; one that stops the vamps using their mind-lock on me, and another that makes me smell like a faeling. He said all the fae and faelings in London are under the Oligarch's protection, thanks to you, so none of them will even come near me so long as I wear this.'

Wow. Tavish *had* been busy, but in a good way.

Katie gave me a lopsided smile. 'So, thanks for telling me, Genny. I know you didn't 'cause you didn't want to worry me, but I'd rather know. And I know vamps can't get me if I stay safe behind a threshold and don't invite them in. That doesn't apply to werewolves.'

She had a point. The counselling must've done more good than I thought, making her look at things in a practical, pro-active way and not just panicking. A lesson I could do with, particularly when it came to dealing with the Autarch.

'You're right,' I agreed. 'I didn't want to worry you. Sorry. I'll tell it like it is next time.'

'Good.' She nodded, packed her stuff away and worked on in silence for a few minutes, then gave a final flourish with her scissors to set me free.

I waggled my foot in relief and she peered at me, grey eyes glinting with mischief. 'Your face looks better now. Less like you've got beetles tunnelling under your skin and more like you're hungover.'

'Nice image.' I snorted, jumping up to peer in the overdesk mirror. Hungover was about right, but even as I looked, the dark circles were fading. I prodded my ribs, no pain. Mad Max's blood had done the business. In fact, I was pretty sure another ten minutes would see me healed of everything other than Malik's rose-coloured bruises. What I needed now was something to eat and a shower. Not necessarily in that order. Spying the room service menu, I asked Katie to order us some breakfast, then headed for the bathroom.

I stood under the hot shower, easing the kinks in my muscles and mulling over Mad Max.

Never mind the mystery of why he'd helped me, the real question was: what was he doing sniffing round me like a hound following a scent? Either he was spying on me, or Malik ... or hell, maybe Malik had asked him to watch out for me? He'd obviously asked someone to buy me new clothes. And that someone might have been Mad Max.

So, if Malik *had* asked Mad Max to keep an eye on me, that would explain why he'd helped me. Even if his help was the *really* tough-love type. But really, why would Malik trust Mad Max? He knew I didn't. And aside from the fact he was a crazy sonofabitch, Mad Max owed his Oath to the Autarch.

Then again, the Autarch might be Mad Max's liege and master, but maybe crazy Max wasn't so insane after all, since he appeared to hate and fear the psychotic sadist as much as I did.

Of course, there was a third option. Mad Max was keeping an eye on me for the sidhe side of the family. Which was almost as worrying an idea as him spying on me for the Autarch.

Shivering despite the steam, I wrapped a towel tightly around myself and grabbed the hotel hairdryer.

The only way I was going to get any solid answers was to do what I'd planned to do before the fertility magic and Mad Max had hijacked my night— speak to Malik in the Dreamscape. I gave my hair a hurried blast of heat, checked my phone and gauged I had just enough time before work to try now. A plus being that Katie could watch over my sleeping body while she was eating breakfast.

Decision made, I touched Malik's rose-shaped bruises on my left wrist, releasing the bracelet hidden there. It appeared with its usual chinking of charms—

Malik's ring was gone.

My mind skidded to a shocked halt. Malik had to have taken the ring, but why?

Unless it was Mad Max? He'd had enough opportunity, and could do magic, though his ability still left suspicion pricking down my spine. But if it had been him, that still the question of why. Damn it. Speculating was pointless. All that mattered was the ring was gone and I couldn't contact Malik that way. I was going to have to speak to him the non-magical way.

And go on the date.

Of course, going on the date could bring me face to face with the Autarch. Something that made me want to run far, far away, and hide.

But I'd already done that once. And I was older now, so maybe, like Katie, it was time for me to deal with my Autarch phobia, instead of letting my terror rule my life. After all, I might not carry a vamp-repelling kit, but I had something way better— the sword Ascalon.

Heart thudding, I took a deep breath and left a message with Malik's answering service to say I was accepting his invitation, and I was free any night this week. The woman at Sanguine Lifestyles politely and efficiently said she'd pass the message on to Mr al-Khan, and rang off.

I stood for a couple of minutes waiting for my pulse to calm, then finished dressing, ate the bacon butty Katie had ordered, paid the hefty hotel bill Mad Max had stuck me with (including two porn pay-per-view films – *Bitch of the Baskervilles* and *The Brides of Cujo,* images from which made me want to bleach my brain – and which I mentally added to all the 'debts' he owed me. I was *so* going to take my pound of flesh using a very large, very blunt blade) and we headed for Spellcrackers.

Halfway there, my phone rang: Detective Inspector Hugh Munro.

'Morning, Hugh. Social or business call?'

'Official business, I'm afraid, Genny,' he rumbled in his

gravelly voice. 'A woman and her son have disappeared, possibly kidnapped, and there appears to be some sort of strange magic involved. I'd like your help, please.'

Crap. 'Of course. Where?'

'London Zoo.'

'On my way.'

Chapter Twelve

Forty minutes later my taxi dropped me off in the small car park opposite the main entrance to the zoo. I checked the other vehicles: three of the police vans designed for trolls (to be expected), about six other parked cars (again, probably usual) and two long limousines with blacked-out windows (definitely not usual). Both limos were backed into the shade of the scrubby line of trees screening the car park from the rest of the zoo, which butted against Regent's Park beyond. Two chauffeurs were leaning against the furthest limo, caps tipped back and smoke curling up between them from their cigarettes. The limos' licence plates both started the same: 112 D 2. The rest of the number was hidden behind the guys' legs. Diplomatic plates. The words 'International Incident' flashed in my head.

That didn't bode well for the victims.

I crossed to the zoo's main entrance.

The shutters were down on the two outside sections between the entrance columns – the zoo didn't open to the public for a good couple of hours yet – but the middle shutter was drawn up to about my shoulder height. The uniformed WPC – the W standing for both witch and woman – standing guard was one I didn't recognise. She greeted me perfunctorily and waved to a zoo employee sitting slumped over the steering wheel of an open-topped utility cart, ready to take me to the crime scene.

The zoo employee – his name badge stated 'David O'Reilly'

– straightened, tossed me a brooding look from red-rimmed eyes and told me to, 'Hop in.'

I hopped in and caught a whiff of something rank. Glancing over my shoulder, I eyed the tarp covering the cart's flatbed. Whatever was piled beneath it was lumpy and stunk worse than a swamp dragon's cave … *Crap!* Bad pun aside, it suddenly clicked that I was getting a ride on the shit wagon.

The cart jerked forward and I grabbed the metal side-bar as the vehicle's electric motor whirred loudly in seeming complaint. We took a left between the reptile house and the Gorilla Kingdom, judging by the signs. David stared straight ahead, broad shoulders hunched inside his green polo shirt like he was cold, a white-knuckled grip on the steering wheel despite the cart trundling along at not much more than a fast walking pace after its initial leap.

Odd smells drifted on the wind and mixed with the shit stink, making my stomach heave. Damn it. I hadn't known a zoo would reek so.

'Does it always smell like this?' I asked.

David shrugged. I took that as a yes and tried to take shallow breaths as I looked around. I'd never been to a zoo before; growing up with the vamp side of my family had, by necessity, nixed most of the normal childhood-type 'day' outings for more than one reason – but wherever the animals were at this time in the morning, it wasn't anywhere I could see from the path we were on. It made the place feel oddly desolate and empty even with the miasma of smells assaulting me.

I opened my *sight*, looking for spells. After all, that was why I was here: whatever had happened had some sort of magical element to it. But other than a few stray bits of wild magic, there was nothing. And as we drove past a sign saying 'African Bird Safari', I realised something else: the place was eerily quiet.

'I thought a zoo would be noisier?' I raised my voice in question.

David shot me a glance as if he'd forgotten I was there. 'What?'

'I guess I just expected to hear the animals more, you know, like bird calls, or a lion roaring, or grunting.' I waved at the sign on the next exhibit that said 'Bearded Pigs', getting a whiff of something earthy and ripe that in no way smelled like bacon.

He frowned, his hands twisting round the steering wheel. When it was obvious he wasn't going to answer, I made a mental note to ask someone else.

Some minutes later, a stomp on the brakes by David brought us to a halt about ten feet away from the crime scene tape stretched across the path. Beyond the tape the path carried on to an area surrounded by leafy, whip-thin trees. Their canopy shaded a round fountain, its water trickling out from beneath a sculptured bronze little girl, kneeling and offering a bird up to the summer sky and freedom: an ironic sort of statue for a place which kept animals in captivity. Behind the fountain, framed by more greenery, I could see a large colourful sign depicting life-sized lions and tigers: the big cat enclosure.

To the left was a picnic spot with slides, climbing frames and swings, and to the right there was an expanse of grass marked as a 'Display Lawn'.

The 'lawn' was crowded, not with animals, but with a good number of London's Metropolitan Magic and Murder Squad; about a dozen uniformed trolls and near enough two coven's worth of WPCs. With that many milling about, whatever had happened was big ... but then with the two diplomatic limos parked outside that was a given.

The lack of press hanging around the zoo was an oddity, though, until I jumped out the cart and saw Detective Sergeant Mary Martin striding up to the police tape. Pale yellow-coloured magic drifted from her like seeds blown from a ripe dandelion head, lifting high into the air over the zoo. A police

Media-blackout spell – and the reason for the lack of journos.

Mary gave me a professional once-over out of pretty brown eyes, before smiling a welcome with a mouth that looked like she'd just been kissed. I knew she hadn't, since she claimed she was concentrating on her career, having recently been promoted to Detective Sergeant for going 'above and beyond' in the Tower of London Abduction case. Mary had gone undercover as my doppelgänger in an attempt to break the case, which was how we'd met.

She waved at my new outfit. 'Nice. Not your usual colour, but it looks good.'

'Thanks.' I twitched at the lilac jacket's hem. 'Colour's a bit impractical.'

'It'd never survive a go-round with the gremlins,' she agreed, laughing, then grimaced. 'Oh, and talking about surviving, you missed last week's poker game.'

The ToLA case was also how Mary had met my flatmates, Sylvia and Ricou. During the follow-up investigation, we'd all become poker pals and friends. Though I'd been wondering recently if 'friends' was all Mary was interested in. Not with me, but with the pregnant pair.

I grinned. 'Sylvia fleeced you again, didn't she?'

'Yep.'

'You shouldn't let Ricou deal.'

'Yeah, I know.' A smile flitted across Mary's face as she lifted the crime tape for me to duck under. 'But they're so cute together when she catches him cheating.'

Cute? Sylvia could do cute, but Ricou? He looked like a stunt double for *The Creature from the Black Lagoon*, all blue scales, bony fins and sharp claws. Unless he was wearing one of his many Glamour spells.

Looked like my wonderings about Mary's interests were on the right track. I prodded. 'So, which of his Johnny Depp Glamours was Ricou sporting last night, then?'

'Oh, the gypsy one from *Chocolat*.' A hint of a blush coloured her cheeks as she headed off at a fast clip, calling over her shoulder, 'Come on, the DI's this way.'

Hmm, the gypsy wasn't one of Sylvia's favourites but Ricou wouldn't have worn it without her agreement. Seemed Mary's interest in being more than friends with the pair might be reciprocated. Not that it was any of my business, nor did I have an issue with it … so long as everyone was aware and happy … Unless Mary's attraction was to do with the leaking Fertility pendant? Something to check out. Later.

I hurried to keep up as we crunched along the slightly rough path and crossed over a small wooden bridge spanning an overgrown ditch. I scanned round, *looking*, checking out the area for any magical clues. But unlike my trip through the zoo and the few floating strands of wild magic I'd seen, there was nothing here at all. Which made me wonder exactly why Hugh had called me.

We reached the big cat exhibit just as Hugh strode through the entrance, almost bumping into us.

'There you are, Genny!' Relief rumbled through his voice as he stopped me with a gentle hand on my shoulder.

At just under seven foot, Hugh's short for a mountain troll, but I'm five four (short for a fae). Not wanting to be talking to the overhang of his chin, I stepped back and looked up.

He'd had his hair cut since I'd last seen him, a week ago, and the inch-high, straight-up black fuzz only just covered his headridge. (Unlike most trolls, Hugh isn't bald; but then he once told me he's got a smidge of human blood in him from way back.) The shorter hair somehow deepened the fine fissures lining his ruddy-coloured face, or maybe it was all the extra responsibility he'd taken on since the disappearance of his old boss, Detective Inspector Helen Crane.

DI Witch-bitch Helen Crane was my nemesis in more ways than one: she was the ex of the satyr I'd promised myself not to think about; had a real downer on me because I was sidhe; and she was the one who'd stolen (as a teenager) the sapphire pendant trapping the fae's fertility. I'd taken it back from her during the ToLA case. She hated me; the feeling was mutual. But I'd felt vindicated in my loathing when she'd proved to be dirty. Her disappearance was good news, sort of, as while I'd rather she paid for her crimes I was still ecstatic she was out of my life for good.

And with the Witch-bitch gone, Hugh had been made up, sort of, and was now (acting) Detective Inspector. Personally, I thought he should have got his full stripe or whatever it was, but he was a troll. Trolls might have been coppers since Robert Peeler started the Met back in the early eighteen hundreds, but it was only recently (after the Indigenous Alien Equality Act) that they'd been given the opportunity to move up out of the grunt ranks.

'We've got three people missing, believed abducted,' Hugh rumbled quietly, after we'd dispensed with the usual brief pleasantries.

'Three?' I frowned. 'You said two on the phone; a woman and her son?'

'Initially we weren't sure about the third.' Hugh pulled his notebook from the pocket of his sharply pressed white shirt. Hugh and neatness have always gone together like a goblin and his bling, but since his (sort of) promotion, he'd adopted a whole new level of smartness. He flipped a couple of pages: 'The woman is Mrs Bandevi Jangali, aged thirty-seven; her son, Dakkhin Jangali, is aged six. Mrs Jangali is an environmental activist.' He glanced down at me. 'She's here taking part in a conservation conference about tigers. Both Mrs Jangali and her son were having a private tour before the conference started. The third person is Mr Jonathan Weir, aged twenty-nine; he's the publicity director for the zoo, and was escorting them.'

My heart went out to the woman, her kid and the zoo guy,

and I prayed whoever had taken them was treating them okay. Or at least as 'okay' as the situation allowed. I'd learned enough from Hugh to know that the first hour was the most dangerous for any kidnap victim. The kidnappers would be high on nerves and adrenalin, and if things went pear-shaped, they were likely to cut their losses – a not-so-cheerful euphemism for cutting their victims' throats, or the equivalent.

The question that jumped into my mind was, 'Why pick here to snatch her? I'd get it if she was working in a country where the situation is volatile, but this is London.'

Hugh bared his pink granite teeth in a grimace. 'Mrs Jangali is also the wife of the ambassador from Bangladesh: Mr Balinder Bannerjee.'

The diplomatic limos in the car park fell into place. Only— 'Surely, she and the kid weren't taking the tour on their own? Didn't they have any security with them?'

Hugh nodded. 'They were accompanied by their personal bodyguards. Two males. They weren't harmed.'

'So they're suspects?'

'It is possible they could be involved in some way,' Hugh agreed. 'Especially given Mrs Jangali's connections and the professional way the abduction was implemented. We're not looking at something random here. The victims were targeted.'

'Is that good or bad for the victims?'

A small puff of anxious dust escaped Hugh's headridge. 'The negotiator, who's on her way, tells me that this suggests the kidnappers are "contingent terrorists". In other words, they've taken hostages because they want to negotiate something in exchange. It could be a ransom, the release of prisoners or publicity for some cause.'

Which explained the Media-blackout spell Mary was maintaining.

'Okay' I gave Hugh a quizzical look. 'Want to tell me why I'm here?'

He consulted his notebook again, then snapped it shut. 'There's something off about the kidnap. The zoo's got CCTV. The recordings show that Mrs Jangali, her son, their bodyguards and the zoo employee entered the exhibit here at 7.33 a.m. As soon as they're inside, the recording freezes. For fifty-nine seconds. At 7.34 a.m. it starts up again. The three victims disappear from the screen and the bodyguards are left standing in the same position. Three seconds later, they look around, realise their charges are gone and call for backup.'

'And they're unharmed?'

'Yes. Unharmed and with no memory of the missing time. There's nothing to be seen on the rest of the zoo's CCTVs. Or on any of the surrounding public CCTV. The three victims just vanish.'

'Magic,' I stated. 'Some sort of Invisibility spell, a Transportation spell or a temporary Portal combined with a Freeze spell...' I trailed off, wracking my mental files for anything else. 'But to be honest, Hugh, it could be any number of spells and my knowledge isn't the most comprehensive. I think your best bet is the Witches' Council.' I gestured towards Mary, who was standing to attention some feet away, and whose mother was on said Witches' Council. 'Oh, and the fae, or the Librarian. Any of them should be able to give you more info.'

Hugh nodded. 'All avenues we're following, Genny.'

'Okay,' I said, then something struck me. 'Why take Jonathan Weir, the zoo employee? I mean, if they could keep the bodyguards out of the loop, why not him too?'

'We don't know, Genny. It's another aspect that doesn't seem to fit.'

'Unless whatever magic was used didn't work on him,' I mused. 'He could've been resistant?'

'He's not.' Hugh flipped over a couple of pages. 'His partner, David O'Reilly, is one of the zoo's keepers. He's stated for the record that Jonathan has no magical abilities.'

'So, I take it you want me to try and gather up any magic that might be around?' It was after all, my party trick.

He indicated the entrance to the exhibit. 'I want you to come in and tell me what you see.'

'*See*, as in magic?'

'Yes, and as in anything else.'

I frowned. I doubted that I was going to find anything the WPCs hadn't, and I was beginning to feel that Hugh had got me out here to leave no stone unturned, rather than in any concrete hope that I could do something. That was totally fine by me. He'd been my friend since I was fourteen: he'd put his job and himself on the line for me more than once. If he wanted me here to dot i's and cross t's then I would. A good result on this could mean a lot for his career and, more importantly, for the missing victims.

And even if there wasn't anything for me to find, that didn't mean I wouldn't do my damnedest to actually discover a clue.

Chapter Thirteen

Inside the big cat exhibit, the roof made the corridor-like place look shadowed and dim after the bright sunshine outside. I wrinkled my nose; it stank of pine-scented cleaner cut with freshly butchered meat and wet fur. My sense of smell was definitely on overdrive, something I was beginning to suspect was down to drinking Mad Max's combination of vamp/doggy blood. Ugh. Hopefully, it was the only side-effect and I wouldn't start chasing sticks, or poodles wearing bridal veils.

I scanned for anything magical. To either side were U-shaped plate-glass windows, looking out over the tiger enclosure. It was more sparse English woodland than dense jungle and, despite a covered area near the first window, presumably for the tigers to sleep in as it was padded with straw, the big cat stars of the show were nowhere to be seen.

But as my eyes adjusted to the dimness, there were plenty of people to make up for the lack of tigers. Four WPCs and three uniformed trolls were stationed at intervals along the corridor, while another troll – Constable Lamber, his mottled beige head a pale beacon against a tall, frothy-leaved potted plant – stood to attention behind four males. The marked similarity of three of them with their short black hair, dark-skinned faces and closed-off expressions made me wonder if they were related: brothers or cousins, maybe. And all three were wearing the same long kurta shirts in a deep green, with heavy gold embroidery down the front and sleeves, over loose white trousers with more gold thread around the ankles – standard

Indian dress, albeit more formal than I usually saw in Southall, London's 'Little India'.

They stared back at me from behind opaque eighties-style aviator sunglasses.

Being stared at like I was a walking zoo exhibit is pretty much the norm for me as the only sidhe in London, and most of the time I don't notice so much, but the men's stares were predatory enough to raise the hair on my nape. I made a note to tell Hugh, and see if anyone else got strange vibes from them.

The fourth male was older; mid to late fifties going by the silver threading his black hair and the deep lines marking his brown-skinned face. Instead of the Indian dress the others were wearing he'd opted for city business style with a white shirt, grey hand-tailored suit and a less-than-sartorial orange and black striped tie. The look made him stand out, as did the anxious, haggard expression on his face. Had to be the ambassador.

'Mr Bannajee,' Hugh's quiet voice confirmed. 'With his Head of Security and his wife's bodyguards.'

I nodded as the ambassador came forward and gave a small bow. 'Lady Genevieve Taylor,' he said, his accent pure public school English. 'It is always a pleasure to greet one of the sidhe fae, even under such difficult circumstances as these.'

'Nice to meet you too, Ambassador,' I said, the polite small-talk feeling odd with his wife and kid missing. 'I'm sorry about your family.'

'I appreciate your concern. It is devastating that they have been taken.' They were the right words, but his tone was the same, polite, which was weird considering his eyes had started darting around like he expected someone to jump out at him … Unless it was shock?

'Ambassador,' Hugh rumbled reassuringly. 'As I explained, Lady Genevieve will inspect the crime scene here and then tell us what magic there is, or isn't. Isn't that right, Genny?'

'I've already looked,' I said slowly, thinking no one was going to like my answer.

'So quickly?' The ambassador's gazed fixed on mine and he leaned forwards eagerly. Behind him the three cool-dude henchmen shifted to high alert.

I gave Hugh an enquiring look. Didn't he want me to tell him what I'd found first?

He gave a barely perceptible nod. 'Go ahead.'

Fine. I took a breath, catching that whiff of butchered meat and wet fur again under the stink of pine-scented cleaner, and said, 'There's nothing. No magic, no spells, not even a stray bit of wylde magic. The place has been scrubbed clean.'

Beside me neither Hugh nor Mary reacted, so my discovery was as they expected.

But the ambassador stared at me, his head half shaking, half nodding as if he couldn't believe what I'd said. Finally he blurted, 'Nothing?'

'I'm sorry, Ambassador,' I said.

'But there must be something!' Distress coloured his voice. 'How else will we find—'

'My apologies, Ambassador.' Henchman One appeared at his elbow. 'But we must take our leave now.'

The ambassador turned to him, launching into a low-voiced passionate tirade in a musical language I didn't recognise.

Henchman One listened then stepped forward, his expression regretful, and spoke to Hugh. 'Inspector, I believe we have helped you as much as we can. You know how to contact the ambassador should you hear any news of his wife and son.'

Hugh nodded, his frustration showing only in his slight frown. 'I do, of course.'

'You may choose to leave,' the ambassador warned Henchman One, 'but I will stay.'

'Ambassador.' Henchman One closed his eyes briefly, as if he didn't want to deal with the man's anguish. 'I am sorry, but you may not pursue this further without permission from the President and the Prime Minister. I fear to do so would compromise our diplomatic status in this country. Please. We should leave now.'

Anger washed over me. How could the stupid man worry about diplomatic status when a woman and kid were missing?

The ambassador shook his head. 'The President would agree with me. We must—'

'No.' Henchman One cut him off again, his tone soft. 'We must not.'

I scowled at the defeated slump of the ambassador's shoulders, thinking it was a damn shame Hugh couldn't just pull them all in for questioning, without Henchman One the ambassador seemed like he'd be more talkative.

The ambassador bowed his head in a stiff goodbye aimed at no one in particular, turned and walked towards the exit. Henchman One followed, striding with silent contained steps, almost as if he were stalking him instead of following him. The sight pricked goosebumps over my skin; despite his regretful stance, there was something off about him, and the other two. As they trailed past us, the nearest one's kurta caught a gust of wind. The reek of butchered meat and wet fur intensified, drawing my attention to near his knees. Marring the green silk there, was a tiny pattern of rust-coloured spots.

Blood splatter.

'The blood wasn't human,' Hugh said thoughtfully, when they'd gone and I told him about it. 'Are you sure, Genny?'

'Positive. But I'm not sure what the blood belongs to. I know the scent's familiar, but I can't quite place it.' I frowned, frustrated. 'The place reeks to high heaven, so it's skewing my perceptions.'

'Reeks?'

'I'm having a sensitive nose day.'

Hugh frowned. 'That's not normal for you, is it?'

I pulled a disgusted face. 'No, I think it's a side-effect of something I drank.'

'Anything I should know about, Genny?'

Hugh wasn't a fan of vamps, especially where I was concerned, but I briefly told him I'd hurt myself and Mad Max had offered to heal me. And that a side-effect of that healing seemed to have upped my sense of smell. 'Still, hopefully it will wear off soon,' I finished. 'And at least it helped me find a clue.'

Grim fissures bracketed Hugh's mouth. 'Yes. Their insistence on their diplomatic status seems out of place in this situation, and makes things difficult for all of us.'

'You mean suspicious,' I said drily, then added, 'not to mention spooky with them hiding behind those mirrored sunglasses.'

Hugh pulled out his notepad and a large troll-sized pen. 'Spooky in what way?'

'Like they wanted a piece of me, or something. Course that might just be because I'm sidhe.' I looked at Hugh and Mary. 'Unless anyone else feels the same?'

She shook her head. 'Not me, sorry.'

'Ask around in a bit, sergeant,' Hugh said, making a note.

'Will do, sir.'

'Maybe it was just me then.' I shrugged. 'And I got the definite impression the ambassador wanted to tell you more, but they weren't interested in letting him talk.'

'Your impression's right, Genny,' Hugh rumbled. 'Though the ambassador did appear to be genuinely concerned for his wife and child.'

'Yeah,' I agreed. 'He seemed upset when I said the place was clear of magic. Though that didn't come as a surprise to you and Mary, did it?'

'It didn't. It was the main reason I asked you here. Mary has a theory about it.' He gave her a nod.

'The place isn't just clean of magic,' she said, 'it looks like it's got a flat sheen to it. I was sure I'd seen it somewhere before. So I had a chat to a couple of the beat WPCs, and we worked out what it was. It looks the same as when you do the magical clean-up after the pixies in Trafalgar Square.'

I blinked. 'It does?'

Mary nodded.

I squinted round. It really didn't look like anything to me, other than clean of magic, but then not everyone sees magic the same way.

Hugh laid a gentle hand on my shoulder. 'We think it could mean there's another sidhe involved. Which is why I wanted you to see for yourself.'

Anxiety itched down my spine. The last time another sidhe had come to London I'd ended up on the run for murder. Of course, Witch-bitch Helen Crane had been in charge then, not Hugh. But—

'To be honest, Hugh, another sidhe hanging around isn't too likely. The gates to the Fair Lands are still sealed shut and the fae aren't taking any chances where Clíona' – a.k.a. my not-so-dear sidhe queen grandmother – 'is concerned. They don't want her getting her hands back on the Fertility pendant.'

'But it could be possible?' Hugh insisted.

'I suppose so,' I admitted. 'Tavish would know for certain. I can ask him, if he's around.' I explained about Tavish going AWOL last night.

'I'd appreciate it, Genny.'

I flipped open my phone, turned towards the windows to shade the screen from the sun, then stopped as I saw the tigers had appeared from their hiding place. They were both lying down, mouths slightly open in the hot sunshine, eyes half closed, obviously relaxed. Had something frightened them away? Something to do with the kidnap? Or was this their normal routine? As I wondered, I realised that now, unlike the unnatural silence when I'd first arrived, I could hear the background noise of animals out in the zoo. As if, like the tigers, the animals had emerged from wherever they'd been hiding. Maybe that eerie quiet had been due to whatever magic had been used to kidnap the victims.

'Hugh?'

He looked up from his notepad. 'Yes?'

I told him my thoughts. His ruddy face creased with interest. 'I'll have someone look into it. No stone unturned is always a good motto.'

I rolled my eyes at his usual mountain troll pun, then called Tavish and got his voicemail. Again. Damn. If the kelpie didn't answer soon I was going to go round and bang on his door. I left another message, filled Hugh in, gave a statement and grabbed a lift in one of the police vans adapted for trolls back to Spellcrackers.

Where Katie told me the pixie apocalypse had hit London.

Chapter Fourteen

I hauled myself on to the huge bronze lion – one of the four in Trafalgar Square – and straddled its back haunches. The metal beneath my legs was still hot from the summer sun, despite it being early evening and the lion in shade. Sitting there, with the musical sound of the square's fountains in the background, was almost enough to send me to sleep. Especially after the exhausting day I'd had.

The damn pixies hadn't left another statue unmoved.

The eagle on top of the RAF monument on Victoria Embankment had taken up dive-bombing the glass-topped pleasure boats on the Thames, leaving scratches on their plastic roofs; the gold wolf's head fountain at the Aldgate pump had been howling randomly at passers-by, resulting in one man being taken to hospital with a suspected heart attack; the griffin at Temple Bar had become an intermittent flame-thrower, leaving scorch marks on nearby buildings; the sphinx at Cleopatra's Needle had whispered childish riddles, smacking down a heavy clawed paw whether the answers were right or wrong; Eros in Piccadilly had targeted passing double-decker buses with badly shot arrows, luckily managing to miss anything alive; and so my day had gone.

In fact, the only statues that didn't seem to be hit by the pixie apocalypse were the pixies' usual targets: the lions here in the square.

Apparently they'd only been two of the little blighters here all day. I'd nabbed the first quickly – it was asleep in the cat carrier ready to get shipped back to Cornwall – and now I was after the last one. Which was currently doing standing back-flips on the lion's head, to the delight of the tourists below.

I eyed the pixie, wondering how much trouble it was going to be as I adjusted my elbow-length gloves. Made of supple swamp-dragon leather they were thick enough to protect from the pixies' bites, but the leather's spongy texture didn't damage the pixies' chitinous teeth (the problem with cowhide). I gave the gloves a good sniff, checking the honey scent of the Pix-Nap cream smeared on them was still strong enough to attract the pixie's attention.

Thankfully the 'sensitive nose' I'd picked up from Mad Max's blood had worn off by mid-afternoon. The sensory input had been relentless, distracting and, not a few times, disgusting to the point that eating had been out of the question. Mad Max must have a strong stomach, but then he was a vamp who turned into a dog so I guessed he was used to it.

Now, though, my nose seemed to have rebelled and I was having trouble smelling anything.

I rolled my shoulders and started inching along the lion's back—

My phone vibrated, making my heart leap; it was late enough to be Malik.

I yanked a glove off, checked the display. Not Malik but Tavish.

'Hey,' I said, my disappointment washed away by relief that he was finally returning my calls. 'I was about to send out a search party. What the hell happened to you?'

'Och, doll, dinna fash yerself,' he said in his soft burr. 'I had a bit of sorting out to do, then I got a mite distracted by a body in the river.'

Tavish is a soul-taster. He long ago promised, under River Lore, not to Charm humans into the water but only to feed on those souls who die in the river, not that he feeds on the whole

116

soul, only the sorrows, guilts and sins weighing it down. But the heavier the soul, the longer it takes, sometimes prolonging his victim's dying for his own pleasure. Not that I had a problem when those souls were usually drug dealers or the like who were in the river by design, usually not their own. End up in the Thames with death staining your soul and all the kelpie's promises are off. Whether you want to die or not, you've no choice but to ride into the depths with him if he finds you.

But that he'd been doing that now filled me with furious disbelief. 'You've been off playing with your food while I've been worrying about your tarot cards and the fae's fertility?'

'Aye, well, it's nae quite like that, doll. The body wasnae truly wanting to die.' His voice held an odd note, not quite sadness; regret maybe, with an undertow of excitement. 'Only 'twas a time afore my other self realised that.'

Did that mean he'd tasted an innocent's soul? Someone who was in the river by accident? And broken his promise? But asking another fae that, or if they'd just taken someone to their death, isn't the done thing. Not to mention, tragic as that might be, I was more interested in getting answers to my own questions.

'Have you spoken to Hugh?' I asked. 'About the possibility of another sidhe being in London?'

'Aye, doll. I chatted to him and the witch Mary Martin nae long ago. 'Tis nae possible, the gates are fully sealed.' Relief flooded through me to such an extent that I realised I'd been more worried than I'd thought; the last thing I needed was any of my sidhe relatives turning up again. 'But I've told him we'll do a wee double-check on the gates, to be sure,' Tavish added.

Right. Better safe than sorry. 'Good. But you could've phoned and kept me in the loop,' I grumped.

'Aye, and so I am now, doll.' He ignored my exasperated snort, saying, 'And I've been doing a bit of checking. I'm thinking I've found your Emperor.'

My exasperation took a back seat. 'I'll bite.'

I heard the soft click-clack of his keyboard. 'I've sent you a screenshot. Tell me what you ken.'

'Okay.' I scrolled through to my emails and viewed the attachment, which showed the same image as the Emperor tarot card had. A dark-haired, hawk-nosed male in his thirties wearing a purple toga and golden laurel-leaf crown, sitting on a golden throne, a golden eagle perched atop the Rod of Asclepius behind him. But instead of holding a silver dagger, this Emperor gripped a golden chain. On the end of the chain, reclining at the Emperor's feet, were two large grey-brown wolves. 'That's him,' I said. 'But on the tarot card he was holding a silver dagger; he didn't have the wolves.'

'Nae wolves, doll. Werewolves.'

'Werewolves? Really?' Surprise mixed with trepidation flashed through me. And I had a sudden memory of Katie telling me she thought the flasher from last night was a werewolf. Fuck. 'Are you sure the two wolves aren't just animals?'

'Aye, doll, I'm sure. I'm sending you some more photos.'

I brought the pictures up on my phone. The first showed a cropped close-up of one wolf's eye; the second showed a front paw. The eye was human, a green iris with a starburst of hazel fanning out from the pupil. The paw was furry but, unlike a normal wolf's paw, was prehensile with a short but definite opposable thumb. Two sure indicators of a werewolf in their animal form.

I almost asked Tavish if the pictures could've been 'shopped, then didn't. The Emperor was a vamp. No way would a vamp falsely advertise having a couple of werewolves at his beck and call, not if he wanted to keep his blood cred. Of course, the fact that he had a couple of werewolves chained like pets meant he was probably pretty much at the top of the vamps' blood-tree anyway.

Which was sort of reassuring in a way. If the Emperor was

that überpowerful then the chances that he knew how to release the fae's fertility from the pendant just rocketed up. Not
that I hadn't believed the cards, but a strange vamp knowing
the solution to London's fae's fertility problem wouldn't have
been my first guess. No, my first had been the Autarch, my
very own bloodsucking nightmare. One I might be getting
reacquainted with soon, if Malik or his answering service ever
returned my call about our date.

I took a calming breath and told Tavish about the flasher
Katie and I'd seen. 'Think it's related?'

'Could be, doll.'

I shared Katie's worries that the werewolves could end up
hunting her because she was a virgin. 'Is she in any danger?'

'Och, dinna fash yerself about that. 'Tis an old story from
the Shining Times, and I doubt there's a werewolf alive who
remembers it, never mind kens the truth of it.'

The Shining Times supposedly came after the dinosaurs but
before man first struck cold iron. Which didn't pin it down
much. Though if anyone would know, it was probably Tavish.
Rumour has it he's a couple of millennia old, but he's always
been cagey about his age, and with his angular, almost classic
sidhe, features I've often wondered if he's older. Maybe even
born in the Shining Times. Which was when the sidhe and
magic and the humans' world first came together, and the
sidhe procreated with any living thing that took their fancy –
like humans, animals, trees, and even the elements – bringing
whole new species into being. Including werewolves, by the
sounds of it.

I frowned. 'Are you saying that werewolves came from the
sidhe? Like the rest of the fae?'

Tavish's snort over the phone was faintly derisive. 'Nae,'tis
different magics that birthed the shifters. And 'tis long lost
now.'

'So Katie's not in danger?'

'Nae more than from any Other. And 'tis unlikely these werewolves will bother with the wee girlie, but we dinna ken what this Emperor vamp is like. So to be sure I'll stir up a scent potion from wolfsbane and mistletoe for her. And for you too, doll. 'Twill encourage the beasts to keep their distance.'

Great. Katie could be in danger because of me. Again. 'Okay, thanks, that puts my mind at rest.' A bit, anyway.

'Mind, 'twill nae smell too good.'

I blew out a breath. 'Doesn't matter if it helps keep her safe.'

'Aye. And 'twill give her something to hang her worries on too, so they dinna bother her as much.'

Like the vamp-repelling kit he'd given her. I told him she'd shown it me, and that I was grateful he'd done that for her.

'Och, she's a good wee girlie, 'twas a pleasure to do, no thanks needed, doll.'

'So, the Emperor's got a couple of pet werewolves I need to watch out for,' I said, digging out a Phone Privacy spell as a group of teens climbed onto the column's plinth to get a closer look at the pixie, now dancing a passable jig. Their giggles and chatter cut out as I activated the crystal. 'Any ideas why the tarot card didn't show them, and why it gave the Emperor a knife instead?'

''Tis possible the werewolves are nae important to our question, doll, and the knife is. But how 'tis difficult to say, with only one card revealed.'

Right. 'So when can I expect the other four to reappear?'

'Och, when she's got something more to tell.'

'She?'

'The spirit in the cards, doll. Who else?'

I had a sudden *duh* moment. Of course. 'But why's it taking her so long?'

'Told you. Answers are nae always there for the taking. She has to search.'

I frowned. 'She didn't for the first card? That was instant.'

'Aye, well, you ken I had already asked. 'Twas why I wanted you to have the reading there and then. The cards were after reminding me you were the key.'

'Okay,' I said, 'so why did the eagle in the card cut the reading short, as if it was holding back info?'

'Ah, her readings are always a bit abrupt, some things are nae always clear even to her, or a question's asked she needs to look into.'

In other words, wait and see. 'So if she's out looking for answers, how do you know we can trust the spirit?'

'Och, dinna fash yerself, doll, the cards are sidhe made. Means the spirit's bound to tell the truth of her findings.'

Disbelief flashed in me. 'Call me paranoid, but that doesn't exactly reassure me, Tavish. Sidhe might not lie, but they don't always tell the truth.'

'The spirit's never steered me wrong yet, doll.'

'Fine,' I said, deciding I'd reserve judgement. 'So the knife's important, but we don't know why. But you don't think the werewolves are?'

'Hmph. Nae to the question's answer. But you're likely to be dealing with this Emperor, so they'll be a consideration. I take it Malik al-Khan dinna say anything about werewolves?'

'Nope,' I said, 'all I got out of him was that there's a vamp called the Emperor; he's badass' – as are most überpowerful vamps, so nothing new there – 'and he's not the Autarch by another name.' I shuddered. 'But I'll ask next time I see him.' On our date. When he confirms it. I stifled my impatience. 'So anything else helpful you can tell me about this Emperor?'

Chapter Fifteen

'**N**ae yet, doll,' Tavish said. 'Could be I'll find out more soon as I get into the Emperor's website.'

Shock rocked me. Tavish is a techno-geek for hire – he's rumoured to freelance for the Ministry of Defence – so for him not to have hacked the website meant it had some serious firewalls. 'You haven't got in yet?'

'Aye, but 'twill nae take long,' he added, determination roughening his voice. 'So 'tis naught to worry about.'

'Okay,' I said, then it dawned on me why he'd been incommunicado. It wasn't the body in the river, or not only that; the arrogant kelpie hadn't wanted to admit the Emperor's security had beaten him. Males and their egos! Good thing he'd won himself major kudos points by helping Katie. Though thinking of egotistical males— 'Oh, yeah, there's something else. Did you know the Fertility spell in the pendant is leaking?'

'The spell is leaking?' Genuine surprise sounded in his voice.

'Yes, if I'm to believe Mad Max. I ran into him' – *well, his roundhouse kick anyway* – 'and, long story short, that's what he told me. I think it's the cause of the problems I have whenever you use your magic, not a side-effect from that Chastity spell.' I told him my theory about my abstinence combined with the leaking fertility magic inadvertently setting me up for my own impromptu fertility rite.

He snorted. ''Tis nae something I'd have imagined being the cause. Any times I've been part of the fertility rites, the magic is nae picky like that, 'tis more indiscriminate. And you ken the witch wore the pendant for all those years and she dinna have a problem with it.'

The witch was Witch-bitch Helen Crane. I sniffed. 'As far as we know Helen didn't have a problem with it, but she's not around to ask.' And it would just be like the evil Witch-bitch to have sicced the pendant with more than one nasty little spell. After all, she'd magically booby-trapped it, so no one who knew she had it, could snatch it from her without the fae's fertility being lost for good. 'Sure you don't know anything? I don't trust Mad Max to give me all the info.'

'Aye, Maxim isnae the most trustworthy source,' Tavish agreed, then added hesitantly, 'but you could maybe ask Ana. She's had a fair bit to do with the pendant over the years.'

We said our goodbyes and I chewed my lip, thinking over his suggestion.

Ana: my faeling niece, and Mad Max's daughter. Her 'fair bit to do' with the pendant had been at the hands of the deranged baby-making wizard Dr Craig, who was the mastermind behind the ToLA case and with whom Witch-bitch Helen had been partners in crime. Helen had shared the pendant's magic with him and poor Ana had been his first victim/experiment. Sadly she'd suffered his baby-making experiments more than once and of the four kids she'd given birth to, only one was actually hers – Freya (her daughter and Mad Max's grandkid) – and now Ana was pregnant again with another of the evil doctor's baby-making experiments. He and Helen made a matched pair.

I was glad I'd killed him.

Needless to say, anything to do with the Fertility pendant wasn't Ana's favourite topic. And while she'd been friendly when we'd met during the aftermath of the ToLA case, and was currently relying on me for regular donations of blood for Freya, that friendliness hadn't lasted past our meeting. My hopes that I could get to know some of my sidhe-sided family had been destroyed like a *cracked* spell.

But hey, at least Ana didn't want to kill me like the rest of my sidhe family, so I counted that as a win. And it wasn't as if we had any friendship to upset if I asked her about my problems with the Fertility pendant. Not to mention I was in the right place to do so, since Trafalgar Square is Ana's home.

Or at least, the entrance to her home is through the square's left fountain, since she lives in *Between*.

Between is the space (unsurprisingly) between the Fair Lands and the humans' world, and is malleable enough that anyone can create their own private out-of-this-world patch ... if they have enough power and the magic likes them. Obviously I didn't; I couldn't even get into *Between* on my own, never mind set up home there.

I squashed the niggling frustration and envy that Ana, a faeling, could do the sort of magic most full-blooded fae would struggle with, when I couldn't even *cast* my own Privacy spells but had to buy them instead, and phoned her. Okay, she probably didn't want to talk about the Fertility pendant, but I didn't want to take the chance that next time the magic decided I needed to get my rocks off, it would pick some poor unsuspecting human and I'd end up fucking him or her to death.

'Genny.' Ana sounded oddly wary, almost as if she was expecting my call. Had Mad Max talked to her? Only as far as I knew she refused to have anything to do with her father, because he was a vamp.

I put on a bright voice. 'Hey, I'm in the square, catching pixies, any chance we could have a chat?'

'I'm not at home right now,' she said flatly.

Not home? But it was nearly ten at night and she was going to give birth at any moment. Though she was an adult, so really not my call. 'Oh, right. Mind if I ask you something, then?'

'I'm busy, Genny—'

'It's about the Fertility pendant,' I said, jumping in with both feet.

Silence, then a sharp, 'What about it?'

'I've been having a few problems with it and when I ran into Maxim last night he told me the spell in the pendant leaks. He said I could end up re-enacting my very own fertility rite if I'm not careful. And I really don't want to end up picking up some poor human and doing him some damage because of it.'

She blew out a dismissive breath. 'You don't have to worry. Helen couldn't stop the pendant leaking, but she bespelled it to *focus* the leak. The magic fixes on anyone you know and find attractive enough that you want to have sex with them, who isn't already in an ongoing sexual relationship.'

Oh. 'Right, so I'm not going to see some hot guy on the Underground who happens to be single and want to jump his bones then?'

'No, I shouldn't think so. Helen didn't want it causing her any hassles like that.'

No, she wouldn't. Helen the Witch-bitch was all about protecting her own interests.

'Okay,' I said, 'but it did sort of fixate on Maxim last night and I know he's your dad, but really, there's no way in hell I find him attractive.' Not to mention the whole icky incest thing.

Another longer silence, then, 'I'll email you a recipe for a Purging Poultice spell which will help, but if you're going to continue living with the pendant, the best way to keep the Fertility magic under control is to have sex on a regular basis.'

Not something I could guarantee doing right now ... though the idea of 'regular sex' with Malik ... was *not* something to think about in the middle of Trafalgar Square, not unless I wanted to take a dip in the cold fountain in the next five minutes. I sat straighter, got my excited libido under control and my mind back on track. 'Thanks for the spell, Ana, but that doesn't answer my question about Maxim.'

An annoyed huff came over the line. 'My father and Helen know each other extremely well, remember, so the spell probably recognised him.'

It took a moment for what she meant to sink in. 'Are you saying that Helen and Maxim have been—'

'Yes,' she interrupted, 'for years. But I do *not* want to discuss my father's sex life.'

I didn't want to either, but— Helen the Witch-bitch and Mad Max had been having an affair, or whatever, for years? Wow, I hadn't seen that coming. Though thinking about it, I should have. I'd known they had a kid together: Jack. Helen had given him up at birth to be a sidhe changeling, and he was now one of the Morrígan's ravens. He was the same age as me and Ana, and was another baby conceived by way of the Fertility pendant. But even knowing about Jack, and that Mad Max and Helen had got it together when she was a teenager, I'd always imagined it had been a one-off. If it wasn't—

'What about Finn?' I asked, my indignation on his behalf breaking my self-imposed promise not to think about him since he'd cut me out of his life. 'Helen jumped the broom with him for seven years. Was she still seeing your dad then?'

'Seriously, Genny,' Ana snapped, 'I am *not* discussing it with you. And anyway, I don't know. I don't want anything to do with Maxim. He might be my father, but he's a vampire. I don't want him near me, or Freya. I never have done. It's down to him that my mother is dead. She was looking for him when the other vampires took her. I don't want the same happening to me, or, The Mother protect us, to Freya. Maxim will never be part of our lives. And if I didn't need your blood for Freya, you wouldn't be either. You're too close to the vampires. It makes you dangerous.'

Well, that told me why my hopes of a happy family friendship had fizzled like a damp squib. Not that I could blame her really. Not when she was only trying to protect herself and her kid.

'Look,' Ana rushed on, 'you wanted to know how to deal with the Fertility spell. I've told you. Either stop living with it or start having sex, I really don't care. And whatever you do, don't get it frustrated by getting all excited and then stopping. Oh, and its response will be stronger if you or the other person uses magic. Now I'm busy, so goodbye.'

The line went dead, leaving me staring morosely at the pixie who was now doing muscle-men poses on the lion's head, despite only having an audience of three pigeons and a bag lady. The old woman gave a desultory clap, and part of me wanted to go back a year or so to when catching pixies and getting booed by the crowds seemed like my only problem.

I sighed. Still, at least I now knew the Fertility spell wasn't going to have me Glamouring passing strangers and forcing them to have sex. And that the only people I had to worry about were friends I found attractive. Which had to be why it was only when Tavish used magic that I got all hot and bothered; I just wasn't that into him.

My phone rang. A tiny flame of hope that it was Ana ringing back died as the display said 'Katie'.

'Hi, hon, what's up?'

'Hey, Genny. Sorry, but Harrods have got problems with their Magic Mirror spells in the lingerie changing rooms again.'

I groaned. 'Thought I got it sorted this morning.'

'No such luck,' she said, commiserating.

I gave the last pixie a considering look. In the last couple of seconds he'd curled up like a cat on the lion's head and was snoring away. I didn't have to catch him – pixies are only really a problem when a pack of them get together – so this one could wait for another day. And the one I'd already caught

127

was easy enough to deal with; the delivery service we used to ship the pixies back to Cornwall was nearby.

'Okay,' I said, sliding down off the bronze lion. 'Tell Harrods I'm on my way.'

Midnight. I got home to find my flat, as usual since Sylvia and Ricou had moved in, was pitch-black. They'd left the blackout blinds down again. I flipped the light switch in a vain hope that the protective Wards hadn't fried the electricity for the umpteenth time, but as usual nothing happened. Sighing, I bumped the front door shut with my hip, dropped the bags of Spellcrackers files I'd lugged up the five flights of stairs and, as I waited for the Ward to release its sticky hold on me, pressed my forehead tiredly against the cool wood of the door.

I'd gone for gold on this last trip to Harrods, stripping and *absorbing* the Magic Mirror spells from the whole store, not just the lingerie section, before the store's resident hedge-witch salt-washed the mirrors. They were going to leave them spell-free overnight as a test before recasting the spells. I'd *absorbed*, as an added precaution, to dispose of it away from the store. The job itself had been relatively quick and easy – I'd been there for less than an hour – and other than feeling like I'd swallowed a set of hyperactive pinballs for once the magic hadn't hit me with any of its quirky side-effects. Or so I'd thought.

But the consequences had crept up on me. Without realising how I'd got there, I'd been staring fixedly at a mirror in the doorway of a Chinese restaurant, silently debating whether my left eye was slightly larger than my right, and if I'd look prettier if the sharp angles of my chin were rounder. A tiny Asian woman, stereotypically old and wizened, had shuffled up to me and pressed a fortune cookie into my palm, breaking my obsession with my looks. I'd thanked her. She treated me to a toothless grin, then shooed me on my way.

I'd kept my gaze on the pavement after that.

Now the damn stuff was nagging me to rush to the nearest mirror and check myself out.

Another quick look wouldn't hurt.

I pushed away from the door, turned and headed towards my bedroom— and let out a strangled squeak as my nose ended up mashed into the rough bark of a small tree. Sylvia, my dryad flatmate.

Chapter Sixteen

'**O**ops, sorry, Genny,' Sylvia breathed, the rustling laughter in her voice belying the apology. 'Didn't hear you come in.'

A crack like a snapping twig, and faint light bathed the living room. The light came from a football-sized globe. It was hovering inside my chandelier, making the long strands of amber- and gold-glass beads sparkle as if they'd been sprinkled with fairy glitter. One of Sylvia's Moonshine spells. Since I couldn't *activate* it I preferred electricity, though the spell *was* prettier.

Sylvia was pretty too. Her green eyes shone bright as spring buds, delicate branches with soft, arrow-shaped leaves curled down to her shoulders (she'd stopped pruning her scalp now she was pregnant, needing the extra boost for the baby), and her diaphanous pink negligée floated around her knees as if shifting in a gentle wind. The negligée was embroidered– appropriately, since her tree was *Prunus avium* – with tiny red cherries down the deep V of its neckline.

'Damn it, Sylvia!' I gingerly felt my nose for damage as I glared at her exposed chest. She heaved an appeasing sigh as she automatically 'dressed' herself in her usual waking Glamour; the green-grey bark-like skin I'd run into morphed into the pale pink smooth flesh of her more usual 'Hello Boys' cleavage, near enough swallowing the hen's-egg-sized sapphire pendant she wore.

The pendant containing the fae's trapped fertility.

All my problems stemmed from that innocent-looking sapphire.

And the damn thing still kept throwing new ones at me.

Though if it weren't for that pendant I wouldn't even be here and it looked good nestled between Sylvia's generous breasts. Which were utterly fabulous, now I was taking the time to look at them. Lush and firm and soft. I frowned at the oxymoron, wondering what her boobs would feel like. I'd been with girls before, when I'd been in Rosa's vamp body; it wasn't my preferred choice sexually, but most vamps don't usually discriminate and I'd been more interested in their venom-infected blood than their bodies, so I'd never really taken much notice of another girl's breasts. Only Sylvia's were fascinating, not in a lusting-after-them way, but full and nicely rounded ...

'Genny?'

... whereas mine were way smaller. Tiny even. In fact, I was virtually flat-chested. I could never get a cleavage like Sylvia's, not even with a padded bra. Maybe I could get a pair of those silicone chicken breast thingies ... or there was always plastic surgery ... hmm, that might be the easiest, especially with my quick healing ... and now I was earning more I could probably afford—

'Genny!'

I jerked my gaze from Sylvia's boobs to her exasperated face. 'What?'

'Why are you staring at my chest?'

'I'm not.'

She gave me a 'pull the other one' look. 'You were!'

Shit, she was right. Embarrassed heat stung my cheeks. What the fuck was wrong with me? Mentally I shook my head, shoving stupid thoughts about plastic surgery where they belonged.

'Sorry, Syl,' I said, stepping back, 'I was just admiring ...' I waved my hand vaguely at her.

'Gosh, 's'okay, Genny.' She smiled, a pleased glint in her eyes. 'My boobies are glorious, aren't they? They're even bigger now I'm pregnant, and Ricou loves them. Says they're—'

'Don't wanna know, Syl!' I quickly held my hands up before she hit me with TMI about her and Ricou's love life. Something she was fond of doing. Dryads don't do personal boundaries well. 'What were you standing around in the dark for anyway?'

'Waiting up for you, of course,' she said cheerfully. 'But, gosh, I really didn't expect you to be so late, and I was tired, so I was just having a little nap.' She looked down, and slowly lifted one foot then the other as she carefully pulled the net of hair-like roots out of the wooden floorboards. The scent of green, growing things filled the room. 'Baby Grace has been kicking like a lumberjack in hob-nailed boots all day,' she added, snagging my hand and placing it on her barely there bump with a contented smile.

Baby Grace. Joy and happiness spread like warm honey through me. Baby Grace was the one wonderful thing to come out of the sacrifice my friend Grace had made to save me last Hallowe'en. I'd unintentionally trapped her soul in her pentacle necklace, but once I'd realised I'd let her go, and her soul had moved on into Sylvia's baby. I wasn't clear if Grace was being reborn, reincarnated, or how it all worked, but for me Sylvia's baby having Grace's soul made her and her mother even more special.

'That's my gorgeous girl,' I murmured, grinning as Baby Grace said hello in her usual enthusiastic way. Then I quickly modified the grin to a sympathetic grimace as Sylvia shot me a narrowed look, one that heralded another lecture about babies and bladders. 'You really shouldn't be waiting up for me, Syl. C'mon, off to bed with you,' I said, gently trying to steer her towards the oak wardrobe hulking near my bedroom door.

Through the back of the wardrobe was Sylvia and Ricou's

own private patch of *Between*; their magically created living space outside the humans' world. Whoever introduced Sylvia to the Narnia books had a lot to answer for; if it hadn't been for them, my protest that my one-bedroom attic flat was too small for us all to share, and that the pregnant pair should live somewhere safer and more comfortable, would've held water. Though, truthfully, while having Sylvia and Ricou as flatmates, was strange at times and not without its complications, it was great.

Sylvia pouted. 'But I wanted to talk to you, Genny. And look, I've got all your stuff ready.' The light globe brightened to full-moon strength as she draped an arm over my shoulders and waved a graceful hand at the floor where there was a large sheet of blue plastic.

The blue plastic was my magic neutralising gear. The sheet was marked with two circles, a large eight foot one with a smaller three foot one offset inside. I'd *drawn* the circles with a mix of ground amber, dried unicorn faeces and my own blood after dissolving juiced-up ricepaper runes – very expensive, very elaborate, ricepaper runes – into the mixture to power it up. The magical ink meant I didn't have to use the traditional sand and salt (cheap, but hell to cart around and messy to clean up) or buy one of the rare etched-by-dwarves silver and copper circle chains (easier to carry, but even with the inbuilt protections they're a magnet for thieves). And though pricy to make, my blue plastic spell-neutraliser kit was worthless to anyone else since it was *keyed* only to me. I was quietly proud of it – the result of hours of painstaking trial and error – and was thinking of patenting it, once I'd worked out how to bring the cost of the runes down.

If I could *cast* my own spells, my life would be so much easier.

I shoved the constant frustration away and gave Sylvia a quick hug. 'Thanks, I appreciate it.'

'Gosh, no worries, Genny.' Sylvia grinned happily. 'It's the least I can do. And, look, I've even put salt out for you.'

'Oh, thanks,' I said again, eyeing the six-inch block of salt sitting in the smaller circle. Sylvia hated salt, always saying that just thinking about it clogged up her sap, so she really was being helpful … so helpful that my 'what's she after' antennae started twitching.

She stroked a finger down the lapel of my jacket. 'This is new, isn't it?'

'Yeah.'

She tilted her head curiously. 'What happened to the clothes you were wearing?'

'Got damaged when I tangled with a spell.' Not a lie, but way better than telling her Malik ripped them off me. The last thing I wanted was an interrogation about my love life, however well intentioned.

'Goodness. Must have been a hard one.'

An image of Malik naked flashed in my mind. *Oh boy!* I swallowed, then managed a weak, 'Yep. It was.'

'Still, the jacket is nice. Not your usual colour, but the lilac suits you. Now why don't I help you out of it' – she grasped the jacket and I let her tug it off, only just managing not to jump as her hand trailed down my spine and came to rest on my hip – 'and while you're doing your spell-*cracking*, I'll mix you up an extra-special Bloody Mary and we can have a lovely cosy chat, just us girls together.' She chuckled low in my ear, squeezed my butt then headed for the fridge.

I watched her, thoughtful. As passes go, it was about as subtle as if she'd flashed me a neon sign. Question was, why? I might have thought it was because of my boob-staring, if not for the salt.

Not that I was too surprised. Sylvia didn't have any gender preference when it came to sex, other than her own, which seeing she was co-sexual and had all the accessories she needed was whatever she wanted it to be. She preferred to be female, though a few months ago, when her mother had sent Sylvia to court me in order to break the curse and she discovered my partner choice was male, she'd offered to 'change'. But that was then. Now she was pregnant and happy, or so I'd thought, with Ricou.

She turned, a highball glass filled with ice in her hand. 'Gosh, haven't you started yet, Genny?' She rattled the glass. 'Hurry up, otherwise this will melt.'

'I'm wondering why I'm getting the special treatment?'

A gleam lit her green eyes. 'Maybe I just want to see you naked.'

Right. 'What about Ricou?'

'Oh, gosh, he'd like to see you naked too.' She smiled a little too widely. 'But he's out on search duty.' Her fingers closed around the sapphire pendant nestled in her cleavage.

Ricou was feeling guilty that he was going to be a dad again, when the rest of the fae were still in fertility limbo. Consequently he was spending a lot of time searching for a way to release the trapped fertility, and not a lot with Sylvia.

'So, you're hitting on me because you're feeling lonely?' A possibility, but doubtful given the way she was clutching the pendant so hard her knuckles were turning white.

'Golly, of course not,' she said, banging the glass down with frustration. 'No. I'm hitting on you because I like you, Genny. And anyway, Ricou and I always share.'

'So you're interested in a threesome deal?'

'If you are?' she said hopefully.

Crap, maybe she really was serious. 'Um, Syl, you know I like you, and Ricou too, but I thought you realised neither of you is my type.' Not to mention she was pregnant, so was this really the time to expand their relationship to include anyone else?

'Fiddlesticks!' She threw her hands in the air. 'I knew this wouldn't work.'

Chapter Seventeen

Ah. 'What wouldn't work?' I asked.

'I told them you were still hung up on Finn. That you wouldn't be interested in me and Ricou. But they wouldn't have it.'

Finn. The cut-me-off-without-an-explanation-satyr-I-wasn't-thinking-about.

I rubbed the ache blooming in my chest.

Sylvia's green eyes filled with sympathy. 'Just because he stopped writing, Genny,' she said softly, 'it might not mean what you think.'

I'd kept writing up until four weeks ago. Not because I was hung up on him but because he was my friend. And I wanted to know if he was okay. Even if he'd never got my letters, he knew there was no way I could contact him other than through his family so he'd have found a way to check why I seemed to be giving him the silent treatment ... if we'd really been the friends, never mind the anything more, I'd thought we were.

Crap. I'd promised myself not to waste any more time on him.

'Who are they, Syl?'

She gave me a long troubled look, obviously wondering whether to push me about a certain satyr. But that subject was done. To my mind, anyway— She started to speak and I jerked my hands up. 'Syl, forget it. Forget him. Please. Just tell me who *they* are, and why they want you to seduce me?'

She shook her head, leaves rustling with a mix of frustration and irritation. 'Goodness, who do you think, Genny? Our mothers!'

Right. The Ladies Meriel and Isabella: Head naiad and dryad respectively a.k.a. Ricou's and Sylvia's mothers. 'Why do they want you to seduce me—' I stopped as it all fell into place. 'No, let me guess: Spellcrackers.'

'Yes.' Sylvia sighed, her shoulders drooping. 'They said we might as well make ourselves useful since we both insisted on staying with you.'

Damn. I knew the satyr herd elders wanted Spellcrackers back but this was the first I'd heard the Ladies had their acquisitive eyes on the business. Well, they could all think again. Spellcrackers was mine, and would be until a certain satyr came back from the Fair Lands, which wouldn't be for at least another two months.

I scowled at Sylvia. 'You've been staying with me for three months. Why are the Ladies plotting now?'

'Gosh, I don't know. Mother wouldn't tell me anything more unless I let her through the Wards. She said she wasn't going to discuss matters of import while on a public roof for all to listen.'

I gaped. 'You kept your *mother* standing outside?'

'Of course I did.' Her expression turned to a mix of despair and mutiny. 'I'm not that stupid. You don't know what she's like.'

Actually, I did. Lady Isabella hadn't been beyond kidnapping me as a way of making me do what she wanted in the past. That she hadn't succeeded was not for want of trying.

'If I'd let her in,' Sylvia carried on, 'she'd have had me locked up in my tree in a heartbeat. She's on about it not being safe here for me and the baby again.'

'Is she crazy? With all the protective Wards and magic here this place is safer than Buck House. Not to mention you can hardly move for all the dryads and their trees she's got camped out around here. They've had to divert traffic round the huge elm that's taken root outside the front door.'

'I told her that, but she's suddenly got this bee in her bonnet that "staying here is dangerous". Of course, it's really about that Ricou. She's still furious that her grandchild is going to be half naiad, and how we're never going to find a suitable tree. She only shut up about it when I agreed to have a go at seducing you.'

'You made an *agreement* with your mother?' Fae don't make or break bargains lightly; the consequences are too unpredictable and can backfire on both parties even if the bargain is kept. I couldn't care less about Lady Isabella, but I did care about Sylvia. 'Why the hell did you do that, Syl?'

Her eyes went wide with shock. 'Oh my gosh, no, it wasn't that type of *agreement*, Genny.' She held her hand up, fingers crossed. 'Just the kid's promise, the sort that doesn't involve magic, you know?'

Relieved, I nodded. 'You had me worried for a min.'

She smiled, then added coyly, 'And, you know, you might have said yes. It would be so much fun.' She paused, obviously waiting for me to have a change of orientation: Sylvia is nothing if not persistent. I gave her a look. 'But, oh well, you didn't, so now I've kept my promise, I'm off the hook. So' – she grabbed the bottle of Cristall vodka – 'how about I make you that special Bloody Mary?'

'It's okay, Syl.' I took the bottle from her and put it down. 'I'll do it myself once I've finished. You go to bed. You and Baby Grace need your rest.'

'I could always stay and watch?' she said, giving me a hopeful look. 'It gets a bit lonely with Ricou gone most of the time.'

Did she never give up? 'No, you really couldn't,' I said firmly.

She pouted. 'Spoilsport.'

'Yep, that's me.' I opened the wardrobe door and gestured inside. 'Goodnight, Sylvia.'

'You know, Genny, you're really not like sidhe are supposed to be—'

'Please,' I groaned, 'not the sidhe sex myth again. Syl, I'm really not gagging for it.' At least I wasn't now, after Mad Max's tough-love Poultice spell. And, thankfully, even before that Sylvia obviously hadn't been hitting my hot buttons. 'Now. Go. To. Bed.'

She gave me one last imploring look, which I pointedly ignored, then, with a loud guilt-inducing sigh, she ducked under the empty hanging rail and disappeared through the back of the wardrobe.

I grabbed the sheet I kept on the wardrobe shelf, closed the door and carefully draped it over the wardrobe's front to stop any peeping eyes.

I stripped off. Not that I needed to be naked to do the cleansing ritual to get rid of the Magic Mirror spell I'd absorbed at Harrods; it was just more practical than neutralising my clothes afterwards. Crunching on half-a-dozen liquorice torpedoes, I sat crossed-legged inside the larger circle, opened the part of me that can *see* the magic, picked up my knife and pricked my left index finger. A bead of bright red blood welled up and I touched it and my will to the outer circle. The circle rose like a glass cake dome shot through with gold.

I gathered the hyperactive pinballs of magic inside me and taking a deep breath, *tagged* the pinballs to the salt block. They fizzled and spat like water on a hotplate as they hit the salt, then, as I hoped it would, the Magic Mirror spell dissolved into the usual thick grey sludge. The fetid smell of rotting vegetables filled the circle – confirmation, if I'd needed it, that the original spell had been altered with deliberate malice and wasn't some sort of accident, same as the last few times I'd done this.

Only now, after my unusual preoccupation with my looks and Sylvia's cleavage, I had an idea what might be responsible.

That urge for plastic surgery hadn't popped into my head on its own. A quick email to Hugh and bit of investigation by the Met's Magic Squad, and Harrods' mutating Magic Mirror spell problem should be sorted. Satisfied I'd got something to go on, I *set* the sludge-filled inner circle. It popped into place like an upside-down sieve made of fine gold mesh.

'Now for the fun part.'

I *focused* on the sludge-covered salt, and *cracked* it.

The magic and the salt exploded, the sludge predictably erupting like a mini volcano. I threw my arms up in front of my face as the sludge splattered me, leaving me feeling cold, wet, and as if I'd been thoroughly slimed by a swamp-dragon's parasitic wyrm.

'And isn't that an icky thought,' I grumbled, flicking sludge off my fingers and watching as it dissipated into the ether. At least the sieve-like inner circle kept the actual salt from hitting me; the stuff stung like sand in a desert storm otherwise. The sludge was magical, so now the spell was neutralised the only physical clear-up involved was washing the salt down the drain in the bath, and stowing my blue plastic.

I tidied up, jumped in a hot shower then emailed Hugh about my suspicions.

The Magic Mirror spell problems at Harrods: think I know what's causing it. The lingerie fitting rooms are filled with promo leaflets for a posh plastic surgery clinic (link to website below). I think they're probably tagged with some sort of Dissatisfaction or Envy hex to encourage new customers to the clinic. Could be worth checking out?

I pressed send then headed for the kitchen to make my Bloody Mary nightcap.

The glass of ice was still waiting for me; Sylvia had thoughtfully bespelled it to stop it melting. I opened the fridge and wrinkled my nose at the fishy reek of the two dead mackerel;

having a naiad as a flatmate has its smelly downsides. At least Sylvia likes her food cooked. Though I couldn't really talk, I thought, as I snagged the carton of lamb's blood and poured a pint into a cocktail shaker. I added a healthy measure of vodka then stuck my hand in the empty cut glass bowl next to the sink.

The glyphs etched around the bowl glowed pink as it conjured some blood-fruit: the magical answer to controlling my 3V infection. The blood-fruit meant I didn't have to rely on G-Zav – the human vamp junkies' methadone – which doesn't work too well for fae, or need to Get Fanged by a vamp to get my regular dose of vamp venom. The bowl and its never-ending supply was a reward from Clíona after I'd helped her out. Seeing as my queenly grandmother wasn't my biggest fan, the paranoid part of me kept expecting her to take it back, or use it to poison me, even though that would effectively break the bargain we'd made. So far, she'd stuck to her word.

Usually I got cherries – the bowl had a thing for Sylvia (with the whole fruity connection they had, she and the bowl gossiped like a pair of silver birches) – or sometimes blackberries, though they'd been noticeably absent since *the satyr* had stopped writing. Occasionally the bowl produced something weird, like today's offering. A fruit, painted silvery gold like all blood-fruit, appeared. It was vaguely pear-shaped, but too knobbly, so I doubted it actually was one.

I poked it and guessed. 'A pear?'

'This is not a pear, but a quince, sacred to Aphrodite' – the bowl's voice took on a conspiratorial tone – 'and you know who she is, don't you?'

'Yep,' I said flatly, 'the Goddess of Love.'

'And of beauty and sexuality,' the bowl added smugly. 'The quince is also the fruit of love, marriage and fertility,' it finished archly.

Of course it was. 'What's it taste like?'

'What else but paradise?'

Gods save me from magical artefacts and their lame sense of humour.

'Thanks,' I muttered, knowing from past experience that saying anything else would get me something disgusting next time, like crab apples. I chopped the quince, popped the pieces into a mincer, cranked the handle (not having electricity sucks) and added the pulp to the blood in the cocktail shaker. I shook, poured the Bloody Mary into the glass and added a good shake of chilli flakes. They'd help disguise the quince if it tasted foul. And, after that paradise quip, I fully expected it to.

I sipped. Under the chilli the blood tasted bitter and astringent. Figured.

I moved to the full-length mirror propped next to my bedroom door (I'd shifted it out of my bedroom to stop Sylvia, and her lack of boundaries, from bursting in every time she wanted to use it) and dropped my towel. Might as well check the Magic Mirror spell was truly kaput.

I stared at my reflection with apprehension. Malik's rose-coloured bruises still marked the front of my body from my breasts down to the faint Celtic knot tattoo which sat low on my left hip, the remains of the spell that had let me borrow Rosa's vamp body. It was now as dead as she was. If not for them, I thought I looked pretty good. My curves might be not be as generous as Sylvia's but I was healthy and in proportion. Big boobs would look odd, I decided. Relief filled me. The nasty influence of the Magic Mirror spell was definitely gone.

I chugged the rest of the blood-fruit Mary down, and stepped back.

Something crunched under my foot.

It was the fortune cookie the old Chinese woman had given me. I'd stowed it in my backpack.

Gingerly, I picked it up. It crumbled in my hand and a blank tarot card zoomed out to hover in front of me.

Pulse speeding with excitement, and a little trepidation, I hurriedly set a Privacy spell (there was too much wood around and no way did I want any of Sylvia's mother's spies hearing about this), swapped the glass for a knife and slashed my index finger.

'I offer my blood solely in exchange for the answer to my questions. No harm to me or mine,' I said, and touched the tarot card.

The little mouth latched onto my blood with gusto. Still no pain, other than a tiny tickle.

'Tell me how to find that which is lost, and how to join that which is sundered, to release the fae's fertility from the pendant and restore it back to them as it was before it was taken,' I asked, repeating my original question.

The mouth stopped sucking. 'Eh, why's everyone so blummin' impatient,' a crotchety voice grumbled. 'Blimey, can't ye let a body have a few moments to drink in peace?'

'Um, sure,' I said, not sure if the voice was male or female. 'Sorry.'

'So ye should be, girlie. So ye blummin' should be. Now keep yer mouth shut till I'm done.' The mouth latched back on and I watched as my blood turned the card red from the bottom up.

An image appeared on the card.

Chapter Eighteen

A blood-red moon hung between two Romo-Greco-style pillars, frowning down at a grey-brown wolf which was baying up at the moon, and a dog with a stick in its mouth. The ground was covered with snow, apart from a black-cinder path leading between the two beasts and into the distance. A nebulous dark shape was clawing its way onto the path from the crimson-coloured river running along the front of the card.

The Moon. Symbolising feelings of uncertainty, of being haunted by the past, and associated with dreams, fantasies and mysteries. Well, it got that right; my past was haunting me in the shape of the Autarch and the Fertility pendant; Malik had the dreams and fantasies nailed, and the Emperor was certainly a mystery. And if I needed any more convincing, the moon was shadowed by a black sickle shape, matching the black gem in Malik's ring; the dog was a silvery-grey Irish wolfhound, like Mad Max in his doggy persona; and the wolf was a were-wolf with distinctive green starburst-patterned human eyes. Which left the dark thing in the river. Wasn't it supposed to be a crayfish? Though since it was meant to represent 'fears that come out of the abyss', the dark shape had it covered.

The card stopped sucking on my finger and I repeated my original question.

The wolf howled at the moon and leaped out of the card on to my arm. I tried not to flinch as its sharp prehensile paws dug into my flesh.

'He knows! He will tell you! For a price!'

'Is he the Emperor?' I asked, double-checking.

'Yes.'

'Is the Emperor a vampire?'

'Yes.'

Good to have what I knew confirmed. 'Can you tell me where to find him?'

'No.'

'Can you tell me what price he wants?'

'No.'

Figured. Rather than get a straight yes or no again, I risked an open question. 'What can you tell me?'

'They are coming.'

Informative. Not. 'Who are they?' I asked. 'And why are they coming?'

'They are the beasts. They come for you.'

My pulse sped. 'Why do they come for me?'

The Irish wolfhound barked and dropped the stick he was holding, then jumped out of the card. Snapping at the wolf's heels, the dog chased it back into the card. As the two hit the snowy scene the moon flashed bright as a halogen light and illuminated the shape that was clawing its way out of the river. It was a monstrous grey and black striped cat, bigger than both wolfhound and wolf.

As a pictorial manifestation of 'fears that come out of the abyss', the cat had a crayfish beat hands down. It opened its jaws wide, showcasing huge sabre-tooth fangs, then shook itself, spraying bloody droplets over the snow-covered ground as well as the stick the dog had dropped— no, not a stick but a silver dagger, half-buried. It looked similar to the one the Emperor had been holding in the first tarot card, only now I could see some of the handle. It was carved twisted bone and eerily familiar—

The cat screamed and the card disintegrated into a mini

snowstorm. The crimson-tinged flakes drifted down to melt like ice on my skin.

I stood stunned. I was pretty sure the dagger's handle was carved from a unicorn's horn. The last time I'd seen a dagger like that was during the demon attack at Hallowe'en. It couldn't be the same knife; that one had gone to hell with the demon. But this one looked similar enough that I wondered if it had the same power— a Bonder of Souls.

Only, why would the tarot cards show it first with the Emperor, then with Mad Max's doggy persona? And should I be more worried about the knife, or that the Emperor's beasts were coming for me? Or maybe they were already here; Katie thought she'd seen a werewolf after all. And I'd been so fixed on the flasher/watcher/shapeshifter being the Autarch that I hadn't believed her.

Damn it. Katie.

If the werewolf had been at the Primrose Hill park to sniff me out, then there was a good chance it had sniffed Katie out too. Tavish might say there was nothing in the old wives' tale about werewolves chasing virgins, but that didn't mean they wouldn't go after her to get at me.

I yanked my robe on and called Tavish.

He answered on the ninth ring and, almost jumping up and down with worry, I demanded, 'Did you give Katie that werewolf-repelling perfume yet?'

'Aye, course I did, doll. I sent it her right after we chatted. Sent some to you too, 'twill be in your fridge. Why?'

The anxious knot in my stomach relaxed slightly. Katie was safe; the perfume should keep the werewolves at bay. And the Ward on her necklace would protect her from almost anything else.

I said thanks and filled Tavish in on the Moon tarot card. 'So,' I finished, 'I obviously need to watch out for werewolves, but what about the knife? Could it be another soul-bonding one? And if it is, why does he want it?'

'Och, Soul Bonders are a rarity. The knife may be another thing entirely. 'Tis difficult to say why, doll, with only two cards revealed. 'Twill be easier to divine once the full reading is complete.'

'So not helpful, Tavish.'

'Aye, well, I told you searching out the answers takes time.'

'What about the fact that the Emperor's holding the knife in the first card, but the Irish wolfhound has it in this one? That's got to mean something?'

'Nae doubt it does, and the cards will tell you in time.'

He sounded preoccupied, but then I could hear his computers beeping and the clack of keys in the background. I tapped my foot, anxious. 'Tavish, c'mon, they're your cards. Give me something to work with here.'

'Aye, but 'tis your reading. So 'tis catered to what's in your mind and heart, nae mine.'

'Okay, then how's this for a theory.' I closed my eyes, trying to fit the pieces together. 'The werewolf on the card said the Emperor's werewolves are coming for me. It felt like a threat, but what if it's not? What if it's just a heads up? I mean, when I asked the werewolf why the Emperor wanted me, the Irish wolfhound chased the werewolf off. And when I asked Malik about the Emperor last night, he started prevaricating, and he was under the Autarch's influence.'

I leaned on the kitchen counter, head in my hand and clutched the phone closer. 'So if we take it the Irish wolfhound, a.k.a. Mad Max, represents the Autarch, and the werewolf represents the Emperor, then the dog stopping the werewolf from telling me things could mean that the Autarch is trying to stop me from finding the Emperor.'

I blew out a breath, trying to ease the tension in my shoulders. 'Maybe what the card's really telling me is that

147

the Emperor's beasts are coming for me so we can do a deal, but that the Autarch is going to try to stop me meeting them. Which could mean the Autarch's trying to prevent me from finding out how to release the fae's fertility from the pendant.'

'Hmph.' The sound of Tavish's fingers hitting keys quietened for a moment. 'Nae sure the Autarch's bothered about the fae's fertility, doll. But stands to reason he won't want you mixing with any outsider vampires, not when he's always had a hankering for you himself. And I ken you said Malik doesnae think much of this Emperor, either. So my money's on the card being a warning for you to take care about the Emperor, and also a warning to keep away from the Autarch and Malik al-Khan till this matter with the Emperor is done.'

Except I'd already agreed to Malik's 'date' ... if he ever phoned me back to arrange it. And the date wasn't only to find out about the Emperor and the fae's fertility. I needed to talk to Malik about us. To work out whatever our relationship was. And I needed to know the beautiful vamp was okay.

Of course, if I didn't go on the 'date' I probably wouldn't need to confront Bastien the psycho, or my phobia.

But then if Malik were in trouble, I'd be leaving him to the sadistic psycho's not-so-tender mercies ... something I wasn't prepared to do.

I decided not to mention any of that to Tavish.

Instead, I said, 'If I stay away from Malik, it makes it harder to find the Emperor. And I'd rather find him before his werewolves find me.'

'Told you, doll.' Tavish's irritation came over the phone loud and clear. ''Twill nae take me long now I've found his website ... as a matter of fact, I'm sending you another screenshot.'

I checked. The new shot of the Emperor looked the same as the last one except now below the Emperor, scrolling across the screen in Romanesque font, were the words: Forum Mirabilis.

'Think it's some sort of vamp chat room?'

'I dinna ken yet, doll. Mirabilis means "Amazing", or "Wondrous",' Tavish replied, his voice still distracted. 'And there's nae much that's wondrous about a chatroom. Anyways, soon as I find it out, I'll let you know.'

'Okay, but there's a couple of things worrying me. First up, why did the cards show a huge cat thing instead of a crayfish? That has to mean something?'

'Hm, could be something or ...' A silence. 'Could be you're more scared of cats than crayfish?'

'I'm not a troll, Tavish,' I said drily, 'and I couldn't care one way or the other about crayfish.'

'Well, the cards dinna always show the literal truth, she may be picking up on your subconscious fears and having herself a bit of fun—'

'Fun!'

'Aye, she's a creative type, so maybe 'tis a subconscious thing from last you were scared—'

Which was ten seconds ago. When I thought of the Autarch. Which meant the thing crawling out the abyss should be a vamp.

'—Or last saw a cat,' Tavish finished.

'The gnome's,' I said flatly. 'The place was full of cats.' And I'd thought of the Autarch there, too.

'Och, well, there you go, doll. Something scared you there and the spirit's matched it with the cats. Told you, she's the creative type. And she can be a bit ornery at times, too'

An ornery creative type? Really? Dismay filled me. I'd rather have a pedantic-tell-it-like-it-is type answering my questions. A feeling that brought up my second, more important worry. 'Are you sure the spirit in the tarot cards is trustworthy? That she can't be compromised?'

He gave an exasperated snort. 'Told you, doll. Those cards are sidhe-made.'

'Sidhe can fudge the truth as well as anyone, Tavish. Seems weird that an out-of-town vamp, however powerful he is, who we've never heard of, knows how to release the fae's fertility. I mean, what if it's a big hoax, or some sort of trap? What if the card's spirit is out there chatting to this Emperor vamp, or to the Autarch, and they're cooking all this up together?'

'She's a spirit. She cannae talk to the living unless it's through the cards. Only others she can talk to is like-minded spirits.'

I stared blindly at my scowling reflection, unwilling to let my 'Bastien' paranoia go just yet. 'She's like a ghost then? So a vamp could've got a necromancer to talk to her?'

'Nae, doll, she's nae so much dead as disembodied and bound to the cards.' Tavish sigh was mildly exasperated. 'Told you, without the cards naeone can talk to her. And right now, there's only you can talk to her anyhows, seeing as it's your reading she's doing.'

Hmm. 'What are like-minded spirits?'

'Just that. Another spirit bound to an item, same as your blood-fruit bowl. And afore you ask, t'only way they can chat is if they're by one another and I have the cards here with me.'

'I thought my bowl was a magical artefact?'

'Aye, doll, 'tis that. It uses the power of the spirit bound to it to make it magical.'

Right. Made sense now I thought about it. 'So how do the spirits get bound to an item?'

'Och, maybe they upset someone, or make a bad bargain. There's nae any way to ken.'

Nasty. And probably didn't make for a happy spirit, which my blood-fruit bowl definitely was not; no wonder it was so snarky all the time. Only it wasn't the bowl my paranoia was panicking about, but the spirit in the tarot cards. 'So there's no way she could be plotting with anyone else?'

'Doll …' Another silence while Tavish obviously gathered

his patience. 'Dinna fash yerself about it. Once the reading's done then 'twill all become clear. And 'twill nae be long before I'm into the Emperor's website. That'll give us more to go on.'

'Okay, but—'

The phone went dead.

I scowled at it, wondering if it was worth calling him back, then shook my head. He knew where I was, and for all his distraction he was an invested in the outcome of the tarot reading as I was. More so, really. So I should probably let him get on with his hacking.

I double-checked the new screenshot of the Emperor's website against the previous one. Apart from the 'Forum Mirabilis' bit, there was nothing new. But the tarot cards said the Emperor's werewolves were coming for me, and never mind the 'heads up' theory I'd given Tavish, I'd be stupid not to prepare for the worst. No way did I want to end up howling at the moon. Only I didn't know much more about werewolves than Tavish and Katie had told me.

Time for some research.

I grabbed a blood donation bag, hooked myself up and pushed through the Ward on the front door and out onto the landing (where thankfully, the Wards hadn't managed to nix the electricity). Checking the Buffer spell on my laptop was clear (with all the extra security around, a thief would have a hard time getting into the building, never mind stealing the laptop. Not to mention, computers were even more susceptible than mobiles when it came to getting fried by magic; Buffer spells only give so much protection), I pulled up the online witch archives. The information on werewolves was in the public section.

I clicked on 'Therianthropic Metamorphosis' and started reading.

Chapter Nineteen

Therianthropes are 'Bitten', 'Changed by Ritual', or 'Born'.

If Bitten, the bite should be done the first day of a new moon for optimum success and can only be performed by an alpha in their beast (half and half) form. The hopeful victim gets their throat ripped out (called, appropriately enough a Death Bite) and it usually takes them until the full moon to recover. If they do. Only one in ten males, and one in a hundred females, survive, apparently. Though a quick side search via Google got me enough happy pictures of New Werewolf Celebrations to think the survival rates must be better than stated.

The only place the bite's legal is Russia, for obvious reasons; the Russian secret service aren't nicknamed the Silent Wolves for nothing. Bitten werewolves, both male and female, are infertile (a note said to see 'Changed by Ritual' for more on werewolf fertility levels). Werewolves prefer to live in dense forested areas. Aren't sensitive to silver, as a lot of fiction states, but are allergic to wolfsbane, mistletoe and ergot, particularly when presented in tincture. They generally live a slightly longer than normal human lifespan, have high resistance to most diseases, but are as vulnerable to death or injury as any other in their human or animal forms. In their beast form (half and half) they can only be killed by removal of head or heart.

'Good to know,' I murmured, hoping if I did come across the Emperor's wolves they wouldn't be in their beast form, and made a note to get Tavish's werewolf repellent out of the fridge.

I clicked on 'Changed by Ritual'. It took me to the secure section of the archives; if I wanted to read it I needed a password. Clicking on the 'Born' link took me to the same protected page.

Curious, I texted Tavish and Katie on the off chance that one of them might reply, despite the late hour. Unsurprisingly, given Tavish's earlier abrupt end to our phone call, it was Katie; only her password didn't work. Instead, I got a security warning. I scowled at it, sent another text to Tavish, then after wasting fifteen minutes on Facebook's Magikville, during which I managed to lose half my spellcaster points and ended up trading a golden goose for a dud magic frog. I gave up on my werewolf research, sealed my full blood bag and headed for the fridge.

As I reached for the door, my phone rang. The number on the screen was Sanguine Lifestyles; the vamp's 24/7 'do anything' service.

My heart thudded against my ribs.

'Ms Taylor,' a woman's efficient-sounding voice said, 'I have a message for you from Mr Malik al-Khan. He would like you to meet him at the Blue Heart, at midnight tomorrow. Can I tell him the time and date will be suitable for you?'

Tavish wanted me to stay away from Malik.

Part of me thought Tavish was right and really, with him on the Emperor's case, I didn't need to 'date' Malik for any more info. Only as I'd decided before, that wasn't the only reason I needed to see him …

But the fae's fertility had to be sorted; it had to take priority.

'Ms Taylor?' the woman's voice prompted.

I should say no. I opened my mouth, but instead the words that came out were, 'Thank you. That time and date will be suitable.'

She rang off and guilt twisted inside me as I opened the fridge. 'The "date" with Malik isn't till midnight tomorrow,' I told the two dead mackerel, sliding the bag of blood in to join the one already there on the shelf below. 'That gives me plenty of time to see what Tavish might or might not find out, so if need be, I can always call it off. All it would take is a phone call.' The two mackerel eyed me balefully.

I sighed and reached past the fish to pick up a small black tub: Tavish's werewolf repellent.

I opened it, took a wary sniff— the stuff ripped up my nose like a six-week-old corpse, and as it hit the back of my throat a coughing fit seized me. A couple of minutes later I managed to slam the lid back on, and swipe the tears from my eyes. Tavish wasn't kidding when he said it didn't smell so good. 'I'd rather wear you two as earrings,' I muttered, plonking the tub back next to the dead fish and closing the fridge with a shudder.

Crap. Katie was going to hate it, if the smell didn't kill her first.

And there was no way I could wear it and work. Only I'd be stupid not to.

Damn it. If only I knew for sure she'd seen a werewolf on Primrose Hill. But to do that I'd need to look into Katie's memory, which was a vamp power I didn't have. And no way was I going to let any vamp near Katie, not after last time. But maybe Malik could dredge something up from my memory. I had seen that shadow after all—

An idea hit me. There was a way I could interrogate my own memory, and not only about the shadow, but about the peeping tom I'd seen looking in the nasty gnome's window shortly before.

Sylvia had done a deal with a local witch company for groceries, and the fridge was set up to magically replenish itself as needed. It only allowed individual things through the Ward at any one time (which was how Tavish had sent me the icky werewolf-repellent), so was safe. But the witch company didn't just deliver groceries; they did spells too. And they worked round the clock.

I texted a request for what I wanted, and got an almost instant, positive reply: 'In stock and sent.' Gotta love an efficient company.

I checked the fridge. On the top shelf, next to the black tub with its repellent, was a small box. The box had a cartoon picture of a smiling, sleeping woman with her head on a pillow of clouds. Printed on the box were the words: 'Morpheus Memory Aid'. It was an off-the-shelf hypnopædia spell beloved by panicked students everywhere. I double-checked the blurb on the back of the box:

> Named for Morpheus, the Greek God of Dreams, the Morpheus Memory Aid sleep-teaching spell is a worldwide favourite of students, lecturers, actors, singers, travellers, public speakers and politicians. Retain relevant facts with overnight ease. Learn a new language while you sleep. Mesmerise—

Hm, not quite what I remembered (no pun intended). I opened the box to find a tiny blue glass bottle, a matching blue sleep mask, and the instructions:

> Drink before sleep while concentrating on the information you need to recall. The potion's patented magics will work alongside your dreaming subconscious to completely focus on the required subject matter, then consolidate and commit every detail (including those normally discarded by our conscious self) in the hippocampus – the part of the brain concerned with memory.

> Warning: Contains alcohol. Do not drive or use machinery immediately after use. Please drink responsibly. No liability

will be admitted for failure of dreamer to achieve expected grade in any test or examination. Do not use if aware of any previous adverse reactions to any of the ingredients (listed below), to previous use of Morpheus Memory Aid or any similar magics (nightmares, night terrors, loss of short-term memory), or if suffering from any of the ailments (listed below) which are known to be contraindicated. Disclaimer: Evidence recalled under the influence of Morpheus Memory Aid is not admissible in a human court of law.

'Ah hah!' I told the glazed-eyed fish as I read the last sentence. 'That's what I thought it said. Now let's see if it works.'

Which, since it was aimed at humans and I'm sidhe, was debatable. Still, only one way to find out, and hopefully without suffering any of its 'adverse reactions'. I had more than enough bad dream material with Emperors, werewolves, monstrous crawling-out-of-the abyss cats, stinging Jellyfish spells or my usual nightmare whenever I thought about the Autarch too much – that my psychotic, sadistic betrothed was about to turn up to claim me for his long-lost bride.

I glugged the potion, which tasted like chemical strawberries with a kick, pulled on the sleep mask and flopped into bed.

My dreaming self stood in the gnome's creepsville room with its high ceiling, fungi-covered furniture and shelved walls stacked with plastic boxes and glass tanks full of more staring eyes and various body parts, some hideously mutilated, than I recalled from my actual visit. Instead of the room being dimly lit, now it was as if a half-a-dozen floodlights illuminated it. My dream vision was sharp enough to see every individual hair on the ginger tom cat crouching on the desk, and I realised that its fur wasn't just shades of orange, but held whites and cream too.

I followed the cat's gaze in slow motion towards the sash

window to see the dark-haired male peering round its edge. The shadows were gone from his face and the details of his features embedded themselves razor-sharp into my mind. Black-brown hair, long enough to show a slight wave, pale skin with a smattering of freckles on the bridge of his straight nose, hazel-coloured eyes tinged with green and edged with thick black lashes, generous mouth parted in dismay to give a glimpse of straight white teeth, and even a thin line of stubble along his left jaw where he must have been hasty in shaving.

I'd be able to pick him out in a crowd of similar-looking men a hundred years from now.

I wasn't going to need to. I knew who he was.

Marc. Katie's boyfriend.

But even as I questioned what the hell Katie's boyfriend was doing casing the gnome's joint, or spying on me, and what I was going to do about it, the dream moved on.

I found myself outside the gnome's house with Katie, her grey eyes rounding with alarm as she pointed at the park, her mouth forming the words. 'In those bushes!'

Then I was racing towards the bushes, the sword Ascalon in my hand, clearly seeing the way the leaves trembled, despite the summer-still air, as if someone had held them back and just released them—

Another shout from Katie and I was staring towards the trees.

Only now my sharpened dream vision showed me an amorphous grey shape, low to the ground, crouched on all fours, its eyes reflecting eerily in the darkness like a cat's, and large enough to be a werewolf in its wolf form. But I was too far away, and the shadows too dense, to be sure that it was a wolf and not some other animal, like a large dog or even a small bear.

The animal slowly backed up and disappeared.

Frustration sifted through me. I wanted to race down there,

grab it by the throat, pull it out into the light and see exactly what it was, but the hovering conscious part of my brain knew the Morpheus Memory Aid potion didn't work that way. It worked to enhance whatever you wanted to remember.

The view of the park disappeared beneath a blinding snow storm. The reek of fresh-spilled blood choked my throat.

And a familiar voice with its not-quite-English accent sounded in my mind.

Genevieve.

Chapter Twenty

*G*enevieve. *You should not be here.*

Malik's voice came again, the urgency in it tugging me out of the dream. For a moment I drifted, then horror slipped inside me as the dream pulled me under again, back to a wide, moon-bright plateau. The plateau stretched out to both sides of me, one edge hugging the steep mountain face, the other falling into the clouds roiling below. The ground was covered with an ankle-deep blanket of snow and wolves were howling all around me, their keening riding the wind that dragged anxious fingers through my hair and sent icy snowflakes to sting my face. I knelt in the snow, blood staining it in a ragged circle, like crimson petals scattered from a rose, as I denied my terror, my revulsion, and schooled my face. I was listening, as I had long ago, to the figure before me talking about … something … that filled me with desolation, even as it lifted my soul with fledgling hope. Only the words didn't make any sense—

Genevieve.

Malik's harsh whisper jerked me awake and the dream shredded like fog chased away by a resolute wind. Adrenalin sped my pulse, my left wrist banded with pain, and I jerked up, ripping off the sleep mask and searching my bedroom for him.

Dawn light streamed through the open window, washing over the sloping white-painted walls, the copper paint on my iron bedstead, and throwing shadows behind the rail holding my clothes. But as I peered at the dark corner, trying to see if he stood there, shaded from the sun, my inner radar kicked in and told me the room was empty.

Disappointment rolled over me. I rubbed my wrist, trying to soothe the stinging soreness there and wondering if I had really gatecrashed Malik's dream, which was how it had felt, or was the nightmare down to the Morpheus Memory Aid backfiring? After all, it wouldn't be the first time magic had gone haywire on me—

My bed was covered in rose petals. Those were definitely nothing to do with the Morpheus spell. The dark crimson petals were scattered over the white sheets like fresh blood on snow. Even with the obvious references to Malik's and my time together in the hotel function room, and the dream I'd just woken from, and knowing I was alone, part of me hoped the velvety petals filling the room with a familiar dark spice scent were a clichéd romantic gesture on Malik's part. Only, I didn't need the unease in my gut to tell me they were nothing to do with romance.

I scooped up a petal praying it was an illusion that would dissipate with touch.

It didn't.

My unease grew. Where had they come from? What were they to do with the dream? What did the dream have to do with Malik? How had I heard his voice if he wasn't here? And more worryingly, if the petals were as real as they felt, how the hell had someone – *Malik?* – got them past the Wards?

I *looked* at the open window. In my sight, it disappeared behind a magical steel shutter. The magical steel shone deep purple and the combination of blood and power fuelling the Ward made it hum like a megawatt transformer. My flat was the safest place in England right now. Or at least it was meant to be. Nothing could, or should, get past the Ward, not even a five-hundred-plus-year-old vamp who normally had an open invitation over any threshold I was behind, thanks to my being stupid enough to give him my blood freely.

Agitated, I swung out of bed, grabbed my robe and hurried into the living room. The Wards covering the flat's front door and the window were, like the one in the bedroom, intact, and a quick scan of the room told me everything appeared undisturbed. I pulled the sheet off the wardrobe leading into Sylvia's *Between*.

The wardrobe, too, appeared undisturbed.

But appearances could be deceiving. Warily, I waved my hand over the wardrobe's handles – intricately carved oak leaves that were recent replacements for the original brass ones – careful not to actually touch them. Robur, the ancient dryad now resident in the wardrobe's wood (and the reason why the wardrobe was no longer in my bedroom), wasn't the cheeriest of folk, and since I'd sprayed him with lemon polish not long after he'd moved in, he'd taken a distinct dislike to me. The wardrobe made an irritated creaking noise and the whorls in the wooden door shifted into an approximation of a face. Hooded brown eyes drilled me with a malevolent glare.

'Everything okay in there?' I asked.

'Why, what have you done now?'

At Robur's accusing tone, I clamped down on my defensive 'nothing', and instead said calmly, 'I'm concerned someone may have bypassed the Wards.'

'Impossible! I would know.'

Arrogant much? 'Are you sure?'

The hooded eyes narrowed to disdainful cracks. 'There are three pigeons sitting on the apex of the roof. The witch who lives the floor below is meditating, unfortunately not skyclad as she should be and she has neglected to light her elemental candles. The witch on the second floor is snoring, despite her extremely shrill alarm attempting to wake her three times. The goblin cleaner is polishing the woodwork on the stairs, correctly, I might add, using a lint-free cloth, unperfumed beeswax and working along the grain—'

'Fine,' I interrupted, before I ended up with another lecture, 'you're sure. I get it. But someone still left rose petals on my bed during the night.'

'Your vampire paramour, I suspect.'

I huffed under my breath, ignoring the insult. 'So he was here then?'

'No.'

'Then how can you suspect?'

His face rippled with distaste. 'You were conversing with another in your dreams. I have heard that ability is one it is possible for vampires to effect.'

Astonishment flooded me. I'd been talking out loud in the dream? Why hadn't Robur woken me? Though hard on that thought came the answer; this was the first time he'd done more than creaked at me since the polish incident. Eager to find out, I asked, 'What did I talk about?'

'Ghosts and blood.'

I frowned. 'Can you be more specific?'

Robur grunted. 'No. The language is unknown to me; I only know because you repeated the words "sanguine lemures" over and over. I was irritated to the extent that I searched for a translation. It is Latin for "the blood of undead ghosts", or some such nonsense.'

The blood of undead ghosts? No doubt Malik could explain what it meant, along with how I'd ended up in his dream or memory in the first place. After all it wasn't like I'd had his blood during our Jellyfish spell-removing episode, except— the jellyfish had been feeding on him, and it had stung me. Okay, so I'd *cracked* its magic and killed it, but I'd definitely got some of its poison in me, possibly along with some of Malik's blood. Was that why I was experiencing his dreams/

memories with him? I filed all my questions away for our 'date' tonight— if I ended up going.

Which I would if Tavish didn't sort the Emperor question first.

'Right, thanks,' I said to Robur. The jellyfish scenario could explain why I was gatecrashing Malik's dream, but it didn't explain the physical presence of the rose petals. 'Are you sure no one's breached the Wards?'

'I have informed you already. No!'

'Then how did the rose petals get in?'

'That ... I do not have an answer for,' Robur said dismissively, his face smoothing back into the wardrobe's wood.

I resisted the urge to kick the wardrobe. The sneaky dryad had eyes everywhere, supposedly, but those petals had still got in without him knowing. Concerned, I called Tavish and got his voicemail. I left a brief message about the Morpheus Memory Aid revealing Katie's boyfriend as the peeping tom, the shadowy animal beneath the trees, which might or might not, have been a werewolf. Now I thought about it, it looked like the grey crawling-out-the-abyss cat on the Moon tarot card. I mentioned my weird blood and snow dream, the rose petals and Robur's comments. I left another voicemail for Katie, and one for her mum too, saying we needed to chat about Marc, a.s.a.p., and for Katie to be sure she wore the werewolf repellent, even if its reek meant she was likely to repel half of London.

Better safe than sorry, as the saying goes.

I grabbed an orange juice from the fridge, exchanging the stink-eye with Ricou's dead mackerel. That they were still there meant Ricou hadn't been home and Sylvia had spent the night alone. I made a note to talk to the absent naiad, tell him he needed to pay his pregnant partner more attention.

My gaze snagged on the shelf below the fish where the two bags of blood sat, my last two donations ready to go to Freya, my niece. The Wards were keyed to my blood, so maybe that was how they'd been breached. By someone who had access to my donations. Someone like, say, oh, Freya's granddad, Mad Max— the Autarch's pet vamp.

Only Mad Max didn't need access to my donated blood; he could've easily siphoned off a couple of pints while he'd had me unconscious and tied to the hotel bed. Then given my blood to the Autarch. The blood would be stolen, so its power over me reduced, but there might still be enough for a small breach. And the petals were exactly the sort of sick joke the psychotic bastard would play. What if Robur, despite his initially reassuring conviction in his own surveillance abilities, was wrong and the Autarch had breached the Wards, even though all the interior ones looked intact? Of course, I hadn't checked the ones outside on the roof yet.

I grabbed a handful of dog biscuits from the jar on the kitchen counter, and stuffed them in my pocket as I made a beeline back to my bedroom window. The Steel Shutter Ward moulded like thick, suffocating plastic around me as I climbed over the low sill and breathed in the scents of honeysuckle, cherry blossom and watercress, undercut with the copper tang of the blood fuelling its magic. The Ward released me, snapping back in place over the window and sending me stumbling into the summer sunshine. A hot breeze ruffled my hair, and the early morning bustle from the Witches' Market in Covent Garden five storeys below rode the air like a distant radio.

I tuned it out, scanning the roof.

In the humans' reality the roof was ten feet deep and stretched in a large squared-off U around the three sides of the Edwardian terraces that hemmed in the garden and cemetery below. The red-brick entrance to St Paul's Church closed off the last side of the garden square. The roof was a great place to sunbathe, and all around the U-shape deckchairs and flower-pots had sprung up as soon as the weather turned warm.

But the section outside my window was nearing thirty foot deep; a new addition thanks to my flatmates. And instead of a few potted plants, we had a peaceful forest glade. Moss and colourful lichens carpeted the roof's surface, multi-stemmed silver birch saplings ringed the glade's edge, and in the centre was a silver-watered pond. If I squinted I could just make out where the original roof edge bisected the pond; one of the reasons I never ventured in for a paddle. The other was the water's occupant. Alongside the pond were four wooden sun loungers with green-and-white-striped cushions. It looked like some luxury holiday retreat instead of a roof garden in the heart of London. It also looked as peaceful and undisturbed as usual.

So far, so good.

Above the glade rose a geodesic dome of magic, the dome's opaque glass-like panels obscuring the view over London's rooftops. That dome was the Ward protecting, enclosing and enforcing the overlay of the forest glade on the humans' world. I *focused* my attention on the pink-tinged panels, scanning carefully for any breaks or breaches.

Nothing.

Relief settled in me. Robur was right. No one, not the Autarch, and not even Malik, had bypassed the Wards. The rose petals had to be a vamp illusion, however real they seemed. I turned to go and double-check, but stopped as the shadow of a tall figure appeared outside the Warded dome. Someone was on the roof, and this early it was unlikely to be one of my neighbours, not least because they usually kept their distance.

Pulse hitching in wariness, I clenched my hand, ready to release Ascalon, and dropped my *sight*.

The magical dome winked out.

Finn stood outside the Ward.

Chapter Twenty-One

'**H**ey!' Finn's moss-green eyes sparked emerald, faint lines creasing their corners as he smiled.

Stunned surprise laced with joy at seeing him again made my heart leap, then my anger and hurt boiled up. I started to demand what the hell he was thinking of turning up expecting a welcome as if we'd last seen each other yesterday—

Suspicion froze me. Finn was supposed to be in the Fair Lands with Nicky, his pregnant daughter, until she had her kid. He wasn't due back for at least another two months. So he shouldn't be here. Wouldn't be here ... Unless, while my inner radar pinged him as fae, this wasn't Finn.

I curled my fingers around Ascalon's ring, and narrowed my gaze. The sharp points of his horns standing a couple of inches above his dark blond hair were the only thing about him that said he was satyr and not human, but then he was wearing Finn's usual clean-cut handsome Glamour. Or almost. The lines at his eyes were new, his face was thinner, and the angle of his jaw was more defined, making him look early thirties. Though, like any fae, how old he looked was irrelevant, the real Finn (who at a hundred and eight was one of the youngest in the satyr herd) had always looked around my age: twenty-five.

The fae's smile faded, and something else ... disappointment, wariness, or maybe a touch of anger ... took its place. 'I thought you'd be happy to see me, Gen.'

He sounded like Finn too. 'How do I know you're Finn?'

He frowned, then comprehension lit his face and he touched

166

his palm to the Warded dome. It flashed bright vermilion and he hastily snatched his hand back.

Yeah, the Ward packs a punch. But then this guy was fae, he'd know that. So why the hell had he hurt himself like that?

'Third time's the charm, Gen,' he said, holding his hand up; his palm was black where the Ward had seared his skin. 'Except it wasn't, was it?' He gave me a lopsided grin. 'Ricou said we were lucky not to kill each other. Remember?'

I did. Tavish had sicced me with a Chastity spell that manifested as a black handprint on my stomach. Finn had tried to remove the spell using his fertility magic. We'd been in the back of a luxury limo cocooned in our own little world by Privacy spells, and the knowledge than no one would interrupt us. If we hadn't both ended up knocked out by the clashing spells the third time he'd tried, things would've gone a lot further than they did … And yeah, only Finn would know he'd said 'Third time's the charm' right before our 'lucky' magical coitus interruptus.

The memory lodged a ball of hurt in my chest. Why the hell did he have to remind me of that particular moment; the last time we'd had fun and been happy together? Damn satyr could've picked any number of things.

'Ricou can be a drama queen at times,' I said flatly.

Finn's shot me a searching look but all he said was, 'So, you're sure it's me now?'

I wanted to say no. I wanted to shout at him to go away. But my curiosity spiked … *or maybe a moment of errant masochism*: I also wanted to know why he'd cut me off.

I stepped through the Ward, shivering as the recognition magic pricked goosebumps over my skin. There was one last check— skin to skin. Stealing myself for his touch, I stuck my hand out, 'Nearly.'

He nodded and clasped my hand in his, taking a deep breath and rolling his shoulders like he was shrugging off a heavy cape. The mouth-watering smell of blackberries swam on the air and his familiar magic bloomed inside me. I gasped as it filled me, then swallowed back a scream as it ripped spiked thorns of desire through my core and almost took me to my knees before Finn gathered me to him.

'Um. You okay, Gen?'

I leaned against him, not sure my legs would hold me, breathing in his warm berry scent, feeling his heart echoing my own heart's fast thudding, and concentrated on crushing the need thrumming through my body. Bastard satyr had sicced me with enough of his sex-god energy to power-up a fertility rite. Boy, was I thankful that Mad Max's Poultice spell had done its job. Damn fertility magic would've had me desperate and begging again. Especially as my libido thought Finn was exactly what it needed, and wanted nothing less than to act on the promise of pleasure still jumping along my nerve endings. Only no way was that going to happen, not when he'd cut me off.

Finally I fought myself back under control, and pushed away from him. 'What the fuck was that for?'

'Well, I wanted you to be sure it was me,' he said sounding contrite, but a flicker of satisfaction crossed his face. 'Sorry.'

Rage sparked. 'No. You're not.'

'Hey, I am sorry, truly, Gen. I've …' He lifted a hesitant hand as if to touch me, then let it fall. 'Okay, yeah, maybe I took advantage. A bit. But I didn't mean to hit you quite so hard. The magic's been playing havoc with me recently, and I've … missed you. Forgive me?'

I'd missed him too. The feeling slammed into me, twisting through my anger. And I knew better than most how the magic could play tricks on you.

Finn's mouth turned down. 'Things haven't been easy with Nicky, either. Not that that's an excuse, but it hasn't helped.'

Yep, I could imagine that coping with a pregnant teenage

daughter wasn't easy, especially one whose pregnancy had been forced on her by a deranged baby-making wizard. Not to mention Nicky ending up in the mad wizard's clutches was down to her own mother, Finn's ex and my Witch-bitch nemesis DI Helen Crane. Helen's betrayal of him and their daughter was something else he'd had to deal with. The Witch-bitch was an evil piece of work if ever there was one.

I shoved my hands in my robe pockets, warring between wanting to hug him for the nasty stuff he'd ended up dealing with, and pounding on him for siccing his magic on me. For bringing back memories I'd buried. For cutting me off. But concern for Nicky, and for him, made me ask 'How is Nicky?'

'She's fine.' His shoulders slumped. 'Well, not fine, but okay,' he added, then the wariness darkened his green eyes again. 'We need to talk, Gen.'

Yeah, we did. I clenched my hands in my pockets. 'You'd better start then,' I said, trying to keep my anger out of my voice.

Finn flinched, so obviously I wasn't successful. He waved at my bedroom window. 'Can we go inside, Gen?'

No. But the excited rustling coming from the silver birches silenced my kneejerk denial; we'd given the trees enough gossip already. And I did want to hear whatever he had to tell me.

'Sure,' I said. 'But I have to go first then pull you through the Ward.' *Only we have to touch again. I'm not sure I'm ready. Or if I want to.*

He nodded as if he'd heard my reluctant words or more likely noticed my hands were still shoved in my robe, then he cast an assessing eye over the dome. 'Looks complicated.'

'It is.' I grimaced. 'And sensitive.'

'Sensitive?'

'Yeah, it's set to activate if it senses we're under threat,' I said, then as talking was easing the anger tensing my muscles I added grudgingly, 'Turns out it can't tell the difference between fear and excitement. The Ward went into lock-down after I signed up Harrods.'

Impressed delight lit his face. 'You got the contract with Harrods?'

'Yep.'

He grinned, leaned in as if he were going to kiss me then, as I shifted back, clasped my shoulders instead, giving them a congratulatory pat. 'Way to go, Gen!'

'Thanks.' I'd worked hard to finalise that deal, and I was proud of it. Now I'd given the police the heads up about the source of the Harrods' mutating Magic Mirror spell, it was going to be a nice little earner. I nodded at the dome. 'It took us two days to get the Ward back on track.'

'Us?'

'Me, Sylvia and Ricou.'

'Ah,' he said, a muscle spasming in his jaw. 'I'd heard you were living together. How's that working out?'

An odd note in his voice made me frown. 'Better than I thought it would. Why?'

He cast another look at my bedroom window. 'Can we talk about it inside? Or is that a problem?'

'Why should it be a problem?'

'Not here, Gen,' he insisted.

He sounded ... jealous? Of Sylvia and Ricou? That was ... weird. And way out of line. He was the one who'd stopped writing not me. I blew out a furious breath to calm myself then stepped back into the magical dome. The Ward slapped shut behind me. I turned, took a moment to *focus*, and shoved my left arm through the Ward's plastic-feeling side. 'You need to hold my hand with your left, and remember: stay calm.'

He stared at my hand as if I'd offered him raw meat to eat (something I'd never do, since Finn's vegetarian) and it clicked he was glaring at Malik's rose-shaped bruises circling my wrist, though why was beyond me; he knew they were there. I raised my brows and wiggled my fingers impatiently. He grasped them and I went to guide him through, then stopped him with a warning look. 'Oh, one more thing, the Ward will strip away your Glamour, so you might want to make sure your clothes are real.'

'I don't make a habit of walking around undressed, Gen.' Amusement glinted in his eyes, and for a moment the teasing, light-hearted Finn I loved was back. 'At least not since that time you *called* my clothes along with a spell.'

'That was nearly a year ago,' I huffed, aggrieved. 'And it was an accident.' It had been our first Spellcrackers job together. I'd been mortified at my erratic magical ability that I hadn't taken time to enjoy the naked Finn eye-candy. 'And it only happened the once.'

'Twice.'

Oh, yeah. Except the second time I'd given in to temptation and done it deliberately. Not that it got me anywhere; Finn had been even quicker at zapping his Glamour back in place than the first time.

I gave a louder huff, and tugged him towards me.

He stepped into the Ward. It held him, the power in it tasting and testing. The air around him flashed with emerald sparks, and I squinted against the glare as his Glamour peeled away in stages, as if it took time to reveal his true form. His T-shirt disappeared. His shoulders and chest broadened, the muscles hardening and becoming more defined. His jeans morphed into a pair of olive-coloured cargo trousers, loose enough to conceal the tail I'd glimpsed only once and which, like all satyrs, he was shy about. His features sharpened, taking on a feral edge, his hair turning from dark blond to a ruffled sable, his horns lengthening, curving and twisting sinuously a foot above his head. His eyes were the last to change: the softer moss-green of his irises flowing into the whites and shading them pale chartreuse as his pupils elongated and flattened into dark horizontal slits.

For a moment I caught my breath, stunned. I'd seen his true form before, but only when he'd been fighting, hurt or angry enough to lose his hold on his Glamour, and while his human shape was clean-cut handsome, now he was— well, jaw-droppingly gorgeous didn't begin to cover it.

'Like what you see, Gen?' he said, grinning like a fertility fae who thought he was on to a sure thing.

Annoyance smacked into me and I shut my mouth. Damn satyr. He'd somehow fudged the Ward: his whole slow-Glamour-strip deliberate.

Before I could call him on it, a loud splash came from the pond behind me.

I swung round, adrenalin speeding my pulse as I dug a handful of dog biscuits from my robe's pocket.

The pond's occupant – a gigantic eel called Bertha – had risen five feet above the water's surface and was doing her usual swaying snake-charmer's dance. Briefly I wondered if I could make a run for the bedroom before she saw me, only my luck was out. She drew back in her ready-to-attack stance, her eyes flashing a malevolent acid-yellow, her mouth yawning wide to showcase her pointed teeth. Her extremely sharp and painful pointed teeth. Bertha and the pond might be eight feet away from me, but I had two sets of teeth marks in my right calf and a deep bite in my left buttock to prove *that* distance wasn't a barrier. Not when Bertha hated me with a single-minded passion that went way past murderous. Which was sort of my fault. I'd stabbed her with a bull's horn. She hadn't been herself at the time, and I'd been acting in self-defence. But Bertha wasn't big on extenuating circumstances. She wanted her pound of flesh— literally.

Going for distraction, I pelted her with half-a-dozen

biscuits. Most of them fell uselessly into the pond, but one caught Bertha under her gills. She hissed.

'Isn't that Bertha, Ricou's pet?' Finn asked in a bemused voice.

'Yep.' I threw another biscuit. It bounced away in another lucky hit above her left eye.

'What's she doing in your pond?'

'Stopping any unwanted visitors from using it as a gateway.'

Bertha shook her head, and slithered over the pond's edge on to the grass.

'Safer not to have the pond,' he murmured.

'Sylvia needs the water,' I said. 'Now she's pregnant she's drinking around twenty gallons a day and there are way too many additives in tap water.' A biscuit hit Bertha's nose: *nearly on target*. 'And Bertha adores Sylvia, she'd never hurt her.' *Unlike me.* The next biscuit sailed into Bertha's open maw. She snapped her jaws shut and, radiating bliss, she wriggled back into the water and disappeared, leaving its surface black and ripple-free.

Relieved, I headed for the open window, ducked through the Ward and stuck my left arm out to Finn.

He shot a last puzzled glance at the pond, started to climb in after me, but froze halfway through and said in a soft voice, 'You should've told me if I was interrupting, Gen.'

Crap. I'd forgotten about the rose petals.

Chapter Twenty-Two

'**Y**ou're not interrupting,' I said flatly once we were both in the bedroom. My bed with its scattering of crimson rose petals was like an accusation between us.

'Okay, I'm not,' he agreed, but his expression said he didn't believe me.

Irritation stabbed me. Finn was definitely giving off the jealous vibe. Question was, why? Our 'couple' status wasn't ever a done deal. And was *so* not now. So him putting on the angry, aggrieved boyfriend act was nowhere near cool. Nor did I appreciate his thinking I was jumping into bed with Sylvia and Ricou. Only ... even without the wrongness of it, the brooding jealous thing wasn't like him so who had woken up his green-eyed monster by yanking his chain? Because someone had: Finn had been acting like a suspicious jerk since he'd turned up. My bed with its clichéd romantic gesture was just another nail, as far as he was concerned.

I stuffed my annoyance down as I gathered the petals into an old shoebox; I'd take them with me if/when I went to see Malik later. Right now I'd sort out the infuriating satyr in front of me. Cinching my robe tighter, I fixed him with a glower. 'What did you want to talk about, Finn?'

He jerked his head at the shoebox. 'What's with them?'

'You first.'

He gave the bedroom a critical scan as if he expected to find someone else there, though with Malik's dark spice scent still hovering like a silent ghost, maybe he had cause. 'Are we alone?'

My irritation spiked again. 'Ricou's out. Sylvia's in *Between*, through the wardrobe in there.' I pointed to the living room. 'And there's a dryad standing sentry in the wardrobe's wood, but otherwise, yes.'

Finn snapped his fingers and at the same time as his T-shirt (disappointingly) reappeared, I felt a Privacy spell settle around us. He cast another look around, his gaze hitching on the shoebox before coming back to me. 'My brothers have been telling me things. About Sylvia and Ricou living here. With you. That the three of you might be an item.'

Wow! The rumour mill had been working overtime, and now I knew what had stoked Finn's green-eyed monster. Not to mention that it made a lot of stuff crystal clear. Briefly I wondered what came first, Lady Isabella wanting Spellcrackers and coming up with her Sylvia-seducing-me plan, no doubt with her dryads spreading spurious pre-seduction gossip. Or if Isabella had got the idea from the satyrs, who'd probably put it about that I was up to all sorts of shenanigans with my flatmates as justification for demanding their investment back. Gods save me from London's fae and their squabbles.

'Well, it's true,' I agreed, anger sharpening my voice. 'Sylvia and Ricou do live here. And you know why? Its neutral territory. Living here means that neither the naiads nor the dryads feel left out of the pregnancy, and Sylvia and Ricou don't have to spend all their time smoothing ruffled feathers.' Not that there were any feathers involved, just scales and twigs, mostly. 'Not that it's any of your business,' I added, even as I wondered if his brothers' tittle-tattle had anything to do with why Finn had stopped writing. 'But hey, seeing as your brothers have been in a chatty mood, maybe they told you they want Spellcrackers back, too.'

Confusion crossed his face. 'What?'

'The herd wants Spellcrackers back,' I said slowly, like I was talking to an idiot. Which I was. 'You made them sign it over to me, but now the curse is lifted so is the reason for giving it to me. If they think I'm an "item" with someone else, someone who isn't a satyr ... well, no doubt they're even more determined not to lose out on their original investment.'

He sunk down on to the bed, dropped his head in his hands. 'Gods, I should've realised they'd try something: I know what they're like.' He sighed and looked up at me. 'I should've got them to agree to back off before I went. But with Nicky and everything, I just didn't think. I'll sort it now. I'm sorry. Gen, this isn't how I hoped our getting back together would go.'

He was sorry! He'd sort his family! He'd expected something like this! He thought we were getting back together!

I threw my hands up, warring between fury and disbelief. 'Finn, I wrote to tell you what the herd were up to. When you didn't write back, I did wonder if the satyr messenger service wasn't passing my letters on, which I was obviously right to. But hell, didn't you wonder why I wasn't writing to you? Didn't you think about trying some other way to contact me? Or asking me what the hell was going on?'

Bewilderment clouded his moss-green eyes. 'How could I? We were out of time sync.'

I blinked. 'Since when?'

'Since two weeks after we got there. I've only just got back.'

I stared at him. The Fair Lands have their own timelines, sometimes in sync with the humans' world, sometimes not. A day here could be months or even years there, or the other way round, depending on who was controlling the magic. And if Finn had been out of time sync, it could explain his silence.

'I did write to you, Gen, but I'm guessing you didn't get my letter.' He reached out to take my hand. 'I'm sorry. I can understand your being angry about that, and with the herd being stupid idiots about Spellcrackers.' He paused. 'You must have thought my silence was deliberate?'

I looked down at my hand in his. I wasn't sure if I wanted to leave it there or take it back. Three months of thinking he'd ditched me wasn't something I could do an emotional one-eighty from in a few seconds. And okay, Finn might not have been totally responsible for his hurtful silence, that was down to his brothers, but he hadn't seemed too surprised that they'd screwed things up for him. And he'd come over here channelling the green-eyed monster on his brothers' say so. He seemed to be letting them mess in his life way too often.

'I did think your silence deliberate,' I said pointedly, then pulled my hand from his and crossed my arms. 'It hurt, Finn.'

He flinched, then he straightened his shoulders and said softly, 'Gods, Gen, I truly am sorry.'

'So am I,' I said, keeping my voice neutral.

He nodded, understanding I wasn't ready to forgive him. The silence between us lengthened, turning awkward, then I sighed and asked, 'Why go out of time sync?'

'Some of the other girls were having problems,' he replied, his relief evident that I'd spoken. 'The Morrígan said they and their babies wouldn't survive the births without a big intake of magic.'

The other girls were the rest of the faeling victims of the ToLA case. Though, unlike Nicky, they'd all signed on with the mad wizard doctor as well-paid surrogates. It would've been a good gig for them all if they hadn't started dying. Deaths that Witch-bitch Helen, as the police officer in charge of the investigation, had covered up.

'So the Morrígan slowed all their pregnancies down,' Finn carried on. 'It added another four months on to everyone's due date, including Nicky's. Other than moaning she was the size of a house she never complained, despite ending up pregnant for thirteen months.' A shudder ran through him. 'Not like some of the others.'

I gaped. 'Nicky was pregnant for thirteen months!'

'Yeah. But like I said, she was brilliant.' Pride shone in his smile. 'The baby's a boy, Daniel Christopher.'

'Wait! She's had the baby?'

'Yeah, two weeks ago. She's talking about keeping him, but' – he raked a hand through his hair and rubbed his left horn in agitation – 'well, he's only two weeks old so it's still too early to know if he's hers or not. Or who the father is. She was the last to give birth so that's why it's taken us so long to get back into sync with London.'

I sat down on the bed next to him. 'Wow. That's unreal.'

He nodded. 'Yep. It is. Even living through it.'

Briefly I touched his arm. 'Is Nicky okay?'

'She and the baby are healthy.' He grimaced. 'She's still got a lot to work through. Psychologically. We all have.'

'Yeah,' I agreed. They weren't the only ones.

We fell into another awkward silence, then Finn gave the shoebox of petals a sidelong look. 'Do those mean that something's going on with someone else?'

My anger blew back up and I almost told him to mind his own business again. But even though the petals might not be the clichéd romantic gesture he suspected, I did have something going on with Malik and, even if it was still early days, I needed to tell Finn that.

But I wasn't up for another emotional confrontation. Not right this minute.

I snagged a petal from the box. It still felt velvety soft and real. As illusions went, this one was top of the range. If it *was* an illusion. I held the petal out to Finn. 'Does it exist?'

He gave me a searching look, then took the petal and examined it thoroughly before handing it back. 'Seems real enough. Why?'

'They weren't here when I went to sleep. Robur, the dryad sentry, says no one's breached the Wards, and the only sending spot is inside the fridge. So how did they get here?'

He stared fixedly at the window for a minute then cupped his hands; a small earthenware pot filled with violets appeared in them. 'The Wards are set to let whoever is inside them *call* something from outside.'

'They are?'

'Yep. It's pretty standard for this type of defensive Ward, in case you get trapped and need to *call* in food or water. Though usual rules for *calling* still apply; you'd have to know exactly where an item is before you could *call* it here.' He held the pot of violets up with a smile. 'These beauties are from my glade. First thing I saw last night, when I got back.'

Hmm. I hadn't been aware of that particular feature, but it wasn't really a security hazard; not with the way entry through the Wards was set up. Except— 'There's only Robur, Sylvia and me here. Robur's not the type, Sylvia's in *Between* and I was asleep.' Not to mention I can't *call* anything other than spells, and only then if I can see them.

'Then I don't know how they got here, unless …' he trailed off, pensive.

'Unless what?'

He stood and put the pot of violets gently on the window-sill. 'Maybe you *called* the petals without realising it. It's been known to happen sometimes with toddlers; they're asleep and next thing a toy will turn up in their cot even though they couldn't have known where it was. It's thought either they were dreaming of it or it's a manifestation of a subconscious want.' His moss-green eyes darkened. 'Though I guess that theory hangs on what you were dreaming about?'

My dreams had been of Malik, of gatecrashing his memory, or whatever the blood-spattered snowy plateau scenario was. And yes, the crimson petals on my white sheets had reminded me of that, and of our time in the hotel penthouse, but no way could I tie the two together as any subconscious want, not when the rose petals had felt like a threat. A threat, I decided,

I'd be better talking about with Malik than with Finn.

'Okay, thanks,' I said, then dived into a subject change. 'So, when are you going back to the Fair Lands and Nicky?'

He eyed the shoebox with a frown. 'You don't want to talk about these and your dreams?'

I don't want to talk about Malik and his dreams with you, *no.* 'Not right now.'

For a moment he looked as if he wanted to argue, then he nodded. 'I'm going back later today. Look, I know you think I'm an idiot for letting my brothers rile me up about you and Sylvia and Ricou—'

'If the hat fits.'

'Guess I deserved that.' He shook his head ruefully. 'But if I'm honest, in a way I wanted to believe them.'

My jaw dropped. 'What?'

'I know, sounds crazy even to me.' Bafflement briefly crossed his face, and he scratched behind a horn. 'I mean, I hated the thought you might have found someone else, but at the same time ... Hell's thorns, that is crazy,' he said, almost to himself. He shook his head then turned to stare out the window, tension tightening the broad muscles of his shoulders under the thin T-shirt. 'There's something I've got to tell you, Gen.' His hand against the window frame curled into a fist. 'Something I don't want you to find out from anyone else.'

I stood, dread settling like lead in my gut. 'Okay, so tell me.'

Chapter Twenty-Three

'Gods, this is a mess,' Finn muttered, before turning to face me with a determined expression. 'Helen's been staying at the Morrígan's castle while we've been there. Not that we're staying together. It's a big place,' he finished quickly.

Shock rocked through me and I sat abruptly back on the bed. Ugh! I hadn't seen that coming. My own green-eyed monster reared up and snarled, surprising me with its strength. But my fury was more than just jealousy. Damn it. Helen the Witch-bitch was pure poison; even if he couldn't admit that before, surely he couldn't deny it now, not after what she'd done to him and their daughter.

I balled my hands, glared up at him. 'How the hell could you let her near Nicky again, after what she did?'

He raked his hand through his hair. 'Nicky doesn't know. She doesn't remember much about what happened, and she was brighter once Helen turned up, so I agreed not to tell her anything.'

I shot him a disbelieving look. 'You agreed?'

'Helen ... yes, I agreed.'

In other words, it had been the Witch-bitch's idea, and she'd somehow persuaded Finn to go along with it. Nothing had changed there then. After all, Helen had persuaded Finn to keep his daughter a secret from me in the first place, despite the fact that we were supposed to be on the fast track to providing Nicky with a curse-breaking baby half-brother. And how the hell was Nicky going to feel when she found out that both her parents had been lying to her by omission? If my own experience, right up until I was fourteen, was anything to go by – my vamp father had been an expert at that sort of leaving-out-the-important-stuff style of communication (such as, the princely vampire he planned to marry me off to just happened to be a psychotic sadistic murderer) – then I could pretty much guarantee Nicky would be shocked, angry and betrayed. Much like I felt now.

When the fuck was Finn going to learn to stand up for himself? And his daughter?

I blew out searing breath. 'You haven't forgotten what Helen did, have you?'

He frowned. 'No, of course not.'

'So the fact that she's responsible for Nicky being pregnant, that she's lied and deceived you throughout all the time you've known her, and she used her position as a police officer to try and ensure I ended up either dead or pregnant, or both, more than once— Oh, and let's not forget she's responsible for the death of my best friend and the continuation of the fertility curse. And you *still* let her stay?'

A puzzled look flickered over his face as if he couldn't believe it himself. 'I know ...' Then his expression settled to resignation and he held his arms out in surrender. 'She's Nicky's mother, Gen. What was I supposed to do?'

'Protect your daughter and keep her mother the fuck away from her.'

'She can't harm her, not with me there.'

'She's already harmed her, Finn! And it's going to harm Nicky even more once she finds out the truth!'

'Hell's thorns, Gen. Don't you think I haven't thought about that? If I could've stopped Helen joining us, I would have. I've told her she had until after the baby's born, then she had to leave.'

Right. So Helen got to Nicky first. By the time Finn had

found out, it was too late. Or she'd made him think it was. Fuck. I wanted to scream with the anger and frustration, and yes, the hurt boiling up inside me.

'You know she's wanted by the police?' I said flatly. 'She can't come back here unless she's prepared to pay for her crimes.' Though even being burned at the stake was way too good for the Witch-bitch.

'Of course I do. And so does Helen. She's not going to return here.'

Not if I had anything to do with it. 'How long's she been there?'

He looked down at the pot of violets. 'A couple of days after we got there. Jack brought her in.'

Jack was Helen's changeling son. And one of the Morrígan's ravens. I narrowed my eyes. 'So Helen was there before the Morrígan took you all out of sync? And you didn't think to tell me this first?'

He half shook his head, then sighed. 'I wanted to tell you from the beginning, but ... hell, Helen said it wasn't a good idea, and even my brothers said not to. That I should just keep it to myself. That you wouldn't be happy' – *I wasn't!* – 'That you wouldn't understand' – *I didn't!* – 'That if you thought there was something going on between me and Helen you might not be waiting when I got back' – *Got that right!* – 'Then when I did, they started bringing up Sylvia and Ricou.'

I stared at him. My own dysfunctional family wasn't any better than Finn's. But at least they didn't try to run my love life for me. Oh, wait, they did. They'd stuck me with the Fertility spell and all its problems. Fuck. 'I don't have a clue what to say, Finn.'

He took my hands in his. 'Gen, I want you to know there's nothing going on with Helen. I don't spend any more time alone with her than I can help, and I don't want to. But she likes to play happy families with Nicky, and she's using it to ...'

He trailed off, colour staining his cheeks. *Embarrassment?* 'It makes things difficult,' he finished lamely.

Why the fuck would he be embarrassed if nothing was going on? Something broke inside me. I'd had enough. I couldn't listen to him tell me any more about the Witch-bitch. He'd always had a blind spot where she was concerned. The suspicious part of me thought she'd sicced him with some sort of spell, in fact he'd sort of admitted that she had, which just made his continuing acceptance of their relationship worse. And if he couldn't break away from her, especially now, then I was done.

I jerked my hands from his. 'You need to leave, Finn.'

His brows knitted. 'Leave?'

'Yes.' I strode from the bedroom through the living room to the front door and yanked it open. 'Now.'

He followed me, an earnest frown on his face. 'You truly want me to go, Gen?'

Part of me wanted to say no. I didn't want to lose Finn. He was my friend. And he had a place in my heart. But his Witch-bitch ex was as toxic as nuclear slag. Almost everything bad was down to her, and no way did I want her to get her evil claws back into Finn and Nicky. But I couldn't stop him from letting her. He had to do that himself. And if she was part of their lives— If he let her *stay* part of their lives, *his life*, then I couldn't stay his friend.

Whatever had broken inside me turned jagged, my throat ached and tears stung my eyes.

I looked at him straight. 'Yes. I want you to go.'

'Is this because of that sucker? Are you seeing him?'

Fury filled me and I opened my mouth, ready to tell him, hell, no! Then, at a nudge from the magic, my rage muted and I snapped it shut. Was this about Malik? Okay, yeah, I wanted both of them. And I knew there was no way I could have my cake and eat it with the two of them. And truth was, I didn't want to. Sharing might be Sylvia and Ricou's thing, but, right now, it wasn't mine. So I'd known a choice was always going to have to be made. And that choosing one would mean losing the other.

But Finn playing happy families with Helen meant the end of Finn and me, even if Malik hadn't been in the picture. So yeah, Finn's half-arsed confession was making my choice easier, but it wasn't the reason I was telling him to go.

'This is about you and Helen,' I said flatly, 'which you'd realise if you took the time to think about what you've just told me.'

'Gen, he's a sucker. A sucker who can order you around against your will. Or have you forgotten?'

'I haven't forgotten anything. Like I haven't forgotten how Malik gave his protection to every fae and faeling in London when I asked, and wanted nothing in return. Or how he was the one who put himself in danger helping me during the demon attack last Hallowe'en—'

'I would have come if I could, Gen,' Finn interrupted, his expression stricken. 'You know that.'

'Yeah, I do,' I snapped, my anger mounting again. 'But you couldn't, could you? And why was that? Oh yeah, because *Helen* stopped you.'

'Because I would've broken her circle. She was working to keep the demon contained.'

She was working to let the demon kill me, you mean. Rage rushed through me. I grabbed his arm and shoved him through the Ward on the flat's door.

'And I haven't forgotten,' I shouted, 'that without Helen, Nicky, your daughter, wouldn't be pregnant and Grace, my best friend, wouldn't be fucking dead in my place.'

He stood on the landing outside, eyes wide with shock, then he shuddered as if casting off a heavy coat. 'Gen. You're right. I'm sorry—'

I slammed the door in his face.

The rage drained out of me, leaving me empty and hollow. Pain flooded in to take its place. I sank to the floor, hands over my mouth, until the sound of his footsteps faded.

Then I let my tears fall.

Chapter Twenty-Four

'What's it this time: nose, boobs or hips?'

I focused on Mary's – Detective Sergeant Mary Martin's – reflection in the full-length mirror in front of us. I'd been so wrapped up in my frustration and anger, and, yes, grief, over Finn, I hadn't noticed her come up next to me.

Behind us, the mirror showed a plush office decorated in warm creams and oatmeal, and accented with enough pink to make it patently feminine without turning it into Barbie's living room. The office was one of many in the upscale plastic surgeon's expensive home-cum-consulting rooms, and was closer to a modern take on a Georgian drawing room than a doctor's surgery. But then if victims feel reassured and relaxed in their surroundings, it makes them easier to fleece.

Currently, the only victims around were the filing cabinets (heavily disguised as a splay-legged oak sideboard). The cabinets were being disembowelled by two WPCs wearing white paper jumpsuits, with matching shower caps and bootees, who were systematically tagging and bagging their contents. The same thing was happening throughout the rest of the exclusive Harley Street address where another ten witches – who along with Mary, made a full coven – were busily gathering evidence.

And there was a ton of evidence to gather. Virtually every leaflet (of which there were thousands still in unopened storage boxes), every magazine and every reflective surface (from the numerous mirrors, through the framed pictures of satisfied customers, right down to the polished brass doorknobs) was tagged with some sort of Dissatisfaction hex.

The place must've been like the eighth circle of hell to work in.

My email to Hugh about the source of Harrods' mutating Magic Mirror spell had set 'Operation Nip Tuck' in motion, and the unsuspecting doctor had received a six a.m. raid from Mary and her girls in blue.

Mary placed a hand on my shoulder, making my own evidence-gathering jumpsuit crackle. 'So, you going to answer me, Genny, or do I have to drag you into the Skin Stripper?'

I gave her a half-smile. ''S'okay, I haven't picked up another hex.' The things were virulent, and throughout the morning we'd all spent time mirror-staring and angsting over our hex-induced bodily imperfections, the cure for which was a stint in the torturous Skin Stripper. 'Just miles away.'

Mary gave my shoulder a sympathetic squeeze. 'Ah. Time for a break, then. Come on, I'll buy you coffee.'

We headed out into the hall, our paper booties scuffing quietly on the thick carpet as we moved past the leaflet boxes stacked along the wall and into the office set up as a temporary canteen. The Ward on the doorway slipped over me like the tickle of feathers.

As per procedure, the room had been physically emptied (even the carpet removed), ritually swept and magically cleansed, then Warded off from the rest of the house. The Skin Stripper was set up in the middle of the floorboards; a three-foot copper tray, surrounded by a tall circular frame off which hung a glyph-covered shower curtain (to preserve a witch's modesty) and a modified shower head which rained salt, not water, on the tray's occupant. Candles flickered in each corner of the room filling the air with the scent of sage, cloves and lemon balm, and along one wall were trolleys containing the Evidence Holding crystals. Against another wall was a stack of picnic-sized cool boxes with 'Property of Metropolitan Magic and Murder' stencilled in blue. We had enough food and drink to keep us going for another couple of days, if needed. Same as any other magical evidence-gathering investigation, the whole building had been Warded shut, and until all the active spells were locked up in the Holding crystals, police procedure said that none of us were getting out.

Personally, I wasn't planning on any of us staying longer than absolutely necessary.

But then speed was one reason why Hugh had called me in as a police consultant. While it took a witch a good five minutes to transfer a spell from its original carrier to an Evidence Holding crystal, it was as quick as snapping my fingers for me. And, of course, the second reason was that I could identify any Magic Mirror spells similar to those used at Harrods.

Mary opened a cool box and handed me an orange juice. 'Let me guess,' she said, 'you've got man trouble, or should I say, satyr trouble.'

I raised my brows. 'I'm that transparent?'

She smiled. 'I'd love to say no, and that it's my superb powers of deduction at work. But yeah, you are, especially since Sylvia texted me.'

'Damn gossiping dryad.' I jabbed the straw into the drink carton. 'It'll be all over London now.'

Mary shot me an admonishing look as she fiddled with the coffee flask. 'Sylvia won't say anything; she was just worried about you.'

I snorted. 'I meant Robur. Sylvia hadn't got up when I left, so the only way she knows about Finn is if the Wardrobe Freak told her.'

'Ah.' She added milk and ten lumps of sugar to her cup. It was excessive even for a witch. Still, Mary was using enough power on the job that she wasn't likely to suffer sugar-abuse bloating any time soon. 'Anything I can do?'

I drained the juice box and crumpled it. 'Lock up DI Helen Crane and throw away the key,' I said sourly.

'Wish I could.' She shook her head in regret. 'The problems she's left us with are never-ending, both down the Yard and in the Witches' Council.'

'I'm more pissed off about the problems she's causing now,' I said, helping myself to a BLT. I'd been relieved to find the cool boxes contained a good supply of the sandwiches and orange juice at break time, since all I'd been allowed to bring in with me was my phone and some liquorice torpedoes (we were all nude under the jumpsuits; good thing it was summer and the paper was the thick, reinforced type). 'The Witch-bitch has only gone and hitched herself back up with Finn and Nicky in the Fair Lands.'

Mary grimaced. 'Ugh. That's a bugger, isn't it?'

'Yep. And when he told me, I chucked him out. So he's probably back there now, trapped in the Witch-bitch's nasty, sticky web, where I've fat chance of doing anything about it.' I ripped open the sandwich and tossed the packet in the bin in self-disgust. Some friend I was.

She frowned. 'You're not responsible for his decision, Genny.'

I pursed my lips. 'I know. But I'm pretty sure the Witch-bitch has him tagged with a Love spell or a Trust Me crossed with a Compulsion.'

'Wouldn't put it past her,' Mary agreed. 'But he'd have to be stupid not to realise it after all this time. Those things need to be topped-up to keep working and from what I've heard it's been a while since those two have been a couple.'

'They've got Nicky,' I said, 'so they'll have had enough contact for the Witch-bitch to keep her claws in him.'

'You're making excuses for him, Genny,' she said gently.

I shrugged in defensive acknowledgement. 'He's a friend.'

'And you want him to be more?'

Part of me still did, yes. But it wasn't that part driving my need to see Finn safe. 'Not so much now, but that doesn't mean I want him tied to that bitch.' Irritably, I picked the lettuce out of my sandwich.

Mary gave me her pensive-cop face as she sipped her coffee. 'You know we've got bacon rolls, don't you?'

'BLT's come with healthy salad stuff,' I explained deadpan, as I squidged the bread back together.

'That you don't eat,' she replied drily.

'Hey, I eat the tomatoes.' I pulled out a slice to demonstrate and popped it in my mouth.

'Only 'cause they're smothered in mayonnaise.' Mary grinned, topped up her coffee, added another three lumps of sugar and stirred. 'And you know you're just feeling guilty for throwing Finn out in a fit of temper instead of convincing him of Helen's evil nature.'

I was. I cut her a frown. 'You taken a psych course or something recently?'

She gave me a mock-stern look. 'So, you also know you'll never convince him she's evil unless he wants you to?'

Didn't stop me wanting to try. Or better still, find the Witch-bitch, hitting her over the head with her broomstick and putting us all out of her misery. I sank my teeth into the sandwich, tearing off a large bite.

Mary poked me on the shoulder. 'So ring him. If nothing else it'll get the guilt out of your system.'

'He's probably back in the Fair Lands by now,' I mumbled after I'd swallowed.

'Leave a message then,' she said. 'Calling him is for your benefit, not his, *capiche*?'

I chewed thoughtfully. Mary was right. Finn and the Witch-bitch Helen and their relationship weren't my problem to sort out, even if I had wanted me and Finn to be more than friends. But leaving him a message to let him know I *was* still his friend and here for him, if or when he came back, would at least make me feel less like I'd thrown him to the wolves.

I dug my phone out.

Chapter Twenty-Five

My phone was dead.

Pushing away ominous thoughts about what that said about my and Finn's friendship, I squinted at the small cherry-red crystal stuck to the back. Sure enough there was a black starburst crack at its heart; I'd fried the Buffer spell at some point. I sighed and showed Mary. 'Third time today. First one went soon as I unplugged the damn phone from the charger then, even wearing gloves, my backup did the same. I dropped them off at the office to get fixed. This one's a spare.'

Mary nodded. 'Electronics and magic, always iffy, especially with a good dose of high emotions.'

I sniffed. Not to mention I was iffy with magic in the first place.

'Those Buffers Sylvia makes are good if a bit expensive,' Mary offered with more sympathy than a fried phone warranted. But then she'd heard me moan about my lack of magical ability more than once.

'They were Sylvia's Buffers.'

'Ahh. You *were* angry.'

'Yep.' And upset, I added silently. I'd call Finn later, once we'd finished here. After all, it wasn't like he was around to answer.

'Want me to let your office know you're fried?' Mary asked.

'Thanks,' I said.

She fished her phone out and sent a text. 'Done.'

I nodded, then as she scrolled through her messages, asked, 'So, any news on the zoo kidnap victims yet?'

'No.' Frustration turned her brown eyes almost black. 'We're going through all the textbook motions, calling for informants to come forward, etc., but other than the usual crazies, so far that's a bust. And there's been no ransom demand of any sort. Which, since they were snatched yesterday morning, the negotiator says there should've been by now.'

'Think it's an inside job?'

'Difficult to say without speaking to the victims' families and associates. Which is hard with the Bangladeshi ambassador still claiming diplomatic immunity.' Her grip on her cup tightened in exasperation. 'Apparently he's spending his time praying for his wife and child's safety at London's Central Mosque. Which is all well and good, but if he'd let us help, we might have a shot at finding them.'

'So, no luck getting that bloodstained kurta the bodyguard was wearing for a scrying?'

'No. The DI's put in a written request, but they've not even come back with an acknowledgement. Even more worrying is that his security refuse to give us anything to use as a *focus*, not even some of the kid's toys.'

'You were going to try a psychic scry?' I asked, surprised. Psychic scrying was way harder and less successful than standard scrying, which used hair, nail clippings, blood or other bodily fluids.

'We were hoping to do a combined. The kid's only six, so something's bound to have ended up in his mouth at some point. I still find Emily chewing on things.' Emily, Mary's daughter, was nine. 'It was a long shot, but anything's worth doing in these situations.' She gave a wry twist of her lips but I could see the worry etching into her soul; abducted children were always the hardest cases for everyone to deal with, even more so for parents. All that horrific imagining of 'things that could happen' combined with the natural protective urges really take a toll.

'Right,' I said, after we shared a quiet moment, 'did anyone else think the ambassador's henchies were a bit off? Sort of predatory?'

'I asked around, but seems like you were the only one, Genny.' She grabbed a pink-iced doughnut topped with a cherry. 'Could be you just freaked them out.'

The only people I usually freaked out were those who didn't have a nearby fae community; usually some place, like the Midlands, where too much heavy industry made it uncomfortable living for most fae.

'The ambassador didn't seem freaked by me,' I said.

She picked the cherry off and popped it in her mouth. 'True. But unfortunately it doesn't give us any sort of clue to go on. What we need is for him to come to his senses and give up whatever information he or his security staff are holding back. My instinct says it's the clue to why the victims were snatched.'

'Think there's anything I can do? See if I can get him to chat to me off the record?'

She ate her doughnut, munching thoughtfully. 'It could work, but only if the DI thinks it's a good idea. I'll run it by him. If he says yes, maybe you could go and see the ambassador once we're finished here. Any idea when you'll be done?'

I headed back out into the hallway and contemplated the long, high stack of leaflet boxes. Each box glowed faintly pink in my sight. Mentally I did the calculations. 'Individually, it'll probably take another seven or eight hours. Or I can *call* them in groups, which will be an hour, two tops.' I gave her a questioning look.

Mary shook her head. 'Sorry, Genny, much as I'd love to say go for it, this one needs to be done individually.'

'Okay,' I said, resolving it would be done in the eight hours or less. I was going to make sure of it. That timescale would see us out of here at around ten. Plenty of opportunity after that for an 'unofficial' visit to the ambassador, if Hugh authorised it, to see if there was any way I could help the kidnap victims. And still leave me enough time to rush home and get ready for my 'date' with Malik.

'I'd better get on with it, then.' I gave Mary a determined smile, grabbed an empty crystal and smacked my hand on the nearest box.

'Great. I'll go and check on the rest of the girls,' she said, then strode off down the hall.

Seven and a half hours later, I sighed in relief as I picked up the tape-cutter knife and opened the last box.

Something white zoomed out to hover in front of my face.

A tarot card.

I snatched up the tape-cutter and ran my finger along its serrated edge. Blood welled, scenting the air with copper and honey, and I pressed the bloodied tip to the blank card. The little mouth latched on, sucking up like a starved vamp. Like before, it tickled, but didn't hurt. Unlike before, I stayed silent until the mouth stopped feeding.

The image appeared on the card. A tall, thin minaret tower, with a covered lookout encircling its top, watching over a building with a shining gold-domed roof. At the building's base, tiny figures were running around in panic as they tried to keep from being barbecued by the flames and lightning shooting down from the night sky.

The sixteenth card: the Tower. Symbolising change, crisis, and chaos. Unsurprisingly, as the building depicted was the minaret at London's Central Mosque, the one near Regent's Park, where the Bangladeshi ambassador was praying for the safe return of his wife and child. Not that I needed the card to tell me the ambassador was in trouble. But the card did tell me

196

that he and the kidnap victims' all had something to do with finding the fae's lost fertility.

Now that was surprising, shocking even. But before I had chance to process the idea, the little mouth stopped feeding.

Heart thudding with anticipation, I repeated my original question. 'Tell me how to find that which is lost, and how to join that which is sundered, to release the fae's fertility from the pendant and restore it back to them as it was before it was taken.'

One of the tiny figures jumped out of the card to land on the stack of leaflet boxes. It was the ambassador in his crumpled business suit and orange and black striped tie.

'He knows! He will tell you! For a price! The beasts are coming! They come for you!'

Right. Nothing new there. Maybe time for another open question. 'What does the Emperor want with me?'

'He seeks Janan!'

Hmm, a nice specific answer, just not an overly informative one. Still, a name was good. 'Who is Janan? Where do I find Janan?'

'Janan is Beloved of Malak al-Maut! Janan will come to you!'

Janan will come to me? 'Who is Malak al-Maut? When will Janan come to me? Why does the Emperor seek Janan?'

'Malak al-Maut is to be revered. Janan will come when the time is nigh! The Emperor seeks to use Janan!'

Revered? Time is nigh? Sounded way too End Of The World for my liking, especially with all the fire and lighting shooting through the sky. 'How does the Emperor intend to use Janan?'

A jagged fork of lightning struck the minaret, setting the mosque on fire and illuminating a huge (compared to the rest of the card's tiny figures) wolf standing in the shadows. The wolf stalked to the edge of the card, the whites of its human eyes stark in its grey-brown furred face, and growled, the sound raising the hair on my nape. The ambassador turned and fled back into the card, rushing straight into the heart of the small inferno. The wolf – *werewolf* – chased him.

And the card flared into bright flames then exploded into ashes that dissipated into the ether.

Fifty minutes later, my taxi rumbled to a halt at the entrance to London's Central Mosque.

I peered out of the window and was relieved to see that the mosque wasn't on fire and that the golden dome was shining serenely against a backdrop of twilit grey sky, unmarred by shooting flames or jagged forks of lightning. Not that I'd really expected any of that, but it had crossed my mind that the ambassador and the mosque might be under a physical attack rather than a metaphorical one.

Of course, that could all change now I was here.

The word from Hugh, via Mary, when I'd asked if I could talk to the ambassador, had been that the diplomatic situation was too delicate without it being fully authorised by someone much higher up the food chain, and then they'd want to know why. Which meant filling them in on the tarot cards and the fae's trapped fertility. Something I was pretty sure the fae would object to. I got the unspoken message. If I wanted to find out what the ambassador and his missing wife and child had to do with the fae's problems, I was ostensibly on my own. Plausible deniability meant that if my visit ended with the shit hitting the fan, the only one it would stick to was me.

So I'd skipped out of the Harley Street crime scene and grabbed the taxi here, giving Mary the excuse (that she could repeat, if need be) I had to rush for a date.

It wasn't a lie. I did have a date – at midnight, with Malik.

And I did have to rush. I checked the time – ten forty: I had an hour and twenty minutes. It should be enough time to have an ambassadorial chat, head home, get ready and then walk to the Blue Heart vamp club in Leicester Square. Only knowing my luck and London's traffic, it probably wasn't.

I offered the driver an extra tenner on top to let me use his phone. After a brief haggle, he agreed one handsfree call for twenty quid; not that he wasn't trusting, or was trying to rip me off, of course. Oh no, he was just worried my magic touch would nix his phone.

Yeah, and trolls keep cats as pets.

I gave him the number and we both listened for the pickup. 'Malik al-Khan.'

My heart gave its usual leap at the sound of his remote, not-quite-English accent.

'Hi,' I said brightly, conscious of the driver's avid curiosity (which I suspected was another reason he'd refused to hand over his phone). 'It's me. I just wanted to let you know I've had an urgent appointment come up, so may end up running a bit late for our meeting at midnight.'

There was a pause and I suddenly wondered if I should've given him a heads up that 'me' meant *me*, or if I was going to end up embarrassed when Malik asked who was calling. Relief flashed through me as he said, 'Genevieve,' then continued in a slightly perplexed tone, 'Why are you calling from another's phone?'

'Mine's fried,' I said, 'so the taxi driver's letting me use his. For a fee. Handsfree,' I finished flatly, partly as a tacit warning, but also as the bitch in me wanted to see the disappointment in the driver's eyes.

'That is … generous of him.' The thread of amusement in Malik's cool voice almost surprised a snort from me. 'Where is this urgent appointment?'

'London's Central Mosque. It's in connection with the situation we discussed the other night.'

'Then thank you for letting me know, Genevieve. I will see you later.'

The phone went dead.

I blinked. I'd been sort of thinking about asking for his help, like maybe he could send out a search party if I was more than an hour late. Evidently that wasn't to be. Still, at least he knew where I was. And why. Which was some sort of failsafe. And my own disconcertion at the call's quick end was nothing compared to the driver's dissatisfaction. No doubt he'd been hoping for some juicy gossip to sell to the papers.

But I'd be stupid to rely only on Malik as a backup, so, after another haggle, I grudgingly gave the driver sixteen pounds and thirty-nine pence (the rest of my cash) and he sent a text to Tavish for me:

> T no 3 appeared. Am at LC Mosque, Regent's Park on spec.
> All connected somehow. Will ring b4 midnight. If not, come find me.

Backup message sent, I hitched my backpack over my shoulder, hopped out and waited until the money-grubbing taxi driver had driven away. Then I pulled out a grey pashmina I'd liberated from a cloak cupboard at the plastic surgeon's (no doubt abandoned from last winter) and covered my head. Not only was it respectful, but people tend to ignore what they expect to see. With luck, it would get me far enough into the mosque to find the ambassador, before his henchmen caught my scent and tried to stop me.

Chapter Twenty-Six

I walked through the mosque's entrance gates and followed the short path through the near-hundred-foot-high archway and up the few steps into the wide expanse of paved courtyard. A string of open arches to my right showed a covered corridor leading to the main door; the other sides of the courtyard were watched over by rows of tall, arched windows, their glass plain. The whole building was a mix of blocky sixties concrete architecture married to the traditional patterns of Islam. It didn't make anything pretty, but it was solid and imposing. The courtyard lights were bright enough to banish most of the shadows without bathing the space in the glare of spotlights. The place was almost empty of people but was filled with the same quiet, weighty peace that infuses most places of worship. A certainty of faith in a higher power. Allah might not be my god, but, nonetheless, his presence was felt here.

As was the ambassador.

He was near the mosque's main door, huddled in a patch of shadow, hemmed in by a male and female. Briefly I wondered where his henchies were, and why they'd left him alone, then checked out the couple. The male was mid-twenties, tall enough to loom over the shorter ambassador, with the black curly hair and dark complexion of the Mediterranean. The female was in her late teens and petite, a pretty dark-eyed brunette with hair that waved over her shoulders, but unlike her Mediterranean pal, her skin was almost vamp pale. The male was dressed in a vest, shorts and flip-flops, clothes not entirely out of place in midsummer in London. The girl was also in flip-flops, legs bare, but then things got odd. Her top half was draped in a hip-length fur jacket more suited to the depths of a Russian winter.

Even without the jacket's out-of-season strangeness, its colour would've snagged my attention. It was grey-brown; the same shade as the Emperor's werewolves on his website picture. And the werewolves on the tarot cards. So was this female a werewolf? Wearing a wolf, or even a werewolf-skin coat? If she was, it seemed to be verging on cannibalistic to me, but hey, what did I know?

Nothing for sure, other than that the Tower tarot card had led me here and showed the ambassador being chased by a werewolf. So whatever was going on had to do with the fae's fertility, the Emperor, and the ambassador's kidnapped wife and child. But however I joined the dots, I couldn't figure out what picture they made.

I kept my head down and glided behind a pillar so I could see without being seen, frustrated that I couldn't *cast* a Listening spell, or at least chance getting near enough to hear without spooking them. Though, really, one look at the ambassador's face told me he wasn't getting good news, while the confident calm of the couple said they were entirely happy with whatever was being discussed ... The female seemed to be doing all the talking ... a ransom maybe? Except ransom demands weren't usually delivered in person, were they? Something to ask Hugh's negotiator. Later. For now, I watched and sent out a careful ping with my Spidey senses.

All three hit me as human.

Damn. My gut still said the girl, and probably the male with her, were werewolves, but then I'd never met any, so maybe I couldn't tell. Not a particularly comforting thought when I was used to *knowing* who was what, no matter what shape they wore.

After a minute or two's more quiet chat, the girl held her hand out, offering something to the ambassador.

He stared for a long moment, hope and fear warring in his expression, then held his own palm out.

She dropped whatever she was holding with a satisfied smile, and I caught a glint of gold.

He clenched his fist, nodded, then backed away. He quickly retreated through the entrance into the mosque's interior.

The girl turned her satisfied smile towards the tall dark male, lifted a pale hand to caress his cheek, then the pair headed for a high archway that led out of the courtyard to the far side of the mosque. If I remembered right, there was a gate there that opened out on to the road.

Indecision nipped at me.

Did I go and talk to the ambassador as I'd originally intended, find out what he was hiding, and what the werewolf girl had given him?

Or did I chase the werewolfy pair?

Interrogating the ambassador was the sensible, safe option.

Only he wasn't going anywhere.

The werewolves were.

But chasing after a couple of werewolves on my own was, well, chasing after the big bad wolves and asking for trouble, especially since I didn't have my damn phone on me so couldn't call for help. But if they were the Emperor's werewolves, then the fur-coated female and her curly-haired pal could lead me straight to the vamp himself. Maybe even to the kidnap victims. And just because I was following the werewolfy pair didn't mean I had to follow them all the way to their hideout. Or that I was going to be in danger. If things started looking iffy I could turn tail; after all, I knew how to run. Plus, if it came to a fight, well, so long as the pair didn't take their half-and-half beast form they were as vulnerable to injury and death as any other human or animal.

And I had my ace up my sleeve, or rather my sword in my ring— Ascalon.

But first I needed to leave a few breadcrumbs for my kelpie backup.

I bit at my finger, the one with the nearly healed scab from where I'd given blood to the last tarot card, and touched a drop of honey-scented blood to the pillar.

Then I hightailed it after the werewolves.

The archway they'd passed through led me to another, smaller, paved area, some summer-browned grass, and, as I'd thought, to a short flight of steps and a gate to the Hanover Gate road. Hoping the furry couple hadn't jumped into waiting transport, I stuffed the pashmina into my backpack, jogged quietly down the steps, took a moment to leave my blood on the gate as I closed it and then checked both directions.

Relief swam through me as I saw the werewolfy pair were nearly at the end of the road, on foot, and heading towards Regent's Park.

I went after them, not worried about being seen or heard; there were enough folk around and, even at this late hour, the traffic was as busy as ever, not to mention the noisy whistles, clanks and excited shouts drifting over from the Carnival Fantastique in the heart of the park. I kept far enough back that I guessed I was out of scenting distance, in case they could do that in their human forms, while cursing my lack of knowledge about werewolves in general.

The pair turned right on to Outer Circle, the road which runs all the way round the park, and moved at a fast walk until they reached the temporary car park set up for Carnival visitors. For a moment I thought they planned to pick up a car, or head for the Carnival crowds, but instead they took the path past the kiddies' boating pond and over the two-step bridge to the far side of the boating lake. I hung back as they reached the vehicle-turning space before one of the park's large and exclusive private houses, watching to see which way they went next.

They took the south path.

It ran along the curving shore of the boating lake, and for a good long stretch had dense bushes to either side, and was pretty much deserted at this time of night. A perfect place for an ambush. Was this their intended route? Or had they twigged they were being followed?

'Okay,' I murmured, 'do I call it a bust and head back to the mosque and the ambassador, or keep tailing you?'

The 'ambush likely' path met a crossroads at a point further on where they could choose to head up to the Carnival, go straight on across the park and ultimately out of it into Primrose Hill village. Or they could turn and cross the bridge towards the Inner Circle, the area containing the Queen Mary's Gardens, a whole heap of the park's utility and college buildings, and two more large, exclusive private houses. Houses which were just the type a vamp with delusions of imperialism would pick for his temporary residence.

If the houses were hosting the Emperor and his gang, then they would take the bridge at the crossroads. Only I wasn't stupid enough to head down the creepy, ambush likely path after them.

But I didn't need to. I could go the long way round through the more open parkland, which would make it easier to see anyone coming and, if I sprinted, still get to the crossroads before them and lie in wait. Yeah, it risked losing them but tailing them was looking more and more like a long shot anyway.

'But first,' I muttered, 'a little added insurance.'

I fished inside my T-shirt, hooked out the chain I was wearing and pulled it over my head. The tiny blue-glass bottle that had contained the Morpheus Memory Aid potion dangled from the chain like a pendant. I'd salt-washed the bottle and filled it with Tavish's disgusting werewolf repellent. Not that I was planning on anointing myself with the stuff – it stank enough that everyone, including werewolves with sensitive noses, would know I was about – but the bottle was fragile enough that it was easily broken. If anyone came at me with nefarious notions, werewolf or not, I'd crush the bottle and even if the obnoxious smell didn't drive them away, it would give me a couple of seconds' distraction.

And a second was all I needed to release Ascalon.

I placed another 'I went this way' drop of blood on the ground. Then, gripping the tiny bottle in my left hand, its neck chain wrapped round my wrist, and holding my right hand with Ascalon's ring at the ready, I started running, sprinting over the summer-dry ground as silently as possible.

The bushes on my right grew denser as I raced past, leeching away the light and shifting with amorphous grey shadows that seemed to be keeping pace with me. Shadows that reminded me of the animal I'd seen on Primrose Hill the other night, the one my Morpheus-Memory-enhanced dream had shown me. My mind told me it was down to my imagination, to being hyper-aware of my surroundings, and that the grey shadows I kept glimpsing out the corner of my eye, and the hair-raising rustles and snaps I could almost hear coming from the thick vegetation, really weren't a pair of huge werewolves licking their lips as they loped alongside me.

I neared the crossroads and slowed, pulse pounding like thunder in my ears, as I looked for a good spying place.

Shock splintered through me as a familiar presence pinged my Spidey senses.

I jogged forwards warily until I reached the crossroads and could see all four paths.

All seemed deserted.

But I knew there was a vamp nearby.

One I could feel, but couldn't see.

The taste of Turkish Delight teased my tongue and my heart thudded with anticipation.

'Show yourself,' I murmured.

Shadows coalesced from nowhere at the start of the bridge twenty or so feet in front of me, twisting like smoke as they took on line and form and detail, until a figure stood, legs apart, arms loose at his sides, his black leather coat snapping around his leather-clad legs in a non-existent wind; the same wind blew his shoulder-length black silk hair away from his pale, perfect face and I caught my breath at his beauty.

Malik al-Khan.

Chapter Twenty-Seven

'Typical flashy vamp entrance, Malik,' I murmured, knowing he could hear me, and wondering why he'd followed me here instead of waiting for me to turn up to our date. Was it concern? Or something else?

The corner of his mouth quirked briefly. 'Genevieve.' His scent of warm leather mixed with dark spice and liquorice curled round me like a teasing summer breeze, making my stomach flutter. Part nerves, part lust. *Mesma.*

Wary, my fingers tensed around the bottle of werewolf repellent; the stuff stank enough that it would work on a vamp too. I trusted Malik. But only if he was the one in control. And since I'd last seen him, I couldn't be sure that Bastien the sadist hadn't been up to his torturing tricks. My gaze skimmed over Malik's beautiful face, down his long lean body, searching for any new nasty spells or possible injuries. Nothing.

'Just so I'm clear,' I said, raising my voice slightly, 'who am I chatting to? Is it you or is this going to be like the other night, with the Autarch doing his remote string-pulling thing, or whatever was going on with that Jellyfish spell?'

Malik touched the faded delta scar on his forehead as if in a brief salute. 'I appreciate why you might be concerned, but with the spell's influence removed, I am the only one who is pulling my strings. I give you my word of honour.'

His word. Good. Neither Malik nor the Autarch would mess around with that. I slung the tiny bottle on its neck chain back over my head.

'Glad to hear it,' I said, the knot of worry under my heart easing as I allowed myself a longer, more appreciative stare. And damn, in all that leather he might be wearing the clichéd, dangerous vamp look that all the Fang-Fans drooled over, but hell, I was ready to drool too. In fact, after our close encounter on the table at the hotel, I was ready to do way more than drool. *And there's no reason I couldn't.* At that thought, desire coiled deep inside me—

Malik's obsidian eyes took on his sleepy tiger look. 'Are you well, Genevieve?'

Oh, yeah. 'Good, thanks,' I said, giving him my best innocent smile. He might have vamp supersenses, but just because Malik could tell what my body was feeling didn't mean I couldn't at least try to keep him guessing.

His look sharpened. 'Is there a reason you are jogging in the park and are not at the mosque?' His question held an edge of disapproval. Hmm. *Irritating vamp better not be getting ideas about doing his whole 'protecting the sidhe' thing again.*

'I was chasing a couple of the Emperor's werewolves.' I shrugged, like it was an everyday occurrence, and started walking towards him. 'Don't suppose you've seen any sniffing around?'

A fine line furrowed his brow. 'Were these werewolves in human, animal or beast form?'

He hadn't denied the possibility that the Emperor or his werewolves might be about. So, did that mean he knew something, but was going to stall me, or what? 'Human, last I saw, but that was nearly ten minutes ago.'

'I see.' He lifted his chin, nostrils flaring, then his frown cut deeper. 'It is possible they have come this way, but I cannot tell conclusively.'

My frown joined his. It wasn't the answer I expected. Or wanted. Annoyed, I stopped a few feet away from him. 'Why not?'

'A werewolf in human form does not carry enough of their wolf's scent for them to be identified by smell alone; it is part of the magic that allows them to be two-natured. I would need to have met them in their human form before I could pick out their scent from the myriad of others that permeate the air about us. As for scenting a werewolf in their wolf or beast form, there are a number of scents upon the air that could be wolf, or a large canine of some description, but with the zoo and the Carnival nearby that is to be expected.'

Right. Good that he was giving me chapter and verse without any prevarication. It meant he was on the level and not trying to hide anything. For a change. My irritation dissipated and I took a step closer. 'So a werewolf in human form smells like a human, and in their wolf form smells like a wolf?'

'Yes,' he agreed, giving me a look that said he had his own questions but was prepared to answer mine. For now. 'They are much more easily identified by sight, or by their blood.'

I blinked. 'They don't smell different, but their blood does?'

He moved closer; his coat brushed against my jeans. I stuck my hands in my back pockets, resisting the urge to run my fingers down his black T-shirt where it stretched over his hard abs. *Later.*

'Their blood has a certain tang to it, yes.'

Malik's voice was low, intimate and turned my knees weak. Embarrassingly, it took me a moment to catch up with his words … Oh right, werewolf blood tasted different. Weird that didn't affect its smell … I got my brain back on to business and looked up at him. 'Have you met any of the Emperor's werewolves?'

A conflicted expression crossed his face, part sadness, part … anger, maybe? 'I have. But not in more than five hundred years.'

Werewolves only live a human lifespan. So not much point describing the couple to him. Though really, since he'd tacitly admitted that the Emperor and his werewolves could be about, it wasn't *what* the couple were that was in question, but *where* they were, and *where* they might be going, so we could locate the victims. But if he couldn't scent them, we couldn't follow them.

Damn. Looked like the werewolf trail was a dead end.

I cut Malik an enquiring look, and asked the big one. 'What about the Emperor? Have you met him more recently?'

His eyes turned cold. 'I have not.'

Nice unequivocal answer, even if his tone had sent a shiver down my spine. Malik really didn't like the imperial vamp. 'So does that mean you don't know where his lair is?'

'I do not know where he might be if he is in London, which is the question you are asking, I believe?'

'Yep.'

He stepped back and disappointment sifted in me. I sighed. *Well, I was the one who'd spoiled the moment.* 'My question is, why do you want to know, Genevieve?'

'I told you. The tarot cards say the Emperor has the answer to releasing the fae's trapped fertility.'

'But what has that to do with the Bangladeshi ambassador?'

Something, but exactly what I didn't know. And I wasn't going to find out staying here. I hitched my small backpack higher. 'How about I tell you on the way back to the mosque? If I can't find the werewolves, then I want to see what info I can get out of the ambassador.'

He pushed his hair back, elegant fingers sliding through its long length. 'The ambassador is no longer there.'

'Really?'

'I looked for you at the mosque first. While there I overheard him having an altercation with his security chief. He had received an invitation for an immediate meeting with the British Prime Minster. The security chief did not want the ambassador to go, but moments later the ambassador's vehicle arrived and I saw him driven away.'

Crap. Tonight was a dead end all round. At least when it came to werewolves, the ambassador and finding his connection to the fae's trapped fertility. I looked at Malik. Though maybe not when it came to other things, like our date. Not that I wanted to head off to the Blue Heart vamp club, but maybe we didn't have to. We could stay here. It was way better. Quiet, private, and with the added advantage of no Autarch hanging around to play the psychotic gooseberry.

I gave Malik a bright smile. 'How about I tell you what the ambassador has to do with this while we take a walk around the lake?'

Chapter Twenty-Eight

Malik slipped his coat off and hooked it over his shoulder. 'A walk would be pleasing, Genevieve,' he said, his voice taking on its earlier intimate tone.

My pulse sped up. Pleasing wasn't the half of it.

He moved closer and traced a line along my jaw, setting my skin tingling. 'Or we could make use of the lake?' Gentle pressure from his hand turned my gaze down towards the water, to where one of the lake's small wooden boats bobbed. I hadn't noticed it before. A boat trip out on the moonlit water was heading into Hallmark romance territory. Not that I had anything against that; in fact, I was all for it. The thought of Malik wielding a pair of oars, in the short-sleeved black T-shirt he was wearing, while I sat back and watched (preferably without any embarrassing drooling on my part) had my heart thudding even faster in anticipation.

'That would also be ... very pleasing,' I said, matching his cool, despite knowing his vamp supersenses had to have picked up the faster tempo of my heartbeat.

'Shall we?' He held out his hand, black eyes glinting with quiet amusement.

I gave him a mock quelling look and placed my hand in his. His cool fingers closed around mine as he led me down to the short slope and to the boat. As I stepped in the boat rocked gently then settled. I sat on the low seat, my back to the pointy end (stern or the bow? I wasn't sure: my knowledge of boats is sadly lacking), and tucked my backpack behind me

213

as a cushion. I stretched my legs out and found the small boat surprisingly comfortable.

Malik jumped in confidently. The boat didn't move, not even the slightest rock. Dropping his coat behind the middle seat, he sat and faced me, legs either side of mine, forearms resting on his thighs, clasped hands dangling mere inches above my jeans-clad legs. He smiled, a teasing lift of his lips and the boat pushed off and seemed to glide out onto the lake under its own power, quiet ripples in the moon-silvered water following in its wake.

'Show off,' I murmured.

His smile widened into a grin with a glimpse of fang and my heart did a little happy flip. Not only was he gorgeous, I'd never seen him so relaxed before. But then most of the time we'd spent together we'd been dealing with some crisis or I'd kept my suspicious barriers up between us. Not without reason; Malik usually knew far more about whatever was going on than I did, and just as usually wasn't keen on letting me in on it.

But for once, whatever was happening with the vamps, Malik seemed to be as out of the loop as I was.

The boat glided over the water, heading under the bridge towards where the lake narrowed and split around a small island covered in small trees and overgrown bushes. A home to the lake's herons.

Malik's hand encircled my right ankle. As I jumped, he said, 'May I?'

Slightly bemused, I nodded, made myself settle back and look relaxed.

He grasped my trainer and pulled it off. It thudded on the bottom of the boat and I had to force myself not to jump again at the cool touch of his hands on my bare skin. Within seconds warmth spread throughout my body, warmth that turned my bones languid and simmered a delicious heat deep inside me.

Gods, if he was this good with just my feet …

I swallowed and asked, 'Reflexology?' less from interest and more to stop my mouth moaning in pleasure.

'It is similar. This is Sokushin Do. It is the ancient Indian tradition of foot massage for healing and pleasure, taught by monks in the temples in Japan. "Soku" means foot. "Shin" means heart. "Do" means way.'

Well, his touch was certainly finding its way to my heart. And other places.

'Now, Genevieve,' he said, his voice weaving round me like silk, 'tell me about this connection between the Emperor and the Bangladeshi ambassador.'

Was his Sokushin Do just a way of softening me up? If it were, I'd happily agree to be softened up like this any time he wanted. I stifled a sigh of bliss then, knowing I was probably going to spoil the moment again, lifted my arm and regretfully released my bracelet. It appeared around my left wrist with its usual chinking of charms. As Malik raised one elegant brow I held it up. 'Don't suppose you took your ring back the other night?'

His hands stilled in their tantalising caressing of my sole. 'No.'

Delighted relief that he hadn't washed through me, quickly followed by annoyance at Mad Max. 'Then I'm pretty sure Maxim took it. I had a run-in with him after you left.'

'You ran into Maxim?'

'Well, it was more the other way round,' I said, thinking of Mad Max's roundhouse kick. I propped myself on my elbows and told Malik everything about the leaking Fertility spell and my night with Mad Max (which lit fires of rage in Malik's pupils, though he didn't bat an eye at Mad Max using magic, so the crazy sonofabitch had been truthful about keeping his wizarding abilities). Then, after a side discussion assuring Malik I was fine despite Mad Max's rough treatment and that the Poultice spell was actually working, I asked, 'So is Max following you or me? And on whose orders?'

'I do not know.' Malik's expression hardened, his hand holding my ankle flexing with restrained strength. 'Yet.'

For a moment, I was gleeful that Mad Max would end up at Malik's mercy, then my glee muted to disappointment that whatever Mad Max was up to, Malik wasn't up to speed with it. Still, if he didn't know about Mad Max, he had to know about my gatecrashing his dream of kneeling in the snow, and talking to someone about *sanguine lemures* – the blood of undead ghosts. After all, he'd told me I had to leave the dream, had pulled me out of it, even. But knowing that didn't make it easier to ask him; not when it suddenly hit me that my dreamcrashing had been a huge invasion of privacy.

'Something else weird happened last night,' I said, pulse speeding nervously, 'I think I accidentally ended up in your dream. Or memory ...' I trailed off as the boat rocked, horror crossing his face and he released my foot, too quickly for me to stop it thumping down on the wooden planks. Then the boat settled and his usual enigmatic mask dropped like a shutter over his face.

'My apologies, Genevieve. I did not intend to bring you into my memories. I imagine that the spell you removed' – he touched the faint scar on his forehead – 'and partly absorbed was responsible. The jellyfish organism had been feeding on my blood, which contained the power of Red Shamrock.' *Red Shamrock vamps could share or even steal memories.* 'I will take more care in future.'

I scrambled to sit up. 'I don't think it was all down to you.' I told him about the Morpheus Memory Aid and that the bizarre side-effect was no doubt brought on by my usual iffy reaction to magic. 'So really I'm the one who needs to apologise.'

He inclined his head in acknowledgement. 'Then we should both endeavour to take more care in future, Genevieve.'

'Probably a good idea,' I agreed with a smile, then said tentatively, 'Your memory didn't feel happy ...' I trailed off as flames flared in his pupils, then snuffed out, leaving his eyes black and opaque. Damn, was he mad? Or what? 'I'm sorry, Malik. I didn't mean to pry' – the magic pricked at me for sort of lying – 'well, not in a bad way. Maybe if you want to talk about it, I could help?'

Something indefinable darkened his eyes. 'Thank you, but the incident happened in the past and it is not one I wish to discuss.'

Hurt flashed in me. Not that he wouldn't clue me in about his memories, but that his tone was the same chill one he'd used before to push me away. Instinctively, I pulled my feet under me. 'Fair enough,' I said, angry at myself, when my words came out less neutrally than I wanted.

He took in a breath, nostrils flaring, then his sorrow and regret slipped like a wisp of shadow over me – *mesma*. 'I did not intend' – he dipped his head, letting his loose black hair obscure his face for a moment, reminding me of Katie when she was anxious, then a brisk wind blew his hair back to reveal his beautiful features set in a grim expression – 'I will tell you of the ... memory, Genevieve. But it is one that is difficult for me to recount and I think it is more pertinent that we first talk of those matters that could be of concern to us now. For the rest, we have the night before us, do we not?'

A knot inside me loosened. He wasn't cutting me off, he was just postponing. And he was right. We did have all night to chat. *And maybe more.* And sitting in a small rowboat in the middle of a moonlit boating lake was as perfect a place as any to do it. So might as well get the less personal stuff out of the way first.

'Okay,' I said slowly, then as he held out his hand in an obvious peace offering, I uncurled my legs and let him lift my other foot and slip my trainer off. I relaxed back as his long fingers started to weave their Sokushin Do magic.

'It may be that I could help you with retrieving the memory you wished to enhance,' Malik said softly, 'if you would allow me to?'

'Thanks.' I smiled. 'I would, but I got what I needed from the spell' – ID-ing Katie's treacherous spy boyfriend – 'but there was something else.' I told him about waking to find my bed covered in crimson rose petals. His frown let me know, as I'd thought, the petals weren't down to him. I added that either I'd subconsciously *called* the petals myself (as Finn had suggested, not that I mentioned him) or that maybe Mad Max might have had something to do with them.

'So what do you think?' I asked.

'I will look into it, Genevieve.' Malik's mouth thinned, his thumb pressing uncomfortably hard into the ball of my foot. I tensed before I could stop. His touch danced lighter and I gave an appreciative sigh then reluctantly got my mind back onto business as he asked, 'Can you tell me about this connection between the Emperor and the Bangladeshi ambassador?'

'You know the ambassador's wife and kid have been kidnapped?' The story was splashed all over the news so I'd have been surprised if Malik hadn't, but it always pays to check. He nodded. 'Well, I got another tarot card. It showed the ambassador under attack at the mosque by a werewolf, so I went to find out what it had to do with the fae's trapped fertility. When I arrived I saw the ambassador talking to this couple and my gut said werewolves. So I added two and two, rightly or wrongly, and came up with their being the kidnappers. Then, as the ambassador wasn't going anywhere, or so I thought, I decided to follow them to see if they might lead me to the victims.'

His hold on my ankle tightened, making me squirm. 'That could have been a rash decision.'

He wasn't wrong, but— I held my arm out and released Ascalon. The silver of the sword gleamed in the moonlight. 'I have this, remember.' He'd seen the sword once before.

'That sword will not protect you from everything, Genevieve.'

'Yeah, I know that,' I said, a little of my exasperation lacing my voice as I let Ascalon slide back into my ring. 'But waving a magic sword around does usually make people think twice. And I'm not totally stupid. I wasn't planning to do anything other than observe from a distance. Plus, I left a blood trail for you to follow, if needed, and I stayed off the "likely to be ambushed here" path.' I winced as his fingers again dug none too gently into my foot. 'Which was when I lost them. If I hadn't seen you, I'd have gone back to the mosque. And I told Tavish what I was about too.' Sort of, anyway.

Wariness crossed Malik's face. 'The kelpie knows where you are?'

'More or less.' I lifted the tiny blue bottle from where it dangled on its chain around my neck. 'He also gave me this. It's werewolf repellent, and believe me, this stuff will clear a crowd.' I let the bottle rest back between my breasts and, as Malik's gaze followed and lingered, couldn't resist a little back arch, then almost swore as I remembered— 'Oh, and I need to let Tavish know I'm okay before midnight, so he doesn't come rushing to my rescue.'

The boat rocked again as Malik lifted his gaze back to mine; the dangerous, dark look in his eyes sent a frisson of desire spiralling through me. 'Then perhaps you should call him and tell him you are safe.' His words carried a hint of question as he offered me his phone.

I kept my eyes on his as I reached out and took it. A tension I'd barely registered left him as I did; he hadn't been sure I'd put Tavish off. Inwardly, I smiled; good to know Malik didn't think anything between us was a done deal.

I sent Tavish a text, not wanting to get into a discussion

as to why I was with Malik when Tavish had warned me off seeing him, then handed the phone back. 'Thanks.'

It chimed with an answer a moment later. Malik's enigmatic expression didn't change as he read, then sent a short reply.

'Do I want to know?' I asked.

He pocketed the phone with a grim twist of his mouth. 'The kelpie cares greatly for your wellbeing, Genevieve.'

So it had been a warning, then. Not such a surprise, really. The pair weren't friends, and only allied with each other because it mutually benefited them both, mostly to do with keeping me safe. And their alliance wasn't something I was going to jump in the middle of. 'So, anyway,' I said, getting us back to business, 'I was planning to go back and ask the ambassador about Janan—'

'Janan, Beloved of Malak al-Maut?' Malik's stunned question interrupted me. I opened my mouth to say yes, only before I could speak red flames of power lit his pupils and he pulled me on to my knees before him. His mouth met mine in searing heat. Startled, I froze, as his lips met mine in a burning kiss.

Show me your memories, Genevieve. His voice came in my mind, almost an order until he added, *Please.*

Disappointment flew through me as it clicked that this was the memory kiss, the Red Shamrock blood power kiss he'd asked permission for in the hotel function room. But hey, this was Malik, and it was still a kiss.

I pressed my body to his, eagerly returning the kiss and murmured, *See them*, in his mind.

Then I was falling, twisting like a leaf in a high wind, images from my past swirling around me in an ever-changing montage, until one particular memory hit as clear and sharp as if it was yesterday, and not more than twenty years ago.

Chapter Twenty-Nine

I was four.

My father, tall and blond and aristocratic, was dressed in his special black suit with the satin lining, the one that matched my stepmother Matilde's sapphire-blue eyes. We were in the great hall of some ruined castle that was our latest home; an empty, echoing acre of grey flagstoned floor, lit by a distant fire. I stood between Matilde and my father, his hand a restraining weight on my shoulder, fearful as I sensed their unease about the strange vampire who visited us.

The stranger faced us. Shadows writhed around him like angry spirits, shredding and reforming in a non-existent wind, shrouding his face in darkness. Only now I could see past them. The stranger was Malik, but he was still a stranger. There was none of the warmth or humour or humanity I was used to seeing; instead a vicious cruelness sharpened his beautiful features.

'Is this the child, Andrei?' Malik's low disdainful voice, with its not-quite-English accent, ran a shiver down my spine, then and now.

'Greet our guest, Genevieve.' My father's hand pressed on my shoulder.

I stuck out my black patent toe, clutched the slippery green satin of my dress and bent my knee in a trembling curtsey.

Malik's insistent fingers gripped my chin, jerking my face up. 'The eyes are truly sidhe fae,' he murmured, his expression as cold and hard and brutal as his fingers. 'I am sure my master will be pleased. All that is left is to confirm the contract. I am to take a sample.'

'Niet.' Matilde spat out the word.

My father hissed. 'It is but a taste, Matilde; no harm will come to the child.' My father offered the stranger a low bow. 'My apologies. You have my permission.'

Malik knelt on one knee before me, avarice and an alien anticipation filling his eyes, and held up a silver dagger. 'Janan, Beloved of Malak al-Maut. Forged by the northern dwarves from cold iron and silver. Tempered in dragon's breath.' The blade gleamed red in the firelight. 'The handle is carved from a unicorn's horn.' Pale light bled from between his fingers. 'And set with a dragon's tear.' An oval of clear amber winked against his palm.

The part of me still in the present recognised the silver dagger. It was the one from the tarot cards. The Bonder of Souls.

In the memory Malik's hand clamped around my left wrist, his power freezing me so I was unable to move, but I heard my bones crack, felt the pain lance through my small body. His nostrils flared with pleasure.

The blade traced a slow, icy-path down my inner arm.

I cried, though no sound came out, my tears mixing with the thin rivulets of my blood to pool on the flagstone floor ... as Malik used Janan to bond my soul to his.

'Genevieve!'

The memory fled, leaving my tongue coated with the sickly sweet taste of strawberries. The taste of the Morpheus Memory Aid potion. Just my bad luck I'd have another adverse reaction to the damn spell. Not that the memory of Malik taking my blood for his master, the Autarch, when I was four was new. I'd just never experienced it with quite such clarity before. Or remembered Malik being quite so detached and pitiless before.

I realised we were kneeling together in the small boat, my

hands balled in his T-shirt and his arms tight about me as if he thought I was about to jump. He wasn't far wrong. My heart thudded in my chest as I looked into his obsidian eyes, now inches away from my own, seeing the flickering remnants of the past in their black depths. 'You hurt me deliberately,' I whispered, hearing both my four-year-old's fear and my current shock in my voice. I swallowed back the ache in my throat. 'You enjoyed it.'

'Yes.' His agreement was desolate in my mind.

'Why?'

'That was who I was, then, Genevieve.'

I stared at him, still stunned. 'I don't understand.'

'Nor would I wish you to.' Sorrow and remorse soothed over my arm where he'd cut me then, the barest touch of *mesma*, offering apology for the pain he'd caused. 'But I will attempt to explain, should you wish me to, though I would prefer not to do so here in the open. Nor will my honour allow me to tell you the whole of it.'

His honour wouldn't allow him? Crap, that meant he'd given his word not to talk, which meant I'd get nothing important out of him. I clenched my fists, wanting to beat him, to scream at him, to make him tell me now. I needed to know all of it; I'd had enough of things hidden, of secrets. But ... I took a shallow breath, then another deeper one, calming myself. He couldn't tell me. And this wasn't the time. I forced back the hurt, both physical and emotional, of the memory ... and concentrated on Janan: the Bonder of Souls knife.

The Emperor had been holding Janan the knife in the first tarot card.

The Irish wolfhound (a.k.a. Mad Max) had dropped Janan into the snow in the Moon tarot card.

The ambassador on the Tower tarot card said the Emperor wanted Janan.

Only Janan was gone. Lost in the demon attack last

Hallowe'en when a sorcerer had tried to use it to steal my body for herself. Long story short, she hadn't succeeded, and the knife had disappeared with her demon master.

The only way the Emperor could get Janan was if he took a trip to hell.

That wasn't going to be an option. At least not if he wanted to come back in full ownership of his body.

But if the Emperor wanted a soul-bonding knife, it followed he wanted to bond souls.

What the hell did bonding souls have to do with releasing the fae's trapped fertility?

Unless that was the price the Emperor wanted me to pay? My soul bonded to his? Some sort of power thing? Fear tightened my gut. What would that mean for me? Except … Malik had my soul bonded to his for near enough twenty years before I'd died one too many times and the bond broke. As far as I could tell, it hadn't done anything at all to me. Or to him.

But Malik knew of both Janan and the Emperor. He could probably join the dots much faster than me. I gave him a narrowed look and said, 'The Emperor wants Janan.'

Something indefinable flickered over his face at my subject change, before his expression turned to his more usual enigmatic one. 'Am I to take it your tarot card told you this, Genevieve?'

'Yes. Do you know where Janan is?'

His black brows drew into a frown. 'Did you not send it to hell with the demon last Hallowe'en?'

A question. Damn it. I hated questions. 'Yep. But maybe something or someone got to the knife before it disappeared?'

He shook his head. 'I know only what you told the kelpie, Genevieve. That does not lead me to think that it would be possible for someone to have retrieved the knife before the veil closed.' Frustration threaded his words. 'Had I been conscious at that time, I would perhaps be more certain.'

224

Which, with the whole 'tranqued-by-the-bad-guy', was about as specific as an answer as he could give. I sighed. 'Okay, so we're pretty sure Janan is in hell. But the Emperor obviously doesn't know that otherwise why look for the knife? So the more important question is: why does he want to bond souls, and whose souls do you think he wants to bond? The kidnap victims', maybe?' I shuddered at that horrible thought.

'The Emperor may not want to bond any souls,' Malik said. 'Janan can also release a soul from its earthly body.'

I snorted. 'Wouldn't it be easier to just kill someone if he wanted to release their soul?'

'No. Death frees the soul. But with Janan the soul can be captured.'

I shuddered. 'Ugh, nasty thing.'

'Not originally. Janan's primary purpose was to keep the souls of the dead safe on their journey to the afterlife. That is why Janan is called, Beloved of Malak al-Maut. Malak al-Maut is the Angel of Death.'

Shock slammed into me. 'Malak al-Maut's the Angel of Death? Why the hell would you use the Angel of Death's knife to bond our souls together?' Horrified and angry, I shoved at him, catching him off guard. He went flailing backwards over the wooden seat behind him and thudded into the base of the boat, eyes wide with surprise. The small boat rocked dangerously and, as if we were in the middle of a rom-com, I lost my balance and tumbled forwards to faceplant, oh so gracefully, between his legs, my nose mashing against a certain hard but obviously sensitive part of him. As mortification spliced through my fury, and his pained grunt reached my ears, there was a clunk of something hitting wood, followed by the quiet tinkling of shattering glass.

Cold liquid drenched my T-shirt, arms and hands.

My anger stalled as my mind tried to understand what broken glass and wetness meant. Then, as the boat steadied and

Malik's hands grasped my shoulders, lifting me away from him, it dawned on me that my fall had smashed the fragile bottle of werewolf repellent.

The reek of it slapped me like a long-dead, heavily decaying fish.

I clapped my hand over my nose and mouth. My wet hand. My lips burned as if I'd pressed silver to them. Then as the metallic tang of the liquid seared my tongue, and my hands started to blister, it hit me that the repellent did actually have silver in it. Silver which, thanks to my vamp blood, I'm allergic to. Shit. I snatched my hand away as my throat closed on a choking cough and, catching a glimpse of bloody tears streaming down Malik's pale face, realised I wasn't the only one hit by the silver in the repellent.

Where's the Hallmark moment now, Gen?

Then, almost faster than I could process, we were out the boat and in the lake. Water closed over my head. Instinctively I snapped my mouth shut, struggling and thrashing to the surface, but a steel grip held me under. I gasped for breath and water rushed down my nose, my throat, filling my stomach and lungs. Hands ripped at my clothes, the cool lake water soothing my burning flesh. Greyness edged my vision and a distant part of me thought I was probably drowning until I was hauled out of the water, coughing and spluttering, and dumped unceremoniously on to a patch of sandy grass.

I collapsed there, retching. Damn Tavish. Why hadn't he told me the repellent had silver in it? The stuff wouldn't have killed me, like it might a young vamp, but if Malik hadn't dunked me I'd have been out of it for who knew how long while my sidhe body healed itself. Not to mention what harm had it done to him. And hadn't that article in the witch archive said silver didn't work on werewolves? The kelpie had some explaining to do, next I saw him.

Finally, my heaves subsided.

I pushed wet hair out of my eyes and discovered I was on the small island just past the bridge.

Other than my briefs, I was naked.

With no sign of Malik.

Chapter Thirty

Ten minutes later, I'd half-dragged myself down to the lake's edge, rinsed my mouth out and was sitting there, hugging my legs, toes tapping anxiously in the water as I tried to work out what to do next. Did I try to find Malik, or see if I could rustle up some help? Though the lack of clothes problem wasn't exactly conducive to accosting strangers, nor was the fact that I had enough aches and pains, and bruises blooming, that it felt like I'd been in a death-roll with a croc. Not to mention a vague fuzziness in my head. The dunking I'd taken seemed to be the cause, or maybe the silver in the werewolf repellent was to blame.

Then Malik appeared.

My aches and pains muted with relief.

He rose up out of the water about fifteen feet in front of me until he was standing waist deep, hair slicked wet down his back, moonlight gleaming on his pale chest, its silky triangle of black silk hair arrowing down to disappear into the water. He looked like some sea god, breathtaking and beautiful and ready to be worshipped. My toes curled of their own volition. He came towards me, the lake getting shallower as he did, to reveal, much to my regret, that he wasn't all-the-way naked. He was still wearing his leather trousers. Damn him.

A hot wind sprang up from nowhere tangling my hair across my face. When the wind dropped, Malik was standing before me. I shuffled a few feet back up the grassy bank and he sank elegantly down into a crouch before me. He held something grey out. When I frowned at it, he wrapped it round my shoulders and tied it gently. As I watched, he nicked a finger on one fang and let it bead with dark, almost black blood.

He offered it to me. 'Freely given, Genevieve.'

The scent of liquorice and dark spice drew me and I leaned forward eagerly, sucking his finger into my mouth. A brief glorious taste burst on my tongue then, disappointingly, his finger was gone. I blinked as the aches and pain vanished and the fuzziness in my mind cleared.

His blood had healed me.

I frowned as I realised his hair was dry, as were his leather jeans, and the grey thing around me was the pashmina; also dry. My backpack was on the grassy sand next to me; the spell Sylvia had put on it to keep my things safe had obviously worked to stop its contents getting wet, which explained the pashmina. But not Malik's dry hair nor the trousers ... Unless that had been the wind ... *some sort of vamp power* ... something to think about later.

'Thanks,' I said, placing my hand on his arm. 'For helping me.'

'You are welcome, Genevieve.' He smiled, then his mouth thinned as he added, 'Though I fear your clothes are unsalvageable. I did not know how much silver the potion held, so I was primarily concerned with removing them before they could do you harm.'

I gave a lopsided grin. 'Seems to be a habit you have, ripping my clothes off.'

His mouth twitched. 'I will replace these as I did the others.'

''S'okay,' I said. 'Think Tavish owes me, not you.'

'The kelpie did not tell you there was silver in the potion.' Condemnation edged his statement.

'Nope,' I agreed. 'But even if he had, neither of us would have thought I'd end up wearing more than a drop at a time, or virtually drinking the stuff. Anyway, I didn't think silver worked against werewolves?'

'It does not. I believe silver can be used as a magical carrier for other ingredients. The sidhe do this, so I have heard. It concentrates them, giving them more potency.'

Figured. My lack of knowledge when it came to sidhe magic was almost as frustrating as my lack of magical ability.

'How about you?' I asked. 'Did the silver do you any damage?'

'Nothing I could not heal.'

'So, I guess I should say I'm sorry for' – *headbutting you in the balls; nice subtle sophisticated moment, Gen!* – 'um, landing on you like that.'

Malik's eyes lit with amusement. 'It was not a … landing I had imagined.'

'Me either.' I gave him a wry smile, then rolled my shoulders. 'But finding out you'd used an Angel of Death's personal blade to bond our souls was a shock.' I raised my voice slightly in question. We were still in the open, but maybe he could tell me something …

He dropped his gaze, broke off a strand of rough grass and twisted it tight around his finger, then let it fall. 'I did not use Janan to bond *our* souls, Genevieve.' He lifted his head. Sadness darkened his eyes then was gone. 'Your soul was bonded to mine by proxy; mine was not tethered to yours. Your future was not mine, but belonged to the Autarch.'

The usual panic rippled through me. I stamped on it. 'Yeah, well, the Autarch can go whistle,' I said flatly. 'That's never gonna happen.'

'No, it will not,' he replied, moving so he knelt before me. 'You have nothing to fear.'

I hit him with a sceptical look. 'Seriously? But you owe him your Oath. What if Bastien orders you?'

Malik's pupils flared with power. 'He cannot.'

My gaze caught on the fading scar on his forehead where the Autarch had branded him with delta, meaning slave. Actions speak louder. 'Fine,' I said, 'you might believe that, but I don't. The Autarch is a sadistic psychopath, nothing's going to change that no matter what you think.'

'We have come to an agreement, Genevieve. He has given his word.'

'C'mon, Malik,' I said, denying the flicker of hope that he might be right. 'You know Bastien better than me. Sooner or later he'll work out a way to get around whatever he's promised.'

He regarded me for a moment, then repeated, 'He has given his word, Genevieve.' But his hesitation told me my suspicion was correct. That he too thought that whatever Bastien had agreed, there was a chance he'd find a way round it. The flicker of hope snuffed out.

'If you say so,' I said flatly.

He frowned. 'Is this why you changed your mind about my invitation?'

'What invitation?'

'To meet with me tonight.'

I shook my head, perplexed. 'I didn't. I told the woman at Sanguine Lifestyles I'd meet you at the Blue Heart as she requested. I said so yesterday.'

His frown deepened. 'I sent a text message today to ask you to meet me at sunset instead. Your exact reply was, "Any meeting must be private at office or not at all."'

'Huh? Well, it wasn't me. My phones went kaput this morning and I've been stuck with the police on a closed crime scene all day ...' I trailed off. I'd left my phones at work to be fixed. Had someone at Spellcrackers been checking my messages? And answering them? But who the hell would do that? Damn it, whoever it was, was due a bollocking.

'You did not have your phone all day?'

I focused back on Malik. 'No.'

An odd hesitation showed in his eyes, then he said, 'After your refusal the other night, I thought you had changed your mind about my invitation.'

Oh. He thought I'd got cold feet. 'I hadn't— still haven't, but …'

'But what, Genevieve?'

Looked like now was the time for our chat. I took a breath and drew the pashmina closer. 'I'll be honest, asking me on a date to a vamp club when you had to know I wouldn't accept' – I gave him a candid look – 'well, it smacks of playing games.'

He treated me to a considering look, then nodded. 'Yes, you are right. I am sorry. I should have stated my concerns plainly and not attempted to force a decision from you. I find your insistence in allying yourself with the witches and fae, to the point where they can dictate your decisions for you, while distancing yourself from the vampire side of your heritage, troubling. And I allowed my disquiet to compromise my good judgement; such a misstep can occur when I am somewhat … volatile.'

I gave him an ironic look. 'You don't say?' The corner of his mouth twitched, then his amusement faded as I said, 'It also made me think the Autarch was behind the invite.'

'I appreciate why you may have thought that, Genevieve.' His gaze turned thoughtful. 'I have given you my assurances that you are safe from Bastien. I understand that you still have some anxiety where he is concerned, but there is no need for it.'

'I wasn't anxious about me,' I said. 'But you. I thought he was doing some strange possession thing with you.'

Amazement crossed his face. 'You were concerned for me?'

'Yes. So once I had time to think about it, I realised I had to accept.'

'You did?'

'I thought you needed help.'

One elegant brow rose. 'You would risk the condemnation of the fae and the witches, and put yourself in danger, to help me?'

'Don't act so astounded,' I said, peeved. 'For one, as you've pointed out, I shouldn't be toeing the witch and fae line. And two, I've helped you before. That time at the Blue Heart with old Elizabetta.'

'That was to help you, Genevieve.'

'It helped both of us, if I remember right,' I corrected. 'And anyway, you've helped me plenty of times in the past. So I couldn't not help you. That's what friends do.' 'Friends' wasn't all I hoped for, but it would work as a start.

His black eyes met mine and for a moment I glimpsed vulnerability in them before he said, 'We are friends?'

I half-smiled. 'Yes.'

'Thank you.'

'You're welcome.'

'It is generous of you, Genevieve, to accept my invitation because of your concern for me.' His expression smoothed into his usual enigmatic mask as he spoke, but not before I saw a shadow of something like disappointment. 'But it was not necessary, even as a friend.'

Idiot vamp. Did he think that was the only reason? I gave him an arch look and said blithely, 'Oh, my concern was part of it, but not all of it.'

'Ah. I see.' His lids half-closed in his sleepy tiger look. 'Perhaps if I were to issue you another invitation, one with a more private venue in mind?'

I grinned. 'I would be delighted to accept.'

We looked at each other, the silence growing, tension charging the air, as something changed between us. As if my acknowledgement that we were friends and I was ready to help him had dissolved an indefinable wall separating us. Part of me almost wanted to shuffle my feet, part of me wanted to gaze at his beautiful face, to take in every detail of him. Another part just wanted to say, to hell with this, and throw myself at him.

Just as that part was winning and urging me to do something, anything, his gaze intensified. 'What if I wish us to be more than friends, Genevieve?' His low voice slid over me like cool satin – *mesma* – its touch both tentative and electrifying. 'Would you still be willing?'

The breath whooshed out of my lungs, my heart stuttered then steadied. Part of me was prepared to say 'yes' without hesitation, but this was too important a decision, and had been too long coming, to do that. He wasn't asking for furtive meetings, or snatched moments, but something more open. More lasting. With ramifications for both of us. The Bastien problem. The other vamps', the fae's and the witches' reactions. But, more than all of that, there was a much more personal obstacle. If Malik ordered me to do something, I had to do it. So far I'd got around that problem by blackmailing him. Only, if we were going to have a relationship, that wasn't an option any more. But then relationships are about trust. So I would have to trust him not to order me about, and in return he would have to trust me not to blackmail him.

I raised my hand, placed my palm over Malik's heart and lifted my gaze to his. 'Yes,' I said. 'I am very much willing.'

He grasped my shoulders, fitting his mouth to mine gently and carefully, then more insistent and demanding, then hard enough to bruise. His tongue thrust against my teeth. A part of me reeled, stunned, not at the kiss but at his rapid loss of control, as though my answer had unleashed him to take what he wanted. I parted my lips instinctively, eagerly, surprised as his dark spice blood invaded me, quickening my pulse and drowning me in a wave of heady desire. My body responded as if a switch had been flipped. I pressed against him, insides swirling in giddy anticipation, nipples budding to aching peaks, molten heat slicking between my thighs. Gods I wanted this. Wanted him. Needed him. I had for so long. And now we could have it. Have each other.

I tangled my tongue with his, pleasure sparking as a sharp fang pierced my bottom lip. Sweet honey and copper-tasting blood exploded in our mouths and someone groaned: me, him or both of us. I slid my hands over his silky skin, rewarding my fingers with the lean, defined muscles of his back, the beautiful indentation of his spine. He sucked hard at my swollen mouth, the rhythmic sensation resonating in my core.

The pashmina fell away, quickly followed by my briefs, leaving me naked, open.

He groaned, a harsh desperate sound, and grasped my hair, trailing rough kisses down my jaw as I tipped my head back to offer him my throat. His hand roved over my breasts, pinching and pulling with brusque touches, bringing forth inarticulate cries for more. I pressed against him, fumbling at his leather jeans, impatient to free him, his fervent growl matching mine as the thick satiny length of him sprang into my eager hold. His hand caressed lower, long elegant fingers parting me with perfect skill, sliding over the throbbing bundle of tiny nerves and pushing deep inside, their marble coolness a glorious overwhelming counterpoint to my own wet heat. For a long moment, time stilled and he held me there, a willing captive on the very edge as the pressure spiralled tighter, and tighter, and tighter …

Mine! The shout reverberated against my throat as his fangs pierced my flesh, his will commanding my release. I screamed, arched against him, and the orgasm rolled me over and over in a tsunami of pleasure, fluttering my heart, stealing my breath and plunging me headlong into soft black-velvet darkness laced with delicate patterns of gold.

Chapter Thirty-One

Distant voices dragged me from the darkness.

I pushed them away, enjoying the warm weight of the leather coat covering me with a familiar dark spice scent and the sated haze swirling through my mind and body. But even if I was sated, Malik wasn't; I'd passed out before we'd really got down to it, an annoying hazard of donating blood during orgasm. But now there was more to come. I grinned at my unintended pun. Oh yeah, so much more was to come. My body perked up, obviously appreciating the thought, and I stretched out under the coat, searching for the beautiful vamp so we could continue what we'd so gloriously started.

He wasn't there. Something neither I, nor my body, was too thrilled about.

I opened my eyes. Above me, I expected to see the night sky. But the view was hazed, as if I were looking through thick plastic. I squinted uncomprehendingly. Then blinked. A dome of magic rose high above me. A blood-Ward circle. And judging by the golden-pink tinge to the magical dome, it was my blood and power fuelling the protection it offered. Either I'd started doing magic while unconscious – unlikely – or something weird was going on.

I looked sideways, vaguely aware my neck felt like someone had chomped on it—

Malik sat a couple of feet away on the sandy grass, leaning against a lump of rock, forearms resting on bent knees, hands loose between his leather-clad legs. His head was tipped back, his eyes closed. Unease slipped down my spine. He didn't look like a happy blood-bunny basking in the aftermath, but more like he was waiting with weary resignation for me to wake up. I glanced back up at the moon; it didn't appear to have moved across the sky much, so I couldn't have been out of it long. I looked back at Malik to find him staring at me with an un-nerving blank expression.

Out of eyes gone solid gold.

'What happened?' I said, or meant to, instead I croaked 'Whahp—' thanks to the killer sore throat.

His eerie gold stare didn't flicker.

Fuck. Had I trapped him in my Glamour? Only he'd said it wasn't possible. Gut clenching, I threw off the leather coat and leaped up—

The ground heaved like I'd jumped on a storm-tossed boat, my stomach roiled, darkness spotted my vision, and I face-planted again. This time into his arms. He lowered me gently to my butt and pushed my head between my knees.

'My apologies, Genevieve.' His not-quite-English accent was formal, his tone empty. 'I fear I took too much blood.' Cool fingers on the back of my neck eased the rapid onslaught of a hammering headache.

''S'okay,' I whispered past the thudding pain in my head. 'Body'll replace it soon. Red cells're turbo-boosted – 3V, re-member.' Though why I was explaining all that to him, a vamp … Only, beneath his empty tone, he'd sounded like his heart was breaking.

His wasn't the only one. Mine felt like it was cracking into tiny pieces too. We finally get together and things were sup-posed to be mindblowing. And they had been mindblowing, and amazing and glorious and any number of other wonderful adjectives, for all of what felt like five seconds … then I'd woken up. Now, for some unknown reason, everything seemed to be going horribly, heart-wrenchingly wrong.

That bastard Cupid must truly have me on his shit list.

My nausea eased, the ragged tufts of grass and sandy earth beneath me coming into focus, and I realised the pain was muting. I raised my head carefully, grateful for Malik's soothing touch at my nape.

I slanted a look at him, crouching elegantly next to me and started with something simple. 'How come we're in a circle?'

His golden eyes flickered. 'The kelpie wished to take you from me.'

Huh? 'When was Tavish here?'

'He appeared while you were ... sleeping.'

Had to be the voices I heard. Annoyance flashed through me. Damn kelpie. One thing for him not to trust Malik, but he should trust my judgement after all this time. Though perhaps I should've expected the interfering wylde fae to turn up; I'd known he wasn't thrilled about me seeing Malik. But that didn't explain why we were in a circle.

I asked Malik again.

Briefly he closed his eyes. When he reopened them, the gold was duller. 'I *cast* the circle.'

'You?! But you can't do magic.' I frowned. 'Can you?'

He held out his hand. A can of Blue Bat juice, emblazoned with the Blue Heart logo, appeared in his palm. 'It appears I can.'

I frowned. Had he just done some kinetic vamp trick? Or— 'Where did that come from?'

'The Blue Heart.' He offered me the can with a flat, eerie stare. 'Drink it, Genevieve. It will assist with your recovery.'

I took it and chugged back half the drink before I realised he'd given me an order. The stuff tasted like goblin piss (Beater goblins in Sucker Town have their own peculiarities when it comes to subduing rogue vamps, as I'd discovered once when I'd been wearing Rosa's body as my vamp disguise). As I started to splutter, Malik clapped a hand over my mouth, pushed my chin up and ordered, 'Swallow. Then drink the rest.'

I glared at him, promising retribution. If he thought giving me an orgasm, no matter how freaking fuck-tastic it was, gave him permission to order me around like some junkie blood-slave, even if it was for my own good, then he was sucking on the wrong sidhe.

I finished the drink, went to throw the can at him, but it was out my hand and *vanished* before I had a chance.

'Tell me you did not just do magic?' I demanded.

'Why would I tell you that, Genevieve, when that is exactly what I did do?' His mouth turned grim. 'It appears your blood not only enhances my own powers, but grants me your magic as well. Much as if you were another vampire I had fed upon.'

Which was so fucking unfair. 'Except I can't *call* stuff,' I said, hearing the thread of a childish whine in my voice. 'Or *vanish* it like that.'

He lifted an elegant shoulder. 'The vampires I feed on cannot necessarily tap all the powers that run in their blood either.' He flicked his fingers and the dome went fully opaque; a Privacy spell. Crap, this just got better and better. I scowled at Malik as he draped the leather coat over my shoulders, saying, 'Put the coat on and fasten it.'

'That's the third order in as many minutes,' I snapped, jerking the coat on, fingers buttoning it up clumsily, as I fought to disobey. 'I thought we agreed you weren't going to do that shit any more?'

In answer, he bit down on his wrist then held it in front of my face. 'Drink.'

Both my hands grabbed his arm, my mouth latching on to the bloody bite like I was starving. I sucked down his spicy blood as if it was ambrosia, my fury mounting even as he pulled me into the V of his legs and my body traitorously responded to where his obvious arousal pressed against my butt.

Bastard, I thought loudly at him.

'You are right, Genevieve,' he murmured against my ear as his hard arm pinioned me around my waist. 'I am indeed a bastard. My father never married my mother, and her people, Christians who worshipped the western god, forced her to give me up when I was seven as devşirme. Devşirme was the tithe paid by those conquered by the Ottomans.'

Surprise made me choke on his blood. He was choosing *now* to tell me something personal about his past? Didn't he know the time for sweet nothings was during the post-coital haze? And not after he'd pissed me off with all his orders. But his words still muted my fury, and raised an instinctive compassion in my heart for the child he'd been.

'You do not need to feel pity for me,' he said coolly, as if he'd read my mind which, with me attached to his wrist like a limpet was a possibility. 'I was trained as a janissary, one of the sultan's elite army, and was proud to swear my loyalty to him and his blood. It was a prestigious and rewarding life, more so than the one I was otherwise destined for as a subsistence farmer in Northern Albania.'

Bully for you, I muttered at him. *But how about we can the personal history and talk about the present? For starters: I've had enough blood. In fact, sucking on you is making me feel nauseous.* Which wasn't a lie. I was feeling sick, just not physically. Though, the way my stomach was bloating up like an over-stretched wine bag, physical sickness was going to be an option in the near future.

'Keep drinking,' he ordered.

I didn't need to pity the child he'd been, or the bully he was being now. But while I might not be able to disobey his 'keep drinking' order, I could dig my teeth into his arm in protest. Triumph sparked as he flinched, then an odd note of remorse hit. I was causing him pain ... or he was causing me pain ... I was getting echoes of what he was feeling, sucking them down with his blood. Damn. If we merged thoughts any more, then between us I was going to get emotional whiplash.

'When I was twenty, Suleiman 1 became sultan. He was my liege and my … friend. He had ambitions to expand the Ottoman Empire; ambitions which succeeded, as history has documented. What history does not detail is the strategy he used to win the Battle of Mohács where he defeated Louis II of Hungary and the Ottoman Empire became the pre-eminent power in Eastern Europe.'

Through my link with his blood, I caught remnants of his feelings for Suleiman: loyalty, respect, an echo of hero worship, and sadness that his liege and friend was long gone; but, above all, a brotherly love. Not that any of that explained why the hell he was telling me all this. Or made me any less furious.

'Suleiman used *sanguine lemurs*, as they were called then.' Malik's voice was stark. 'Revenants.'

Revenants are the skeletons in the vamps' closet, the monster side of the vamp myth, the one that isn't supposed to exist. Unlike the usual 'lucky' recipients of the Gift (3V-infected humans who are carefully nurtured over months, or even years), revenants are made instant vamps through a forbidden ritual. One day human, the next a bloodthirsty, bloodsucking monster with less impulse control than a greedy two-year-old. All they want to do is fuck, feed and kill, and not necessarily in that order. Though 'want' isn't quite right, as after a few days they don't usually have any higher functions left, and most end up shambling corpses; the true undead.

The penny started to drop. Malik carried the revenant curse in his blood, though he'd overcome it. Damn. Whatever the reason I was getting this story, I knew it wasn't going to have a happy ending. The thought almost snapped the tether of his order and stopped my own feeding.

'After the battle, Suleiman gave orders to keep no prisoners,' Malik carried on in a low voice. 'It was a good strategy. It sent a message to our enemies, plus we had neither the manpower nor the supplies to support the extra mouths. But his true reason for the order was to destroy the revenants. They had been corralled along with the vanquished enemy, and had continued to feast unchecked until the monsters died with the dawn. There was no way to determine which of the living or dead might be infected; one bite and a drop of blood can be all that is required for the curse to manifest. Suleiman paid the dragons to burn every one until they were nothing more than ashes to be scattered to the four winds.'

His blood told me he'd been one of those who'd directed the massacre, and I tasted the horror and shame he still felt at that memory. It coated my throat, made it hard to swallow.

Was that when you were made revenant? During the fighting?

'After the battle, Suleiman dispensed with the vampire's services, the one who had made the revenants. When the vampire left, he took something of mine. I hunted him down. Offered myself in exchange. That was when I was afflicted with the blood-curse.'

He stopped. And this time I felt grief, failure and soul-deep revulsion and hatred. For what he'd become, and for the vamp who'd made him both evil and a monster.

The vamp that did this to you is the evil monster, I said firmly, my own anger rising. *Not you.*

Bitter denial trickled through his blood, and then he gently ordered, 'Stop now, Genevieve.' My mouth and hands let go of his wrist, and I gasped, slumping as he released his mental hold on my body. 'You have received back all but a small part of the power I acquired from you when I fed.'

I rubbed my neck and jaw, easing the stiff muscles there, swinging between anger, the need to comfort him and wondering what the hell he was talking about. 'Explain.'

A weary sigh chilled my nape. 'It was too dangerous for me to carry your magic, Genevieve.'

I twisted to kneel between his legs, relieved to find his almond-shaped eyes were back to their normal obsidian black. 'Dangerous?'

Malik traced a finger over the pulse in my throat. It jumped at his touch. 'I became close to losing control of the revenant when I took your blood. It is why I took more than I intended.'

My chest constricted. It was his biggest fear; that he'd go insane with bloodlust, start killing and spread his revenant curse. Personally, I couldn't see it; after all, he'd kept himself under strict control for centuries, always feeding from other vamps, however difficult they made things for him, and never from humans. Or even me. Until now. But then that's phobias for you. Still, it was understandable after the trauma of seeing an army destroyed by a pack of animalistic revenants, only to become one soon after. I shuddered. It also sort of made sense of his ordering me about, but—

'But more than that,' Malik continued, 'the danger is also due to the Emperor. He is the one who gave the Gift to Bastien.'

Chapter Thirty-Two

I stared at Malik, horrified. 'The Emperor is Bastien's master?'
'He is.'

Fuck. Bastien might be the Autarch, and have gained his autonomy centuries ago, but if the Emperor was his master, there was a pretty good chance he could waltz back in and start ordering Bastien around like he was a baby vamp. And Bastien owned Malik's Oath.

Malik raked a hand through his hair. 'I cannot risk any other knowing I have the ability to access your magic in this way, Genevieve. It would make you too vulnerable.'

He had it in one. If I wanted to keep my freedom then there was no way any vamp who had power over Malik – be they Bastien or the Emperor – could be allowed to know what Malik could do with a quick slurp of my blood.

But greater than the threat to me was the havoc that sort of power could cause between the different supernatural races. The Emperor might be European Head Fang, but unlike in the UK, vamps in Europe weren't mainstream; there was just too much prejudice and superstition against them from both non-magical humans and the European Witch Councils. It kept the vamps in check and often in hiding, fearing for their nearly immortal lives. Whereas with the Live and Let Live Tenets of the UK witches and vamps, and the vamps recent step up to celebrity status ...

I raised my brows. 'I'm guessing that the vamp set-up in the UK looks pretty attractive to the Emperor?'

Malik inclined his head in agreement. 'London, in particular.'

Damn. No wonder Malik had made me drink all my power back. If the Emperor was already interested in taking over, then a vamp able to use a sidhe's power would definitely add a high shine. 'Fuck, Malik, if you'd just explained what I needed to do I'd have done it. You didn't have to order me.'

'My apologies, Genevieve. The revenant is more easily controlled if it is not provoked.'

I frowned. Okay, so maybe I'd have wanted to know what the big deal was before I'd agreed, but— 'You mean if *you're* not provoked?'

'The revenant is not I,' he said, with an odd stiffness. 'I am not the revenant.'

'What does that mean?'

He gave me an empty stare. 'We are not the same.'

Did he think he was possessed, or did he have some sort of weird alter-ID thing going on? Though with what he'd told me of his past, and the emotions I'd gleaned from his blood, or maybe our blood, it wouldn't be a surprise if he did. 'So what, you think of the revenant part of you as separate?'

'If you wish.'

O-*kay*. Probably better if we left the philosophising for another time. Like when we didn't have to worry about the Emperor or what he wanted. 'So,' I said, glancing at the opaque dome, 'if you're feeling yourself again, we need to work out how I'm going to speak to the Emperor about the fae's fertility. And find out what he and his werewolves have got to do with the Bangladeshi ambassador and his missing wife and kid.'

'It is something to consider,' Malik said, 'but first …' He picked up a pebble from the ground, took my left hand and, pulling us up to our feet, dropped the stone into my palm and closed my fingers over it. 'Travel safe, Genevieve.'

I had a split second to think, *oh shit*, before his eyes flashed gold, my stomach lurched and the island and boating lake vanished.

I landed hard—

On the gravel roof outside my flat. A second later my backpack appeared.

I took a wary scan around. The roof was empty, the majority of windows I could see were dark, and above me the stars twinkled happily despite the haze of sodium light polluting the night sky.

The exasperating vamp had sicced me with a Translocation spell.

It could take a full witch coven hours to *cast* one of those, and even then they didn't always hit the target.

And Malik had *cast* it just by picking up a stone.

Like it was no harder than blinking an eye.

Even channelling a sidhe's power, that was fucking scary.

But how the hell had he even known how?

The annoying vamp was going to have to come up with a lot of answers next time I saw him.

More disturbing though was the fact that it sounded like there was a vamp throwdown in the offing. Something Malik obviously wasn't interested in discussing with me, judging by my involuntary quick exit. No doubt the idiot vamp was trying to protect me again by keeping me out of the loop. But with the tarot cards pointing the finger at the Emperor for info on releasing the fae's trapped fertility, and with the kidnap victims to find, no way was I going to twiddle my fingers while Malik did whatever Malik was thinking of doing.

'No doubt some stupid Lone Ranger impression,' I muttered.

So, next step was … speak to Tavish. He was as invested in finding the answers as I was.

I scrambled up, dusting myself off with a groan. Malik's Translocation spell had dropped me on my butt, hard enough to jolt every vertebra in my spine. At least his leather coat had stopped me getting gravel burn, even if it did drag around my feet.

I grabbed my backpack, gathered up the long coat like I was some Victorian maiden about to flee, and pushed my way into the Warded dome. It clung like extra-sticky glue, evidently recognising me but not entirely happy at letting me through. Had to be my vamp-recycled blood.

As the Ward snapped into place behind me, I heard an ominous splash. Damn. Bertha the eel had woken up. I turned, hoping to make a dash over the roof garden for my open bedroom window, to find the huge eel was high-tailing it at me like she was going for the world record of 'fastest slithering thing on the planet', along with 'jaws wide enough to swallow a cow and sporting an impressive set of razor-sharp gnashers'. What the hell had Ricou been feeding her? Super-size shrimp dinners? She had to have tripled in size since I'd seen her that morning. Okay, maybe I was exaggerating, but, Bertha's bite is way worse than her bark. The size she was now, she wouldn't leave just teeth marks in my calf, she'd have half my leg off.

I waved my hand at her, shouting, 'Biscuit!' and then pretending to throw the non-existent biscuit.

Bertha ignored my ruse, and kept coming.

Crap. My only chance was to backtrack through the Ward, climb down the roof ladder and use the front door.

The Ward wasn't interested in letting me leave.

I was caught between it and the freak of an eel. Trapped.

Damn Ward really didn't like my recycled blood.

'Now would be a good time for some help,' I muttered. Only help wasn't coming. Not at this time of the night. And while I had Ascalon, and the blessed sword would make short work of the giant eel, no way did I want to hurt Bertha; it wasn't her fault she didn't like me. Not to mention she was Ricou and

Sylvia's beloved pet. Only I already knew I wasn't fast enough to outrun her ...

Maybe I could Glamour her?

I'd have to touch her. And hell, I'd never tried to Glamour a fish, or whatever Bertha was. But I had nothing else—

I yanked up my magic, ducked under her looming jaws and slapped my hand on her slippery slimy neck.

Blue light, not gold, sparked from my fingers.

What the—

Bertha froze.

I gaped for a second, then turned and ran, threw my backpack through the open window and dived headfirst after it into the dark room and crash-landed onto the wooden floorboards. Panting, I grabbed the low windowsill and pulled myself up to check on Bertha.

She was still frozen. An odd nimbus of flickering blue light, like an aura, or the blue flames that flared in Malik's pupils when he used vamp magic to stop time, surrounded her long fishy body.

I stared transfixed. There was only one explanation.

Malik wasn't the only one who'd gained extra powers from our exchange of blood. I had too.

And I could use them.

I was still staring, bubbling with excitement that at last I might be able to wield some sort of magic, when my bedroom door slammed open behind me. I turned. A black shape rushed me, grabbed the back of the leather coat and hauled me up to dangle about six inches above the floor. I choked, the coat's collar cutting off my air. My gaze fixed on a pair of swirling turquoise eyes. Pulse racing, I kicked out, getting a lucky foot in, and my captor yelped and flung me back. I crash-landed in a heap for the second time in as many minutes.

There was a crack and a football-sized globe bathed the room in light; one of Sylvia's Moonshine spells.

Tavish was hunched over by the bottom of my bed, hands between his legs, eyes now murky grey with pain, the beads on his dreads flickering from bright turquoise to the same muddy colour.

'Genny!' Sylvia cried from the doorway, her head of blossomy twigs quivering with concern. 'Oh my goodness, are you all right? Tavish said you were with that vampire at Regent's Park, and that he wouldn't let Tavish see you. What happened? Did he hurt you?' Sylvia moved to look down at me, spring-green eyes sparkling with concern and curiosity. 'Why aren't you getting up? Do you need to be healed?'

'I'm fine,' I croaked, rubbing my throat. 'Or I would be if that stupid kelpie hadn't tried to strangle me.'

Tavish snorted. 'You kicked me!'

'You were choking me!'

He shifted gingerly. 'You didnae look like yourself for a second, doll.' His words were part apology and part question. ''Twas as if darkness slicked your soul like oil on water, but 'tis washed away now.'

'Yeah, well,' I grumbled, 'if you started looking at folk's shells instead of checking out their souls to see if you can take a sneaky mouthful, then maybe you'd recognise them more often.' Idiot kelpie and his soul-tasting habits. Though his comment made me frown. Was my odd-looking-soul moment down to my recycled blood? Maybe it was like the Ward not quite recognising me? Not that that let Tavish off the hook.

'You did look weird, Genny,' Sylvia exclaimed. 'Your eyes had these tiny blue flames. They're gone now, though,' Sylvia said, moving to peer down at me. 'What were they for?'

'It's a power thing,' I said, still hardly believing it. 'I froze Bertha.'

'You did?' Sylvia gasped. 'Oh my goodness, is she dead?'

'No such luck,' I muttered, then louder, 'she's fine. It's just a temporary freeze so I could avoid her.' I looked out the window. Bertha was back in her pool, head stuck up like a vigilant periscope, eyeballing the point where I'd entered the Ward as if she expected me to reappear any moment. 'She doesn't like me.'

'Oh, I'm so glad you didn't kill her,' Sylvia said, obviously relieved as she offered me a hand. 'She's so sweet, and of course she likes you. Bertha loves to tease, that's all.'

I huffed as I untangled my legs from the heavy coat and let her pull me to my feet. 'By taking chunks out of my arse?'

'It's a nice arse.' Sylvia grinned, then stroked her finger down the coat's lapel. 'This is nice too, though it's a bit big for you. Have you been shopping again?' She tilted her head, pursing her cherry-red lips. 'No wait, I recognise it. It's that vamp's coat, isn't it?' Her eyes widened, and before I could stop her, she'd pulled the collar open. 'Oh, you've been Fanged.' She peered closer, enveloping me in her sweet cherry-blossom scent. 'More than once, I'd say too. Oh my, Genny, are you all right? He didn't hurt you, did he?'

'No—' I shifted away, taking me, my Fanged throat and Malik's coat out of her curious reach and felt a prick of magic that wouldn't let me lie – he had hurt me when he half-drowned me – and that made me add, 'not in the way you mean.'

'Genny!' Her head twigs shook with determination and she crossed her arms. The movement drew my attention to her 'Hello Boys' cleavage, and envy filled me as a familiar pinballs of magic jumped to life inside me; Harrods' Magic Mirror spell. *Damn, I'd thought I'd got rid of that.* Before the hex could get its 'plastic surgery' tendrils into me again, I quickly averted my eyes to Tavish.

He was giving me a look that said a lecture was coming my way, so I went on the offensive. 'And there was no reason for you to check up on me, either.'

The beads on his dreads flashed crimson with anger. 'Aye, there was, doll. Given what I found.'

'What did you find?' Sylvia questioned.

Malik using my magic and me out for the count. Something Sylvia didn't need to know. I risked a quick apologetic glance at her. 'Sorry, Syl, but is it okay if I speak to Tavish alone?'

Her eyes rounded in astonishment for a moment, then she gave me a conspiratorial wink. 'Course, no probs, Genny. I wouldn't want to hear anything that Mother would want to know anyway. It'll drive her crazy if she thinks she's missing out on things and she can't force it out of me.' She patted her barely there bump. 'And Baby Grace needs her sleep. See you in the morning.' She turned then looked over her shoulder. 'Oh, and before I forget, Katie dropped your phones off earlier. They're charging on the landing.'

'Thanks,' I said, and we waited until the wardrobe door clunked, then Tavish set a Privacy spell. Lust sputtered, then, to my relief, snuffed out, and I reminded myself to check my emails for Ana's Poultice spell so I could keep the leaking Fertility pendant's side-effect in check. Though hopefully I wasn't going to need it, not if there were to be more nights like tonight with Malik ... Of course, first we needed to sort out a few more ground rules; like when things started looking iffy, talking was the way to go, not packing me off home like some delicate damsel who needed protection.

'So, you've been sharing blood and power with the vampire, doll,' Tavish said, breaking into my thoughts. 'And now the pair of you can use each other's magics.'

Chapter Thirty-Three

'**Y**eah.' I gave him a considering look. 'Malik wants it kept quiet. Says it's dangerous and I agree with him.'

Tavish snorted. 'Well, you're nae wrong, doll. But I ken we decided 'twas best you stayed away from him and the rest, till we know what's what with this Emperor.'

Yeah, well I decided it wasn't best, Mr Grumpy. And as I wasn't about to debate it with him, I hit him with my next attack. 'Oh, and thanks for telling me there was silver in that werewolf repellent.'

His gills snapped shut in embarrassment. 'Aye, well, you were nae meant to use more than a wee drop. 'Twould nae have harmed you then.'

As I'd thought. Still, he should've told me. I shot him another scowl to show I hadn't quite forgiven him yet, then filled him in on the Tower card and my visit to see the Bangladeshi ambassador; the werewolves having something to do with the kidnap victims; the Emperor wanting Janan, the Bonder of Souls; and that given my quick trip home it didn't look like Malik was going to help me get to the Emperor, since it looked like there was a throwdown in the offing between the Emperor and the Autarch. I finished with, 'So apart from the long-term problems that a vamp takeover bid could cause all of us, we're no closer to finding the Emperor or what he wants in return for the info about releasing the fae's fertility from the pendant.'

'Hmph. I'll be chatting again to the vampire, doll, and see what this vampire takeover business 'tis about. 'Tis maybe naught but a storm in a teacup, but so long as they keep to their agreements'– the beads on his dreads flashed a warning red – 'it doesnae matter who's in charge. So dinna fash yourself about the blood-suckers.'

I stared at him. I *was* going to worry about the blood-suckers. Malik, and a few others who were my friends. And I did think it mattered who was in charge. But Tavish and I obviously lived in different worlds, and I wasn't going to waste my breath arguing with him about it. I already knew he and Malik were allies, not friends, only drawn together by what the other could offer …

Damn it, that was it. Malik wanted Tavish's help in killing Bastien – an idea I was fully behind. Only I'd always had in the back of my mind that with Bastien gone, Malik would be the new Head Fang, not some evil interloper like the Emperor. And Tavish wanted me protected until the fae's fertility problem was solved … which was why Malik had sent me home. Into Tavish's waiting arms.

Crap. The annoying pair had double-teamed me again, first with Tavish's text, which I didn't get to see, and then with their little chat while I was out of it. Maybe I should just save time and trouble for all of us, and buy the bubble wrap myself.

'So that's it?' I glowered at Tavish. 'You're going to talk to Malik and I just have to wait for the next card to turn up?'

'Och, doll, 'tis the best thing.' He patted my hand. 'Safer too, what with the Emperor's werewolves running about. And 'twill all sort itself out once the last two cards turn up and the reading's complete; the spirit in the cards hasnae failed me yet.'

Yeah, but there's always a first time. I gritted my teeth. 'What about the Emperor's website? Have you hacked it yet?'

His dreads twisted with frustration. ''Twill nae be long now, doll, but I do have a wee thing of interest to show you.' An electronic tablet appeared with a small audible pop to hover in front of us. Tavish plucked it out of the air, tapped the screen and handed it to me.

It showed the home page for a plant nursery:

Bodmin Moor Plant and Herb Nursery ~ Specialists in mediaeval and modern herbs, herbaceous perennials and rare bulbs ~ Growing since 1775.

I cut Tavish a bemused look. 'Um, why am I looking at this?'

Tavish reached over and tapped 'News'.

A picture of Katie's 'boyfriend', Marc, filled the screen. He was standing next to a slightly older man, both of them smiling for the camera, holding up three cards with gold coins stuck in the middle of them. The caption read:

Nurseryman Carlson Fowey and his nephew Marc Fowey with the three prestigious Royal Horticultural Society gold medals awarded at this year's Chelsea Flower Show; the first year Marc has taken full responsibility for the nursery's exhibits at the show.

I wasn't enlightened. I frowned at Tavish. 'You going to fill me in?'

'You told me that the lad, Marc, here, was spying on you at the gnome's,' he said. 'This is why. He was there to do business. Apparently, one of the gnome's cats was sitting on the windowsill and the lad went to speak to it, glanced through the window and saw you, got a mite curious and then a wee bit embarrassed when you caught him watching. So he rushed off instead of keeping his appointment with the gnome.'

Hm. 'And you believe him?'

'Aye, doll, his tale is true enough. The nursery does business with many of the gnomes, nae just Gnome Lampy.'

I pursed my lips at the smiling Marc and his medals,

reluctantly remembering that Katie *had* mentioned he worked with plants. I couldn't deny his story was plausible, given that whole 'the simplest explanation is usually the one', only unease still niggled at me. Marc and his uncle were doing business with the gnome, who was in no way a nice guy. Though, really, the gnome was pretty much stereotypical, albeit a tad more obnoxious than most. So my unease was probably just my 'Katie paranoia' kicking in.

I turned to Tavish. 'So, there's nothing to worry about?'

'Aye, but to be sure, I've asked a body I ken, who stays down that way, to check out this nursery.'

'Okay, thanks,' I said grudgingly, relieved and glad at least that he'd helped in this— until his next words.

'Och, and I told Katie's mother all about it. I ken you wouldnae want her worrying.'

I stiffened. 'Tell me you told Katie too? Before you told her mum?'

His 'why would I do that?' expression said it all. He hadn't. Perfect.

Tavish gave me a sharp-toothed smile that told me he'd dropped me in it with Katie deliberately – a joke, payback for some slight, or just him being ornery – then he said he'd let me know as soon as he had any news, and left.

As soon as he'd gone I grabbed my phones from the landing outside ... and discovered about twenty texts from Katie, starting with the expected snippy one which informed me Marc had already told her about the 'gnome mix-up', before Tavish had done his 'Sam Spade' thing, which he wouldn't have had to do if he'd just spoken to her first. Oh, and some friend I was, getting Tavish to do my dirty business, and blab to her mum, instead of trusting her to know that she'd have told her mum anyway.

Damn. I was going to have to do some serious grovelling. Still her aggrieved tone let up a bit with the rest of the texts, all updates about Spellcrackers –things were all 'running like clockwork', which was good news, despite making me feel oddly redundant. The childish part of me wanted Spellcrackers to fall to pieces without me, to show no one else could run it as well. Mentally I slapped myself, saying I should be grateful that everyone was super-efficient at their jobs.

Katie's next text had my jaw dropping in shock.

Finn's just walked in the office!!!! Did you know he was coming back? Why didn't you tell me?

The text was sent mid-afternoon. I stared at it, heart pounding, thoughts and questions bouncing like balls I couldn't catch till I snagged the important one: if Finn was still here I had a chance to talk some sense into him about the Witch-bitch Helen.

I called him.

His phone went straight to voicemail.

I started to call Finn's brother, then stopped as I remembered the herd were on my shit list. Instead I read the rest of Katie's tests. They told me what I wanted to know: Finn had turned up looking for me, discovered I was holed-up all day with the police at the Harley Street crime scene, poked around the office for a couple of hours, then said he had to go back to the Fair Lands. He'd asked Katie to tell me he'd be back soon.

'Soon!' I spluttered at the phone. 'When the hell is soon? Tomorrow? Next week? When?' And why the hell couldn't the aggravating satyr tell me that himself— Maybe he had. Frantic, I scrolled through the rest of my messages—

And found the one, sent late afternoon, from Malik:

My apologies, Genevieve. I am unable to meet you at midnight. I would be grateful if we could rearrange our meeting for sunset. Malik.

'My' answer to him, five minutes later, was as he'd told me:

Any meeting must be private at office or not at all.

Stunned, I stared at the text until the pieces snapped into place. Finn had been at Spellcrackers. My phones had been at Spellcrackers. Finn, if he was about, was always the one who fixed the phones ...

Damn interfering satyr had sent 'my' answer to Malik. And if I needed any more confirmation, four other texts – all Spellcrackers' business calls – had been answered too. But just because Spellcrackers didn't deal with vamps, and even if he hated suckers, and Malik in particular, it didn't give Finn the right.

'Back less than a day and you're already up to your old tricks,' I ground out.

Furious, I texted him, not caring he wouldn't get it until whenever the fuck 'soon' was!

You have no right to answer my texts. No right to make arbitrary, high-handed decisions on my behalf, about my work or my personal life. Oh, and yes, Malik *is* my personal life.

Fuming I jabbed send.

Stupid, irritating males – all of them – trying to run my life for me.

Half an hour later, I'd showered, eaten the BLT sandwich I'd found in the fridge (thanks to Sylvia's magical delivery service), drunk my nightly blood-fruit Mary, and my rage had muted to a pensive simmer. I checked on Bertha again. She was still swimming back and forth, doing her vigilant-periscope patrol, no doubt hoping I was going to reappear so she could get a bite in.

I sighed, not sure what I could do about the vengeful eel. She was here to stay, for at least until Sylvia had her baby, so I had six more months of dodging and running across my own roof ahead. I lay back in bed, staring at the white, sloping attic walls of my bedroom, and twisted Ascalon's emerald ring on my finger.

I'd called Malik.

My calls went straight to voicemail.

Damn. I needed to talk to him. No way was I going to wait for second-hand info from Tavish. But talking to Malik was impossible when the vamp wouldn't return my calls. And, with dawn fast approaching, hunting him down to talk in person wasn't an option. At least not until after sunset, sixteen or so hours away. Frustrated, I rubbed my wrist and the hidden bracelet there: the quickest, easiest way to talk to Malik would be in the Dreamscape, but to do that I needed his ring, which I still didn't have—

An idea struck. Maybe I could use another Morpheus Memory Aid to gatecrash his dreams – like I had when he'd been dreaming about the *sanguine lemurs* – and then somehow twist the dream so I could talk to him?

Only it was a crap idea. Turning up in his dreams by accident was one thing ... but jumping into them deliberately? An apology probably wasn't going to cut it.

Except right now he owed me. He was the one who'd sent me back without talking things through. If we were going to have any sort of relationship, he knew he couldn't do that. No way was I going to be the princess in the ivory tower. Not to mention I'd told him I'd help. Help did not mean sitting things out on the sidelines. Especially when he had a fight on his hands and I needed info about the fae's fertility from the vamp he was up against. And especially not when Malik could use the power in my blood.

He was a kickarse vamp already, add in my own power and I doubted even Bastien or a millennia-and-a-half-old Emperor could stand in Malik's way.

'Easier to ask forgiveness,' I muttered, and ordered another Morpheus Memory Aid spell.

In the time it took to walk from my bedroom to the fridge, the box was waiting for me next to Ricou's smelly fish.

I took the spell back to bed, thumped my pillows into submission, and finally admitted what had been staring me in the face.

Malik could do magic.

And, okay, he'd got a power boost from my blood, but having the power didn't mean you knew what to do with it. You had to learn how to use it before you could *cast* spells (though, if you were me, learning was a complete waste of time). Malik had *drawn* a Blood-Ward circle, which was basic enough that I could do it, and then he'd cast a Privacy spell, a simple enough magic, though not so simple that I could *stir* one myself. But hey, a vamp of Malik's age could possibly manage it. But then he'd gone and pulled that complex Translocation spell out of thin air. Like it was nothing.

And the only way he could have done that was if he'd studied magic.

No one studies magic unless they have an ability to use it and, other than sorcerers who trade their souls for their magical powers, the only way you get magical ability is from one or both of your parents.

Like Mad Max. He'd inherited his magical abilities from his sidhe mother. And my own half-sister, Brigitta, had taught him to use them.

So, if Malik knew how to do complex magic (even if he needed a boost from my blood to actually do it), it followed that he'd been born with that ability.

So, it also followed that before Malik had become a vamp—

He hadn't been fully human.

With that oddly disturbing thought, I snapped the sleep mask on and chugged back the sickly strawberry-sweet

Morpheus Memory Aid potion in the hope I'd find him in my dreams.

My dreams were a bust. Full of huge amorphous grey beasts chasing me through Regent's Park, and every time their sharp fangs snapped at my heels, I jerked awake, terror pounding my heart in my chest. Only to fall back asleep minutes later to be chased again. Classic nightmare with added werewolves. A frustrating side-effect of the damn Morpheus Memory Aid. In the end I did the only thing possible: I snagged a bottle of vodka out of the freezer compartment and took it to bed with me.

A banging noise woke me from a deep, dreamless (thankfully), alcohol-assisted sleep.

Hot summer sun streamed in through my bedroom window, reflecting squares of light and shade high up on the sloping walls. The angle told me it was still early morning.

The banging came again.

'There is a troll knocking on the front door,' Robur the dryad's eerie voice boomed out of my bedside table drawer. I jerked upright and the empty vodka bottle thudded to the wooden floorboards, clinking against the other one already there. It takes a lot of alcohol to affect my fast sidhe metabolism.

'Why does everyone have to make so much noise?' I muttered, grabbing my head.

'It is the shiny black troll with the gold specks.' Robur's voice was, if anything, even louder. Payback for the lemon polish incident. 'The one who is stepping out with your landlord, Mr Travers. I discern from the wood beetles who inhabit the dresser in Mr Travers' kitchen that the troll has his police uniform on and appears to be on official business.'

The pounding hit a new, urgent note.

'Please hurry before he scratches the wood.' Robur's piercing words hammered into my fragile morning-after skull.

I pulled on my robe and hurried, as directed, to the door. I yanked it open as the large troll who was stooped down outside banged again. Luckily for me, his huge black fist bounced off the Ward (invisible to him, as all magic is to trolls) and sent purple ripples up and down the open doorway.

Constable Taegrin of the London Metropolitan Police's Magic and Murder Squad gave me an apologetic look. 'Sorry to disturb you, Genny.' A small black cloud of anxious dust puffed from his headridge and settled on his shiny bald pate and the shoulders of his stab vest. 'But Detective Inspector Munro was worried; you've been ignoring your phone.'

I had a vague memory of stuffing my phone in the fridge when I'd grabbed the second bottle of vodka after waking from another fleeing-from-monsters nightmare. Crap.

'He wants you back at the kidnap scene at London Zoo,' Taegrin continued. 'I was nearest, so he's sent me to pick you up.'

Chapter Thirty-Four

Covent Garden to London Zoo is fifteen minutes by road. On a traffic-free day. But I've never known London to have a traffic-free day, so we were in for a long, slow drive which I wasn't looking forward to. Especially after it clicked with my hangover-fuddled brain exactly how we were getting there. Parked beneath the leafy canopy of the large elm guarding my building's main door was a Magic and Murder Squad police van. Built to accommodate trolls (obviously, since Taegrin was driving), they lack a certain human-sized comfort.

Once we were safely buckled up (with me riding shotgun so I didn't look like a suspect, but thanks to the adult booster seat and my dangling legs, looking like a seven-year-old instead), it took Taegrin all of a minute to tell me what the score was. The Bangladeshi ambassador had agreed (presumably after his midnight meeting with the Prime Minster) to hand over his bodyguard's bloodstained kurta, so it could be used to scry for leads in the hope it would pinpoint the kidnap victims' location. Hugh wanted me at the scrying, though as scrying was on the list of things I couldn't do, when I asked why, Taegrin didn't know.

After that he was quick enough to realise I wasn't up to sparkling conversation; the two-part Hot.D (short for Hair of the Dog) potion I'd rushed out and bought from the Witches' Market was probably a big clue.

I knocked back the first part, my mouth going dry at the chalky taste, and slumped on my booster seat waiting for the spell to take effect. Hot.D spells are meant to postpone any hangover for twelve hours, but as the witch I'd bought it from said, 'You ain't human, dearie, so I ain't guaranteeing nuthin'.'

Taegrin chatted quietly as the van trundled along about his weekend with Mr Travers. The pair had spent Sunday walking the Troll Trail on the Thames – a sort of troll spiritual pilgrimage that involved crossing all the bridges, and included the occasional stop at participating 'watering holes' to sluice their blowholes. They'd set out at dawn from the Queen Elizabeth II Suspension Bridge at Dartford (the last bridge before the sea), headed upriver and, even with the required 'watering hole' stops, had reached Battersea Bridge by sunset.

'That's seventeen out of the hundred and one bridges, Genny,' Taegrin said proudly. 'Not bad going for a day's trekking. Now we're planning on how we're going to tackle the rest. We thought …'

The initial stupor phase of the Hot.D hit, and I listened with half an ear, watching the sun glint off the gold specks in Taegrin's polished black skin, happy for them both and, since I'd sort of introduced them last Hallowe'en, basking in a vague mother-hen-like delight that they'd found each other through me.

My pulse sped as the Hot.D kicked in with a caffeine shot.

I checked my phone.

Three missed calls from Hugh when he'd tried to contact me.

And a message from Malik.

My thumb hovered …

At some point before the vodka had induced its dreamless sleep, I'd sent him a text:

We need to talk. You know I need to see the Emperor about the fae's fertility. Ignore Tavish and don't cut me out of the loop. Whatever's going on, I can help.

And here was his answer. I swallowed, heart thudding erratically against my ribs. *Only the caffeine.* Pressed the button:

> Genevieve. I fear it is unwise for there to be any more direct communication between us. Should you require any assistance, in any matter, know that Maxim is tasked to put your needs above all others, including himself. Your servant, Malik.

I frowned. Why the hell was he telling me to talk to Mad Max?

I reread the message, disbelief closing my throat.

The words didn't change.

He'd dumped me. By text. After what happened at the lake. Fury ripped through me. Okay, so I got that he'd 'lost control'. That he was worried about his curse. And that he'd discovered he could use my magic. I got that it all scared him. And I got he probably thought he was protecting me. But even if Malik did think that fucking 'direct communication was unwise', he could at least call me and tell me in person. Not send a fucking text.

And if the bastard vamp thought that was the end of it, well, he really didn't have a clue. I'd had enough of males doing what they thought was right. Or just doing whatever they wanted. Or not giving me answers. It pissed me off. Not to mention this wasn't only about him, or me, but about the fae's trapped fertility. I resent my text, adding:

> Stop fucking around, Malik. V important we talk. Meet me at midnight at Tir na n'Og, tonight, or I tell DI Munro to open the letter.

I pressed send. Now he had to have 'direct communication' with me, or I'd shop him to the cops and witches.

The van braked to a stop and Taegrin's bass rumble in my ear took on meaning. '... so we think we should reach the Thames head by the August New Moon.' He turned to grin proudly at me.

'That's great,' I said, forcing my mouth into a smile as I mentally shoved Malik and his fury-inducing texts somewhere where the sun shone hot, and knocked back part two of the Hot.D potion, almost gagging on the bitter aftertaste. Calm, clarity and a sense of purpose spread through me, smoothing out my emotions. Good thing too, as I had a job to do.

Taegrin pointed at the glovebox. 'There's consultant ID badges in there, Genny. Best if you wear one.'

I snagged a badge, followed him through the zoo, and to the tiger exhibit.

We entered the same shaded corridor as before with its U-shaped windows looking out on to the tiger enclosure. I skirted past a yellow 'Warning: Wet Floor' sign, leaving footprints on the recently mopped floor and nearly gagging on the reek of chemical pine-scented cleaner. About halfway along the corridor, Hugh, Mary and a coven's worth of WPCs were gathered around a salt and sand circle with something green lying in its centre. As I neared I realised it was a folded piece of clothing; the blood-splattered kurta belonging to the kidnapped woman's bodyguard.

Hugh turned, his pink granite teeth gleaming as he smiled a concerned welcome, then I jerked to a halt as the pine smell was gone, replaced by another, more familiar scent.

Blood. Its metallic odour was flooded with adrenalin, its very freshness telling me it was recently spilled. Without conscious thought, I inhaled deeply. Underneath the coppery aroma slid another. Meaty and rich with the smell of wet fur. I'd smelled it before, here, yesterday. Only now that recognition was deeper, more visceral than a day-old scent warranted, as if it was one I'd known long ago—

Static flashed in my mind.

The zoo corridor disappeared.

*

I stood at the centre of a wide, moon-bright plateau. It stretched out to both sides of me, one edge hugging the steep mountain face, the other falling into the clouds boiling below. The ground was covered by an ankle-deep blanket of snow, unmarked as far as I could see. For a moment all was still, silent, a breath out of time …

I was back in Malik's dream/memory. The one I gatecrashed the first time I used the Morpheus Memory Aid.

A distant wolf howl split the air, icy snowflakes stung my cheeks and a chill wind whipped my hair over my eyes. I pushed it back, and the snow-covered plateau was no longer white and pristine. Instead, pools of fresh blood stained the white expanse around me like a scattering of crimson rose petals.

The blood-scent intensified, laced now with arousal and the sweetness of ripe figs.

Rage curdled in my stomach.

Genny?

The voice was a distant rumble, like thunder in a far-off storm. *Hugh.*

Static flashed again.

I looked down.

A man sprawled naked in the snow at my feet. Black curls matted his scalp. Green eyes, vivid against the dark olive of his skin, gazed up empty above a long aquiline nose and thin, sculptured lips. Splinters of bone gleamed sharp and white in the red ruin of his throat. Thick black hair furred the hard muscles of his chest. Below his ribs, a long wound gaped wide, the flesh ripped open by something sharp and clawed, the ragged end of his aorta dangling into the internal cavity; evidence that his heart had been ripped out. A tangle of intestines wriggled over the lower edge of the wound, glistening slick and wet as they spilled from his abdomen on to the snow.

A distant analytical part of my mind catalogued the dead

male's injuries, and concluded they were recent. So recent, so immediate, in fact, that his body hadn't caught up with the reality of his demise. Since, from the thatch of black hair between his wide-spread legs, his sex still jutted, still erect, and still smeared with the girl's blood.

A growl jerked my gaze to my right.

To a ten-foot circle cleared of snow. Ash marked out the circle. Glyphs glowed with magic around its circumference. Inside the circle was the girl. She was on her hands and knees, head thrown back, long dark curls streaming over her shoulders, her prepubescent body naked except for a wide leather collar around her neck. A thick chain stretched from the collar to a spike driven into the rocky ground at the circle's heart.

Genevieve!

Malik's voice calling my name was drowned out as the growl came again.

From the girl.

She lowered her head and glared at me with eerie yellow-green eyes.

Shock sliced through me as I recognised her, despite her being a few years younger than when I'd seen her last night.

She was the girl at the mosque. The one in the fur jacket.

The werewolf.

The girl snarled, lips drawing back over longer-than-human canines.

Genevieve!

My name was a sharply ordered imperative.

Static again.

Figures appeared in the distance, grey shadows loping over the snow, racing towards me. Hot flesh seared my palm. I squeezed my hand and warm wetness trickled from between my fingers to complete the pattern in the snow as the muscle I held pulsed one last time.

'Dead.' The girl's whisper was a taunt on the wind. 'My mate dead. You've killed him. Taken his heart.'

You must leave, Genevieve. Now!

'They are coming,' she screamed.

Static.

'Coming for you.'

My eyes snapped open and I found myself lying on the ground, staring up into a huge furry face. It looked down at me with unnerving yellow eyes, swiped a pink tongue out to lick its muzzle and yawned wide enough to showcase a stomach-churning set of canines. *My, what big teeth you have, oh Furry One!* Panic knotted my throat— until I breathed in the scent of pine cleaner, and my mind caught up with the fact I was back at the tiger exhibit at the zoo; and there was a reassuringly thick pane of glass separating me from the pointy-toothed tiger eyeballing me like I was his next meal.

My pulse slowed and I realised I wasn't lying on the ground but on a thin foam mattress covered by a silver-foil survival blanket. The only person about was Mary, chattering quietly away on her radio. I shut her and the tiger with its pointy teeth out and tried to sort through what just happened.

The damn Morpheus Memory Aid spell, combined with Malik's blood I'd drunk, had to be backfiring again, this time not even waiting for me to sleep; instead the spell was just throwing me straight into a memory/flashback.

Malik's memory/flashback.

And a disturbing one at that.

Not that I'd expected any of Malik's memories of the Emperor and his werewolves to be good, not after Malik had gone hunting him and ended up sicced with the revenant curse by the evil imperial vamp.

Who had to be a truly foul piece of imperial shit indeed if he chained up prepubescent girls and forced them to

268

become werewolves. Because I was betting that was the ritual Malik's memory had shown me. Ugh. Definitely a disturbing memory to have. Not that the Fur Jacket Girl had seemed upset or traumatised by what was happening to her. No, she'd been raging about her mate being killed. That I'd killed him. Shouting that *they were coming. For me.*

My pulse sped up. It was the same as the Moon tarot card warning.

Only it wasn't me who'd killed her werewolf mate in the memory, Malik was.

So was the memory a true one? Or had my subconscious added its own little twist at the end there as a reminder? Not that it mattered when I was pretty sure the Emperor's werewolves were coming for me, anyway. And at least the memory had confirmed one thing; the werewolves were definitely the kidnappers. The smell of werewolf blood on the bodyguard's kurta had dropped me into Malik's memory/flashback.

So, did that mean all werewolf blood smelled the same? Nah, too unlikely. The blood probably belonged to a werewolf Malik knew. Since the male was dead it had to be Fur Jacket Girl. So who was she to Malik? Someone he cared for? The rage he'd felt suggested that. Though his memory wasn't something you'd want to see happen to anyone, whether you cared for them or not. More importantly, his memory meant Fur Jacket Girl had been one of the werewolves here at the zoo.

Which was disturbing in an entirely different way.

Malik had said he hadn't seen any of the Emperor's werewolves for more than five hundred years. So, as Fur Jacket Girl was still around, then she had to be a good half a millennia old. Except werewolves only lived a human lifespan. So either Malik was lying – something I knew his honour wouldn't allow him to do – or I was working on faulty info from the witch archives. Or more likely, incomplete info, since I'd never got into the password protected files. No doubt if I had, they'd have told me some werewolves did live longer than human lives.

And no doubt Malik could've told me that too. If I'd bothered to ask him.

Crap. I needed to speak to him. If he hadn't known what was going on last night, I was betting he did now. Only the text-dumping vamp had cut me out of the loop. And yes, I was pretty sure it was all down to his screwed-up protective instincts and his deal with Tavish, but damn, didn't the idiot vamp know, that all cutting me off would do, was make me furious? And didn't he know that no way was I going to hole up in some metaphorical ivory tower, however much he wanted me to, not when people were missing and the fae's fertility was still trapped? So what was his point, really?

I clenched my teeth, swallowing a frustrated scream.

The silver blanket covering me rustled and Mary looked up from her phone. 'Oh good, you're awake.' She crouched down next to me, hitching her black trousers at the knees as she did, a relieved expression on her face.

'Yeah,' I said. 'Sorry, I was thinking.'

'Thinking?' She grinned. 'I thought it was called fainting. You did a good job of it too. Like a tree toppling.' She demonstrated with her forearm. 'Awesome faceplant. Or it would've been if the DI hadn't caught you. We tried to wake you, but you were way out of it.'

'I don't faint,' I grumbled, as my eyes caught the remains of the sand and salt circle. 'Any luck with scrying for the kidnappers?'

Chapter Thirty-Five

Mary grimaced. 'Nada. The blood on the kurta was too old.'
Damn. If the scrying was a bust then I needed to find Hugh and tell him the blood was werewolf. I started to get up—

Mary slapped a heavy hand on my chest and pushed me back down. 'Stay there until the DI gets here,' she ordered. 'He'll probably want the medic to look at you again. I'll let him know you're conscious.' She thumbed her radio and started giving more orders.

Medic? Again? Hugh was going overboard on looking after the definitely-did-not-faint sidhe. For which I was grateful, but … I did a quick mental inventory to make sure all my fingers and toes, and everything in between, felt normal. Everything did so there was no point lying here, waiting for a – no doubt efficient, but human – medic to tell me I was okay as far as they could tell. I mouthed at Mary to cancel the medic, and, brushing away her exasperated hand as she tried to keep me prone, I sat up.

It put my head on a level with the tiger's. It was sitting on its haunches like a patient dog, less than a foot away from me. The sunlight streaming down highlighted the black stripes marking its orangey coat, and silvered the white fur haloing its lower face and jaw like an old man's beard. Its long whiskers were almost translucent in the glare. And its stripes weren't symmetrical as I'd always imagined, but fanned out from a point between its eyes as if someone had haphazardly painted them in. It was the first time I'd even been so close to a wild animal, and it was beautiful and awe-inspiring.

Movement in the undergrowth caught my eye. Another tiger padded up. It lay down with lazy grace a few feet away, its long tail twitching slightly. The first tiger flicked its black-tipped ears and half-closed its yellow eyes, but otherwise ignored its pal. Both stared at me as if I was the most captivating thing they'd seen this year. But unlike the predatory gaze I'd have expected, the tigers looked more as if they were waiting for my next trick.

I frowned. Was that natural? I pinged them, the possibility of werewolves giving me the crazy idea that they might be weretigers. Got nothing but animal back. But then when I'd pinged the werewolves all I'd got back was human, so maybe that's how they felt to me. I tapped on the glass, mouthing hello. They just kept staring. I pulled a face, stuck my tongue out at them, told them I knew what they were. Still nothing. I caught Mary giving me squinty eyes, so I bit the embarrassment bullet. 'Do you think they're weretigers?'

She looked at me in silence for a long moment, then said, 'Did you hit your head when you fainted?'

I huffed. 'I didn't faint.'

'If you say so.' She grinned then said, 'Okay. Weretigers, or ailuranthropes to give them their proper name, became extinct' – she frowned – 'on 21st June 1758, in Hunan province in southern China, when the last one went loco and mauled eight teenage girls. The girls died and the locals trapped the weretiger in its animal form and stoned it to death.'

I blinked. 'That's … very specific.'

'Mum was looking at something in the witch archives the other night, to do with weres, proper name, therianthropes.' Mary's mother was on the Witches' Council. 'It stuck in my memory.'

The hair on my nape stood on end. 'Really? That's a weird coincidence.'

'Why weird?'

'Because I asked,' I said, mulling over how likely it actually was a coincidence, or was the Witches' Council somehow aware or even involved in what was going on. 'And because I was just thinking about werewolves.'

'Werewolves, proper name, lycanthropes, are the only therianthropes that aren't extinct,' Mary said blandly.

'I know,' I answered just as blandly. 'What was the problem your mum had?'

She gave me her cop face. 'Why do you want to know, Genny?'

I hugged my knees, debating what to tell her, if anything, saved from making a decision when Hugh appeared.

He hunkered down next to me, concern creasing his face and offered me one of the takeaway cups he was carrying. 'How're you feeling, Genny?'

'Good, thanks.' I wrapped my fingers round the cool cup, inhaled the welcome scent of orange juice. 'Now I'm awake.'

He patted my shoulder gently. 'The medic wanted to take you to HOPE' – the Human and Other Preternatural Ethics clinic where they treated all things magical – 'but as your vitals were stable, I thought if you stayed here it would be easier for us to talk.'

'Yeah, we need to,' I said, then got to the point. 'It was the blood on the bodyguard's kurta. Its scent was the trigger and knocked me into a sort of vision.'

'The scent knocked you into a vision?' Interest lit his cloud-grey eyes.

I glanced at Mary listening a few feet away. She was a friend, but she was also a witch, and her mother was on the Witches' Council. And they'd been looking into wereshifters. My paranoia hit: I still had a nasty taste from Witch-bitch Helen interfering in my life. I dug a Privacy crystal out, set it, then filled Hugh in on nearly everything; the tarot cards, the ambassador at the mosque, the werewolves, and Malik's memory (which I asked Hugh to call a 'sort of vision' to respect Malik's privacy). 'Only none of that tells us why the werewolves kidnapped the victims from here,' I finished. 'Or where they're holding them. Or what they gave the ambassador. Or what it all has to do with the fae's trapped fertility.' I gave him a hopeful smile. 'Any ideas?'

Hugh's ruddy-coloured face creased with worry. 'That's a lot of information, Genny, and I'm not happy that Tavish has involved you with the fae again, or with the vampires, but what's done is done. And I can see why you agreed to help.' He tapped his cup thoughtfully. 'As for everything else, most of what you've told me is uncorroborated and circumstantial.' He held his hand up as I started to disagree. 'But I'll get the blood on the kurta checked for werewolf identifiers, which will give us something concrete. And I'll put an official request to the Oligarch's office to speak with Malik al-Khan.'

I scowled. 'Told you, I'll be talking to him myself, tonight.'

'You also told me Malik is being difficult.'

I'd actually told Hugh Malik was being an idiotic, irritating vamp, but hey. And Hugh had a point. Despite my 'blackmailing' text, Malik might still go all Lone Ranger on me, but he wouldn't ignore an official request from the police. And this was about the victims. I nodded. 'Sure. Whatever works.'

'Good.' Hugh said, giving my shoulder a satisfied pat. 'This is why I wanted you here, Genny. I hoped that with a closer look, your sensitive nose might pick up a recognisable scent. Which it seems it has. Admittedly, it was a bit of a long shot, but with three victims' lives at risk ...' His mouth split in a smile, pink granite teeth gleaming. 'No stone unturned is always a good motto.'

'Ha ha, Hugh.' I rolled my eyes at him. 'But glad I could

help, even if it's not much. Though my "sensitive nose" disappeared yesterday. I'm not sure why it picked up the blood smell so strongly.'

'Smells associated with traumatic and/or important events often bring strong memories or flashbacks. Which seems to be the case here, albeit second-hand.' Anxious red dust puffed from Hugh's headridge. 'But there's something else that worries me in all this. These tarot cards. For a question dealing with the fae, they seem very focused on getting you involved with the vampires. Are you sure the cards haven't been tampered with?'

I raked a hand through my hair. 'It's crossed my mind. But Tavish assures me it's not possible. And I trust him.'

'Tavish is the àrd-cheann, and as such he is the one fae, other than yourself, who has regular dealings with the vampires.'

Right. Tavish's dealings were with Malik. And I trusted Malik too. Only for the last few months he'd been under the sway of the Autarch, thanks to that icky Jellyfish spell. The only way I'd trust Bastien was if he was a pile of ash, even then not so much.

'I'm not saying there is a problem with the cards,' Hugh continued, 'but ...'

'Be on my guard,' I finished for him.

'Yes,' Hugh agreed. 'Now, I'd like you to tell Mary about your vision. The event is obviously magical and distinct enough that she may know something that can help, either you or the kidnap victims.'

'No stone unturned?'

'Exactly.'

I laughed, deactivated the Privacy spell and Hugh explained what he wanted to Mary.

Mary looked intrigued. 'You had a vision? Was that why you fainted?'

'I don't faint,' I grumbled.

She grinned, getting out her notebook. 'Fell over, then. Or tripped.' She scratched a note, muttering, 'Ms Taylor did not faint but tripped, and this enabled her to experience a vision.' She looked up and gave me a beatific smile.

I stuck my tongue out.

'Ladies, please.' Hugh's long-suffering sigh was belied by the amused glint in his eyes. We laughed, Mary took notes about the dead man in the snow and the young girl in collar and chain inside the circle, while I drew what I could remember of the glyphs.

Mary gave me a quizzical look. 'You know I said Mum was looking into therianthropes in the witch archives? This was the ritual. I can ask her to compare the glyphs to check' – she looked at Hugh – 'if that's okay with you, sir?'

'It is,' Hugh said. And as Mary took photos and emailed them, Hugh handily asked the question I wanted to. 'Why was your mother looking at this particular ritual?'

'There was an unauthorised user alarm on the private archives.'

I stiffened. I had a horrible feeling I knew who the 'unauthorised user' was— Katie: when she'd done her own werewolf research.

'Mum was tracking what they'd been looking at,' Mary carried on, 'in case it was anything dangerous. There's some pretty ancient spells in there. This is one of them.' She cut me a look. 'It's part of that weretiger story I told you about.'

'What weretiger story?' Hugh asked, and Mary filled him in.

'Um. When exactly did the unauthorised user access the archives?' My question got me piercing stares from Hugh and Mary. I tried not to look guilty on Katie's behalf, and no doubt failed.

'The night of the "Harry Potter" spell in Leicester Square,' Mary said, her cop gaze pinning me where I sat.

Damn. It had to be Katie. It was too much of a coincidence otherwise. 'Okay,' I said, 'before you start interrogating me, if the ritual I saw of the girl in my "vision" chained up in the ash circle is the same one that was being looked at in the archives, what's it for?' I asked the question, though really I knew; I just wanted to be sure.

Mary pursed her lips, debating, then blew out a breath. 'Okay, but if it's needed for prosecuting someone, you'll have to get a warrant to ask the Witches' Council for permission to view it.'

Hugh gave a slightly insulted rumble. 'Of course,' I said, patting him consolingly on the arm; the witches were always a bit close-mouthed about their secrets.

Mary lowered her voice. 'It's a ritual for changing a human into a therianthrope.'

I stopped myself from pumping my arm and shouting, 'Yes!'

'I take it this isn't the same ritual that's in the police manual?' Hugh's deep voice rose in question.

'No,' Mary agreed. 'It's nothing like the Death Bite one. This one has some seriously revolting stuff.' She shuddered. 'Well, like your vision, Genny. The human has to be a virgin, and the whole ritual is barbaric. That last weretiger killed in China? There's a note in the archives saying they think he was the last pure blood-born weretiger, and the reason he mauled all those young girls was because he was trying to replicate the ritual, to make himself a mate.'

Which all tracked with Malik's memory. Young Fur Jacket Girl had called the dead male her mate. And she'd evidently been a virgin.

A pensive frown lined Hugh's forehead. 'Werewolves have no more magical ability than a non-magical human, other than their inherent shapeshifting, so there's still the strange lack of magic at the kidnapping to be explained.'

'Which I still maintain looks like when you clean up after the pixies,' Mary said.

'But the *àrd-cheann* is adamant that there is no possibility of there being another sidhe fae in London.' Hugh looked at me. 'How confident do you think he is about that, Genny?'

'I think Tavish is pretty sure—'

My phone rang.

'Aunty?' A girl's high-pitched voice.

My mind did a fast turnabout from werewolves and sidhe to my faeling niece, Freya, and the fact she was calling me in the middle of a school day. Had Ana, her mum, gone into labour?

'What's the matter, Freya? Is it your mum? Is the baby coming?'

'You have to get here quick,' she shouted. 'Granddad says they're coming.'

They're coming! I clutched the phone, stuffing my instant panic away. Not Ana, then. 'Where's here,' I said, forcing calmness into my voice, 'and who are they?'

'Home, and I don't knoooow!' It was a scared, frustrated whine. 'He can't frogging tell me. He just shook me by the scruff and ordered me to phone you.'

Home for Freya was Trafalgar Square. Or at least, that's where the entrance to her home was, through the left fountain. Which was also the watery abode of her great-grandpops, the fossegrim, the fountain's fae guardian. Though why he'd be ordering Freya to phone me was odd; the old water fae wasn't exactly *compos mentis* during the daytime, nor much better at night, not to mention we'd hardly spoken more than a couple of times.

A dog growled in the background; a low urgent warning.

My heart stuttered as I realised Freya didn't mean the fossegrim, but her other granddad. Her vampire granddad. The one who wasn't supposed to be anywhere near her. Mad Max.

Freya yelped. 'He wants to know how long, Aunty?'

I looked at Hugh. 'I need to get to Trafalgar Square. Freya's in trouble, and Ma—' Conscious of Freya listening, I stopped myself from saying Mad Max, changing it to, 'my cousin Maxim is with her. He says they're coming.'

The same alarm thrumming through my veins etched Hugh's face, then he went into full DI mode. 'I'll get you a car and driver, Genny.' He lifted his radio. 'At the zoo entrance. Should be twenty minutes tops from here, with a siren.'

Chapter Thirty-Six

We sped along the morning's route from the zoo back into the centre of London. I sat hunched in the back of the police car, muscles tense, hitting Freya's number on my phone and getting shunted direct to voicemail every time, questions whizzing around my head like a flight of manic garden fairies.

How did Mad Max know they were coming if he didn't know who they were? Were they the same 'they' that the tarot cards warned me were coming? The Emperor's werewolves? But why would they come for Freya? And why would Mad Max go to Freya and get her to phone me? If they were dangerous, he'd led them straight to her. And why wasn't Freya at school, where she'd be safe? Where was her mother, Ana? Was Ana even okay? And why the hell wasn't Freya answering her phone? Why was Mad Max there anyway? Why wasn't he tucked away in his daytime sleep instead of running round London in his dog shape?

Damn it. I didn't trust him. Vamps weren't exactly altruistic to start with but Mad Max took the prize for selfish. He might have 'helped' me with his Poultice spell, but that didn't mean he wouldn't sell me out at the drop of a dog biscuit. Never mind that he was the Autarch's dog and I could be heading into a trap. Not that it would stop me, not when Freya was involved. And truly, for all Mad Max's faults, this was Freya, his grandkid, and he was all about protecting her. Which still didn't mean this wasn't a trap for me. Just not for her. Gods, I hoped not anyway.

Deciding after the sixth voicemail that I should do something more constructive than going insane with worry, I started phoning for help. Trouble was, the only help I could get wasn't going to arrive at Trafalgar Square any sooner than I was.

Desperate, I leaned forwards, tapped Mary's shoulder. 'How many Stun spells have you got?'

She twisted to look at me, a wary expression on her face. 'Stun spells are police issue only, Genny.'

I gave her a flat look. 'My niece is in trouble. Probably from werewolves.'

'There're the two of us.' Mary jerked her head at the driver; a five-foot-nothing witch, with dark cornrowed hair and golden, freckled skin a few shades darker than my own. I'd met her at the Harley Street/Magic Mirror crime scene where she'd introduced herself as Dessa – short for Odessa – and who was manoeuvring the cop car through the traffic with an easy confidence that carried an edge of glee. 'And there's another WPC and a troll constable heading there from Old Scotland Yard.' I hadn't been the only one phoning. 'Plus I've called in the Peelers.'

Peelers. Non-magical human coppers, so called because of Robert Peel (who started the Met) and the fact they had no juice. 'Peelers are cannon fodder when it comes to magic.'

'Trained cannon fodder who can deal with the crowds.'

'Also cannon fodder,' I said, fingers digging into the plastic seat backs. 'How many Stun spells, Mary?'

The siren hooted its *wha wha* warning as Dessa slowed through a junction. We held our breath as she zipped the car through a narrow gap between a delivery lorry and a souped-up four by four, then we were speeding up again.

Mary held her baton up. The jade mounted in the silver tip winked the bright green of a Stun spell in my sight. 'The usual one in the baton,' she said, 'and one here.' She tapped the jade pin in her shirt collar.

'Only two,' I said, dismayed. 'Dessa?'

The cornrowed witch sniffed. 'I'm a plod, so baton only.'

'Stuns are time- and ingredient-heavy spells to *cast*, Genny,' Mary said, frustration making her words harsh. 'It makes them expensive. And please don't ask for one, it's against regs for civilians to have them and if we're caught, I'm suspended and you're in jail. The DI won't be able to stop it.'

'I'll take my chances,' I muttered.

'If something happens to Freya,' she carried on, 'you don't want to be in jail. We haven't got time to argue, plus we've got your back.'

Crap. She was right. And more than ever, this was one of those times I desperately wanted, no needed, to be the all-powerful magic-wielding sidhe I imagined I would have been if not for whatever the hell was wrong with me.

'Thanks,' I said, grateful, but wanting more.

'Here, take this.' Dessa dug in her uniform shirt pocket as she overtook a beat-up white van, and held up a clear plastic packet with a pink plaster in it. A nicotine patch.

I blinked. 'I want to knock them out, not stop them smoking.'

'Sh—ugar! Wrong one!' She fished again, held up another plastic packet. This one contained a blue patch and the label read: 'Power Nap Patch ~ Restore your Get Up and Go.'

Was she mad? 'Um, seriously, Dessa.' I met her brown eyes in the rearview mirror. 'If there're bad guys threatening my niece, I want them out, not hyped up on caffeine.'

'Trust me. This'll knock anyone out in three seconds flat.' She flipped it in the air. I caught it. 'It's got chamomile, valerian, and synthetic morphine. The caffeine only kicks in after forty mins; it's slow release.'

The baggie had the slippery feel of spell plastic – it would vanish as the spell was activated – and a peelable 'sticky' to attach it to my palm until I was ready to *tag* someone. Neat. I almost dropped it as Dessa added, 'Oh, and it's got a touch of aconite.'

'Aconite's poisonous!' Mary exclaimed.

'So's that patch if you eat it,' Dessa warned. 'But slap it on a "collar" and it drops them straight into happy snooze land.' As she wove through the busy traffic, she explained how she'd confiscated the Power Nap Patches from a hoodoo witch with a stall in the black part of Covent Garden market. The witch had been doing a brisk trade as she'd neglected to stamp the patches with the traditional poison mark: the black skull and crossbones in a circle. Apparently there were no ill effects so long as the patches weren't eaten or used more than once a week; something else the hoodoo witch hadn't told her customers. And they were cheap, or at least cheaper than Stuns, to make.

'You and I are going to have a serious chat, constable,' Mary said firmly, once Dessa finished.

Dessa's mouth turned down. 'Yes, sarge.'

'Sounds like it might be a useful spell,' I said neutrally as I peeled the covering off the sticky and stuck the baggie to my palm. 'Maybe it could be licensed ...' I looked up – we were driving through Piccadilly Circus – and met Dessa's gaze in the rearview. I winked. She half-smiled back. I'd try to make sure Mary didn't give her too much grief for the spell.

A minute later we turned into Haymarket. *Straight on, then left into Pall Mall, and we're there.* I rolled my shoulders, releasing the tension there. *C'mon, c'mon, not far now.* Only the traffic in front of us slowed. 'There's some hold-up ahead.' Dessa craned her neck as the car slid to a halt behind a black cab. 'Looks like a breakdown.' She moved to give the siren a burst.

I touched her arm. 'No. We're too close; the wrong people might hear it.'

'Your call. But we won't get past all this without it.'

Crap. Dessa, with her flashing lights and siren, had got us this far in what had to be the longest fifteen minutes of my life. But Trafalgar Square was still half a mile away. I ran at least ten times that every morning; when I wasn't hauled out to a crime scene. 'I'll run,' I said, opening the car door. 'You two catch up as soon as.' I jumped out into the middle of the road, slammed the door, and started sprinting up the queue of stalled traffic; so much easier than trying to dodge the pedestrian jungle. Under the background noise of cars, buses and people, I heard Mary shouting something, then another door slammed and her pounding feet echoed mine.

What felt like an aeon later, but was probably no more than two or three minutes, I slammed to a halt at the top of the stairs leading down from the north terrace of Trafalgar Square. I caught my breath, scanning the square. It wasn't as crowded as I'd expected. But as always there were folk lounging on the rims of the fountains, some dangling their feet in the water. There was a queue for ice creams at the café. A crowd of tourists were taking photos of the pixies playing on the huge bonze lions ... Automatically, I clocked their numbers: eight pixies, seven up from yesterday, and the lions were sparkling with pixie dust— a problem for another day ... And another, smaller tourist group watched over by one of the square's heritage wardens, were snapping pictures of the hawk used to keep the pigeons from the square; the bird was perched on the black and gold railing caging Nelson's Column, and was eyeing the crowd with an imperious tilt to its head.

I curled my fingers around the Power Nap patch, sweat licking fear down my spine. The sparse crowd should've made it easy to find Freya and Mad Max, but there was no sign of them. I upped the focus on my inner radar ... three witches; two somewhere near the column, and another further away, behind and to my right – Mary. And a weird ping towards the far corner of the square … I frowned trying to work out … but it was gone before I could ID it. And I still couldn't *sense* hair or hide of Freya or Mad Max.

I phoned Freya, but again it went straight to voicemail. I snapped the phone shut, wanting to scream or hurl it at someone, anyone— Instead, I took a steadying breath and continued scanning the square. Damn. There was nothing out of the ordinary, nothing, no one for me to find, or fight, or extract info from. Time to go knock – figuratively, anyway – on Freya's door.

I jogged down the steps angling towards the left fountain.

'*Ciao, bella*,' a male's voice called from my right. '*Io sono qui*.'

I almost dismissed the loud and mostly unintelligible voice – no one with nefarious deeds on their agenda was going to draw attention by calling out 'Hello, beautiful' and whatever the rest was – but some instinct made me turn. The male was about ten feet away. Adrenalin hit, hyping my senses. In one long second I took him in. Black curly hair, cut short to his head; vivid green eyes, hard and watchful despite the wide grin on his olive-skinned face; tight jeans, open-necked shirt displaying thick black chest hair; his arms outstretched, a bunch of red roses, tied with ribbon, gripped in one hand – the picture of the stereotypical Latin lover enthusiastically greeting his girlfriend – and looking enough like the dead male in Malik's snow-plateau memory to be a relative. Latin lover had to be the male werewolf I'd glimpsed at the mosque.

And in the hand not carrying the roses, glinting gold in my *sight*, Werewolf Guy was holding some sort of ready-to-go spell.

High-pitched barks, followed by low ominous growls, came from my left.

My pulse sped as out the corner of my eye I saw two dogs jump out of the fountain: a smallish fluff of silver and grey fur

– Freya in her Norwegian elkhound shape – closely followed by Mad Max's giant white-haired Irish wolfhound.

Of course, now they turn up.

Werewolf Guy changed course towards the dogs, drawing back his arm to throw the glinting gold spell.

Not at my niece, you don't!

'Hey,' I yelled, willing time to stop and freeze around him. Almost predictably, my cool new vamp power didn't put in an appearance. *Brute force it is, then.* I charged, catching heads turning in the crowd, along with Werewolf Guy's startled expression. At the last moment before I barrelled into him, I ducked and shoved my shoulder into his stomach. He doubled over with a grunt, air whooshing out his mouth. I clamped my arms round his thighs, heaved and flung him over my back; for all I'm small for a sidhe, I'm way stronger than most humans. I whirled to find Werewolf Guy jumping lightly to his feet as he came out of a roll, still holding the roses— and the spell. Crap. He'd recovered acrobatic quick. Not that I truly thought it would be that easy.

Cameras flashed, and a few tourists clapped, obviously thinking we were some sort of street show.

He grinned, showing crooked but definitely human teeth, and swivelled back towards the dogs. The Irish wolfhound had the smaller, fluffy dog by the scruff, dragging her back towards the fountain. Werewolf Guy raised his arm. Determined bastard! I threw myself at him and slapped my palm, with its Power Nap patch, against his in a parody of a high five. Purple sparked as the spell activated. His eyes met mine, triumph gleaming in their vivid green for a second, before they rolled up inside his head and he crumpled. Shit. I'd got him— But not before he'd thrown his own spell.

Stomach churning, knowing I was too late, I jerked round to see a coin glinting gold as it spun through the air.

Straight at its target. The dogs.

In a blur of vamp-related speed, the Irish wolfhound grabbed the elkhound by the scruff and flung the smaller dog out of danger. She yelped as she landed in the middle of the fountain, disappearing in a cascade of displaced water. Then in almost in the same motion, the Irish wolfhound launched up, mouth open, and caught the gold coin. He dropped to all four paws with an audible thud, and froze, head hanging unnaturally still.

Mad Max and I stared at each other, less than ten feet apart.

Waiting …

I didn't like him. He was a twisted selfish vamp who had no compunction about using anything or anyone in whatever way it suited his purpose, and he certainly didn't worry about who might or might not end up hurt. And I definitely didn't trust him. For the exact same reasons. But despite the fact he'd tried, on more than one occasion, to use my friends as 'hostages' to force me to give him my blood (Mad Max wasn't the sort to even think of straight-out asking), he'd done it for the sake of Freya's mother, Ana, and for Freya herself. Which even now didn't make me feel overly charitable towards him, nor did the fact that he was sort of family. Nonetheless, I still found myself wanting the spell to not do whatever it was supposed to do, to him.

Which currently looked like …

Nothing.

He spat the coin out.

It hit the pavement with a tinkling sound, rolled in a wobbly semi-circle then fell on its side.

I *looked*. Whatever magic it had, it was gone.

The Irish wolfhound sunk to his haunches, pink tongue lolling in a manic doggy grin, diamond-encrusted dog-tags catching the sun. *Well, that was a bleedin' anticlimax, wasn't it, Cousin?* Mad Max said in my head. *Thought things might get a tad more exciting than that.*

Fury, along with a rush of relief, swept over me. I shot a quick glance at Werewolf Guy – still clutching his roses, but now snoring away – then snagged the coin, strode over and grabbed the Irish wolfhound by his throat.

'If whatever fucking idiot scheme this is,' I ground out, 'hurts even one hair on Freya's head, I'll remove your balls with a blunt blade and wear them as earrings as I scatter your ashes on the Thames.'

Promises, promises, Cousin, he drawled. *If I didn't know you better, I'd almost believe you meant it.*

I squeezed harder, almost choking him. 'Believe it! Now what's going on?'

Oh, stop getting your knickers in a twist, love, this one's nothing to do with me. The dog licked his nose, nonchalantly. 'It's *down to you and your friend, the Turk.*

'Malik? What's the hell's he—'

A sharp bark cut me off, and I found myself sprayed with water. I released Mad Max, swiped at my eyes, and glared down at a soaking wet Freya as she finished off her shake. 'You need to go back home, pup.' I pointed at the fountain. 'Where it's safe.'

She shoved her wet doggy self between me and the Irish wolfhound, and curled her lips in a snarl.

I tapped her on the nose. 'Don't you take that attitude with me, pup. You know he's not supposed to be visiting you, so he's in the wrong here, never mind he's your granddad—'

'Genny!'

I turned my head to see Mary, her hand pressed to her side as if she had a stitch, staring down at Werewolf Guy in dismay. He was twitching as if he were a statue the pixies had tried to animate. I grimaced. It looked like the Power Nap patch, or something, was disagreeing with him.

Chapter Thirty-Seven

I pointed at Freya. 'Get her back home,' I ordered in a low voice to Mad Max. 'Make sure she stays there, and later, you and I are going to have a long chat.'

Freya barked an obvious, 'No!'

'Yes!' I told her.

She growled— and Mad Max snatched her up by her scruff, threw her in the fountain again then trotted calmly after her.

A round of applause from the crowd reminded me we had an audience. *Damn. Next thing the paps will turn up, and I'll be on the front pages again.* At least the heritage wardens were keeping the rubberneckers out of the way.

I jogged over to Mary as she lifted her radio. 'I need a HOPE ambulance. Code six three one – unidentified magical casualty. Trafalgar Square. How long?' It crackled unintelligibly. ''K, I'll hang on.' She pointed at the twitching werewolf. 'What did you do to him?'

'All I did was tag him with Dessa's spell,' I said. 'He was fine a minute ago. Better tell the medics he's a werewolf.'

'Unidentified is clearer. That way they won't make mistakes. Why's he holding the roses?'

'Camouflage?'

'I meant,' she said pointedly, 'why is he still clutching them? He's unconscious. He should've dropped them, shouldn't he?'

'Maybe. Or maybe it's something to do with the spell's side-effects.' I bent to check him out.

Mary grabbed me. 'Leave him,' she ordered. 'Standard ops with un-ID'd spells. No touching the victim, and he needs to be in a circle. Here' – she handed me a lump of green spell chalk from her pocket – 'draw one. About eight feet across. At least he's on stone, it'll make it easier.'

I started drawing a circle, crabwalking around the still twitching werewolf.

'Cripes,' she muttered, which was Mary's answer to swearing with a precocious nine-year-old daughter. 'I should never have let Dessa give you that spell. It's got aconite in it. If he really is a werewolf, it could kill him.'

Aconite? Oh, yeah, wolfsbane. I scowled. 'He's not a good guy, Mary.'

She shot Werewolf Guy a frown. 'We don't know that, Genny.'

I snorted. 'He was throwing spells at my niece! And he helped kidnap three people. Good guys don't do that.'

'What spell?'

'This!' I stopped drawing and showed her the gold coin. It glinted in the sunlight.

She peered at it. 'There's no spell.'

'Not now. Mad Max sort of ate it.' I glanced at where he was sitting next to the fountain like he was auditioning for Guard Dog of the Year, and getting not a few admiring looks from the crowd. There was no sign of Freya, so hopefully she was tucked up safe at home, in *Between*.

'Max looks fine,' Mary said. 'Maybe you were mistak—'

Werewolf Guy howled in pain, his twitches turning to jerks, and blood started leaking from his nostrils, mouth and ears. A horrified buzz came from the crowd, and I caught more of the inevitable camera flashes. Blood always brings out the ghouls. Werewolf Guy let out another howl, his spine arched, veins standing out like black cords in his neck. An answering screech came from above. The hawk, trained to scare the square's pigeons. Werewolf Guy convulsed as if invisible hands were trying to tear him apart.

'Finish the circle,' Mary shouted. 'Quick before he shifts.'

I dragged the green chalk over the flagstones, only a foot to go ... Time seemed to slow ... Werewolf Guy's eyes snapped open. He flung his arm out. They flew from his hand, scattering in a shower of red petals. The petals landed on the grey slabs, like the pools of blood staining the snow in Malik's memories. Werewolf Guy smiled at me with victory in his eyes. Above me the sound of wings buffeted the air. Gut clenching, I looked up. The hawk hovered, a dark shadow against the clear summer sky. It opened its beak wide, screeching again as it vomited a stream of green magic. The magic twisted and twirled, morphing into a verdant jade serpent, fang-filled jaws hinging wide, as it arrowed straight for me. I raised my hand, *focused*, and *called* the magic snake, aiming to snatch it from the air—

Something shoved me aside. The Irish wolfhound, wiry hair brushing my face as he leaped, snapped his jaws on the jade serpent. I stumbled, falling atop Werewolf Guy. For a moment he trapped me in his arms, holding me tight, then a flood of magic washed over me, spreading out over Trafalgar Square like the pressurised shockwave after an explosion. I glimpsed the hawk hovering; Mad Max shaking the serpent like a terrier with a rat—

Mad Max, the hawk and Werewolf Guy all vanished.

I sat on the stone edge of the left fountain, half-listening to the splash of water and the background rumble of traffic, as Mary, Dessa, and a dozen Peelers from the local police station finished taking statements. The Peelers had turned up a few minutes after it all went down, and along with the heritage wardens had managed to corral the majority of the bystanders into a makeshift witness waiting area, using the square's café as their base. Even without the free tea/coffee/juice on offer, the majority were eager to hang around and recount everything exciting they'd seen.

And what they'd seen, according to Mary, came with the usual add-ons of imagination and conjecture. Some thought the hawk was an eagle, or a vulture, or even a remote control toy; Werewolf Guy's hair colour was everything from blond, through red, to his actual black; and the 'dogs' varied from 'a brace o' wee terriers' to a pack of rabid wolves— that particular witness was currently getting the third degree.

I was waiting to get my own third degree (as per Mary's instructions) from Hugh. Waiting for Tavish to phone me back about the gold coin; I'd emailed him a set of pictures. And for Freya to shift from her doggy shape to human, which she was refusing to do. But most of all for Ana, Freya's mum, to turn up.

I reached down to Freya, lying sphinx-like by my feet, ears pricked forwards as she watched the square with an unwavering doggy stare, and ran my fingers through her thick silky fur. It had dried in the sunshine, and I could just make out the darker tint on the ends, all that was left from when she'd magically dyed her hair green a couple of months ago. Attention seeking, Ana had told me with a long-suffering sigh. Freya's dad had left during the ToLA case, after discovering what his brother, the deranged baby-making wizard behind all the abductions, had been up to. Supposedly, it had all come as a big shock to Freya's dad.

Yep, and I was a goblin queen.

Freya grumbled low in her throat, flattening both ears in a sulky 'leave me alone' gesture. I stopped petting her. Where the hell was her mum? School was nearly finished for the day, Ana wasn't here waiting for her daughter to arrive home, and all my calls kept getting her voicemail. My paranoid imagination was running riot, involving Ana in various awful scenarios with the Emperor, his werewolves, Bastien, or more likely, giving birth on the Underground.

I pushed my uneasy thoughts aside for another ten minutes until they hit critical, and dug Werewolf Guy's gold coin in its clear plastic evidence bag out of my pocket (after a 'discussion', Mary had agreed I could hang on to it until Hugh said otherwise). I turned it over, examining it for any clues I might have missed the last twenty times I'd looked at it. It was a little larger than a pound coin, had a golden eagle on one side, a man's head crowned with a laurel wreath on the other and Romulus Augustus writ Roman-style around the coin's circumference. It didn't take a genius to add coin and Werewolf Guy together, and come up with the Emperor, even without the face on the coin looking like the picture on the Emperor's website.

Romulus Augustus was the last western Roman Emperor. His reign started on All Hallows' Eve in 475 when he was around fifteen, and lasted for all of ten months, until he'd was deposed and shipped off to the Castel dell'Ovo on an island in the Gulf of Naples, from where he later 'disappeared' a.k.a. Accepted the Gift and became a vamp. Of course, Wikipedia didn't mention the becoming a vamp bit. Or that the Emperor was Head Fang of Europe and Bastien's master.

Or that the Emperor's werewolves had just dog/spell-napped Mad Max instead of me.

'Idiot dog,' I murmured, wondering again why the hell he'd pushed me aside.

Freya nipped my ankle and regarded me out of accusing doggy eyes.

'Not you, pup. Granddad Max.'

She whimpered then tucked her head on to her front paws.

I frowned down at her where she dozed in the sunshine, her black nose twitching occasionally. I could understand Mad Max sacrificing himself for his grandkid. But even with me donating my blood to Freya, there was no way I could see my self-seeking, use-anybody-and-don't-give-a-fuck-who-gets-hurts cousin deciding to save me by playing snake-catching hero.

Hugh's huge figure cut out the sun. 'Maxim's actions appear to be out of character,' he said, echoing my own thoughts.

'Yep,' I agreed, looking up at Hugh's ruddy face, deeply creased with worry. Two major incidents in less than a week were taking their toll. 'Anything more from the witnesses?' I asked, though to be honest I didn't expect there to be. If there had been Hugh would've been acting on it, not talking to me.

He shook his head as he sat, large hands cradling a mug of milky coffee. He took a sip, then looked pointedly down at the dozing Freya. I got the message: we needed her to shift to talk, but she wouldn't, and he had an idea to persuade her. I tilted my head to show I understood, and he started the ball rolling. 'Run through what happened one more time for me, Genny.'

I did, ending with, '... the hawk threw the Snake spell, Max intercepted it, and was zapped away instead of me.'

Hugh nodded encouragingly. 'So you think the hawk was using the Snake spell to remove you from the scene?'

'Well, me or Werewolf Guy,' I agreed. 'We weren't that far apart.'

'Only the Snake spell didn't touch the werewolf male, but he still vanished. So the spell was more likely for you.'

'Yep, that's what I thought too.' I grimaced and held up the plastic evidence bag with its gold coin. 'But that still doesn't explain this, or why Werewolf Guy threw it at the dogs.'

Hugh held his hand out and I dropped it in his palm. He opened the bag and sniffed, lifted it up to catch the sunlight, then held it like he was weighing it. 'It's solid gold, and going by the smell, it's as old as it looks.' He sealed the bag and offered it back. 'It's probably an extremely valuable antique.'

I took it back. The plastic was slightly gritty from his skin.

'So why throw it at a couple of dogs, even if he knew who they were?'

'It could be payment of some kind.'

'Payment? To Max for me?'

'Yes. This looks like a classic set-up to me. Max uses Freya to get you here.' Freya's ears pricked up at her name. 'The werewolf male tries to snatch you, your niece warns you and the plan goes pear-shaped.'

It actually made sense, especially if you knew Mad Max. 'Why did he snatch the Snake spell, if he was part of the plot?'

'You were *calling* the spell, trying to catch it.'

'Yeah.'

'And if you caught it, it wouldn't have worked, would it?'

'No.'

'So we'd have the spell as evidence, and would be able to trace it.'

Which was partly why I'd tried to catch it. That and not wanting to be *tagged* by an unknown spell, of course.

'So,' Hugh carried on, 'Maxim catching the Snake spell before you could achieves two things.' He held up two large fingers, and out the corner of my eye I saw Freya raise her head and fix Hugh with anxious eyes. 'One: it makes sure no evidence is left, and two: Maxim is safely removed from the crime scene and not available to answer questions.'

I heaved an exaggerated sigh. 'Sounds just like Maxim to cut and run when his plan goes wrong. Bet he turns up later with some story about how he escaped.' Freya stood, ears back, hackles raised. I made a show of ignoring her. 'So there's not much point looking for him, is there?'

Freya nudged my hand with a wet nose, then barked, loud and insistent. 'Quiet, pup,' I said, patting her head, as if she were just the dog she was pretending to be.

Hugh nodded, adopting his blank-stone cop's face. 'Yes, we've got better things to do than look for Maxim.'

The puppy shook like she was shedding water, magic prickled over my skin, and then Freya took her human shape. Her blonde hair was gelled into spikes, the tips still dyed green like her fluff-ball fur, school tie pulled loose round her neck, and her overlarge white shirt messily tucked into her maroon skirt. A backpack appeared slung over one shoulder; she dropped it to the ground with an irritated thump.

I'd asked her once what happened to her clothes when she was a dog; she'd shrugged, saying whatever she was wearing just went away, and then came back again, and wasn't that what happened with everyone?

I squashed a pang of envy. So what if she could change into a dog, and back again, complete with magically reappearing clothes, without breaking a sweat, despite the fact she was a faeling, not a full-blood fae, with a mix of sidhe, fae, vamp and human blood. Much like myself, who couldn't do anything with magic other than *crack* it, *absorb* it like some freaky sponge, or use it ready-made, and who didn't even get to keep the cool vamp powers. I wasn't jealous of *her*, exactly, but maybe of her and everyone else's abilities. And I had to wonder why she, an eight-year-old kid who was sort of my niece, ended up with magic powers and I didn't.

Freya clenched her hands into fists. 'Granddad Max didn't do the things you said! You've got to look for him! He's in trouble!'

Chapter Thirty-Eight

'**W**hat makes you think Granddad Max's in trouble?' Hugh asked, his gravelly voice matching his stony expression.

'Because he was scared!' *So there!* She didn't say it but she didn't have to. It was in the jut of her chin.

'Scared of what, Freya?'

'The werewolves, of course.'

I leaned forwards. 'Did Granddad Max tell you they were werewolves?'

She pulled a face. 'No. I heard you all talking. Granddad Max couldn't tell me what they were.'

'You mean he didn't tell you,' I said.

'No, Aunty. I mean he couldn't.' She huffed. 'I asked him. That's what he told me.'

'Freya,' I said gently, 'just because he told you he couldn't, doesn't mean he didn't know.'

'It does! Granddad Max doesn't tell lies. Or not much to me anyway. I can tell.'

Nice qualification!

Hugh leaned forward with interest 'How can you tell?'

She sniffed in an attempt to play it cool, but her blue eyes sparked with excitement now she had our full attention. 'I can smell when he lies, like I can smell when the girls at school lie too. And when Mum does; lies smell like burned toast.' She folded her arms, daring us to not believe her. 'And I can smell when they're scared.' She wrinkled her nose. 'That smells like dead fish.'

News to me. I wondered if her senses were better because of her dog shape, her vamp genes, or both. I patted the stone rim of the fountain next to me. Freya gave me a wary look, obviously wondering if sitting would commit her to something she didn't want, so I raised my brows. She glowered and plonked herself down.

'Okay,' I said, bumping her shoulder gently with mine. 'I get that Granddad Max was scared, but if he didn't know who was coming, how did he know to be frightened of them?'

'He had a dream about it. It woke him up.'

Dreams. Right. 'What sort of dream?'

She shrugged. 'He didn't tell me. Just said he knew they were coming for you, and he had to warn you.'

'Then why the h—eck didn't he tell me that,' I asked, feeling another urge to wring Granddad Max's neck.

'He didn't know where you were, did he? That's why he got me to phone you.'

'Why didn't he phone Genny himself?' Hugh asked.

She gave him a scornful look. 'Duh. He's a dog. Dogs can't use phones, can they?'

Duh indeed. 'So why couldn't you have told me that when I first asked you?' I asked.

'Granddad Max said I had to stay furry 'cos it's easier to run away with four legs instead of two.' She rolled her eyes to show what she thought of that idea. Not a lot. 'And when I'm furry I don't smell so much like you. He didn't want them getting me by mistake.'

I frowned. 'You smell like me?'

'I drink your blood every day, don't I?'

Duh again.

'Granddad Max said the less we told you, the quicker you'd get here. And that he couldn't guard you till you were here.'

'Max wanted to guard me?' Surprise sparked in me. Then I got it. The last text Malik had sent me. When the irritating vamp had dumped me. He'd said: *Maxim is tasked to put your needs above all others, including himself.*

I looked at Hugh. 'She's right. He was trying to protect me.'

'I told you he was,' Freya grumbled.

I gave her a hug. 'I know you did, thank you.'

'So you're gonna look for him, aren't you?' she said suspiciously. 'Now I've told you everything?'

I nodded. 'Yes.'

'Even though you said you wouldn't?'

'I said we wouldn't if he was helping the baddies.' Which it didn't seem he was.

'We'll make sure he's looked for, don't you worry.' Hugh smiled at Freya. 'So lies smell like burned toast, fear smells like dead fish, is there anything else you've picked up that might help us?'

She gave him a look from under her lashes. 'When people have sex it smells like coconuts.'

Hugh's mouth opened, then closed again. His ruddy cheeks coloured with embarrassed heat.

'Behave,' I muttered. 'Hugh was asking if you'd smelled anything today that might help us find Granddad Max, like if you caught any of the baddies' scents?'

She looked out over the square, her nose twitching. 'The bird that dropped the Snake spell smelled like Uncle Jack.'

'Uncle Jack?' Hugh asked, just as a woman's voice shouted, 'Freya!'

I jerked my head up. Ana was rushing towards us as fast as her huge baby-bump would let her. Despite her hurried waddle, she looked cool and elegant in a sleeveless dress, her pale blonde hair falling in a sleek waterfall to her hips. Relief filled me at the sight of her, despite her elegance making me feel hot, dusty and in need of a shower. But then she hadn't spent the morning getting up close and personal with the floor at the zoo, followed by a tussle with a rose-wielding Werewolf Guy and a snake-spitting hawk.

'Mum,' Freya shouted loud enough for the whole square to hear, 'Granddad Max's been kidnapped.'

Of course, I'd rather do all that over again than have to deal with an obviously frantic, ready-to-pop-any-day-now, desperately angry Ana.

She sank into a crouch in front of Freya, pulling her daughter to her protectively. 'Are you all right?' she said, patting the squirming Freya.

'She's fine,' I said soothingly.

Ana shot me a frightened, furious look. 'Why was Maxim here, Genny? You know he's not to come anywhere near Freya.'

As I opened my mouth to try and explain, Hugh said gently, 'Ms Fossel, perhaps we could have a word?' He rose to his feet. *Thanks, Hugh,* I thought, grateful. 'I'm sure you could use a nice cup of tea,' Hugh rumbled quietly, indicating the café. 'Shall we?'

She looked as if she were going to object, then rose and clutched Freya's hand. 'If you insist, Inspector.' She jabbed a shaking finger at me. 'And you, keep Maxim away from my daughter.'

'Muuum?' Freya wailed. 'Granddad Max is in trouble!'

'Maxim can look after himself.' She pulled on Freya's hand and turned.

I watched them walk to the café, understanding why Ana was angry – the vamps had tortured and killed her mother (my half-sister) and she was terrified they'd do the same to her and Freya. Still, it hurt she blamed me instead of Mad Max, her vamp father; he was the one who'd got Freya involved.

Suddenly, Freya pulled free and ran back to me. 'Mum smells of coconuts,' she whispered. Then she was gone, disappearing into the café, along with a telling-off from her mum.

Bemused, I propped my elbows on my knees and my chin on my hands. Ana smelled of coconuts? Ana had been having sex? *That's* why she hadn't been here, and why she hadn't answered her phone. But why would Freya tell me? Did it have something to do with finding her Granddad Max, or was she just trying to embarrass her mother because she was angry with her. And who was Ana having sex with anyway? Was sex even advisable in her hugely pregnant state?

Mary sat next to me. 'So that's Andrea, she's your what? Second cousin or something?'

'Niece is easier,' I murmured. 'And she's decided she wants to be called Freya now. It's her middle name.'

''K,' Mary acknowledged. 'She looks a nice kid. Nine, isn't she?'

'Not till September.'

'Nearly the same age as my Emily. They're all about pushing boundaries at that age.' She sighed. 'Oh, and telling you how their friends' mothers do everything so much better than you do. It makes life difficult.'

'Yeah, I s'pect it does.'

She patted my shoulder. 'Ana's just scared, Genny, so she's opted to kill the messenger.'

'Yeah, I know,' I said. 'So at what point can't you have sex if you're pregnant?'

Her brown eyes widened. 'Interesting change of subject.' She cut a look to the café, then said, 'Sex is possible right up to birth, if you're careful, and if you feel like it. Some even have sex as a way to start labour. Me, I ballooned to the size of an elephant as soon as I hit my third trimester, and Emily spent most of her time dancing pointe on my bladder. Sexy, it was not.' She shrugged. 'But everyone's different.'

Freya was telling the truth about her mum, not that I'd doubted her, but she could've been mistaken. 'Thanks,' I said.

'Think it's important?'

'To do with the werewolves and them taking Mad Max? Doubt it, but you never know.'

'Well, I know something that is important.' Excitement laced Mary's voice and she showed me her phone. The screen had a shot of a gold coin.

I held my own gold coin in its plastic evidence bag to the screen. The coins could've been twins. 'Snap.'

She laughed. 'So, you want to guess, or shall I tell you?'

I sat straighter, heart pounding. Hugh's comment about the gold coin being thrown at Mad Max as payment of some kind came back to me. 'The Bangladeshi ambassador sent it to you,' I said slowly. 'It was given to him by the werewolves the other night at the mosque in some sort of exchange for his wife and kid.'

'Yes. He's just come through with the info. Knew you'd get it!' Mary shot a finger at where Dessa was leaning against her cop car, mouthing, 'You owe me.' Dessa pulled a face. Mary turned back to me. 'The ambassador hasn't opened up about anything else, though, like whether he knew they were werewolves, or what the coin means. But with your gold coin, at least we have corroborating evidence that the two cases are connected, and that his wife and kid, and the zoo employee, were taken by werewolves, presumably the Emperor's. And here's the other interesting thing' – her expression said she was on a roll – 'guess what else the square here has in common with the crime scene at the zoo?'

'Easy,' I said, smiling. 'It's been cleaned of magic in exactly the same way.'

'Spoilsport.' She gave Dessa a half-hearted thumbs-down making the cornrowed WPC grin happily. Mary huffed and whipped out her notebook. 'C'mon then, how do you know?'

'The hawk did it,' I said. 'In the square. With the magical green ribbon snake.'

'Ha ha. Very funny.' She shook her head. 'Oh, and it's a Booted Eagle not a hawk. The square's bird warden ID'd it.'

An eagle? Well, it went with the whole Roman imperial theme.

Mary waved her notebook under my nose. 'Specifics, please.'

'Okay,' I said. 'Well, Freya said that the bird smelled like her Uncle Jack. Jack is one of the Morrígan's ravens. He's also a changeling. Ergo, the eagle is also changeling. Changelings are human babies raised by the sidhe in the Fair Lands and given sidhe magic. So the eagle changeling used sidhe spells in the kidnaps, and that's why the zoo, and here, look like a sidhe's cleaned up all the magic.'

Mary fingers whitened where she gripped her pen then she gave me a not so friendly look. 'You know,' she said quietly, 'that's the one thing all us witches fear about our babies, that we'll wake up to find them stolen. Taken to be a changeling. And all we're left with is a stupid *ùmaidh*.'

Stupid was right, since *ùmaidh* means dolt or dim-witted. But then most *ùmaidhs* were made from something inanimate like a fresh cut log, or the longer lived ones from animals – I'd heard piglets were a favourite – so anything more than basic sentience wasn't part of the spell.

I touched Mary's arm. 'Won't happen. For one to make an *ùmaidh*, the sidhe would have to offer up a chunk of flesh and sever part of their soul. It's a big sacrifice to make for something that's only going to live for a couple of weeks at the most.'

Mary's mouth twisted. 'Yes, I know, but they'd get the stolen baby in exchange.'

True. Only if a sidhe really wanted to steal a baby they'd be more likely to leave a Glamoured sprite behind than an *ùmaidh*. Way easier. But I didn't tell Mary that. And really she didn't need to worry anyway. I did tell her that.

'Reason being,' I carried on, 'the sidhe have agreed not to

steal any kids from London. They can only take them with the mother's agreement.' Grianne, my faerie dogmother, had told me that little gem, back when I'd accused my sidhe queen grandmother, Clíona (through Grianne), of stealing Freya's Uncle Jack when *he'd* been a baby. 'Well' – I added the proviso Grianne had also told me – 'they can't so long as there's a queen on the British throne. Which there is now. It's an old agreement going back to Boadicea.'

Mary's eyes widened with surprise. 'Truth?'

'Yeah.' I frowned. 'How do you not know that?'

'I've never heard of it.' She tapped her pen thoughtfully. 'Weird. I'll have to ask Mum, see if she has. It would certainly put a lot of our worries to rest.' *If it's true.*

She left it unsaid. Not stupid enough to say it might be a lie to my face. Though to be honest, I was wondering if Grianne had somehow told me it wrong too … or if I'd let some cat out of a bag I wasn't supposed to … but that mystery was for another time.

'So,' I said briskly, 'we know the eagle is a changeling, and he/she used the jade ribbon snake to wipe the crime scenes clean magically, but it wasn't just the magic that disappeared, but the eagle, Werewolf Guy and Mad Max too.'

'Which means the snake also held some sort of Translocation spell, or it opened a portal.' Mary flipped back a couple of pages in her notebook. 'One of the witnesses said he saw a large black shadow fall from the eagle, so that might indicate the portal option.'

I nodded. 'Yeah, but a portal to where?'

'I don't think it can be far; those types of spells take a lot of power,' Mary mused. 'It might even have gone to a nearby van. We had a shoplifting perp who was doing that with goods before we nicked him …' Her face lit up. 'We nicked him when he lifted something we'd planted and we were able to scry for it. So it doesn't matter where the portal went, because we can find it. Or find Mad Max, anyway, using that gold coin he had in his mouth.'

I handed her the coin in its plastic bag. 'I picked it up, remember, after Mad Max dropped it, is that going to be a problem?'

'Not if we keep you with us, and the coin's got lots of scratches on it, so his saliva should be all over it. The main scrying kit is still back at the zoo, but Dessa's got a portable kit in the car.' She jumped up, but I stopped her with a hand on her arm.

'I know why the Emperor wants me – sort of, anyway,' I said. 'But why would his werewolves kidnap the ambassador's wife, her kid, and the zoo employee?'

'I don't know, Genny. But right now, why doesn't matter. Let's see if we can find them first, then we can worry about that.' She hurried over to Dessa, and I fished my phone out to check my messages. Nothing from Tavish, which was odd considering he'd said he'd got into the Emperor's website, and I'd sent him the pictures of the gold coin. I left an update then checked the rest.

Most could be left till later, but Katie wanted me to call, urgently.

I phoned the Spellcrackers' office private line. 'Hey, hon,' I said, 'how's things?'

'Where are you, Gen?' Finn said sharply. 'We need to talk.'

Chapter Thirty-Nine

Surprise at unexpectedly hearing Finn's voice flipped straight into anger. He was supposed to be back in the Fair Lands. But since he was here, and wanted to talk, he could start with an explanation.

'What the hell were you doing answering my personal texts, Finn?'

'You know why, Gen,' he said, exasperated. 'You can't go seeing the sucker out in public.'

'That's my decision, not yours.'

'Yeah, it is,' he agreed, stumping me. 'And you're right; I probably shouldn't have sent that text. I know jealousy isn't cool, but it's more than that, if you want to keep Spellcrackers.'

And here it was: his usual emotional blackmail. Well, I'd made my decision and even if Malik was a cowardly text-dumping over-protective idiot vamp, and our relationship was more likely off than on, I was sticking to it. No way was I going to let Finn, the satyr herd, the witches or anyone else dictate my choices in life. Not to mention if Finn *was* back for good, then Spellcrackers wasn't mine to keep anyway. I nudged my backpack nearer with my foot, resisting the urge to kick it, and dug out a Phone Privacy spell.

'Threats are even less cool than jealousy, Finn,' I snapped as the spell activated and the noise from Trafalgar Square muted. 'Oh, and my keeping Spellcrackers is sort of a moot, as you're back.'

'I know, Gen,' he said, his exasperation turning to apology.

'I've been talking to Tavish, and like him I'll back you all the way. Hell's thorns, I think the herd owe Spellcrackers to you for all the hassle they've caused.' He paused. 'But things will be a lot easier if you stay away from the sucker. If you can, that is.'

Shock rocked through me. Part was his comment about 'staying away from Malik, if I could', though what Finn meant by that was a mystery. But mostly it was down to: 'Did you say you're willing to go against the rest of the satyr herd? To let me keep Spellcrackers? Don't you want it?'

'Gen, I enjoy the job, but a lot of that is working with you. I don't feel any great need to be the boss and to be honest, with Nicky and the baby to look after, I could do without the added responsibility. So, yeah, I'll back you.'

Sincerity rang in his voice, telling me he meant every word. A bubble of happy excitement expanded in me. Finn backing me, and backing down as boss, didn't mean I'd win, but it meant I could fight with a clear conscience, knowing that I wasn't taking anything from him. Only— 'What about you? What will you do?'

'Work for you, of course.' He laughed like it was a joke, though his words held a serious note.

I blinked, astonished. 'You'd want to work for me?'

'Gods, Gen, I'd be happy to.'

I let that idea sink in. We were friends, we made a great team and we'd always had a lot of fun working together. Okay, so it would be different if I was the boss, not Finn. But there was no reason why it couldn't work ... my happy bubble deflated ... except of course, there was. Malik for one. And Finn's evil ex, the Witch-bitch Helen Crane. She might be stuck in the Fair Lands, but she hated me enough that I doubted I'd seen the last of her.

Finn seemed to read my mind. 'Gen, I know you're upset about Helen, but that's over. And if you're thinking the sucker's going to be a problem, then he doesn't have to be. I know about last night. But I want us to be together and I hope we can sort things out.'

I nearly dropped the phone in the fountain. He knew about me and Malik, and he still thought *we* could sort things out? Never mind how the hell did Finn know— Tavish! 'Tavish had no right to tell you.'

'He didn't, Gen. Sylvia told me.'

'Sylvia?' I said, even more betrayed that *she'd* gossiped about me. We were supposed to be friends. 'She had no right, either.'

'Hell's thorns, Gen.' Finn's exasperation boiled up again. 'It's not like it's a secret; all the dryads are talking about what happened on the boating lake last night.'

Crap. I'd forgotten about the trees on the island. They'd have had a ringside seat, literally, and now it would be all over London. Even if Sylvia hadn't told Finn, someone would've given him a blow-by-blow account soon enough. I wanted to crawl under a stone somewhere and hide. Not that I regretted what had happened with Malik, or wouldn't do exactly the same again (though obviously somewhere *way* more private), but hell, why couldn't the damn dryads gossip about anyone else for a change? Not to mention Finn was taking what happened with Malik awfully well, but then I *had* chucked Finn out for playing happy families with the Witch-bitch Helen, so maybe he knew he didn't have a jealous leg to stand on. Not that I wanted him to be jealous. Still, I hated that he'd found out like that. And I needed to tell him that things between us couldn't be sorted out. Not the way he wanted anyway. Only that wasn't the sort of discussion for a phone call.

'Finn, look, I think we should meet up later. Once I've finished here.'

'Sylvia was worried about you,' he replied, as if I hadn't spoken. 'The trees said it was pretty violent, and with Ricou not around she needed someone to reassure her that the sucker hadn't hurt you.' He stopped, then said hesitantly, 'Did he hurt you, Gen?'

'What? No, of course not.'

'Sylvia said she wasn't sure, she'd asked you, and you told her not to worry,' he went on earnestly. 'I know he can order you around, Gen. If you can't tell me, there's ways of getting round it. Just say something, like, oh, he's a bad client. You don't have to protect him.'

Damn it. This was why he was taking things so well; he'd cast Malik as the bad guy, me the damsel in distress and himself as the white knight riding to my rescue. Typical. 'Finn,' I said, trying to keep the irritation out of my voice. 'I'm not protecting Malik. He didn't force me to do' – the magic pricked at me, stopping me from lying – 'what you think.'

Silence. Then, almost as if to himself, he said, 'Sylvia told me the trees said there was some accident and the sucker forced you to drink his blood. But that was all.' A pause as he obviously worked things out. 'Did something more happen, Gen? Something that he didn't force you to do?'

Yes, a lot more. But I thought you knew that. My chest constricted at the pain in his voice. Shit. I bent over, hugging myself. *Way to put your foot in it, Gen!* And what the hell was I supposed to say now?

I took a fortifying breath. 'I'm sorry, Finn,' I said quietly, 'it was ... he was ... I didn't mean for you to find out like that. I was going to tell you when you got back.'

Another, longer silence. Finally: 'You're working with the police on something to do with those kidnappings, aren't you?'

He'd changed the subject. I didn't know whether to be relieved, or cry. I scrubbed my face. 'Yeah.'

'Right. I'll hold the fort here until you're done.' His brisk businesslike tone came out harsher than usual. 'We can talk about this then.'

Crap. Not a subject change, just a postponement. Only I'd

made my choice, and never mind Malik was an idiot, I wasn't going to change my mind. Finn needed to know that. 'No—'

The phone cut out.

I stared at it, warring between heartsick I'd hurt him and annoyed, both at him and myself.

A hand waved in front of my face. 'Earth to Genny!'

I looked up to find Mary smiling quizzically at me. 'What?'

'We're going scrying, remember? For your Cousin Maxim? You get to come along for the ride.'

'Oh, yeah. Sorry.'

'C'mon, then,' she said, and as I followed her to Dessa and her police car, she told me the plan. It sounded like we were going to be driving in ever-expanding circles around Trafalgar Square until they got a hit. All I had to do was sit back and enjoy the ride.

I slide into the back of the car – which was like an oven after being parked in the blazing summer sun – and, as Dessa pulled out into the slow-moving traffic, stifled a yawn. Damn, looked like my restless night, thanks to the Morpheus Memory Aided nightmares, was starting to catch up with me. A nap would be good. Only I had a lot to try to make sense of. I leaned my head back on the seat, thoughts of Mad Max, werewolves, kidnap victims, gossiping dryads, Finn and Malik spinning like dervishes in my mind ...

Malik/I strode through the twists and turns of wide shaded corridors, his/my hand on the sabre's hilt, pantaloons ballooning about our legs, the tall headdress on our head an odd but familiar weight. Our slippered feet marched purposely past the ornately arched and curtained doorways, behind which flowed the constant murmur of female voices. The guards – plump, ebony-skinned eunuchs – bowed their heads, murmuring soft-voiced greetings.

'Abd al-Malik' – *Servant of the King* – 'welcome.'

I slipped further into Malik's dream/memory, acknowledging them, accepting their respect, but not stopping as the dream/memory drew me along its path.

Soon I halted at the entrance to a small courtyard garden. Gleaming mosaics patterned the courtyard's walls in a geometric design that spoke of the Middle East, fan-shaped palms cast welcome shade, a breeze carried exotic floral scents and the quiet splash of the corner fountain was a soft relaxing music. Above, the sky stretched an endless blue, a blazing sun throwing down a fierce midday heat.

In the centre of the courtyard sat a woman in her mid-twenties swathed in layers of jewel-encrusted fabric, topped with a short embroidered waistcoat. Her glossy brunette hair cascaded in was to her hips from beneath a fez-style hat atop a headscarf, also encrusted with its own fortune in gems, as she tended to the black-haired baby girl lying on the colourful rug in front of her. The baby was in the middle of being changed, arms waving, legs kicking free, giggling as her mother tickled gentle fingers over her tummy. Sitting on the rug close to them was another child: a solemn-looking girl of about six, her hair the same glossy black as the baby's, dressed in a miniature version of the mother's bright, jewel-covered outfit. The girl cradled a doll in her arms, rocking it back and forth, her mouth murmuring a quiet lullaby.

The memory stilled as if I'd pressed pause.

I, not Malik, recognised the girl. It was Fur Jacket Girl, the werewolf I'd seen at the mosque, and then again in the memory I'd had at the zoo, where she'd been chained in the ash circle in the snow, her mate lying dead nearby. This was her as a child.

Malik had *known her. She'd meant* something *to him. That's why he'd been full of rage and had killed her mate.*

Even as shock stuttered within me, the memory started up again.

311

Behind the woman and children stood a tall boy of around nine or ten, head down, arms crossed over his thin chest, bad-temper radiating from his stance. He was dressed in a miniature version of Malik's/my clothes: a tall headdress atop his turban, pantaloons, and a floor-length crimson coat that brushed the gem-sewn slippers on his feet. And secured through the embroidered belt around his waist was a curved sabre, similar to the one I carried, a man's blade and not a child's toy.

I stepped into the courtyard and the woman looked up, giving me a smile full of welcome and love.

'Malik, *canımın içi*' – *light of my soul* – she called. 'You are home. Safe. I trust the campaign goes well?'

The memory sharpened and I drank in the woman's beauty; her huge, thickly lashed, dark eyes, porcelain-pale skin touched with the sun's blush, the perfect lines of her cheek and jaw, the tiny black crescent inked at the corner of her lush mouth.

The moment broke as child-Fur Jacket Girl jumped up and flung herself at me. I caught her, lifting her high in the air to a delighted squeal, then kissed her cheek as I carried her back to her mother. I set her on the rug as her mother offered me the baby. As she did, her sleeves fell back to reveal intricate tattoos like black vines twisting up her arms. Dropping an affectionate kiss on the woman's forehead I took the chubby baby into my arms and tickled her tummy as her mother had done. She smelled of sweet herbs and aloes. I laughed as she giggled with innocent happiness.

A sharp cough vied for my attention and I saw a shadow flit through the woman's eyes. I handed the baby back and turned to the boy. He was still staring at his slippered feet, his bad temper more pronounced.

'Emir,' I said, sketching a bow.

'*Çorbaci*' – *Commander* – 'Abd al-Malik. Welcome.' He

returned my bow. Then he raised his eyes to mine, his mouth splitting wide in a knowing grin.

The memory froze again.

I, not Malik, knew that grin, even with its slightly crooked, still human teeth.

Last time I'd seen the boy I'd been fourteen and it was our wedding night. He hadn't been a child then but a six-foot-tall gangly fifteen-year-old. Or at least, that was the age he'd looked; as a vamp he was however many centuries old. But it didn't matter how childish he appeared in this dream/memory, no way could I ever forget the spiteful way his lips curved. Or the lust for others' pain that shone in his large, doe-like brown eyes.

He was the Autarch – Bastien – my psychotic murdering betrothed.

'Hello, my sidhe princess,' the boy-Bastien said, as if we'd last met days ago instead of eleven years.

Terror-induced adrenalin flooded my veins. I forced myself to take a calming breath, and then another. This was Malik's memory, twisted into nightmare. A side-effect of the Morpheus Memory Aid interacting with his blood. Just like at the zoo. Nothing more. Bastien wasn't real, which meant he couldn't hurt me. But despite my mental bolstering, I still flinched as his hand clasped the scimitar and he rolled his shoulders back in the same way that had been a prelude to him wielding another sword on my faeling friend that betrothal night. Finally killing her after days of torture. And I couldn't stop myself instinctively shuffling backwards to put more space between us until I bumped into the courtyard wall.

'You're not real,' I whispered.

He laughed, darting to me and pinching my arm. It hurt, and I froze, shaking with panic. 'Real is a mutable term, princess,' he admonished. 'Particularly when you are trespassing in someone else's memories.'

I swallowed. 'Yours?'

'Come now, sidhe. Let's not spoil our reunion with stupidity.' He threw his arms wide to encompass the woman, the girl and the baby. 'This vision of domestic sentimentality is certainly not something I would desire to relive.' He leaned towards me and I pressed myself harder into the wall as he sniffed. 'And then there is the nasty little irritation that you stink of Abd al-Malik's blood.'

This is a nightmare. Nothing more.

Only even as I told myself to wake up, I knew I wouldn't. Somehow I'd blundered – *or been pulled?* – into the Dreamscape; where dreams and reality mix.

And now I was trapped there with the one person who churned my guts liquid with horror.

The boy-Bastien's nostrils flared again. 'Not only *his* blood, but sex too. My, my, what have you and my ever-faithful commander been up to, my lovely bride, that you smell so deliciously tasty?'

No way was he biting me. Or fucking me. Or using his sword on me. I'd die first. *Or, said the scared child-voice in my mind, more likely after …*

'But sadly, I am not allowed to play with you, my princess.' He stepped back and I sagged against the wall in relief. 'Not yet, anyway, not until my pact with my commander is done. But them I *can* play with' – he indicated the woman and children on the rug, then lifted one elegant brow – 'so which one shall I pick, my bride?' He pointed a contemptuous finger at the woman. 'Shall it be the beautiful Shpresa, my father's favoured *Ikbal*, despite her opening her legs for any who choose to defile her? Or her youngest, Aisha, the little parcel of precious humanity that squeals like a stuck pig at her knees and takes all her attention?' He moved to stand behind the child-Fur Jacket Girl cradling her doll, and reached out to stroke her hair, jealousy twisting his mouth. 'Or perhaps her other daughter, the delectable Dilek.' Child-Fur Jacket Girl frowned, feeling his touch if not hearing his voice, and hunched away from him. 'Such young flesh Dilek has, so very pure and innocent.'

Nausea roiled in my stomach at the thought of what he might do. At what he might make me watch. Again.

The dream/memory started up again; this time it scrolled in front of me like a film I was watching.

Boy-Bastien bent to Dilek's ear, saying something in a language I didn't understand. A look of fear, quickly masked, crossed her face, and she turned to yell defiantly at him. He laughed nastily, pinching her cheek and, as she batted him away, grabbed her doll, holding it tauntingly aloft. She shouted, desperately jumping up to rescue the doll from him.

The woman, Shpresa, looked up from swaddling the baby, her expression the resigned one of mothers everywhere when children goad each other. She called out sharply, gesturing at Bastien to give the doll back. Bastien nodded, holding the doll by its head and feet as he offered it to the crying Dilek. As she went to take it, he shot a 'watch this' look in my direction and shoved the doll into Dilek's small chest. She stumbled back and he jerked his arms gleefully apart, ripping the doll's head from its body and tossing the decapitated parts into the corner fountain.

Dilek burst into anguished tears. Her mother gathered her up into a hug, and spoke to Bastien in a disappointed tone that indicated this wasn't the first such incident. He shrugged his bony shoulders, a mock air of contriteness not quite hiding his satisfaction. Shpresa spoke again, pointing at the baby, and he sidled past her, surreptitiously yanking Dilek's hair as he did so. As Dilek bawled louder, Bastien snatched the baby up, gripping her under her arms and dangling her at arm's length. She wriggled, little arms and legs waving as he gave me a calculating glance and the dream/memory halted again.

'Babies are such fragile things,' he said, throwing the

squealing baby into the air and catching her just before she hit the paving slabs. 'Much like a child's doll. Don't you agree, my lovely sidhe?'

My heart thudded with impending dread. 'Put her down.'

He smiled. 'Come and join me fully in the Dreamscape.'

'No.' The word was out my mouth before I could think.

'A pity. She is not as sweet as sidhe blood, I warrant, but sweet enough for me to indulge myself.' Bastien licked his lips and buried his face in the baby's tummy. She squirmed with a pain-filled gurgle, then he turned her to face me. Fang marks pierced her small round stomach, bright blood dripping from the tiny, neat holes. 'Shall I feast on this plump chicken, tear its tiny limbs, suck on its marrow, crack its head like an almond and gorge myself on its infant mind? Shall I do all that while you watch and listen to its screams? Or will you join me, my princess?'

No fucking way. But despite knowing the baby was only part of whatever twisted nightmare/illusion Bastien was making, my fear of what he might make me watch unglued my feet. I took a step towards him and said, 'Yes.'

The baby, the woman, the child-Fur Jacket Girl and the courtyard disappeared.

The white sloping walls of my attic bedroom snapped into focus around me.

It was night. The room dimly lit by the moonlight shining through the window. I was dressed in my usual sleep vest and shorts. But even as my mind tried to reject the change, a hand gripped my throat, fingers digging in, almost but not quite choking, and jerked me up on to my feet so Bastien could stare down at me. The gangly boy was gone; in his place was the grinning, teenage six-foot-plus Autarch. He flashed sharp fangs, a triumphant expression on his teenage face.

Chapter Forty

'Well, well, my lovely sidhe princess. I am delighted you have agreed to join me fully in the Dreamscape.' He raked his gaze down my body then his mouth twisted. He ripped my vest top down the front and prodded disdainfully at the rose-coloured bruises marking my breasts and belly. 'Although I must remark you were prettier at fourteen; now you appear to be damaged goods.'

I punched him in the gut. He doubled over, the metallic stink of recently ingested blood belching from his surprised mouth, his fingers loosening on my throat. I followed with an uppercut to his chin, snapping his head backwards. Then I reached up, grabbed his ears, yanked his head down and headbutted him on the bridge of his nose, hearing the satisfying crunch of bone. I shoved him, wondering why he wasn't fighting back. Was it surprise or luck? And how long before I ran out of both? He staggered slightly, and as he swiped at the blood streaming from his broken nose, fell on to his butt, laughing.

I clenched my right fist.

A ball of angry dragonfire erupted from the emerald ring on my hand.

And Ascalon sprung into my grip.

I didn't know if you could die in the Dreamscape, but if you could, then I was going to kill Bastien.

Adjusting my grip around the knobbed hilt, I slashed it through the air, aiming for where Bastien's neck would be when he automatically ducked.

317

He didn't duck.

The sword hit his shoulder, the sharp blade slicing through his torso as if he wasn't there. It exited the other side of his body and I moved back, automatically falling into a ready stance as I held my breath, eager for the top half of him to tumble off and blood to spurt like we were in some sort of CGI film.

It didn't.

Instead he laughed again and, as time seemed to slow, his doe-brown eyes filled with viscous red blood, blotting out his pupil, iris and sclera. Mesmerised, I stared, expecting the blood to spill like tears down his cheeks. Instead, bone cracked as his nose reset itself, the blood on his face disappearing back into his skin as he healed. His lips curved in a cruel smile and he jumped up, stuck his arm out and closed his fingers around my neck again. His nails dug into my throat, piercing the flesh with needle-sharp pain, and I felt hot wetness trickle down my chest.

My pulse thundered in my ears. Ascalon had cut through him. The sword was blessed and bespelled to kill all unless they were an innocent. Bastien was no innocent. But Ascalon had done nothing. Did that mean you couldn't die in the Dreamscape? Yet I'd hurt him. He was hurting me now. And I was bleeding. So why the fuck hadn't it cleaved his torso in two? Why wasn't he dead? Had I imagined I'd hit him? Maybe he'd moved vamp-fast and I hadn't registered it.

Gritting my teeth, I tried again, a two-handed thrust up through his gut, aiming for his heart. Again the sword met no resistance, only this time his body seemed to shimmer translucently for a millisecond. Then he chopped at my wrists and elbows in quick succession. I cried out, agonising pain shooting through both arms as bones broke, and the sword clattered to the floorboards from my useless hands.

'Stop moving, my pretty sidhe, else I will rip out your throat.'

He leaned closer and opened his blood-soaked eyes wide. 'Losing the muscle, sinew, tendons, blood vessels, cartilage, windpipe and voicebox *hurts*. Even one as difficult to kill as you will find it hard to heal that.'

He was right. I *knew* he was right. I *knew* I might not heal it at all. I *had* to do as he said. It was the only way ...

I frowned at the thoughts in my head. They sounded wrong ...

He touched his tongue to his fangs. 'Or don't. I would enjoy fucking you while you suffocate and drown in your own blood.'

Panic froze me as memories of my wedding night and him killing my friend, Sally, slammed into me. I *had* to do as he said. I stopped struggling. His pressure on my throat increased, almost cutting off my air. I forced myself to stay still, to stare back stoically as my lungs heaved for breath, to concentrate on calming my pulse, even as my vision greyed around the edges. He watched me intently for what felt like hours, then his hand at my throat relaxed slightly. I gasped for oxygen before I could stop myself.

'I see you understand, my pretty sidhe.' He sighed. 'Although I find it disappointing.' He hooked his fingers into my briefs and tore them off. Fear clenched my stomach and I forced myself to stay still. He contemplated me like I was a bug pinned under a microscope, and started poking at Malik's rose-petal bruises again. I tensed, skin crawling at his touch, the small pains insignificant to the fiery ones in my wrists. As his prodding moved lower, I desperately searched my mind for what little I knew about the Dreamscape. The only time I'd been here before was via Malik's ring: I'd put the ring on to enter and he'd taken it off to make me leave. Or rather, to wake me up. While I was here, I was asleep in real life. That meant all I had to do to escape was wake up. But without Malik's ring to remove, I didn't know how. It hit me I was trapped in the

Dreamscape with Bastien. Despair filtered into my mind. My recurring nightmare made real.

He gave my throat a quick squeeze. 'Now, I am going to ask you a question. I know a sidhe cannot lie, but know I want you to answer only yes or no. No prevarication, do you understand?'

'Yes,' I gasped, my lungs struggling for breath.

'You reek of Malik and sex,' he said, voice soft. 'Has my commander filled you with his seed, my bride?'

Shock sparked like lightning. '*What?!*'

'Answer me.'

'No,' I croaked. Where the hell was this going?

He frowned then slid his hand down my belly and between my legs. I shuddered in fear and disgust as his finger penetrated for an instant. He brought it up to his nose, sniffed and then licked it.

'You are correct,' he said.

Indignant anger rose. He hadn't believed me. 'Sidhe,' I spat, 'can't fucking lie.'

His mouth thinned. 'He has wanted you for a long time. He has even marked you.' He poked a bruise on my left breast and I forced myself not to squirm. 'But he has still not made you his, even though the spell should have done away with his resistance by now. It is a puzzle.'

It wasn't the only one. For some weird reason, it sounded like he wanted Malik and me to have sex. Had encouraged it, even. The utter improbability of the Autarch 'matchmaking', allied to my earlier indignation, shattered something in my head. 'What spell?'

He touched his forehead. 'The one lodged within the delta brand.'

The sadistic Jellyfish spell I'd removed. Bastien's gaze narrowed as he saw recognition on my face. 'Well, well, my princess, it seems I underestimated you ...' He licked his lips, his gaze skating hungrily down my body.

Think! There had to be a way out of this.

'You are not afraid of me,' he said thoughtfully. 'Why not?'

I stared at him. He really was insane as well as psychotic if he didn't think I was scared.

He tapped my forehead. 'You are afraid here, but not here.' He tapped over my heart. 'You were before, but now you are not. Why not?'

I blinked. He was right. In the last few seconds I'd lost my mind-numbing terror of him. Not that I didn't think he'd hurt me, but he wasn't the big, bad, bogey-vamp of my fourteen-year-old nightmares any more. He was just another sucker, after all— And suckers could get into your mind. Make you think and feel and see anything they wanted with a combination of *mesma,* vamp mind-mojo and illusion. And I was the stupid idiot who'd forgotten it.

Bastien squeezed my throat. 'There are not many who do not fear me, my sidhe princess. I find it *interesting.*'

May you live in interesting times.

The ambiguous Chinese saying flashed in my head, and I decided it was time this got interesting for him.

'You're not real,' I whispered. 'You have no substance. You are nothing but your thoughts in the Dreamscape.' That was why the sword, Ascalon, hadn't cut him. I'd have realised it earlier if not for my stupid childish panic. His other injuries had just been him playing with me. Using them to convince me that if I could hurt him, then he could hurt me. I stepped back.

His fingers didn't unclench, but they didn't rip my throat out either.

'You're not here,' I said with more emphasis, lifting my arms as the pain and illusion they were broken vanished. 'You. Are. Not. Real.'

'I am real, sidhe.' He waved his hand and the beautiful woman, the girl, the baby and the young Bastien, with Malik standing next to them, reappeared behind him. The five were in the sun-bright courtyard with its gleaming mosaic walls the same as when I'd first seen them in Malik's memory, but the picture overlaid my bedroom like a holograph or a vamp-conjured illusion. 'Just as they were real once. My loyal commander couldn't save them— Save us,' he amended, with an oddly conflicted expression, 'when the Emperor came before.'

'You. Are. Not. Here,' I said, and taking a deep breath, I walked straight through him and out of my bedroom door.

'Now the Emperor comes again, my sidhe princess.'

I woke up in the back of the police car.

'And only you can save ...' His voice faded like morning mist banished by the sun.

The car was parked in a layby in front of a row of local community shops; a launderette, a newsagent, an off-licence, a boarded-up video rental place, a Subway and a butcher's. And I was alone. A scrawled note on my lap, addressed to Sleeping Beauty, said Mary and Dessa were checking out a possible hit on their scrying and would be back soon. Something I was grateful for, as my reaction to tangling with Bastien suddenly made itself felt.

I just had time to stick my head out of the open car window (having discovered I was locked in) before my stomach revolted. Vomiting into the gutter, I tried not to think about exactly how and where Bastien had touched me. It didn't matter that he hadn't shown up physically, that our meeting had been in the Dreamscape; it still felt like he'd violated me. I heaved again, catching sight of the feet of passers-by in my peripheral vision. No one stopped; the one advantage to puking your guts out from the inside of a marked police car. Even if the police were nowhere in sight.

My heaves finally subsided and I grabbed a bottle of water from my bag, rinsed away the sour taste of regurgitated orange juice (thankful I'd had nothing more than that and vodka for hours), then used the rest to sluice my mess down the nearby drain, wishing I could flush psycho Bastien away as easily. I shoved the empty bottle back in my bag. Next time I ran into the sadistic bastard in real life, I was going to kill him.

Though I might ask him a few questions first. Like why he was so hot for me and Malik to get together? Whatever the reason, there was no way it was for my, or Malik's, benefit. Bastien was the spoilt, spiteful, dog-in-the-manger type; the type that would break their unwanted toys rather than sharing ... as he'd done to child-Fur Jacket Girl's doll in Malik's dream/memory.

Part of me didn't want to think too closely about that dream/memory. Didn't want to speculate who the woman was. Or what part she and her three children, especially Bastien, had played in Malik's past life. But another part couldn't not think about it. I dug my phone out along with a fresh bottle of water (a replacement, thanks to the same spell that was on our fridge), and drank it, my heart fluttering like an anxious bird's, as I did some Googling.

Malik's memory had taken me to a harem. Though the place had seemed so much less decadent than I'd always imagined harems to be – not that I'd thought about them much – the silent, ebony-skinned eunuchs standing guard over unseen chattering women, along with what Malik had told me about being friends with Suleiman, an Ottoman sultan, meant the place couldn't be anything else but a harem.

Various sites told me that Muslim households had a harem – secluded, protected living quarters for the wives, concubines, children, female relatives and (in the past) slaves – whether it be one room or many, like those in the famous Topkapi Palace, Istanbul. Malik's memory had showed him right at home in the harem, but the only males allowed were eunuchs or relations. Malik was *so* not the former, which meant he had to be the latter.

Brother, uncle, cousin, nephew, son … *husband*.

The woman, Shpresa, had been in her mid-twenties. As had Malik. Bastien had called her his father's *Ikbal*— favourite concubine. Said that his commander – *Malik* – had tried to save the woman and her kids … *save us* … from the Emperor.

Did that mean the woman was Malik's wife? That they were Malik's kids? Only if it did, then Bastien, my psychotic, murdering betrothed, was Malik's—

Son?

Denial and horror hit me like a sucker punch to the gut. My stomach heaved again, and I only just managed to keep the water down. I slumped down in the back seat, wishing I could crawl home, take a blisteringly hot shower and huddle in bed with a bottle of vodka or ten for a week.

Only that wasn't an option.

Ten minutes later, Mary returned, jumped into the car and slammed her door with a frustrated bang, which made my head ring and told me clearer than words that the scrying hadn't panned out. I swiped a furtive hand over my damp face – not from tears, well, not *just* from tears, but from retching half-a-dozen times more; my Hot. D postponed hangover had decided to make its appearance (figured, I wouldn't get the whole twelve hours out of the damn spell), complete with a headache that felt like imps were munching on my brain.

Mary twisted to face me. 'We're going to head— Cripes, Genny, what happened to you? You look like warmed-up death.'

'Took a Hot. D this morning.' I cut a squinty look at the sunshine. 'Got an early rebound.'

'Those things are barely legal.' She gave me her cop face then wrinkled her nose. 'You've been sick?'

I nodded, then wished I hadn't as a wave of dizziness swept over me and my stomach rebelled.

Her mouth pinched with worry. 'Are you going to be okay?'

Unsaid was: we were in the middle of a scrying. Stopping now would mean losing the trail. But before I could say I'd survive, Dessa dived into the driver's seat clutching a bag of fast food.

My stomach heaved again at the greasy smell and I clapped a hand over my mouth, missing what Mary said next.

'Here, Genny, have this.' A hand shoved a small lavender-coloured envelope under my nose with a picture of a serene-looking woman on the front. The spiel underneath said ~ *Revive the Perfect You!* A Reviver, or a Cinderella as they're known in the trade. Cinderella spells were expensive.

'It's legit,' Dessa added as I hesitated. 'Not like the Power Nap patch. Present from my mum. I've been keeping it in case I ever land myself a hot date.' Her face scrunched up in a wry look. 'I've got a toddler, a job and no time. I need to be prepared and I need all the help I can get. Only downside is a headache the next day.'

'Thanks,' I said, taking the envelope; another postponed headache had to be better than hours of vomiting. 'I'll get you another.' I pulled out the pale lavender patch – it smelled of lavender too – peeled off the backing and stuck it, as per instructions, on the back of my neck. For a second nothing happened, then it felt as if I'd been cocooned in cool silk for about five minutes. As the feeling dissipated, I felt like I'd just had a week's relaxing spa holiday; my worries and fears were surmountable, and no matter what life, or a sadistic vamp, threw at me next, I could handle it.

'Wow!' Mary said. 'I didn't know those things were that good. You look a million quid, Genny.'

'I feel it too.' I grinned, eyeing my healthy-looking, perfectly understated made-up face in the rearview mirror and smoothing my hand over my glossy hair. My clothes all looked and felt like stylish, high-end stuff, instead of the chain store basics they actually were.

'Seriously, girlfriend,' Dessa said, shaking her cornrowed head in admiration, 'that Cinderella's the business. If I wasn't straight, I'd be panting right now.'

I reached out and squeezed her shoulder, grateful. 'Thanks, Dessa. I needed this.' I turned to Mary. 'Before we get back to scrying I've got a question about werewolves.' Or about Fur Jacket Girl in particular. If she really was the young girl, Dilek, in Malik's memory – *his daughter?* – who'd been changed into a werewolf, she had to be nearly as old as Malik. 'Do you know how long they live?'

Mary frowned. 'Interesting question. Don't suppose you're going to tell me why you're asking?'

'I will, but later, okay?' I said, deliberately not looking at Dessa.

Mary got the message. 'Okay. Well, the archives say that if therianthropes get the Death Bite, then they live a normal human lifespan. If they're Born therianthrope or Changed by Ritual, then they can live hundreds of years, though I don't know why exactly. Something about them being both animal and human, which all shifters are.' She shrugged. 'So that doesn't really make any sense. But I've only read the first section. There're pages more.'

'Thanks,' I said. So it *was* possible for Fur Jacket Girl to be half-a-millenia old. Which meant she *was* more than likely Bastien's sister and Malik's daughter. She was also one of the Emperor's werewolves. I hadn't a clue how that all fitted together. Or even how I felt about it.

'Right, ladies.' Mary held up her scrying pendant. 'Time to get back to work. See if we can't find this missing Irish wolfhound.'

*

Half an hour later we were still driving around searching for another hit. Then, as we passed the fifteen-foot bronze of Freddie Mercury rocking it outside the Dominion Theatre, my phone rang. Unknown number.

'You need to come to the Carnival at Regent's Park.' The voice was muffled, as if the person was trying to disguise it. 'Your dog is here.'

Pulse speeding, I pressed speakerphone and tapped Mary's shoulder. 'My dog is at the Carnival?'

'Yes. The Irish wolfhound. He's here.'

Mary made 'keep talking' motions with her hands. I nodded and said, 'The Carnival's a big place. Where exactly is he? And who are—'

The phone went dead.

'Hung up,' I told Mary, disappointed not to have more info. 'Still, at least it's a lead.'

'It's a trap,' she said briskly.

'Then why not tell me exactly where to go?'

'So you can't tell the police, of course. And once you're in among the crowds, it's easier to snatch you and make you disappear.'

'Nice,' I muttered. 'But we're still going to follow it up, aren't we?'

She gave me her cop face. 'The police are, yes. *You* are not. Now let me have your phone so I can see if I can get a trace on that call.' She held her hand out. I handed the phone over with a scowl, determined Mary wasn't going to leave me to sit this one out while she and her witches in blue went looking for Mad Max. By the time Dessa pulled into the temporary Carnival car park opposite Regent's Park Mosque, I'd managed to convince Mary to let me tag along.

'But only if you remember you're a civilian, Genny,' she said firmly. 'No running off on your own again, especially not after what just happened in Trafalgar Square. You're their intended target and I'm not losing you. I'm bending the rules as it is letting you join the search, so either you agree to stick with me or I'll take you into police custody for your own safety and lock you in the car until we're finished.'

Looking into Mary's implacable face, I saluted smartly. 'Yes, ma'am!'

'Okay,' Mary said, 'let's get organised, shall we?'

Chapter Forty-One

I nodded then realised Mary's question was rhetorical, as she went into full Detective Sergeant mode. She and Dessa scryed again for Mad Max – using a visitor's map of the Carnival this time – and came up with a possible hit in the north section nearest the zoo. It should have made Mad Max an easy find, if the north wasn't the section with over a hundred of the smaller shows, all crammed together in what was meant to give visitors 'a surprise around every corner'. The surprise for us would be finding Mad Max at all, as the search was going to be like looking for a tick on a dog's back.

Mary snagged some extra manpower from the nearby investigation at the zoo, and within half an hour the section was divided up and five separate search parties, each consisting of three WPCs and a troll – I got to tag along with Mary, Dessa, another WPC and Constable Taegrin: 'safety in numbers' as Mary said – headed out.

The Carnival Fantastique has always been a place for Others to make a living, either by exploiting their own, or another's, rarity. And the north section of the carnival was the area reserved for the less usual acts. So the place wasn't only crammed with shows but was also chock-full of visitors, the majority human, but with a smattering of fae, faelings and Other folk, all eager to catch sight of something, or someone, different.

Finally Mary's scrying crystal flashed faster as we turned into a short, dead-end lane with only four stalls, all of which had seen better days, and a corresponding scarcity of visitors: two women at a spell and potions stall looking at a marble pestle and mortar; a burly man buying a phoenix burger (in a fireproof bun) from a fast food bar manned by a chipped concrete troll; no one at the Ring-a-Rat, which wasn't a surprise considering the weird-looking, two-headed rodents scuttling around the stall's circular track; and at a herbalist's barrow near the willow wall making up the end, a young couple who were more interested in each other than any herbs, judging by the way they were lip-locked together.

The tourists (apart from the lip-locked couple) looked round as the five of us invaded the lane. The women's eyes widened with curiosity while the burly man grabbed his burger and high-tailed it away, to a narrow-eyed frown from Constable Taegrin.

Mary checked her crystal against the map. It pointed at the decorative willow wall blocking the end. 'We'll have to double round.'

Something about the location snagged my memory and I jogged to the wall. At its centre was a woven willow arch backed with mirrored foil. A label stuck to the foil quoted: *Extend your garden vista safely: won't scratch, chip or crack.* And as I squinted at my distorted reflection, it clicked where we were.

'We won't need to,' I called. 'This is an entrance to one of the Other areas. It's got a Look-Away on it.'

Out the corner of my eye, I saw the lip-locked couple pull apart. The girl – a pretty, freckled redhead – nudged her boyfriend, who was well worth the tonsil tangling, if tall, dark and handsome flipped your switch; obviously it did hers—

And Katie's too.

I stared in disbelief.

Tall, dark and handsome was Katie's new boyfriend. Marc.

Marc's eyes met mine curiously for a moment then, as he

realised who I was, colour stained his cheeks and he turned away, suddenly very interested in showing his redhead *girl-friend* whatever was on the barrow.

I clenched my fists, wanting to grab him and ask him what the hell he was playing at. This was going to break Katie's heart when she found out. Crap. I knew the guy was too good to be true.

'You all right?' Mary said quietly as she and Dessa joined me.

'Yeah,' I muttered, glaring at Marc's back. 'Sorry—' I stopped as, from behind another section of willow screen, two more figures appeared: an older male I recognised as Marc's uncle from their picture on their plant nursery website, and a small, squat and disgustingly familiar gnome: Mr Lampy. The gnome was followed by one of his cats, its tail held high. Marc bent to stroke it, nearly managing to hide himself under the stall as he did so. Well, looked like he *had* been telling the truth when I'd caught him spying on me, about speaking to one of the gnome's cats before doing business with Lecherous Lampy. Not that it made me feel any better. Neither did the fact that as the gnome saw me, he waved, mouth splitting into his awful denture-filled leer.

I half-heartedly lifted a hand in greeting then suppressed a groan as he rushed over.

'Ms Taylor, how fortunate to see you here.' His beady eyes leered from behind his round glasses. 'Doing a bit of shopping are you? I've got some juicy worms marinated in sugar syrup with deadnettles if you're interested? Jarred for portability? I know you fairies like those.'

Dessa made a choked noise behind me as I said, 'I'm not a fairy, Mr Lampy, I'm a sidhe. And I'm not shopping. I'm here on official business.' I waved a hand at the four police officers. He had to be blind if he couldn't see them.

'Of course.' The gnome nodded his lichen-covered head

agreeably. 'I won't hold you up, then, but you haven't forgotten about my licences, have you?'

Out-of-season desiccated dead garden fairies are hard to forget, much as I wanted to. 'No,' I said. 'I'll get back to you as soon as I can, Mr Lampy.'

'Wonderful, Ms Taylor.' He turned away, then spun back and leaned in way too close to my chest. I stepped back, bumping into Dessa. 'There was another small item,' the gnome said in a conspiratorial voice. 'The pathway on Primrose Hill seems to have developed a problem. Perhaps you could look at it sometime?'

Pathway? I frowned … Oh, right, there was a small patch of *Between* tagging Primrose Hill to some of London's other green spaces that acted as a shortcut for a lot of fae. It wasn't really anything to do with me or Spellcrackers, but …

'What's the problem?'

He clasped his sausage-like fingers over his pot-belly. 'I'm not really sure, Ms Taylor. I haven't seen it for myself, just heard a rumour.'

'Fine. I'll look into it.' Anything to get rid of him.

'Wonderful.' The gnome gave me anther denture-blinding smile and hurried back to his stall. The freckled redhead was still there talking to Marc's uncle. The gnome's cat had been joined by another, and the pair were under the barrow, ears flat and bottle-brush tails suggesting a spat was in the offing. But Marc had obviously made himself scarce. Damn. I was going to have to break the bad news about him to Katie; so not a conversation I wanted to have.

'Juicy worms?' Mary murmured. I shot her a look and she held her hands up. 'Hey, just asking.'

'Sorry. Disgusting client.'

'Yeah, I can see that,' she agreed, her sympathy only just edging out her mirth, then got back to business and indicated the willow arch with its mirror. 'How do we get through?'

'Just walk,' I said. 'It's an Illusion spell designed to stop anyone entering by accident.' I stepped towards the mirror, only to have Mary's hand clamped on my arm.

'Genny,' she warned, 'we're doing this by the book, remember? Which means we need backup.' She thumbed her radio. It crackled into life.

I sighed impatiently as Mary gave out orders, then pursed my lips at the pretty redhead, wondering if she knew her boyfriend was chatting up seventeen-year-olds on the side. And wondering why she wasn't slapping the disgusting gnome for so patently leering at her cleavage while bagging up what looked like a sheaf of A4 pages and various concoctions for Marc's brother. Why on earth would a nurseryman want all those magical ingredients? Curious. I pinged him: human. The girl, though, had a touch of fae, or maybe witch, blood—

'Okay.' Mary clicked off her radio, and I put the gnome and Katie's treacherous boyfriend away to deal with later. 'Backup's on its way in ten.' She motioned to the other WPC. 'Constable, wait here for them, and while you do take statements from the stallholders.' She extended her baton with its jade-tipped Stun spell and pointed it at the mirror. 'Constable Taegrin leads the way, as he's less likely to be affected by any magical attack. I'll go next, then Constable Dessa. Genny goes last. That way if there's anything dodgy on the other side, she'll be protected.'

Taegrin nodded grimly as Dessa extended her own baton with a ferocious snap. 'Yes, ma'am!'

'You know I could snag your Stun spells before either of you could blink, don't you?' I said drily.

Mary shook her head. 'Doesn't matter, Genny, you're still a civilian. Now, is there anything you can tell me about what to expect?'

I shifted through my mental Carnival files, and as it clicked exactly which Other area this was, an errant moment of mischief made me say, 'A few shows, nothing special.'

'Let's go, then.'

Taegrin ducked under the willow arch, disappearing through the mirror. Mary and Dessa followed, and like the good little civilian I was, I brought up the rear. The mirror's illusion slipped over me like a chill breeze, and I found myself standing between my three protectors, in a visitor-free clearing, ringed by half-a-dozen exhibition tents. And when I say exhibition, I mean *exhibition*!

I'd read the shows' listings on the Carnival's manifest, but words on paper couldn't compare. For a moment I stood and stared with the rest.

Tents one to three, respectively, offered: *Dwarf Smelting ~ Golden Showers a Speciality*, *Sing-a-Long Sea Shanties with Susie the Siren* and *Swan Maiden Dancing*. Though if the gaudy painting of a swan-headed girl, scantily clad in white feathers and wrapping her long legs round a pole, was right, it definitely wasn't the usual 'suitable for children' show.

Standing in front of the next tent were two male centaurs, all arrogant expressions, handlebar moustaches and oiled, pumped-up muscles. The sign above them offered *Heavenly Rides*. Tent five's door flap was down, its sign turned round with 'Closed' scrawled across it in purple ink.

Sitting outside the last, rainbow-decorated tent was a small, green-skinned, pointy-eared leprechaun in a green cloak with his nose in a book titled *Silver-Tongued Devil*. At his feet sat a hairless cat in a blue-knitted jumper, leg in the air as it studiously washed its junk, and surrounding both were stacked huge foot-high balls of multi-coloured string. Behind them stood a massive bull-headed figure, hand on cocked hip, wearing a Spandex one-piece in shiny pink that did nothing to hide the figure's melon-like boobs, nor its thick salami-like erection flanked by what looked like a pair of overlarge apples. A rainbow-shaped sign hanging in the tent doorway challenged all-comers to *Chase the Minotaur to the Pot of Gold ~ String £50!*

'Fifty quid for a ball of string,' Dessa muttered, breaking the stunned silence. 'Even for a pot of gold, that's a bit rich, isn't it?'

The bull-headed figure pointed an admonishing pink-lacquered finger at her. 'I'll have you know fifty smackers is peanuts, luv,' he said in a surprisingly high-pitched voice. The Spandex was as tight as it looked. Or maybe he was a she. 'Why, the King of the Dark Elves himself forked out a thousand times that for the honour of chasing me.'

'He's not worth it,' the centaur on the left said, sneering through his moustache. 'You fancy a ride, witch, then I'm the one to put your money on. Old Mini over there lives up to his name.'

'Yes, indeed!' The other centaur looked down his nose at the pink-Spandexed minotaur. 'I can categorically say that with Mini, what you see is certainly not what you get. That's nothing but a distasteful plastic extension.'

O-*kay!*

Mini the Minotaur stuck both hands on his pink-covered hips, thrust them out and shrilled, 'I'll have you know Major-Me is a truly fully-functioning part of me.'

The leprechaun gave us a tired look from under bushy green eyebrows. 'Bespelled,' he murmured.

'O'Keefe!' Mini cuffed him on his pointy ear and squeaked, 'Shut up!'

'What's bespelled?' Dessa asked.

O'Keefe jabbed his thumb over his shoulder at Mini. 'His strap-on.'

I choked, swallowing back a laugh.

'A bespelled strap-on?' Taegrin growled. 'More like an offensive weapon.'

Mary rounded on me, accusation in her eyes. 'Nothing interesting!'

I widened my own eyes in mock innocence. 'How was I to know you had a thing for ginormous strap-ons?'

Her scowl promised retribution. 'Right,' she said briskly, turning to address the stallholders and holding up her badge. 'We're looking for an Irish wolfhound. His name's Max.'

The silence was deafening. And no Mad Max rushed up, wagging his doggy tail in greeting.

'We know he's here,' she carried on, showing them the scrying crystal, which was now glowing a deep blue, indicating Mad Max should be near enough to see if not actually touch. 'So who wants to tell me what they know?'

The two centaurs snorted and suddenly seemed to find their hooves extremely interesting. Mini produced an industrial-sized file from nowhere and proceeded to give his pink-painted nails an unneeded manicure. O'Keefe stared at us for a long moment, bushy green brows drawn down, then he hawked and spat a huge gob of mucus. Its trail left a rainbow-like arc shimmering in the air as it flew an impressive ten feet to his right and splattered in front of tent five. Multi-coloured phlegm illuminated something lying on the grass, which, now it'd been pointed so disgustingly out, was easy enough to see glittering in the hot sunlight.

Before Mary could stop me, I jogged over, checking the *something* for spells – none – as I did, and scooped it up. I turned, dangling my find from my finger. 'And here we have an obvious clue.'

'What is it?' Taegrin rumbled.

'Max's doggy choke-chain collar,' I said. 'Complete with his diamond-encrusted dog-tags.'

Dessa frowned at Mary. 'Think it's a plant, or did he manage to drop it for us to find, Sarge?'

'Hmm.' Mary tapped her radio on. It crackled to life. 'How close is that backup, Constable?'

'Search group three is here now, ma'am,' the constable's tinny voice replied. 'The others shouldn't be long. And DI Munro's on his way from Trafalgar Square. ETA: thirty minutes.'

As she finished speaking, three more WPCs and Constable Lamber, his mottled beige headridge dusty, appeared in the circle of tents. They all cast quick hairy eyeball at the exhibitions, nodded to Mary, and joined Dessa and Constable Taegrin, waiting for instructions. The centaurs and Mini eyed them with professional disinterest but, as they obviously weren't customers, dismissed them. O'Keefe, the leprechaun, just hunched deeper over his book.

Mary strode over, looked at the dog-tag I held, then at the tent with its closed sign behind me. 'It's probably a trap.'

Whether it was or not didn't matter; it wasn't like we were walking into it on our own, not with half the Met's Magic and Murder Squad about to put in an appearance. I shrugged. 'We'll find out for sure when we check it out.'

She looked at me, indecision warring in her brown eyes. 'What's supposed to be in the tent?'

I took a couple of steps back to the tent doorway and flipped the closed signed over. It showed a picture of a golden bow and arrow, and a crystal ball. Written along the outer edge of the bow in fancy gold script was: *Divine Love with Cupid*.

I waggled my brows. 'So wanna go see a god about a dog?'

Mary rolled her eyes at me, then said, 'Let's do it.'

Chapter Forty-Two

Despite Mary's easy agreement, and my saying that whatever trap might be inside Cupid's tent had probably been scrapped long ago thanks to the very obvious police presence, it still took a long, toe-tapping fifteen minutes for Mary to organise our backup to her satisfaction. She also took time to organise a search of all the other tents, inside and out, and to interrogate the leprechaun and the others for any extra intel on 'Cupid'. But, much to Mary's annoyance, all of them to a minotaur claimed they'd never set eyes on the 'Divine Love god'.

Though they did reveal Mad Max had trotted past them, tail wagging happily, into Cupid's tent about an hour or so before we'd turned up. No one had been with him. Or, at least, they hadn't noticed anyone. Not that any of them had been paying attention. So for all they knew Max the doggy could've had a whole army with him hidden beneath a See-Me-Not veil. And no, none of them had looked up either; so no one had seen any eagle, or any other birds, other than the swan maidens. Stellar witnesses they were not.

Once Mary was sure they had no more beans to spill, she deemed us – us being Mary, me, Dessa and Taegrin – ready to beard the love god in his tent.

'Right, no messing about this time, Genny,' Mary told me as Dessa unzipped the tent's entrance, Taegrin on standby to enter first. 'Tell me what we can expect of Cupid.'

'Far as I remember, he's a cambion.'

Cambions are born of a witch and an incubus, or a wizard

(a witch's son with a human) and succubus. The actual pairing could vary. And since cambions have long been considered 'another type of witch' (something the witches themselves have always been careful not to dispute, lest it reflect badly on their own 'human' classification) cambions benefited greatly from the witches big 'human rights' thing in the eighties. Of course, the real difference between a cambion and a witch or wizard, apart from their parentage, is their appetite for sex magic and their gift for prophecy. Which sort of explained why this cambion called himself Cupid and was telling fortunes.

Mary gave me a resigned look. 'So this guy's not only a comedian, but a *bona fide* magician like Merlin?'

'Yep,' I agreed.

'Cambions are demons,' Dessa suddenly piped up.

We both stared at her, shocked.

'Half-demons anyway,' she amended as she crossed herself.

'Incubi and succubi are minor demons,' Mary replied in a neutral tone, 'but cambions, like us witches and wizards, have been classified as human since the *Malleus Maleficarum* was discredited back in the eighteenth century. Do you want to sit this one out, Dessa?'

'No!' She shook her head vehemently and adjusted her stab vest. 'This is my job.'

'Right,' Mary said, after a few moments' silence that told me, without any need of a cambion's prophetic abilities, that Dessa could look forward to an uncomfortable chat in her near future. 'The tent's surrounded,' Mary carried on, 'so whoever's in there isn't going anywhere.' She paused, extended her stun baton with a sharp snap (she'd still refused to give me one, much to my disgust), and motioned to Taegrin. 'Lead the way, constable.'

Taegrin lifted the tent flap and led the way. Mary, Dessa and I followed.

Straight into an illusion.

Years ago, before the lesser fae sealed the gates to the Fair Lands, and barred the sidhe from London, the Carnival Fantastique was famous for its illusions. The sidhe would take any idea and, using nothing but magic would build illusions so powerful that folk told stories of climbing towers in fairytale castles, feasting in mediaeval banqueting halls, swimming through tropical seas, dallying in enchanted woods, hiking up snowy mountains and many more. Now, with the sidhe locked out, most illusions were cast by half-rate magicians, and were as rough and shaky as the wooden scaffolding their fairytale towers were built on.

But going by the illusion the four of us were now standing in, half rate, rough and shaky didn't apply. As hard as I *focused*, I still couldn't see the tent beneath the magical sheen of the illusionary room.

The room itself was straight out of an Elizabethan-era castle: flagged stone floor and dark wood-panelled walls, candles flickering in sconces, fire burning merrily in the huge walk-in fireplace, the smell of herbs and woodsmoke scenting the air, and a massive four-poster bed with velvet drapes and enough tassels, fringes, and cushions to fill a hearth-witch's haberdashery shop. And on the table next to the bed waited a golden flagon and five golden goblets.

We were expected.

Not really a surprise considering we were visiting a prophetic Cupid.

Cupid himself was half-reclining on the four-poster, the silk sheets artfully arranged to preserve his modesty. But he wasn't the stereotypical winged, curly haired cherub of legend. This god of love was definitely the grown-up adult version. The firelight licked golden shadows over his long, leanly muscled and obviously (apart from those pesky sheets) naked body, his hair was dark, sleek and cut short to his head, a mediaeval-looking gold chain hung around his neck and draped down to his navel, and he regarded us arrogantly with cool blue green eyes.

I squinted in the dim light as I realised both the grown-up Cupid and the room looked vaguely familiar.

'Ooh, my,' Mary murmured in astonishment. 'That's—'

'Jonathan Rhys Meyers,' Dessa said, her gaze fixed unwaveringly on the figure in the bed. 'Got everything he's done on DVD. I loved him as Steerpike in *Gormenghast*. But his new Tudors series is the one I've been watching lately.'

Recognition clicked. Cupid had cast himself as the young Henry VIII!

And Dessa had the hots for the actor playing him … which meant the illusion wasn't by chance.

Which also meant Cupid/Jonathan/Henry – Hell, I was sticking with Henry; it suited him – had plucked his illusion from Dessa's thoughts. Except cambions couldn't do that. But there was something that could. A Wishing Web. I'd never been in one, but I'd read up on them for the Carnival – the spell woven in the web picked up on a person's subconscious fantasies. The Carnival had approved three applications, all for kids under eight, and they'd been set only to trigger for specific wishes. No one in their right mind would license one for adults; their deepest, darkest fantasies are far too dangerous.

I upped my focus. Now I was *looking* for it I could see the dark emerald lines of the spell stretching through the dim room in all directions, hidden beneath the sheen of the illusion. It wasn't so much a web, but more as if thin laser-like beams randomly crossed the room at all angles. Each emerald laser beam bristled with tiny sticky fibres. Fibres that were floating around us like fine cactus spines, and in Dessa's case had already dug themselves into her skin.

Hence, the Jonathan Rhys Meyers scenario.

Crap. I needed to find the Web's power source, and shut it down—

'Ladies!' Henry shifted one long lean leg so the sheet slipped a couple of enticing inches lower, patted the bed next to him and held his hand out. 'Will you not join me? Please?'

—hopefully before the fucking orgy started (no pun intended).

'Oh, boy!' Dessa took a step towards him.

I grasped Dessa's upper arm. 'Oh no you don't.'

'Hey, single mum here,' she growled, jerking her arm back and catching me by surprise in the stomach. I doubled over, wheezing. She packed a punch, even though the stab vest I was wearing took the brunt. 'I gotta take whatever opportunities I can get,' Dessa muttered, starting forward again.

I straightened, grabbing for her wrist and pulling her round to face me. Her eyes were glazed, pupils fully dilated, almost eclipsing her dark brown irises, her mouth slack. 'Believe me,' I gasped, clamping my hand round her other wrist as she tried to shove me away again, 'this isn't an opportunity you want, Dessa. He's not real. And you're working, remember?'

'Who cares,' she snapped, still struggling.

'A little help here, please,' I called, then my stomach sank as I caught sight of Mary and Taegrin. They both stood still as stones, beatific expressions on their faces as they stared up at … whatever. Damn it. Mary I could understand, but what the hell was in the illusion that it could affect a troll?

Deal with them in a minute, Genny, I told myself as I narrowly missed getting kicked in the shin by Dessa.

I shook her, hard enough to rattle her teeth. When that didn't work I *called* the tiny spell fibres sticking in her. As they pulled out they stretched, spinning out into long thin threads. Frantically, I started *absorbing* them, winding them around an imaginary spool inside me, determined to contain them before they dug themselves into any of my own fantasies.

Within seconds the last of the threads slid of Dessa's skin. She stopped struggling, blinked a couple of times, pupils contracting, then frowned. 'Sorry, Genny. Don't know what came over me.'

'It's a Wishing Web,' I said, relieved she seemed herself again. 'Once you're caught in it, it's hard to get out.' I shifted uncomfortably, the spool inside tickling as it tried to unravel. 'It jacks into your subconscious, and doesn't stop till it's worked through your fantasies or the power in the spell runs out.'

'Clever girl,' Henry boomed from the bed. 'But if I can't have that one, then this one's just as plump and juicy with unfulfilled wishes.'

The room around us shivered like a dog shaking itself. The Elizabethan look wavered, and rearranged itself into the interior of a rough wooden houseboat. The bed was still there, but it had lost is posts and cushions. The fire still burned brightly, but inside an cast-iron stove complete with piped chimney. And leaning against the wall was a guitar. I recognised this scene; it was from *Chocolat*; the film was one of Mary's favourites. I scowled at Henry, still artfully naked in the bed. Unsurprisingly, given the new setting, Henry had morphed into Johnny Depp, his hair slicked back in a ponytail like the gypsy character in the film.

Mary laughed, a loud delighted sound. I sighed. Of course, Mary's fantasies would include this Johnny, or whatever his character was called; she'd only been talking about Ricou wearing a Glamour of the character the other morning at the zoo. Except as I watched, Johnny continued to morph. His skin took on a faint blue-grey tinge, his ponytail rose up into a headcrest, and fluted fins framed his face until he was part Johnny and part Ricou, as if the two of them had been Photoshopped together. The whole effect was weirdly disorientating.

Or maybe I was dizzy because the houseboat was still shaking.

Nausea roiled up in my gut. I dropped Dessa's wrists and clapped my hands over my mouth, praying the BLT I'd eaten after taking the Revive spell wasn't about to revisit.

The shaking stopped.

My stomach settled. Relief filled me until another delighted laugh snapped my attention to Mary. She was gazing, star-struck, at the bed.

Johnny/Ricou was no longer alone.

Chapter Forty-Three

Johnny/Ricou had moved so he lay on his side, elbow bent, head propped on his hand. His other hand, more Ricou's than Johnny's going by the blue webbing between his long-clawed fingers, was spread low over the softly rounded stomach of the female figure lying on her back in front of him.

Sylvia.

A naked and hugely pregnant Sylvia. Her magnificent 'Hello Boys' boobs were tipped with pointed, cherry-red nipples, her bushy head of twigs, heavily laden with pink and white cherry blossom, was spread out over the pillows, and more pink and white flowers bloomed at the juncture of her thighs.

Wow. I'd known Mary had a thing about Ricou and his Johnny Depp Glamours, but I hadn't realised she had a thing about the pair of them together. As fantasies go, that was fine by me, if not for the fact that I was about to get an up-close-and-personal ringside seat of her fantasy *ménage à trois*, and no way did I need to see the three of them doing whatever Mary's subconscious was about to conjure.

Not to mention: where had the other cambion, or whatever she was, come from? Somehow I couldn't believe Cupid was powerful enough to cast himself into two illusions. Of course, the bed was massive, its base about three feet off the floor, and the drapes round the base ... well, draped, hiding the space beneath it. A space large enough for half-a-dozen more cambions. A cheerful thought. Not.

Sylvia gave a sly 'come hither' smile, the expression

uncannily like one the real Sylvia had given me two nights ago when she'd hit on me. Mary made a tiny eager noise, and Johnny/Ricou trailed his webbed blue hand up to cup one of Sylvia's jiggling breasts. Sylvia squirmed in delight, her own hands zeroing in on the flowers between her legs, fingers plucking at the blossoms. Johnny lowered his head and swiped at one cherry-red nipple with a long purple tongue. She giggled, legs parting and blossoms flying as her fingers picked up speed. Johnny/Ricou grinned, his 'shopped face contorting bizarrely, and held out his hand. 'Mary, come and join us, luv!'

There was a soft thud, then another, and Mary – minus her stab vest and Stun baton – shoved me and Dessa aside, unbuttoning her blouse with quick jerky movements as she rushed towards the pair on the bed.

Oh. Crap. This was so not going to happen. This might be Mary's fantasy but that didn't mean she actually wanted to experience it, and even if she did, she'd want it to be with the real Sylvia and Ricou, not with whoever the cambion and his pal were under their illusions. I *focused* on the Stun spell winking on the end of Mary's baton, *called* it, caught the firefly of green magic, and, after a brief internal debate about which figure was the cambion, lobbed it in resignation at Mary's back. It hit dead centre, exploding in a flash of mint-scented green, and unsurprisingly, Mary collapsed in a Stunned heap.

'Wow!' Dessa's loud exclamation made me turn to her. She wasn't looking at the unconscious Mary, but down at herself. 'You know, I haven't been this big since I stopped breastfeeding.'

'What?'

She lifted her head. Gold flecked the brown of her irises. Unease crawled up my spine. Had the gold flecks been there before, or were they new? Gold meant something was … wrong … Then all thought left me as Dessa ripped off her stab vest, shirt and bra, revealing a pair of breasts way bigger

346

than Sylvia's, with large areolas the colour of bitter chocolate. 'Look!' She grinned, bouncing them. 'Gorgeous, aren't they?' She pulled a sympathetic face. 'Shame about yours, Genny.'

I blinked. Looked down. I was as flat as a pancake. Again. I tore my own vest off to double check, patting myself down. Nothing but tiny bumps. I started to undo my shirt buttons, panic shooting round my gut as if I'd swallowed a set of hyperactive pinballs. The familiar feeling stopped me cold—

I'd had it before. The Magic Mirror spell. The one from Harrods. Shit. Not again. Even as the knowledge clicked, my fingers were still frantically pulling apart my buttons as if on autopilot, and the realisation was lost.

'Here, you can share mine.' Dessa grabbed my hands, and cupped them to her own breasts, giggling.

Lust and surprise flashed in me at the soft, generous weight of her. I'd never touched the breasts of anyone as well en-dowed as Dessa; the only women I'd ever been this hands-on with – literally – had been vamp venom junkies, and I'd always been more interested in blood than sex at the time. Only now I wanted— No, I needed sex. Never mind that I was basically straight, and Dessa was female, that didn't seem to matter. Not when she seemed to like my hands on her body as much as I did. I brushed my thumb along the freckles trailing across the mound of her left breast like a shooting comet, then squeezed gently, mesmerised as her nipples instantly contracted, thrust-ing eagerly into my palms. She gave a happy moan, her own hands slipping inside my shirt, and I discovered, even flat as a pancake, the slightest touch from her was enough to drag a desperate groan from my own throat.

As she moved my blouse aside, I moulded her with my hands, fascinated by both her body's reactions and my own. She pressed her palms over my smaller nipples were pushing against the smooth satin of my bra, rubbing the tender, aching points. Another, deeper groan escaped me. Bending her head, she dragged down my bra, and quickly fastened her mouth over me. I gasped, my fingers digging into the lush fullness of her, as the slick wetness of her tongue played over my sensitised skin, flicking and teasing ...

The boat shifted, rocking us gently on our feet, then settled.

... I gazed down at his black silk hair, the obsidian gem gracing his earlobe, his lips teasing my breast. Desire flooded my veins, need, sexual and something more, something stronger, fluttered inside me at his nearness; and as his teeth nipped, I threaded my fingers into that black silk, wanting him to pierce my skin, wanting him to have my blood. To have me. I arched into him, physically and mentally, telling him with my thoughts I wanted all the pleasure he could give me, to share that pleasure with him, and telling him that I was his, however he wished. He complied readily, sucking me deeper into the heat of his mouth and biting down, hard. But instead of the delicate sharpness of fangs, clumsy human teeth tore into my flesh. The unexpected pain threw my head back in a scream. I shoved him away from me—

And watched uncomprehendingly as Dessa stumbled back and fell.

She lay there, panting, dark blood staining her lips, her irises solid golden orbs, gazing adoringly up at me.

For a moment I gazed back, confused. Then, as the honey-copper scent of my own blood reached me, my mind cleared and it dawned on me what had happened— what was still happening. The Wishing Web I'd absorbed and spooled was unravelling inside me, its sticky fibres sliding deep as they hooked into my long-held fantasies ... *of Malik ... of giving him my blood ... not because I had to, not because the 3V forced me, not for any reason other than I wanted to* ... I shoved the thoughts away, hitching my bra up, heedless of the bloody bite – I'd heal – and buttoning my shirt as I did so. Now wasn't the time for whatever fantasies the Wishing Web had pulled out of my psyche. Not when I had a more immediate and horrific problem to deal with.

Dessa. I'd trapped her in my Glamour. Never mind that it was illegal and would win me a quick one-way trip to the guillotine. Never mind I could've killed her if we'd got as far as orgasm, leaving her daughter without a mother. Bad as both of those things were, I had an uneasy feeling that releasing Dessa wasn't going to be as simple as I needed it to be. She was a witch. She had to have been Glamoured by a sidhe at least once before (during a fertility rite, otherwise she would never have become pregnant). And we were trapped in a Wishing Web. Despite Dessa's Jonathan Rhys Meyers fantasy, it looked like, deep down, she wished for something else, but whether it was sex with another female, or with a sidhe, I didn't know.

Or really, for all I did know, she was gazing happily up at a creepy magically 'shopped merging of Jonathan Rhys Meyers and me. Which was kind of disturbing given the way she was lying half-naked on the sun-drenched grass—

I blinked.

The houseboat was gone. In its place was a manicured lawn, littered with early autumn leaves, half of it covered in bright sunshine, the rest deep in the shadow cast by the grey-stone walls of a half-ruined Norman manor house. To my right was a huge arched stone entrance, the door half ajar. To my left a copse of trees rustled in an almost chilly breeze. In the distance the deep waters of a moat sparkled.

I knew where this was. Knew what had happened here on my fourteenth birthday, on my wedding night. *It's an illusion*, the rational part of me cried, *ripped from your memories by the Wishing Web*. Memories I'd revisited in shocking clarity only an hour or so ago in the Dreamscape with Bastien.

'My sidhe bride.' His voice was light, chiding, gentle. A lie. 'Mildly entertaining as it is to see you toy with the witch, I wish your attention now.'

It's not Bastien. It's the cambion.

A sword appeared next to me, its point stuck in the grass, its bejewelled hilt quivering as if it had been thrown there.

'Unless, of course,' Bastien's voice said, 'you wish me to cause her, or the other witch, some damage, with that pretty sword.'

I glanced at Dessa, still lying oblivious in the sunshine. And across at Mary, still unconscious from the Stun spell. Horror choked my throat. I swallowed it back. He might be the cambion, but it was my memories the Wishing Web was channelling into this fantasy. And both of them were easy pickings. Innocent victims he would gleefully torture while he fucked them. It was what he'd done to Sally, my faeling friend, all those years ago, in the grand hall of this very house.

Sweat broke on my skin. My heart pounded in dread. No way did I want to relive that horror.

Illusion! Nothing more!

But it didn't matter what I told myself. Between my memories, and the Wishing Web, the illusion was now as dangerous as the reality.

I scooped up Dessa's shirt, slapped it on her chest, and grabbed her head. Ironically grateful that my Glamour forced her to be my puppet, I told her to put her shirt on, get Mary, and get both of them, and the still stone-like Taegrin, out of the tent, and then to keep everyone else out.

She scrambled to her feet, yanking on her shirt as she rushed to do my bidding.

A sigh behind me. 'You disappoint me. I was hoping for some entertainment while we continued our conversation, which you so rudely ended earlier.'

I gripped the hilt of the sword, it wasn't Ascalon but it would do, and turned. Keeping him occupied would give them chance to escape—

My eyes met those of the sucker I'd always wanted dead.

I smiled. As fantasies go, this one was turning out to be a killer.

Chapter Forty-Four

Bastien, my psychotic, memory-hijacking betrothed, and Malik's – *son?* – smiled at me. A trickle of fear dripped down my spine. I reminded myself that he was just another sucker, not to mention that *this* Bastien was nothing more than the product of my imagination and the Wishing Web. Surprisingly, my conjured illusion of him looked different from when he'd 'appeared' in my Dreamscape daymare.

Now he was wearing jeans and a Blondie T-shirt, of all things. It made him look more like the tall, gangly fifteen-year-old he'd been when he'd Accepted the Gift. His features and skin tone were a mix-up of Mediterranean and Middle East, and I searched them for any resemblance to Malik, disturbed when I realised they had the same shaped mouth, the same sharp jawline, though Bastien's brown eyes were round, and heavily lashed, in a way that gave him a limpid, almost girlish look.

In fact, now I wasn't looking at him through panic-warped eyes I realised that, with his unruly dark hair and good looks, he'd probably be a candidate for a lot of people's wet dreams. If they didn't know how sick he was inside.

His looks also reminded me of the crush I'd had on him at fourteen.

Bastien grinned. 'You always did like watching me, my sidhe princess,' he said, the illusion evidently picking up on my memories. 'Peering at me from behind curtains, inside wardrobes, all wide-eyed and innocent, like a timid mouse fascinated by a cat.' He licked his lips. 'It made dallying with your faeling friend even more exciting, hearing your heart flutter like a trapped bird's, hearing your breath hitch at the things we did, all the while knowing that soon I would do the same to you, that I'd be the first to pierce you in every way.'

Of course, once he opened his mouth ... My hand clenched around the sword's hilt, grateful Dessa and Mary were gone. 'Her name was Sally,' I said flatly, tightening my grip on the sword. 'You killed her.'

He shrugged. 'I am rash and impulsive. I often regret the consequences. As I did after I dealt with the faeling: she met her death much too soon. I am sure she could have provided a few more days' amusement for our wedding celebrations, if I had but curbed my impatience.'

I suppressed a shudder. 'I'm sure Sally would've been thrilled to know that.'

'She thought she could take your place, my sidhe. It was an insult.'

'You killed her because you got off on it,' I spat. 'You got off on torturing her. And you were going to do the same to me before Malik stopped you.'

'Be ready to run, Genevieve. At my command.' Malik's voice came out of his mouth. They were the words I'd heard in my head that long ago night when I'd been standing in front of Bastien, in my wedding dress soaked with Sally's blood, frozen with terror.

I took a step back, surprise and dismay washing over me.

'Be ready to run, Genevieve. At my command.' This time Bastien said it in his own voice, his tone bored. 'You presume, my princess, that I did not know what Malik, my ever-faithful commander, my always-loyal shadow, was doing. He told you to run, ordered you to so you had no choice. Then he chased you down like a frightened rabbit, feasted on your blood and your life, and threw your dead body down in front of me like

353

a sacrificial offering.' He tapped his head. 'I was with him in here. Listening, watching, experiencing. So how could I not know what he was doing all along?'

'No.' I shook my head in disbelief. The bastard was trying to trick me. Again. 'If you knew he was saving me, not killing me, you would've stopped him.'

'Saving you?' He laughed, derisive. 'Malik wasn't saving *you*, princess. He was saving me, from myself. It is what he has always done. What he still does.'

Saving him? Did that mean Bastien really was Malik's son? I wanted to ask, but couldn't force the words out. 'What the hell does "saving you" mean?' I demanded.

'We had waited so long for you.' He shrugged. 'As such we would have regretted using your death for a mere few days' entertainment. So Malik prevented me from doing so.'

Icy betrayal slid into my heart. I tried to ignore it, but the voice in my mind said the bastard was speaking truth, that Malik hadn't saved me out of an altruistic sense of honour, but because it was all part of whatever game he and the Autarch were playing at that time. And were still playing now. If the psycho was right.

Briefly, I closed my eyes, breathed in the scent of smouldering leaves, and remembered this was *my* fantasy, dragged from my subconscious by the Wishing Web. Was this what I feared deep down? That Malik's interest in me was all part of some psychotic blood-sucker's plan? That I was just a pawn? That even though I'd accepted a relationship with him, wanted him, I didn't trust him? If so then I was seriously messed up about him. Though, if I thought about it logically, nothing about this fantasy made sense. I wanted to kill Bastien. I always had. If it hadn't been for the feelings of panic and terror that overwhelmed me at fourteen I'd have searched him out in his daytime sleep and, instead of running away, I'd have killed him then.

So, why wasn't I trying to kill him right now? With the sword, my bare hands, or whatever, instead of discussing the ins and outs of plots that might not exist, and worrying that my psyche, when it came to Malik, was really fucked up. Either this Wishing Web was more sophisticated than most, or something stank. And it wasn't the burned … *meat*?

No, not meat, but flesh.

My eyes snapped open.

There was a figure on the grass between us, on its back, arms and legs outstretched, the hot sunshine beating down on it. Twelve silver-dipped daggers had been driven through the figure's wrists, ankles, forearms, calves, biceps and thighs. The blades all missed bone, but sliced through the thickest part of the figure's muscles. I could tell because the figure looked like one of those anatomical drawings, the ones where the skin's been stripped to reveal what's underneath. Except the bodies in those drawings don't look like over-cooked meat. They don't smell like it, either. Their eyes don't roll in their sockets as they look at you. And they don't have a full set of vamp fangs: two sharper canines either side of the needle-thin venom fangs.

'Genevieve.'

And they never speak.

Malik?

'As you can see, my lovely princess, Malik even took your place to ensure I was distracted while you made your escape.' Bastien smiled like the cat that got the cream.

My stomach heaved, and I lunged away as I doubled over, vomiting on to the grass, and thankfully not on … *was it really Malik? Had the sadistic prick done this to him back then?*

I heaved again. Forced myself to stop, wiping my mouth on my sleeve. I pushed to my feet, reaching in the same motion for the sword I'd dropped—

It was gone.

The Autarch was grinning. A wide fang-filled grin that asked if I'd got the joke yet.

I did. The Autarch was here. In this tent. Controlling what illusions the Wishing Web put out, maybe even adding to them, if that was one of his vamp powers. That realisation settled me. I didn't care how or why, or that most vamps couldn't go out in daylight, just that now I'd have a chance at the psycho. The other sword might be gone, but I clenched my hand; I still had my ace up my sleeve, or rather, ring on my finger. Ascalon.

'So your fantasy is watching me puke my guts out,' I said flatly. 'Can't say I'm impressed by your imagination.'

He flung his arms wide. 'This is not imagination but another cherished memory, my princess.'

Well, that answered the question of whether the sadistic prick had made Malik suffer ... He had. I clamped down on my desire to run the psychotic monster through. First I needed to find out what he wanted. Because this was the reason for the phone call telling me 'my dog' was at the Carnival. To get me here, to Bastien. The only thing that didn't mesh with that scenario was Mad Max's kidnap and subsequent escape, presumably, from the Emperor's werewolves. *That* suggested some sort of pact between Bastien and the Emperor ... Or the werewolves. Which was more likely, since Bastien and Dilek a.k.a. Fur Jacket Girl were apparently brother and sister. And, if Bastien's words to me in the Dreamscape were anything to go on, he wanted me to save him, Dilek and Malik too, from the Emperor. Bastien was no doubt going to tell me his 'save us' plan next. Though whatever the plan was I seriously doubted it was going to have my best interests at heart.

Time to cut through the bullshit.

'So,' I said, 'you and your pet dog have got me here. What's the deal?'

He threw his head back and gave a fang-filled laugh. 'You

are delightful. Naïve, but delightful, my princess, if you think I'm the one with the plan.'

'What the hell does that mean?'

'I see I shall have to spell it out,' he said. 'I am the Autarch. I have a certain mercurial reputation, well deserved and well maintained.' He pointed down at Malik— *no, not Malik, just an illusion*. 'When he deprived me of the enjoyment of your body, your blood and your death – in all eyes but his, mine and yours – my subjects would have considered me weak if I had not vented my anger on someone. Malik insisted it be him and no one else. Personally, I always prefer someone else; his constant need for atonement detracts from my own pleasure.' He gave me a look as if to say, 'Poor me, no one cares what I want, I have to suffer so.' I grimaced in disgust. 'But if terror no longer fills my subjects' hearts and minds as their thoughts turn to me, they would soon plot for my messy demise.' He shrugged. 'And we cannot allow that.'

'Fine. I get the politics. You're not the one with the plans. Malik is. You're the figurehead and he's the power behind the throne. The kingmaker. Isn't that what you're trying to tell me?'

He tilted his head, considering. 'Kingmaker?' A happy, if scary, smile spread across his young-looking face. 'Yes. This is true. I was a prince. Malik made me his king. Remind him of that, my sidhe, next time you speak to him.'

I shook my head, not believing him. 'Why the fuck would Malik make you king? If he was that powerful, he could make himself king.'

He arched a sceptical brow. 'With his curse?'

I gritted my teeth. 'What's his curse got to do with it?'

'My princess, do you really think that vampires anywhere would accept a revenant, someone who could turn into a blood-thirsty mindless corpse at any moment, as their liege lord?'

'They accepted a psychotic, murdering bastard like you.'

'Those that lived did, yes,' he agreed prosaically. 'Those that Challenged me to my face died horribly. As did those that plotted behind my back.' He threw his arms out with a flourish and gave a low bow. 'You see before you the magician's assistant, my princess. The pretty distraction to divert the eye. No one sees my loyal shadow coming, not until the darkness takes them.' He grinned. 'You see, I am not the only psychotic, murdering bastard.'

Was it true? Was Malik the one in control? Or was Bastien still playing games, trying to make me think that? But why? What did it gain him, to make me distrust Malik? Or was that it? Was Bastien trying to drive a wedge between us? But again, why? Especially after he'd seemed so disappointed we hadn't had sex. I swallowed back bile at the memory of how the bastard had violated me, and tightened my fist around Ascalon's ring. And what the hell did it all have to do with the Emperor? Though really, second-guessing Bastien was a waste of time; he was the type to sell his own mother, so anything coming out of his mouth was suspect. Time to poke back.

'If Malik's the one in charge,' I ground out, 'then he doesn't want me to know, otherwise he would've told me. So why are you enlightening me?'

He licked his lips. 'The pleasure of knowing you know.'

'Bullshit.'

'Not entirely. I do derive pleasure knowing this causes you emotional pain, princess. Not as much as I wish; I much prefer to cause physical suffering.' He plucked a dagger from Malik's— *no, the figure's* left thigh, held it up so the sunshine hit it. The blood glistening on the blade bubbled, and smoke spiralled. He plunged the knife down into the figure's stomach. The figure made a strangled noise as if stifling a scream. I stopped breathing for a moment. Illusion, nothing more. *Wasn't it?* Bastien met my eyes. His were flat and hard, all signs of insanity gone. 'You are here, bean sidhe, because when the time comes for you to choose, I want to ensure that you know what your choices are.'

Now we were getting to it. 'What do I have to choose?'

'Not what, but who. You think Malik al-Khan is your dark knight, your protector. I am here to tell you, he has taken on those mantles for our sake, his and mine, not yours.'

'Seriously, if this is meant to make me save you and Malik from whatever you've got going on with the Emperor, trying to turn me against him is going the wrong way about it.'

'It is not Malik who will need saving from the Emperor, it is I, my lovely bride. I have already tried to tell you this.'

I clenched my ring. 'Well, listen up, buddy, I'm happy to kill you now, and save the Emperor the trouble.'

'But you will not.'

I released Ascalon and bared my teeth in a smile. 'Bet you can't give me a good reason not to.'

Chapter Forty-Five

'If you kill me, princess,' Bastien said, 'you will have lost that which the Emperor wants from you in return for information about releasing the fae's trapped fertility.'

It was a fucking good reason. It was also a fucking cryptic reason. And it threw up a whole slew of questions. I went for the most pertinent. 'How do you know what I want from the Emperor?'

'You told my loyal shadow, did you not?'

A question for an answer. Which meant Malik almost certainly hadn't told him. 'How do I know you're not spinning me a line?'

Glee wreathed his face. 'I believe you will have to trust me, my lovely sidhe. To that end you will find that I have sent an extremely useful gift to the *àrd-cheann*. A cybernetic Trojan Horse, if you will, to help you both in your quest.'

What the hell did that mean, other than— 'You know there's a saying about not trusting Greeks bearing gifts, don't you?'

'Ah. Luckily I am not Greek, but Ottoman.'

Right. And *that* was supposed to make me trust him? Still, he was right, I couldn't risk killing him. Not yet. I clenched my hand round Ascalon, and as if it felt my frustration, the sword slowly shrank back until it was a chunky emerald ring on my finger again.

Bastien smiled smugly.

Goaded, I snapped, 'You know Malik wants you dead.'

Bastien shrugged dismissively. 'He will not act on it.'

I snorted. Malik had already acted on it; he'd made a deal with Tavish for help to do the deed. 'I wouldn't be too sure of that.'

'My life is worth more to him than any other, even his own, my princess. It always has been.'

He said it with such confidence that I had to ask, 'Why?'

'Because I have long been that part of him that he cares for above all else.'

Again with the cryptic. Irritated, I jumped in with the question I'd avoided before. 'You mean because you're his son?' My voice rose slightly as my doubt, or hope, that he'd deny it crept into my words.

'A question you can ask him when you next see him,' he replied, not even blinking. 'When you do, I want you to give him a message.'

I narrowed my eyes. 'Why can't you give it to him?'

'Malik is not currently taking my calls.' Impatience crossed his face. 'And I can no longer reach his mind. There is … something preventing me. It may be Malik himself. I do not know. Tell him that too.'

Unease pricked me. Why wasn't Malik talking to him? Bastien had said Malik was safe from the Emperor, hadn't he? No, he'd only said that he, Bastien, would need saving … 'What makes you think I'll see him?'

'Why, my faithful hound will lead you to his side, my bride. How else will you save me?'

Mad Max would take me to Malik? To save Bastien? Surprise and suspicion washed through me.

'When he does,' Bastien continued, 'tell my shadow these words exactly: I have honoured the agreement between us. I will not harm the bean sidhe, but due to your incessant vacillating, I have made the choice for you.'

Ice trickled down my spine. 'What the fuck does that mean?'

'You have heard the message you have inspired, sidhe. It

informs all of my decision, now make sure you deliver.' He reached down to yank the dagger from the figure's stomach at our feet and lifted it in a salute. 'Until anon, princess,' he said, and vanished.

Crap. He'd disappeared too quickly for it just to be vamp speed, so it had to be an illusion. Which meant he was still here. And I had one more question.

'Come back here, Bastien,' I shouted. 'Now. I haven't finished with you!'

He reappeared, his expression a mix of curiosity and calculation. 'My, you *have* changed from that timid little mouse, princess.' He raised a brow, and again I saw a resemblance to Malik in his face. I shoved the disturbing image away and said, 'Tell me how to find that which is lost, and how to join that which is sundered, to release the fae's fertility from the pendant and restore it back to them as it was before it was taken.'

'Well, well, would that I could, my princess, it would be a wonderful moment, would it not, if I had something you wanted?' He threw his head back and laughed, and my heart sank. My growing suspicion was wrong. Fuck. I'd been sure he was in league with the tarot cards, sure he was somehow the 'Emperor', and knew the answer.

His laughter cut out and he pointed an accusing finger at me. 'That mad bitch who is your mother is the one you should be asking, not I.'

Yeah, well, if my fruitcake of a mother ever put in an appearance, I would. Until then, I was being led around the nose by a set of crotchety tarot cards—

Bastien vanished again.

Fuck. I had to catch him. He might not know the answer, but he knew more than he'd told me. I rushed for the exit—

A hand grabbed my ankle.

And I faceplanted into straw-like grass, suddenly realising

362

as I did that the cambion's illusions were gone. The tent was back. Empty of anything other than a large black cauldron, a small table and the huge four-poster bed. I jerked round to look at the figure lying on the floor, my leg captured in its iron grip, hoping it was no longer a skinned, dried-up body.

A male – small, naked, with a purple tinge to his wrinkled black skin and a pair of short, scaly red horns sticking out of his forehead – was clutching his stomach with his other hand, blackish-red blood bubbling through his fingers every time he sucked in air.

'It's not supposed to go like this,' he whispered.

Crap. Had to be the cambion. And he was injured.

'Let me go,' I muttered, tugging my foot. 'I'll get someone.'

He did, but not before gasping out, 'Dog. Under the bed. Hurt too.'

Mad Max!

I went for help.

Outside I found Hugh and five other trolls gearing up for my rescue with saline magic extinguishers (similar to a standard fire extinguisher but painted blue with a silver band). There was no sign of Mary, Dessa, or strangely any other witches, or any of the other tents' occupants. There were, however, a couple of medic teams from HOPE with their usual mix of mundane and magical fixes. I shouted out the Wishing Web was down, that the cambion and Mad Max were injured, and that the Autarch was hidden inside. Hugh and his constables disappeared into the tent, quickly followed by the medics.

The cambion was carted off to HOPE. He wasn't injured as such, but was instead hosting a Sagan spider – a sort of symbiotic pet that lives off the host's blood and flesh in return for a magical boost – which was why the Wishing Web had been so powerful. The creature was half-absorbed into the cambion's chest, and was the source of the bubbling blood.

Either the Autarch had killed it when he'd plunged the dagger into the cambion's illusion of the sun-tortured Malik, or the spider had died when its Web overloaded with too many fantasies coming too fast. Hugh said they couldn't be sure until all the evidence had been checked out by the Magic and Murder Squad's witches, and the cambion was in a position to talk further. He was suffering magical blowback from the spider's death, and was being stabilised so they could surgically remove the spider's remains.

'Ick,' I said, grateful I'd never got too close to the wrinkled, horny little male. And glad I'd dropped Mary with the Stun spell, even if she, Taegrin and Dessa were also at HOPE getting checked out. I'd told Hugh I'd Glamoured Dessa, but as she hadn't shown any symptoms once she was out of the tent, he agreed to leave that tiny incriminating detail out of my statement. For now. If it was going to come back and bite me (and no way was that thought Freudian), we'd deal with it when it did. As for my actual bite wound, which had the medics pouncing on me thanks to the blood staining my shirt, I said I'd caught myself on something blunt (Dessa's teeth!), and that it was already healing (itching like a vamp venom bite as it did!), so was nothing to worry about.

Neither was Mad Max. Injury wise anyway.

A call-out over the Carnival's loudspeakers had turned up a vet (from Brighton on a day trip with his wife and three kids), who pronounced Max the dog was suffering from concussion, judging by the blood-encrusted egg-shaped bump on his head, and had been given some sort of sedative but was otherwise a 'fine specimen of the breed, and if his owner was ever interested in putting Max to stud, he knew of a suitable bitch, and would be happy to put Max's owner in contact'.

Hugh grinned, pink granite teeth shining, as he handed me the vet's business card and repeated his offer. 'Thought you might like to pass that on to your cousin, Genny.'

'Ha ha,' I said. 'Even if it were possible, I think he's got enough offspring already.'

Hugh laughed and settled himself carefully into an overlarge, canvas director's chair with *Mini the Minotaur* stencilled across the back. 'So did you get any useful information from Max?'

I grimaced. 'Not much, the sedative's obviously screwing with him.' Dealing with the crazy sonofabitch was bad enough when he was lucid, but trying to get anything out of him when he was drugged made me want to bleach my brain: I was never going to look at a poodle the same way again. 'But he did say that the Autarch can astral-project which explains how he popped in and out so easily.'

'Astral projection is rare,' Hugh said, taking out his notebook and a large troll pencil. 'And I understand it is dangerous without the proper preparations to return the spirit to the body.' He made a note. 'Does Max know where the Autarch's body is?'

'Nope,' I said, shifting uncomfortably on my makeshift seat, one of the leprechaun's huge balls of string. I wasn't sure if a spiritwalking Autarch was better or worse than a daywalking one. 'But apparently I don't have to worry about the werewolves coming after me since Max has done some sort of deal to deliver me to the Emperor in return for the werewolves letting him escape.'

Hugh leaned forwards. The director's chair, while large, still creaked ominously. 'A trap?'

'Supposedly. Only Fur Jacket Girl appears to be Bastien's long lost sister and I think they're in cahoots. So Max delivering me up to the Emperor is probably something to do with the Trojan Horse thing Bastien mentioned he'd sent to Tavish.' Knowing my luck psycho Bastien's plan would involve me sweating it out in an actual wooden horse, which would be hell seeing as Regent's Park was currently trying to put the

Sahara to shame. I chugged back the last of my bottled water as I waited for Hugh to add to his notes, then said, 'Hopefully we'll find out more when Tavish phones back.' I'd called him, and yet again my call had gone to voicemail. Hugh had sent a unit to check on him. Damn kelpie better have a good reason for being incommunicado.

Hugh nodded. 'But Max can't tell you what the Trojan Horse is?'

'Nope. He seems to be blindly following whatever instructions Bastien drops into his head. I can't work out if Bastien's got him under mind-lock or if Max is knowingly doing the sheep thing. But that might be down to the sedative.' Or the crazy sonofabitch's fixation with poodles. 'It's possible we might get more out of him when he pops out of his doggy form at sunset.'

'And he couldn't tell you anything about what's going on between the Emperor and the Autarch?'

'No, but I'm pretty sure there's some sort of showdown or attempted takeover in the offing. And Bastien seems to think I'm his winning card ...' I trailed off as I realised I'd missed something and slapped my forehead. 'Crap. You know I asked him about the fae's trapped fertility?' Hugh nodded. 'I should've quizzed him about the kidnap victims from the zoo too.'

'It's doubtful you'd have learned anything, Genny.'

'Yeah, but I should've asked.' I picked at the plastic tab on the bottle, angry at myself.

Hugh flipped back a couple of pages in his notepad. 'What about Malik al-Khan? Does Max know where he is, or what his involvement is in all this?'

'No.' Questioning Mad Max about Malik had drawn a complete blank. Looked like the pyscho hadn't given that set of instructions to his pet dog yet. So I was going to have to wait to find out what Malik's 'involvement' was. Just as I was going to have to wait for answers to the rest of Bastien's cryptic barbs. 'Damn vamps and their games,' I muttered, systematically crushing the empty plastic bottle. 'All secrets and plots and double dealing.'

Hugh gave my knee a concerned pat. 'Do you want to talk about it, Genny?'

I dropped the bottle, my anger dissipating to misery. Stupid tears stang my eyes and I scrubbed my face, took a breath and told Hugh about Bastien's story that he was just the front vamp, and that Malik was the real power behind the throne, and that while I knew Bastien was a lying, psychotic sack of shit, he was right, Malik *was* always the one with the plans.

'So, looks like Malik's been playing me for a fool, that he and Bastien are not only fang buddies, but' – I hugged myself, my heart cracking as I forced the words out – 'they're father and son, or whatever, and I'm just a pawn in whatever long game they've got going.'

'Genny.' Frown fissures bracketed Hugh's mouth. 'Good relationships are built on mutual respect and trust. To build that respect and trust you need to get to know each other, learn what matters, and accept each other for who each of you are. It takes time. As does attraction, if it is to develop into love. If that is what you feel you and Malik al-Khan could have together, then my advice would be to speak about this to him.'

I let that sink in. I knew Hugh didn't like the idea of me getting together with Malik, or any vamp, and that he'd put his personal feelings aside to give me his encouraging words of wisdom. I put my hand on his familiar gritty one, heart full of love and gratitude for him. 'You're right,' I said, 'and I had planned to talk to him, anyway.' I gave Hugh a wry smile. 'Sorry for dumping on you, but thanks for letting me.'

'Any time, Genny, you know that.' Hugh returned my smile, then his face hardened. 'But as soon as this involves more than some personal issues between you and Malik al-Khan, then let me know. And we'll deal with it together.'

'Okay, thanks, Hugh,' I said, happy and even more grateful to know he had my back, as always. 'I will.' I grabbed another water – damn sun was like a furnace, even sitting in the shade – and half-drained it in a couple of gulps.

'You're drinking a lot, Genny,' Hugh said, 'are you sure you're feeling—' An owl hoot interrupted him; his phone. He checked the screen, shook his head – not Tavish then – and stood up, walking off as he starting speaking.

I frowned at the water, thinking I *was* drinking a lot, as Constable Lamber, his mottled beige head dusty, ambled over.

'Hello, Genny.' He smiled showing teeth worn down from chomping on too many butter pebbles. 'I just got back from HOPE. That cambion chappy asked me to give you something, said it was important. I should run it by the guv first, but he's busy, and 'spect you'll tell him anyway.' He held out a card.

Tarot card number four.

Chapter Forty-Six

My heart thudded as I took the tarot card. 'Thanks. I will. Tell the DI, that is,' I told Lamber, frantically fishing my small flick-knife from my backpack as he ambled away. I cut my finger and offered it to the card, giving it the usual spiel as its little mouth started sucking up my blood.

The image appeared. A woman. I stared at her, stunned. She was beautiful with huge, thickly lashed dark eyes, pale skin, perfect features and glossy, brunette waves down to her waist. Shpresa, the woman from Malik's memory, his favourite *Ikbal*. Her face was so impressed on my mind I'd have recognised her even without the tiny black crescent inked at the corner of her lush mouth.

Shpresa sat on a red velvet throne, wearing a long white gown dotted with spots of crimson, a spiky crown of twelve stars atop her shining hair, and holding a silver dagger in one hand. Her other hand rested on her hugely pregnant belly. At her feet reclined a grey-brown wolf, and around her throne stretched a field of snowdrops, their delicate white flowers nodding as if in a gentle breeze, scattered with the odd crimson rose.

A distant part of me registered this card was the Empress. That she was holding the knife Janan, the Bonder of Souls; that the wolf at her feet was a werewolf, judging by its green human eyes, and the white snowdrops with the crimson roses matched her gown and echoed the 'blood on snow' motif the tarot cards had punted before in the Moon tarot card. The blood on snow in Malik's first two dream/memories. And the rose petals on my bed.

The little mouth stopped sucking. Still I stared, my mind spinning with suspicion.

'C'mon, luvie. We ain't got all day, y'know.'

The card's crotchety voice jerked me into action. 'Tell me how to find that which is lost, and how to join that which is sundered, to release the fae's fertility from the pendant and restore it back to them as it was before it was taken.'

The Empress gave me a sad smile. 'He knows! He will tell you! For a price! The beasts are coming! They come for you! He seeks Janan, Beloved of Malak al-Maut! To use!'

'I know all that,' I said, frowning. 'What else can you tell me?'

'The Emperor is here.'

Duh. Like that was news. 'Where is here?'

'You must save my children.' A single tear dropped down the Empress's cheek.

Her children were Bastien and his sister Dilek, a.k.a. Fur Jacket Girl werewolf. And she wanted me to save them. Well, colour me surprised. Though to be fair, the card could be referring to London's fae as her children. They were, after all, the whole focus of my question. And despite the Empress looking like Malik's *Ikbal*, she was the symbol of fertility, sexuality and motherhood, as shown by her obvious pregnancy. Playing it safe, I asked, 'Who are your children?'

'You must save them.' Another tear joined the first as she comforted her beachball-like belly. 'Even the unworthy.' The tears became a torrent and the card disintegrated into a soggy mess that vanished into the ether.

Even the unworthy? There were some among the dryads I considered unworthy, but hell, she was laying it on a bit too thick. And the whole 'save my kids' was way too coincidental coming right after Bastien. Looked like the psycho vamp did have a direct line to the tarot cards.

I phoned Tavish.

This time he answered.

'I've had another card,' I said, too aggravated to ask why he'd ignored my other calls, and told him about it, Malik's dream/memory and Bastien's 'visits', repeated my message that the psycho vamp had said he'd sent some sort of Trojan Horse 'gift' and laid out how the tarot cards were basically sending the same message as Bastien: I had to save him. Finally, I finished with, 'Oh, and guess what? Bastien can astral-project. Does that make him the sort of like-minded spirit that the tarot card can talk to, or not?'

'Doesnae make much odds if it does, doll,' Tavish replied, sounding tired. 'The cards are sidhe made. The card's spirit has to give a true reading. If she says the vampires are part of it then they are, even if we dinna ken how.'

'Wanna bet she knows, and is holding out on me?'

'Och, doll, 'tis possible. But 'twill nae be much. And truth-fully, 'tis the Autarch's gift that's concerning me now. 'Tis an audio book of Homer's *Odyssey*—'

Excitement swirled through me. 'The Trojan Horse thing. 'Close enough. What's it say?'

'Well, that's the problem, doll. I've tried listening to it, but all it gives me is a log-in page with the username "Genevieve Nataliya Zakharinova" and then asks for a password. I ken that's your given name, so I tried your date of birth and a few other things, but I havenae managed to find it as yet.'

Fuck. What was the point— Of course, that's why the psychotic prick was harping on about our wedding date. 'The password's my fourteenth birthday.' I rattled it off, holding my breath until I heard Tavish's slightly disgusted snort. 'Is that it?'

'Aye ...' he trailed off and I listened impatiently to the clacking of computer keys. Then they stopped.

C'mon then, tell me. I gritted my teeth to contain my impatience.

A sigh came over the phone, half satisfaction, half irritation. ''Tis full access to the Forum Mirabilis' website.'

'And?'

Silence. Then, ''Tis police business and too much for the phone, doll. Tell Hugh Munro I'll send what he needs over with Finn.' He said a quick goodbye and rung off.

Finn was at Tavish's? I blinked at the phone, stunned. Then my pulse started a nervous tattoo. Finn was coming here! And I wasn't sure I wanted to see him so soon after our earlier conversation. I grabbed another water, drained it dry in a few anxious gulps. I didn't want to discuss the ins and outs of our friendship, or answer questions about Malik. Not when I was feeling raw from Bastien's snide digs. And what the hell was Finn doing at Tavish's anyway?

I told myself to suck it up; Finn was bringing much needed info about the Emperor. And as Hugh was off the phone, I brought him up to speed.

When I'd finished, Hugh filled me in on his own phone call.

'That was HOPE. They think we've identified the contents of the cambion's cauldron,' he said, anxious dust puffing from his headridge. 'One of the WPCs thought it smelled like it was the herbal mix the witches use at their fertility rites, so the tech-bods at HOPE have done a rush check. It's similar, though with some unusual additives' – he flipped his notebook open – 'ambergris, horny goat weed, cantharides, and powdered garden fairy, to name the easily identifiable ones.'

'Crap,' I muttered. 'That's some heavy aphrodisiacs there. Not all of them legal.' I scowled at the water bottle I held. I hadn't even noticed picking it up, let alone drinking half of it. Was that what the matter was with me? I'd been in the tent inhaling the stuff, getting all hot and bothered same as Mary and Dessa, only if I was suffering aphrodisiac overload, then

372

shouldn't I be desperate to jump someone's bones, not drink a swimming pool dry?

'Yes,' Hugh agreed with a heavy frown. 'Once the cambion comes round he's got some explaining to do.'

'Talking of powdered garden fairy,' I said, slipping off my shoes, and giving in to an odd urge to dig my bare toes into the dusty ground. 'There's this gnome, Mr Lampy, I'm doing a licensing job for. I'm sure there's something dodgy about him. And he's got a stall here at the Carnival.' I told Hugh where it was, then filled him in on Katie's treacherous boyfriend, Marc, his lip-lock with the freckled redhead, and his uncle buying spell ingredients from the gnome. 'Of course, the two nursery-men might be legit,' I said, 'but if you're going to check the gnome out, might be worth looking at too?'

'Genny'– deep crevices lined Hugh's forehead – 'just because the lad has more than one girlfriend, and associates with someone unsavoury, it doesn't mean he's a criminal.'

'I know. It's just … I'm so angry for Katie.'

Hugh shook his head, but said, 'I suppose it won't hurt to get them all checked out, along with the gnome.'

I shot him a grateful look. 'Thanks,' I said and made a mental note to tell Katie before anyone else did, so I didn't end up in her bad books again. Hugh made some notes, and I glugged down more water. Gods I was hot, and weirdly the idea of stripping-off clothes and throwing myself on the dusty, sun-burned grass and rolling around on it naked was beginning to feel like a great idea. I wriggled, trying to get comfortable as Hugh thumbed on his radio and started issuing orders. Mindful of Hugh's advice, I picked up my phone and sent another text to Malik:

Sorry about last texts, can explain and won't give Hugh the letter. Also, have had two visits from Bastien (Dreamscape and astral) saying I had to save him from the Emperor or I'd lose the chance of finding the fae's fertility. He also said to give you this message verbatim: 'I have honoured the agreement between us. I will not harm the bean sidhe, but due to your incessant vacillating, I have made the choice for you.' So V Important we talk. Meet me at midnight, please. And remember, whatever's going on with the Emperor and Bastien, I can help.

I went to hit send, then stopped and added:

Is Bastien your son?

Before I could change my mind, I sent the text, then shoved the phone back in my pocket and opened another water, thinking astral projection must come in handy for a vamp stuck in his daytime sleep.

Hugh patted my shoulder gently. 'That's your sixth, or maybe seventh bottle of water, Genny. You all right?'

I glanced up at his cloud-grey eyes, squinting against the too bright sun, as I dug my toes into the straw-like grass. 'Not sure. I feel like I haven't had a drink for weeks. And I don't mean alcohol ... ' Damn. That was it. I pulled a face at Hugh. 'I took a Hot.D and a Reviver earlier. It's just the hangover catching up.' I knocked back the last of the water, waved the empty bottle at him with a rueful smile. 'Don't s'pose you've got another?'

'Looks more than that, Genny.' Worried fissures lined his ruddy face. 'Hot.Ds usually have a hydrating effect. Look at your hands. They look like an old person's.'

He was right. The skin was all dry and wrinkled. Like I needed intensive hand cream treatment, or something. 'Huh. Maybe it's a weird side-effect of the Reviver.' I upended the bottle again, the plastic creaking as I sucked all the air out of it.

Hugh stood, his large bulk blocking out the sun.

'Shade,' I murmured. 'Nice.'

He cupped my elbow, carefully helping me up. 'Come on,

Genny. I'll get Lamber to take you to HOPE. Get the docs there to check you out for any problems from that spell mix the cambion had.'

'Can't go.' I yanked out of his hold as desperation dropped me to my knees and thrust my hands into the dusty grass. My flaking skin shimmered gold as the brittle stalks crackled against my fingers. But it wasn't enough. I collapsed full-length, rubbing my face into the earth. Still not close enough. My fingers clawed at my shirt, popping the buttons. I needed more skin—

Water poured down on me.

I flopped onto my back like a starfish and opened my mouth wide, letting it rain over me. Gods it felt good, ice cold, wet and *salty*. Ugh. I jerked up, spluttering as I got a mouthful of saline solution. I swiped my hair and the stinging water from my eyes, and scowled at the person crouching next to me. Finn.

His hair looked as if it had grown since yesterday, his bracken-coloured horns almost hidden in the dark blond waves. He was wearing dark suit trousers and a smart, short-sleeved shirt, cream with a thin ivy-green stripe, the collar open. It was his usual summer business style. And he looked good enough in his handsome human Glamour that I wanted to tear the clothes off him. The thought of the two of us rolling around on the dusty earth, naked, clenched things low inside me. I curled my hands into the grass and stifled that thought. Maybe the cambion's cauldron mix *was* affecting me. Though Finn's salt-drenching seemed to have solved my 'hot and thirsty' problem. And seemed to have cleared my head. Not that I was feeling overly appreciative.

'Thanks,' I muttered, glaring at the blue fire extinguisher he had his hand on.

He grinned cheerfully. 'You're welcome, Gen.'

I sniffed. 'I wasn't being grateful.'

'I didn't think you were.' His grin widened. 'Looks like I'll have to make do with the view instead.' Wickedness lit his moss-green eyes as they flicked down then back up to my face.

I looked down. Sighed. If there was a wet T-shirt contest to be found, my boobs would be taking point and leading the way. As there wasn't, they'd just give anyone too close an embarrassing poke. Great. Still, at least I had boobs, and not the mosquito bites that the Magic Mirror spell kept inflicting on me. I pulled the soaked shirt away from my chilled skin, flapping it gently; in this heat it and my bra should dry in no time. On the plus side, the soaking had almost washed away the bloodstain from Dessa's bite. Maybe the day was looking up.

'Gen?'

I looked back at Finn; his grin was gone.

And maybe it wasn't. 'What's wrong?'

'The Forum Miribilis. It's not good.'

Chapter Forty-Seven

'It's an auction site,' Finn said to me and Hugh. 'The online auction runs all the time, but once every ten years they hold a real-time "Special Auction" in conjunction with the Carnival Fantastique on the Summer Solstice, which is tomorrow night. That auction has a listing of rare items for people to bid on. Plus there's another section, a bit like "Want it Now" on eBay. People list hard-to-find items that they want to buy, either for cash or by offering something in exchange, then the Forum's procurers step in to source the lots. If they do, the site's updated ready for the real-time auction.' He flicked his fingers and *called* an electronic tablet. 'Tavish downloaded screenshots from the website.'

I peered over Hugh's shoulder as he read.

Forum Mirabilis
Where anything can be ordered, bought or bartered: contraband spells, banned substances, exotic slaves, rare epicurean delicacies, magical beings or even your heart's desire, if you are prepared to pay the price.

Finn brought up another screen and, with a grim look at Hugh, said, 'We think this might be related to the kidnap victims at the zoo.'

The screen showed an entry from 'RiverCat1': Wanted: Female ailuranthrope. *Panthera tigris* – any subspecies preferred, though would accept any female ailuranthrope of any big cat species. Must be pure bred, not bitten, and of breeding age.

There was a tick in the column headed: Sourced.

'Weretigers are obviously not as extinct as everyone thinks,' I muttered.

There was a note added to the 'Sourced' column: 'Subspecies *Panthera tigris tigris* (Bengal tiger). Female comes with one pure-bred cub, also *Panthera tigris tigris* (Bengal tiger) – male; aged six. Lots can be offered separately or together.'

They were going to auction off the ambassador's wife and her kid. I hugged myself, chilled despite the summer heat. 'That's sick.'

Hugh rumbled agreement. 'However, it does explain the Bangladeshi ambassador's insistence on his diplomatic immunity.'

'Damn. He's worried about people finding out, isn't he?' I said. 'Though really you'd think that would be the last thing on his mind.'

'The longer a secret is locked in fear, the more impossible it becomes to release it, even when a more immediate danger threatens.' A puff of worried dust escaped Hugh's headridge. 'But now we know the motive behind the kidnap, it should be easier for us to help the ambassador.'

'It doesn't explain why they took the zoo employee too.'

'No doubt we'll find out,' Hugh said, 'when we find him. Which is more important right now.'

'This should help.' Finn handed the tablet to Hugh. 'There's a lot more info about the Forum in it. It's been around since Roman times in various guises, but now all the pre-organisation, leading up to the actual auction date, is done online. It also talks about the gold coins the Emperor's werewolves throw around.'

'They're a recompense of sorts,' Hugh rumbled angrily.

Finn nodded. 'They're given as payment to the person who

has had something taken from them by the Forum procurers. The person can either choose to keep the coin and realise its monetary value, or use it to attend the auction and buy back that which has been taken.'

'You mean those who've been kidnapped?'

Finn shook his head. 'Some of the Forum's listings are of things, not living beings.'

Right. 'So you're saying whoever's got the coin can turn up at the Forum, hand over the coin and get their relatives or item back?' It was too easy. 'What's the catch?'

'It's not a straight exchange. The coin's only an invitation to attend the Forum and barter. The coin-holder is asked for additional payment of some sort.'

'Like what?'

'Apparently it's different for everyone. It's to discourage coin-holders from turning up or, if they do, to make sure the Forum doesn't lose out.'

'Crap,' I muttered. 'It's probably some Faustian or first-born child thing. But at least the coins are a way into the Forum.' I looked at Hugh. 'We've got two: the ambassador's, and the one the werewolves threw at Max. So we could use them to infiltrate the auction, couldn't we?'

Hugh nodded. 'An option to consider, Genny. Though I hope it won't come to that. It would be better all round to stop the auction before it even begins.'

I shot him a wry grin. 'Is this where you tell me to stop trying to teach you to suck eggs?'

'Your input is always welcome.' Hugh's pink teeth sparkled in a gentle smile. 'If it wasn't, I wouldn't ask for your help. 'Now we have this' – he waved the tablet – 'to give to the IT bods at New Scotland Yard, there's a good chance we can find the exact auction location. I'll get it off to them right away.' He called Constable Lamber over, showed him the tablet and started issuing instructions.

A sudden thought hit me. 'Am I on the auction wanted list?'

Finn shook his head. 'Tavish did a thorough search.'

Relief washed over me. 'Good to know I'm not going to end up on the auction block.'

'Yeah,' Finn agreed, clasping my shoulder. 'I hate to say it, but the Autarch did a good thing giving Tavish this info.'

I snorted. 'Only because he's got a showdown scheduled with the Emperor. He's probably worked out that if the police get in on the act, it'll weigh the odds in his favour.'

'Ahh.' Finn gave me a 'should've known' look. 'Still, at least it gives the victims a better chance.'

'Yeah,' I agreed, hoping it would save them, and determined to help any way I could. Only, unease pricked at me. The Empress card had said 'save my children' – Bastien and Dilek, presumably – and helping the police nab the Emperor would do that. But if the Emperor was nabbed before I got a chance to ask him my question about the fae's trapped fertility, where did that leave me and the fae? Okay, so it might be that the Emperor's price for telling me the answer was to get him out of clink. Only while Hugh might be pro-fae, I doubted the human law would see that as a good reason to let the Emperor go, so realistically, it wasn't a price I could pay.

Crap, maybe I'd made a mistake giving Hugh the info about the Forum. Maybe this was what Tavish meant when he said he'd had a prediction that I could screw things up, and leave the fae's fertility permanently trapped? Only he was the one who'd sent the info over. Damn. I needed to speak to him.

Heart thudding, I called. And got his voicemail.

Keeping my voice low, I started leaving him a worried message—

Finn's hand closed over mine and ended the call. I looked at him in surprise. He slung an arm round my shoulders and subtly turned us so we faced away from Hugh. 'Tavish and I already talked about this, Gen,' he said quietly. 'If the Emperor ends up in goal, then it could work in our favour. We can get him out, free and clear, the same way Tavish planned for you last Hallowe'en, if you were ever arrested for that human's death. We'll make the Emperor an *ùmaidh*.'

An *ùmaidh*. A temporary changeling. The sidhe don't only leave them in cradles when stealing human babies, they and the lesser fae use them, if needed, to escape human law. An *ùmaidh* might not 'live' long, a month at most, but then human justice for fae and vamps is swift and fatal. Severing part of your soul and sacrificing some flesh, then forging it to a fresh cut log or an animal, isn't a huge price to pay if you've got a one-way ticket to the guillotine.

I frowned, murmured. 'Can one be made for a vampire?'

'Tavish says yes.'

Right. 'Good to know,' I muttered. 'Though would've been helpful if he'd bothered to return my calls and tell me.'

'I think he's got a lot on his plate just now.'

I shot him a narrow look. 'Like what?'

'When I went round, there was another fae there, but I never saw who she was.'

'She?' I asked, curious.

'Yeah.' Mischief flickered in Finn's green eyes. 'They appeared to be having a domestic, as far as I could work out.'

I gaped. 'Really? Tavish has a girlfriend?'

'Seems so, yeah.'

'Wow. When did that happen?' I pursed my lips. 'Wonder if Sylvia knows? Nah, she can't, she'd never have kept that to herself.'

'Yeah, she and the rest of the dryads do like a bit of juicy gossip,' he grumbled. 'I've already had most of the herd ask me what my early morning visit to you was about.'

I poked him. 'Blame your brothers for gossiping about me being an item with Sylvia and Ricou. It caused Sylvia hassle with her mother.'

Faint heat coloured Finn's cheeks. 'Look, forget about that now, Gen. There's something else we need to sort out.'

Oh, yeah. The whole Helen/Malik/Spellcrackers/Finn working or not for me thing. So not something I wanted to get into. 'Now's not really the right time, Finn.'

'Not that, Gen,' he said quietly, then pointed at the cambion's tent. 'Hugh says you've been hit with a massive dose of fertility rite magic, about five times more than normal, even without taking into account the rest of the stuff the idiot had in his cauldron. Add that to the Fertility pendant problems Tavish says you've been having, and it's not surprising you were rolling round on the ground.'

'It was pretty surprising to me,' I said, then mock-grumbled, 'as was my impromptu shower.'

'You're drying out' – Finn glanced down – 'which is a shame—'

'Hey!' I stuck my finger under his chin and pushed upwards. 'Eyes up, okay?'

He gave me a quick grin, then sobered. 'So the fertility rites were about increasing the fecundity of the land long before the witches co-opted them for making baby witches.' He waved an arm at the semi-circle of tents. 'Look at it. The place is halfway to a drought, and the shows have sucked the natural magic dry. The ground is starving. It was reaching out to all the fertility magic inside you. You're lucky it didn't *absorb* you.'

Swallowed by the earth. I shuddered. So not a great way to die. 'Guess I should say thank you again, and mean it.' I gave him a rueful look. 'Thank you, Sir Knight, for saving me. With your trusty fire extinguisher.'

'You'd have done the same for me.' He smiled. 'Even if I didn't need saving.'

I stuck my tongue out at him. 'Just give me an opportunity. But truly, I am grateful, Finn. So thank you.'

He brushed a damp strand of hair from my forehead.

'You're welcome, Gen.' He lifted my hand and dropped a kiss on my palm, sending a shiver through me that had nothing to do with the shade. 'Though there are other ways you could show your gratitude, if you were so inclined, my lady.'

'Hmm.' I shot him a repressing look. 'And what ways might those be?'

'I'm sure we can think of something fun.' He winked. 'After we've got this sorted.' He pressed a butterfly-light finger to the hollow of my throat, making my heart skip a beat. He touched his wet finger to my mouth and I tasted salt. 'As soon as the saline dries,' he said, gaze turning serious, 'the fertility magic will come raging back. Believe me, I know.'

I licked my lips. There was one sure fire way of getting rid of all that magic. Sex. The thought coiled desire low inside me. 'What do you suggest?' my mouth said, before my brain had time to censor it.

He waggled his brows. 'Want to come and visit my glade?'

Shock flashed in me. A satyr's glade was a sacred place, and they only ever shared them with their loved ones. It was tantamount to a declaration for him to invite me. In fact, after what he knew had happened with Malik, I had to wonder why Finn was even thinking about showing me his glade.

My thoughts must have shown on my face. 'Hell's thorns, Gen, you must know I care a lot about you and our friend-ship, even if I have been an idiot recently' – he rubbed behind his left horn in exasperation, then sighed – 'other things may have changed, but that hasn't. But I know that you said you've moved on, too.' A muscle jumped in his jaw. 'So I don't want you to think there're strings to this or that this is about sex. Unlike here, my glade's private, safe and overflowing with life and magic. The ground there will accept the fertility inside you gently, without hurting or trying to *absorb* you.'

It sounded great, if I ignored the disappointed voice, grumbling about no sex, in the back of my mind.

'And if you don't do something like that soon,' Finn warned quietly, 'the magic could end up forcing you into a sex-a-thon.'

'I vote for option two,' I said, then shook my head, my mouth was damn well going to get me into trouble if it didn't stop. 'Sorry, not sure where that came from.'

He clasped my face, his palms warm and slightly rough against my cheeks. 'That's the fertility magic talking, Gen. And much as I'd love to, I know that isn't what you want from me.' Sorrow darkened his green eyes. 'But I hope our friendship is. And I also know that if I take a jealous hike over something that happened with the vampire' – his expression hardened – 'which might not have been your choice, without us talking about it, then I'll lose any chance of keeping our friendship.'

'Finn.' I put my hands over his. 'Malik didn't force me.'

'You're hyped-up on fertility magic, Gen. It can influence you and get out of hand pretty quickly. Believe me, I know.' He did, it was how the Witch-bitch Helen had tricked him into getting her pregnant with Nicky; ironically enough using the same Fertility pendant that was giving me problems now. 'So, what I'm saying,' Finn carried on earnestly, 'is that I'm back and I want us to see if we can work things out between us.'

I pulled away from him. 'Finn—'

'C'mon, Gen, even if this thing you have with the vamp is serious, he shouldn't stop you seeing your friends.'

'Finn, that's not going to happen, I make my own choices. And I don't want to lose your friendship, but—'

'No buts.' He took my hand and gave me a half-grin. 'I'm not going to give up on us. And I give you fair warning, I'm hoping to persuade you to choose me. But if it's not to be, then I can't promise to be happy about you and the vampire' – his fingers tightened around mine – 'but I will try, so long as you are. I don't want to lose your friendship either, Gen.'

Wow. Only—'What about Helen?'

'You were right. I shouldn't have let Helen talk me into keeping things from Nicky. I went back and had it all out with Nicky. Turns out she remembers more than she was admitting, but was worried I'd be hurt if I found out what her mum had done, so she was keeping quiet.' His face turned grim and angry. 'I have a suspicion that Helen might have put a *geis* on her, but I can't prove it. But it's all out in the open now. Nicky and I are back here. Helen isn't with us and she's not going to be.'

I blinked, trying to take it in, wondering about his quick attitude turnaround towards Helen from yesterday. 'That's a lot of sorting out in just a night?'

He shook his head. 'A night here but nearly three weeks in the Fair Lands. I didn't want to rush things, but I also didn't want to miss any more time here, so I persuaded the Morrígan to take us out of timesync again.'

Three weeks. So his decisions weren't quite the spur-of-the-moment ones I'd thought.

'Gen, if we're not to be, then that's up to you. But I want us to continue working together, with you as the boss if things work out with the herd, but most of all, I want us to stay friends.'

Oh boy. Part of me thought he sounded too good to be true, but another part was happy, ecstatic even, that he'd come to his senses about the Witch-bitch, and about everything else he'd said. I hadn't wanted to lose his friendship. Though whether we could work things out … well, it was early days. And there was still all this stuff with the kidnap victims, the Emperor, and the fae's trapped fertility to deal with first. But Finn was right, before any of that, I needed to get rid of the fertility magic otherwise I'd be no use for anything; paying a visit to his glade sounded like the quickest, easiest way to go.

Hugh agreed when I explained, then said, 'We need to plan around this "trap" of Max's, in case we need to use it to gain entry into the forum. How long before you can come to Old Scotland Yard?'

I looked at Finn and he said, 'A couple of hours should do it.'

Hugh nodded and we all agreed to meet then. Finn grinned as he slung an arm round my shoulder. 'So, Gen, you ready to come and commune with the magnificence that is' – he gave me an exaggerated wink – 'nature in my glade?'

I groaned and elbowed him (gently) in the gut.

Chapter Forty-Eight

'The entrance is through there?' I frowned at the impene-trable tangle of greenery. It was about twelve feet high and wide, and crowded round a double-stemmed oak tree. Ground level was a dense mix of sharp-spiked gorse and stinging nettles. Above, dark-leaved rhododendrons were twisted with convolvulus, the weed's white trumpet flowers dotting the greenery. Finger-thick blackberry stems sporting wicked-looking thorns and hard, unripe fruits arched out of the tangle, swaying in the summer breeze like the feelers of a monster triffid.

We were in one of the rougher, less-used areas of Primrose Hill park. The wide-spread branches of the oak cast a heavy shade, but other than the bushes beneath it, the area around the tree was free of anything but rough grass for a good thirty or so feet. It meant no one would be likely to use the oak as an illicit trysting place, and anyone using the entrance would have a clear view before either popping out of thin air or disappearing, as we were about to do. Something that would either freak humans out or make them too curious; a trait that doesn't just kill cats.

'It's not as bad as it looks, Gen,' Finn said encouragingly. 'Though it's a touch more overgrown than I remember.'

'Thought you said this was a regular shortcut?' The shortcut led through a section of unclaimed *Between* – the space join-ing the Fair Lands and the humans' world – to London's other parks and green spaces, including Wimbledon Common, home to the satyr herd (and wombles, though the satyrs get a bit ansty when anyone mentions that), and Finn's glade, obviously. Supposedly the shortcut was a five-minute walk which was way quicker than fighting through London's traffic for more than an hour, with the added advantage that we'd get to Finn's glade before the fertility rite magic forced me to commune with the earth or rethink the option of a sex-a-thon with Finn. Not that part of me wasn't doing that anyway.

'It is a regular shortcut, or it was anyway. I haven't used this entrance in a couple of years, though.' He held out his hand. 'Just imagine it parting like a pair of curtains, put a bit of juice behind the thought, and stick close to me.'

'Yeah, me doing spontaneous magic,' I muttered, linking my hand with his, which was warm and firm and filled me with totally inappropriate ideas about how it'd feel on my body. 'Like that's really gonna happen.'

'Hey, have some faith, Gen,' he said, plunging into the thicket and pulling me behind him.

I yelped, felt the gorse scratch at my ankles, the brambles snag at my clothes, then the magic slipped over me like grass tickling my skin and darkness swirled as we left the humans' world. Cinders crunched under my feet as I stepped on to the path: the safe way to travel through unclaimed *Between*. Paths mean you get to where you're going, and don't end up lost or falling prey to the cannibalistic half-formed— semi-evolved spirits hungry for magic and flesh. Finn tugged on my hand and I took another step. My bones seemed to lighten as if gravity had lessened and for a second I felt energised. Then fierce sunshine made me squint, loud bellows followed by high-pitched screams assaulted my ears and I gagged on the stench of shit and sulphur.

'Hell's thorns!' Finn yanked me down behind an ochre-coloured boulder the size of a small car. 'No wonder it's so overgrown, a herd of swamp-dragons have moved in.'

I peered round the boulder. About twenty huge beasts, the size of double-decker buses, looking like a mutant rhinos with scales, small vestigial wings and long whip-like barbed tails, were lumbering through the steaming yellow smoke of an apocalyptic-style landscape, snatching at the charred remains of trees. Around another fifteen or so swampies were wallowing in the massive bubbling sulphur craters, sending rivers of liquid sulphur cascading over the craters' edges. The liquid sulphur shone red like streams of super-heated blood and I could just see its fey-like blue flame as it burned.

Swamp-dragon is a misnomer. The name comes from their first appearance back in the mangrove swamps in Java, Indonesia, in the 1690s. It was thought to be their natural habitat before it was discovered the swampies were just on walkabout after emerging from the Kawah Ijen volcano in the east. They'd made enough of an impression last time I'd run into them, I'd done research.

Good thing about swamp-dragons is they have less intelligence than a cow, aren't the fastest creatures for their size, and, unsurprisingly given the nose-stinging environment, have absolutely no sense of smell.

Bad thing is they're omnivores and will munch on anything they stumble across. Usually after stomping on it like they're playing whack-a-mole: their standard method of disabling prey, despite being able to breathe fire. So long as we could run fast, dodge their tractor-wheel-sized feet, and stay on the cinder path, we'd be okay. Probably.

Another high-pitched scream came from above us, followed by a tiny body thudding onto the boulder then bouncing off to land at my feet. A garden fairy, his throat slashed, still twitching in the last throes of ecstasy as he died. I blinked at it, and then, as another screaming, entangled pair zipped past us, it clicked that this had to be where Lecherous Lampy the gnome was getting his out-of-season stock from. The heat from the swamp-dragons had accelerated the fairies' life cycle, and being small and fast, the swampies weren't likely to eat them.

They would us.

I looked at Finn. He'd dropped his human Glamour. His horns curved a good foot above his head, his body still athletic but shoulders and chest broader, muscles thicker, more honed. The angles of his face sharper, feral and even more gorgeous than his clean-cut handsome look— Lust coiled tight in my belly. Forget stinking, stomping swamp-dragons, I wanted to hole-up with him somewhere for at least a week. No, make that a month. I closed my eyes, forced the feelings back.

'So,' I said, adding an airy note to my voice, 'want to go back, or run for it?'

'Run for it?' He shook his head. 'Hell's thorns, Gen, are you crazy? One slip and we'd be swampie pancakes.'

A low chuffing cough sounded behind us.

We turned as one.

A dark grey cat, striped with black and the size of the tigers in the zoo, crouched belly low to the ground about ten feet away. It stared at us out of gleaming green eyes, ears flat to its skull, tail swishing from side to side as if readying to pounce.

'What the fuck is that?' I muttered.

'Haven't a clue, Gen,' Finn replied just as quietly, 'but it doesn't look friendly.'

The cat gave another low chuffing sound and its lips drew back, seemingly in a grin, exposing more of its long sabre-tooth fangs.

'It doesn't,' I agreed. 'And it's blocking the exit.' Coincidence or deliberate? I sent my inner radar out. 'It pings as an animal. No magic, nothing like human or fae in there.'

'My take too.'

'I'm guessing it could be some sort of ailuranthrope?' I said, though I'd never heard of a weretiger, or even a normal tiger, that strange grey and black colour, not to mention the big cat looked suspiciously like the one that had climbed out of the abyss on the Moon tarot card. The card had said, 'The beasts are coming.' Maybe it hadn't been talking about the Emperor and his werewolves after all.

'Whatever it is,' Finn said grimly, 'there's only one of it, and nearly forty swampies.'

'Think we can take it?' I asked, dropping my backpack and kicking it out of the way.

The cat gave a guttural growl.

Finn made a similar low sound. 'Is the sky blue?'

I looked up. Blue sky wasn't always a given in *Between*. It was now, if you ignored the smoky yellow haze from the sulphur.

'Okay,' I said. 'How about I try to scare it, and if it doesn't run, you do your horny bit.' Then we were high-tailing it to the nearest hotel in the humans' world. 'On three, two, one—'

I jumped up, yelling and waving my arms, and ran at the cat.

It sat back on it haunches, a 'you've got to be kidding me' look on its face.

I skidded to a stop, Finn's arms going round my waist as he dragged me back. 'Guess that answers the question whether it's an animal or not,' I said, glaring at the cat.

'Oh, he *is* an animal, Ms Taylor,' a familiar smarmy voice said. 'But not *just* an animal.' A squat figure appeared out of the charred foliage at the base of the twin-stemmed oak tree: Mr Lampy, the wrinkles in his round face deepening as he gave us a wide smile, his ultra-white human dentures blinding. The mustard-coloured lichen mapping his bald pate ruffled in the hot wind. His bare feet crunched on the cinder path as he strained forward, pulling what looked like the bastard child of a wheelbarrow and a chariot behind him. He stopped once he was fully through the entrance, produced a dirty hanky from his tweed jacket and mopped his face.

'What's going on?' I demanded.

'I'm guessing an ambush of some sort,' Finn breathed against my ear. 'You run for it while I hold the cat off. Keep to the left of the cinder path and look for a copse of goat willow by a small stream; the entrance there will bring you out on Wimbledon Common near the windmill. Speak to Dimitris' – Finn's closest brother – 'and he'll bring help.'

It was a sensible plan. Running the swampies' foot-stomping gauntlet wasn't that hard. I knew how to run, even if the recent chaos had meant I'd missed my usual morning exercise the last few days. But I wasn't going to leave Finn to deal with the big cat and the gnome on his own, however sensible-sounding his plan. It didn't feel right, not when there were two of us, and two of them. But as I was about to object, another grey and black striped big cat slunk through the entrance behind the gnome as if it were embarrassed to be here. Then as if to seal the deal, a third big cat bounded through, skidding to a clumsy halt next to the others. Fuck. No way could we outrun all three of them.

The gnome gave a satisfied sniff and tucked his hanky away. 'Glad you decided to take my suggestion and look into the path here, Ms Taylor.' Crap, I'd forgotten he'd asked me to do that. 'It really does make things easier for me.'

'Easier?'

The gnome waved at the three big cats. 'The boys here have a little problem they need your help with, Ms Taylor.'

'Gen,' Finn's voice was barely audible. 'Run.'

The gnome's beady eyes flicked warily at Finn. Stupid satyr with a hero complex. It was going to get him killed one day. I clenched my fist and released Ascalon. The blessed and be-spelled sword sprang into my grip and I shifted into a ready stance. 'Fine,' I said, 'let's chat.'

A strangled surprised noise came from beside me. 'You've got a sword?'

Oh yeah. Finn didn't know about Ascalon. Amazing what you miss when you disappear for three months. 'Yep.'

'You know how to use it?'

'Yep,' I said, baring my teeth at the gnome and his boys.

'Good.' Finn's voice was a satisfied growl.

The gnome reacted, but not by backing off as I expected. He shook his head as if me producing Ascalon was somehow disappointing. Then the horrid little male, who was obviously far stronger than he looked, grabbed the embarrassed-looking cat by the scruff and threw him at me. The big cat yelped, all four paws stuck out as he flew at me with a horrified expression on his feline face. Reluctant to kill him with Ascalon when he wasn't so much attacking as being sacrificed, I leaped to the side, only just missing skewering him. He landed on his paws less than a foot from me and for a second we froze, staring into each other's eyes. Then shock ripped through me as a burning sensation engulfed my hand, the cat's eyes lit with reflected green fire, and Ascalon vanished back into its ring.

'He's an innocent, Ms Taylor!' the gnome called. 'Your sword won't work when there's an innocent around.'

Fuck. I scrambled back from the big cat who was still frozen. 'Gen!'

Finn's warning shout jerked my head up in time to see the nasty gnome rubbing his hands together, then tossing them in our direction. A dozen cotton wool balls flew towards us, buzzing like angry bees. *Security Stingers ~ the Ultimate Intruder Deterrent.* Crap. If the spells got us we'd be asleep and helpless in seconds. Luckily once the stingers launched, they didn't deviate too far from the original target area—

'Split!' Finn pushed me away, obviously having the same idea.

I turned and sprinted along the cinder path that led to help. A couple of stingers buzzed my head, their sticky threads trailing my face like grasping cobwebs. I stumbled, nearly went down, then *cracked* the threads, feeling the magic slice my forehead as the spells disintegrated. Blood dripped in my eyes as I ran faster—

Something thudded into my back, smacking me to the ground. Pain shot through my head as it bounced off the cinders. More pain burned down my back as claws punctured my skin and the hot heavy weight of a big cat pinned me. I yanked my magic up, flung it at the animal. If I could catch him in my Glamour, he would have to obey me.

A fat mud-covered hand clamped a silver bangle studded with jade and citrines round my left wrist: a police-issue manacle. My magic cut out as if it had been ripped from me. I screamed as someone shouted, 'Get off her!' And the Stun spells in the jade chips ignited.

My body convulsed as if I'd been zapped with high-voltage electricity.

'Hurry up and change, boys, and get them in the cart,' the gnome's voice ordered. 'We need to get moving before the beasts take an interest.'

'Both of them?' The man's question was a low growl. 'Going to slow us down.'

'The Forum Mirabilis is in town. The satyr will bring a nice price at the auction. Those horns alone are worth a good few thousand each, and he's a sex fae; I can get a king's ransom for his—'

Unconsciousness took me.

Chapter Forty-Nine

Insistent fingers prised my lips open where I lay on my back, groggy from being yanked from unconsciousness. A small piece of meat, raw and still warm, landed on my tongue. Gamey-tasting blood infused with a strange, wild magic trickled down my throat. A hand clamped my mouth shut, pinched my nose, forcing me to swallow. I resisted, struggling, determined not to give in this time, concentrating on the firelight seeping beneath the tape closing my eyelids. My lungs began to burn. Despair and fury flooded me as, same as the last however many times, the instinctive need for air and the lure of the blood made me swallow before desperately gasping for oxygen like a landed fish. The meat slid into my stomach to join the rest where it congealed into a heavy solid lump, the magic in it seeming to snuff out.

Where was Finn?

Was he okay?

I sent out my senses, searching for him. Nothing other than the two humans; the gnome's boys, cats, or whatever the fuck they were. Only there'd been three of them. Where was the third? And the gnome? Where had they taken Finn?

Gods, I prayed he was still alive. The memory of the gnome's comment about the money he could make for a satyr at auction was like a fist squeezing my heart. Tears of rage and anguish pricked my eyes as I damned myself for not running when Finn had first told me. Then maybe they wouldn't have caught both of us and I could've brought help.

Something sharp pricked my arm ...

Only unlike the other times, I didn't float back into sleep but hovered on the cusp, pulse pounding erratically as I realised I was frozen inside my own body. Terrified they'd up the dose of whatever, I fought the panic using my childhood trick: *one elephant, two elephants* ... I needed to know what was going on if I was going to get out of this ... *five elephants* ... Find Finn ... *seven* ... *nine* ... my pulse slowed as calm spread through me.

'She's under,' a male said, sounding tired.

'You sure, son?' It was the same growling male who'd said taking both Finn and me was going to slow the cart down.

The tape was peeled carefully from my eyes. I could feel it happening, but the sensation was odd, no pain even when I felt the tape snag a couple of lashes. Anaesthetic? Only the human sort didn't work with my sidhe metabolism ... unless they were using the stuff meant for animals. Enough of that even worked on vamps. Crap. Someone lifted my eyelids. I got a snapshot of a vaguely familiar pale face and dark hair before a penlight blinded me ...

'Pupils not reacting so she's under.'

... He was one of the two males I'd seen hanging round the gnome's ...

A couple of buttons on my shirt were popped, sparking unease even as I realised I was still dressed. Something cold touched my chest. 'Heartbeat's stable too.'

... Shit. Of course he was familiar. He was Katie's treacherous boyfriend. Marc. Damn. Not only was he two-timing her with some redhead, now he *was prodding my breast* ...

'The bite's healing up,' Marc said. 'Same as the cuts on her face and her back where you clawed her.' Accusation threaded the words. 'Don't think it's going to fester.'

'How she get bit by some human anyway?' Growling Male said.

'Don't know,' Marc answered quietly, and relief filled me as my shirt buttons were closed. 'But I don't think it's interfering.'

Interfering? With what? Footsteps sounded as the two males moved.

'Bloody hell,' Growling Male said, his voice coming from further away now. 'Yous thought this time it was gonna work for sure. Why ain't she shifting yet?'

'Who knows?' Marc snapped. 'Maybe the stuff the gnome gave you for the circle is wrong. Maybe there's something missing from the ritual. Maybe whoever he got to hack the witch archives copied the wrong ritual. Maybe she can't shift because she's already too magical. I told you we shouldn't trust him.'

Shifting? Ritual? Witch archives …

'Told you, son, more magical the better, so long as they ain't one of them fae who already shift to somethin' else, like a tree. That's what the notes reckoned was wrong with those girls that chink weretiger tried the ritual on.'

… chink weretiger …

A loud noise. Stone hitting stone. 'Don't fucking call me son, Carlson,' Marc shouted. 'I'm not your kid, and after this I never want to see you again. This is all kinds of fucked up wrong. We can't just kidnap a woman and force her into the shift.'

… Fuck. They were trying to make me into a big-cat-shifter. Like them.

'Heh, s— lad, I knows it ain't right, but I promised yer Da when he passed, I'd find yer a mate. He was ma brother. Ain't gonna break ma promise to him.'

'Da would never have wanted this.'

'Ain't wanting it either, Marc, lad. But we tried gitting a female through that Forum an' you seen the money those folk are putting up for that Bengali cat and her kit. Ain't no chance for us to match it.'

'I told you putting that listing on the Forum was a fucking stupid idea, Carlson. Information on the internet goes viral in seconds.'

'Forum said it were private, lad.'

'Nothing's private on the internet. All that stupid listing did was tell everyone we weren't extinct. I've already seen a load of blogs speculating about us.'

'Ain't nothing to be done now, lad. Yer twenty-four in a few days. Already long past yer prime. You need a mate.'

'I don't want a fucking mate.' More stone crashed against stone.

I didn't want him for a fucking mate either.

'Yer want to live, don't yer, boy?'

'Not like this. What's the point of living if I have to spend my life mated to a woman who hates me? If I hate myself?'

'Heh, s— lad, she ain't gonna hate you. Not soon as the mate bond takes. The magic'll see to that.'

Mate bond. What the hell was that?

'This is wrong,' Marc snapped, and silently I shouted agreement. 'I told you, that girl I've been seeing, Claire. I was going to talk to her, I'm sure she'd have agreed to the ritual willingly. She's desperate to be more than human; she wouldn't care what it meant. We didn't have to do this.'

'An' I told you, lad. It weren't gonna work, that redhead might have a smidge of something magic in her, but it ain't enough. An' anyways, she ain't no virgin—'

'She says she was!' Marc exclaimed. 'She told me thrice.'

Was this guy for real? The thrice rule only worked for full-blood fae, not someone with a drop of magical blood.

'Lad, the gnome ain't guaranteeing that thrice rule works for a faeling. And even if yous was to try, even if it looked like it was working right, that redhead ain't telling truth about being a virgin, so yous both be dead soon as yous mated.'

They died if the mate wasn't a virgin? Well, if they thought I was good to mate with Marc . . . no way in hell was that going to happen, even without the dying bit.

'Better that,' Marc said, 'than kidnapping this poor woman.'

'She's a fairy, lad. Ain't no comeback by the law when it comes to them.'

For the freaking last time; Not. A. Fairy!

'She's a person,' Marc snapped.

'She's a fairy. Heck, we've been catching her sort for the gnome. Ain't hear you sticking up for them, lad.'

'They're garden fairies, Carlson. She's as different from them as we are from the tigers in that stupid zoo. And the fairies were already dead from natural causes. We didn't kill them.'

'Ain't killing her, lad. Just making her shift.'

'What if she doesn't shift? Then she'll die,' Marc said angrily. 'That's the same as killing her. Then what you going to do, Carlson, give her dead body to the gnome so he can cut it up and sell it like the garden fairies?'

'Ain't gonna come to that, lad. She'll shift.'

Even I could hear the doubt in his voice. Damn.

'What if she's not a virgin?' Marc asked quietly.

'Told you, lad, I got the feeling right here.' A hollow thump sounded, like a fist on a chest. 'Got it first outside the gnome's in the park other night. I don't get that less they're intact.'

Oh boy, was his feeling wrong. Stupid fucking idiot. He really needed to get his facts right. Not that I'd wish whatever ritual they were doing on anyone else.

'I can't feel anything,' Marc said.

'Course not, 'cos yous still an innocent yerself. Yous needs to go through the ritual afore you cans.'

He was lying. I could hear it in his voice. Question was, why?

'Anyways, it was her or that young blonde yous been sniffing around.'

Katie! If they'd touched her, they were dead. Hell, they were dead anyway. They'd just be more dead.

A menacing growl reverberated through the air, raising the hairs at my nape. 'Told you, Carlson. Stay away from Katie.'

I opened my eyes, blinked in relief and then frustration as I realised it was only my eyes I could move. I stared up. Firelight chased shadows over the rough-hewn rock. We were in a cave.

'Aw, lad—'

'The ritual is wrong,' Marc's yell cut him off. A stone flew over my head, crashing into the cave wall at the back. 'The gnome must've stitched you up. That's why she's not shifting. You're working on the wrong information, Carlson.'

'Look, so— lad, maybe the ritual needs a bit more time,' Carlson said placatingly. 'Ain't doing yous any good brooding 'bout it now it's done anyways. She's gonna be hungry once she shifts. Ain't a bad idea if yous go hunting, get us all some victuals. Yous needs to keep yous strength up for the mating too.'

I was lying on – the muscles of my neck freed and I turned my head – a pile of dark furs atop a bed of hay mixed with herbs. I made out the clean scent of sage and something minty which smelled oddly enticing. But even with the herbs, hay and smoke from the fire filtering the air, I could still smell the sulphur and shit reek from the swampies. Good. They hadn't brought me too far into *Between*, then.

The two males sat either side of the fire, just inside the low gaping slash of the cave's entrance. Beyond them, it was night outside. How long had I been here? Was this the same day, or longer?

Carlson turned his head slightly, his gaze meeting mine without any visible reaction. His eyes were glowing eerily, reflecting like a cat's.

I tried to shout, but my voice was still gone.

'I'm not mating with her.' Marc's voice was firm as he stood, his head nearly brushing the cave's roof as he raked his hands through his dark hair. 'Better she dies than be forced into something she hasn't agreed to.'

'If that's how yous feeling, lad,' Carlson said, his eyes not leaving mine. 'Then fair enough. But if yous so concerned 'bout her feelings, ain't it better if yous give her the choice? Might be she'd choose to live as yous mate, 'stead of dying.'

Marc stilled with his hands on his head. After a long moment, a frustrated growl came from his throat. 'Yeah, you're right. It's not my decision to make. I can't change what we've done to her, can't take it back. But we can explain what's what, then let her decide for herself.'

Fuck, this guy Carlson was good. Though if he thought I was going to jump on the get-mated-instead-of-dying bandwagon, like his pal Marc, he could think again.

'Might as well fetch a brace of those rabbits we saw.' Marc's tone said he was resigned. 'I'll just check she's okay first.'

'Nah, yous git out there and hunt boy,' Carlson said, 'And check on Steve while yous out there. Make sure he ain't gitting any trouble from that goat-man. Ain't wanting them swampies to git him.'

Finn. He was somewhere nearby. They had him. Captive, but alive. Relief made me limp.

'Okay,' Marc said, pulling off his T-shirt, then he dropped his jeans, showing the cave he went commando. He took a deep breath, expanding his chest, and seemed to fall to the floor. As he did so his human shape morphed into that of a grey and black striped big cat. The shift was fast and seamless and, even more worrying, I couldn't feel any magic. If I couldn't feel it, then there was less chance I'd be able to use it to fight them. I pinged him. Only animal came back. Seconds before he'd pinged human. Well, that answered that question. Ailuranthropes, and possibly all therianthropes, hit my inner radar as human or animal depending on what shape they were in.

Big Cat Marc padded out the cave and disappeared into the night.

Carlson stood, picked up a backpack from just inside the entrance, then grabbed what looked like a brush torch. He shoved it into the fire, making it flare up, then came towards me. He was wearing jeans, his chest bare other than a wide bandage wrapped round his lower ribs. Grim satisfaction trickled through me. He was injured. Maybe Finn had got a horn in before he'd been captured.

Carlson dropped the backpack down, jammed the fiery torch into a hole and crouched next to me. I glared at him as he lifted my head, pulled something from behind me and fastened it around my throat. Not constricting, but tight enough that I could feel it was stiff, like new leather. A loud click at my nape, the chink of something metallic, and he lowered my head back into the furs. It took me a stunned moment to realise he'd put a collar and chain on me.

A sudden image of Malik's memory of the snow-covered plateau with Dilek a.k.a. Fur Jacket Girl werewolf, naked on her hands and knees inside an ash-marked circle, tethered by a leather collar and chain, slammed into me. Whatever had been done to her, this male was planning on doing to me.

Terrified panic rose up in me. I shoved it back. Forced my hand to slowly clench around Ascalon's ring. Marc the innocent was gone. Carlson the guilty was easily within sword distance and, if the damn anaesthetic would wear off so I could move more than just my fingers and head, I was going to kill him.

Carlson the guilty moved to sit cross-legged out of my reach. He looked impassively at where I lay, the fire throwing half his face into shadow. 'Yous ain't no virgin, girl.'

Chapter Fifty

I stared at him. It was a statement, not a question, surprising me, even though I knew he'd been lying earlier. Then I recalled his easy manipulation of Marc. However stupid he'd initially sounded by supposedly not checking his facts, he wasn't. 'No, I'm not,' I said calmly, then realised my mouth had unfrozen and I could talk again.

'S'pected as much.' He patted his chest. 'Yous don't feel quite right.'

'Then why didn't you check?' I asked, working on the age-old maxim that if the baddie wants to talk, let him; there's always a chance he'll tell you something you can use against him. Of course, I didn't really have any other option than to let Carlson talk. But I was curious. Somehow, for all his manipulations, I couldn't see this guy letting Marc try to mate with a non-virgin if it meant the younger male would die. Not that I'd have wanted Carlson to check. If I had my way he wasn't leaving this cave, so there was no chance of him kidnapping any other poor girls, *virgo intacta* or not, ever again. 'All it would've taken was a simple medical examination,' I added.

'Ain't only the physical that counts,' he said. 'Yous gotta be able to take the shift. Gnome says yous probably magical 'nuff it'll work. That's why I were watching yous in the park.'

'I heard,' I said flatly.

He nodded, telling me he'd known I'd been listening. 'Gnome said I should take the blonde, but ma nephew likes the girl. Knew he ain't gonna agree to using her.'

The blonde was Katie. Whether Marc agreed or not didn't make me like him any better. He was out of Katie's life, for good.

'Lad wanted this redhead. Only, like I says, she definitely ain't a virgin. I seen her with the gnome one time.' His mouth turned down. 'If yous know what I mean.'

Ugh.

'She got habits,' he added.

Poor girl.

'An' once yous no longer intact, then even if yous shift, the mating kill yous.'

Nice. 'So even though you thought I might not be a virgin,' I said, voice dry as dust, 'and even if I did shift, then this mating would kill me and your boy, Marc, you still decided I was the one. I'll be honest, leaving aside the whole kidnapping and performing magical rituals on me against my will thing, doesn't sound like you're on to a winner with me. So why bother?'

'We always birthed girl an' boy kits till this last generation. Now we's got four boy kits in need of mates. Ma nephew's the first. If he ain't getting a mate soon, he ain't gonna live. If all of thems ain't getting mates in next five years, then our pride is dead. Adults ain't living once kits all gone.'

I snorted. 'C'mon, you can't really expect me to believe that?'

'We's already lost seven male kits,' he said softly. 'We's descended from old, old tigers. Tigers ain't livin much past they be twenty or so. Ma nephew's twenty-four. Soon as his animal soul moves on, his human soul goes with it. Only thing keeps us all living is if we's mated an' having kits.'

Shifters had two souls? Was that the explanation for their long lives, the one Mary hadn't got around to reading in the witch archives?

I narrowed my eyes. 'But you're older than him, and you're not dead.'

'I's two hun'red an' fifty-six. We's ain't ageing much once we's mated, not till one of us passes. Ma mate, Shona, passed last month. It's why I's doing the ritual. I's dying soon anyways. But if the ritual working, then ma nephew gets a mate an' he'll live.'

And shifters didn't die as long as they were mated. It would've been interesting if I wasn't chained up. Still, I felt some satisfaction that Carlson was dying, slightly less that Marc was too. Though if Carlson thought I was going to feel pity for them …

'But I'm not a virgin. So the ritual was never going to work.'

He leaned forward. 'The ritual ain't finished yet. If yous shift, then we knows the ritual works. Not like when that chink weretiger tried it an' killed them tree girls. It may be too late for ma nephew, but ain't for our other kits.'

It all fell into place. He'd gone ahead with the ritual because even if it didn't work out fully, he'd hoped to learn enough for next time. I was a fucking experiment.

'So yous can sit up now, girl.'

The anaesthetic vanished from my body, aches and pains rushed in and I groaned and sat up before I could stop myself.

'Sorry,' he said in a tone that didn't sound it. 'It takes yous like that.'

I groaned again. Less from the pain and more to give myself time to scope out the cave. Ice slid down my spine as I saw I *was* in an ash circle, glyphs glowing at intervals around the circle's edge, like the one Dilek had been in on the snow-covered plateau. Carlson was sitting outside the circle. I straightened, shoving aside the thick chain dangling from the collar banding my neck. It disappeared beneath the furs, so presumably was attached there. But there was enough slack in it to strangle him, if I could get him close enough. But then if he was that close, I could skewer him with Ascalon.

I looked him in the eyes. 'What takes you like that?'

'The mate bond. Means I's got control of yous. Your body

anyhows.' He smiled, showing normal human teeth. 'The ritual worked, girl. First part anyways. Yous got a part of me in yous now. Means I gits to tell your body what to do, and it does it. Yous can nod your head.' Something shifted inside me and I started nodding, anger and fear ripping into me when I couldn't stop, couldn't even talk. 'Yous can stop now,' he said.

My head jerked to a stop. I glared at him, feeling the strain in my neck where I'd tried to resist him, and an alien magic – his – fluttering to life in my stomach. 'That's sick.'

'Ain't lasting for ever, girl. Just till the mating's over. So's yous ain't ending up hurting yourself during the first joining. Cats ain't built the same as humans.'

No way did I want to even guess what that meant. 'Thought you said it wouldn't work if I wasn't a virgin.'

'This bit does. Next bit don't. Probably.'

'What does that mean?'

'Means we's both likely gonna die soon.'

Which didn't answer my question, but I got what he was planning. He might not think mating with me was going to succeed, but he wasn't going to pass on the chance. He was dying anyway, so he had nothing to lose, even if I did. Except I'd died before, at least three times, and I was still here. Being sidhe and virtually immortal has its advantages. Maybe he was the only one about to snuff it after all. Preferably with a lot of help from me. And, unlike normal cats, it didn't sound like he'd got nine lives to play with.

'If it works,' I said, 'I'll kill you.'

He stared at me unblinking. 'If mate bond takes, girl, yous ain't gonna be feeling like that.'

That's what he thought. No way was I going to be forced to mate for life with him, or with anyone.

'But if I is dying,' he added, pulling a square-shaped cloth-wrapped package from the backpack. 'I knows there's a chance you ain't, you being a fairy an' that.'

'I'm sidhe,' I snapped. 'Not a fairy.'

He shrugged. 'If the lack of mate bond ain't killing you, then I want yous to look out for ma nephew and his kin.'

I snorted. 'You've got to be kidding. There's more chance of me taking a swampie home as a house pet.'

'The blonde girl of yours likes ma nephew.'

He meant Katie. I laughed harshly. 'She doesn't know him. And she's never going to after this. He'll be dead.'

He nodded, a sharp dip of his chin. 'Yous ain't necessarily wrong. Anyhows, if yous surviving, girl, it's all here. If yous ain't, then the pride knows to come looking for it.' He tucked the cloth-wrapped package carefully back in the backpack, then jumped lithely to his feet, dropped his jeans – another fucking commando – and unwrapped the bandage from his torso. Underneath was a raw wound, still trickling with blood. Damn. It looked like someone had carved a chunk of muscle from his left side, right down to his ribs ... nausea roiled in my stomach as I got it. He'd carved chunks off himself. Chunks he'd forced down my throat. Chunks that were now fluttering faster inside me.

He swiped a hand across the wound. It came away covered in blood. He flicked the blood on to the ash circle. I gasped as the circle set and his unfamiliar magic stretched inside me, as if something warm, wet and slippery was sliding around beneath my skin, a beat reverberating through me like I had a second heart. Carlson fell to the floor, morphing seamlessly into a chunky grey and black sabre-toothed cat. The cat crouched low on its belly, hackles raised, and let out a scream, part challenge, part something else.

My stomach cramped, doubling me over.

The cat screamed again.

My head jerked up, a film passed over my eyes and the light in the cave brightened as if bathed by halogen spots, even as the colour drained away to leave everything, even the flames, in shades of grey.

The cat peeled its lips back and hissed. Part of me was fascinated by the sharp detail of the stripes in its coat, its long, quivering whiskers; another part of me smelled the gamey scent of its blood. And wanted more. Wanted to tear its flesh and crack its bones. I threw my head back, letting out my own scream, the sound vibrating oddly in my still humanoid throat.

The other cat crouched lower, muscles bunching for attack, ears flat, tail swishing.

My stomach cramped again, pain and anger and hunger goading me.

The cat growled low, demanding my obedience.

No way.

I leaped, pushing off with powerful hind legs, claws extended, attacking—

The collar tingled with magic then tightened to a chokehold round my throat, snatching me back even as that alien magic ripped part of me clean away. I soared through the air to land on the other cat's back. It yelped in surprise, then pain, as I clamped my mouth on the back of its neck, sabre-fangs sinking deep, slicing through muscle, tendons and bone to meet with a snap that jarred my head. The cat beneath me froze in submission, its heart pounding, breath panting from its parted mouth … *Like the man part, it didn't want to die. It wanted to take me as its mate, to have more kits …*

The blood scent from its wound called. My stomach cramped a third time.

This cat wasn't my mate. It wasn't worthy.

It was prey.

I shook it.

Snapped its neck.

Killed it.

Fed.

Chapter Fifty-One

Something warm, wet and rough licked my cheek. My eyes snapped open, and I stared up into a huge furry face. It looked down at me with curious copper-coloured eyes, huffed as if to say, 'Get up, lazybones,' and yawned wide enough to showcase a gut-liquefying set of sharp, white, sabre-toothed fangs—

I threw myself away, rolling until I slammed up against the invisible wall of the ash circle, the heavy chain and collar choking my throat, and froze, staring at the big cat a few feet away, whiskers gleaming amber, the very tip of its tail twitching. Gradually what I was looking at sank into my mind. The big cat's coat was a mix of glossy golds, bronzes and dark reds, marked with black stripes. It looked as if someone had given an orange and black tiger a funky metallic dye job. If I ignored the black stripes, its coat matched my hair. And unlike the tigers in the zoo, its pupils were oval, like a domestic cat's. Or mine.

'What are you?' I croaked, heart pounding erratically in my chest.

Its ears pricked forward, the look on its face saying, 'You're kidding me, aren't you?' Then, as if I was no longer interesting, it went and flopped down at the cave entrance.

I huddled there, trying to catch the thoughts running round my head like a frantic mouse. Who was the gold cat? Was it another shifter? Was the funky gold cat why I thought I'd shifted into a big cat and eaten Carlson? But there was no way

I had, not when I was still stuck in the circle, still collared and chained. Not that I wouldn't have killed Carlson …

There was no sign of his grey and black striped cat body. Or his human one. His backpack was still here, its contents strewn across the floor: the cloth-wrapped package containing the ritual (ugh), phone (no use here) and a bottle of water (damn, I was thirsty). His discarded jeans and the bloody bandage were piled next to it. There was no sign of him. Not even a bloodstain on the cave's floor. So had the gold cat chased him off? Eaten him? And where had it come from? More important, what did it want with me?

Not a lot, I realised, as the gold cat rested its head on its (very large and no doubt very sharp-clawed) paws next to the cold remains of the fire, and dozed in the sulphurous-coloured sunlight coming through the entrance. Not far from the gold cat was my own backpack. Which was an unexpected bonus. I took a calming breath – the cat could wait – untangled myself from the chain, then scrambled up and paced my magical prison looking for a way out.

The chain easily let me move to the edge of the ash circle, but I couldn't cross the ashes or get a handle on the magic in them to *crack* it. Nor could I break the padlock on the leather collar, or the chain, which was obviously thick enough to hold the big cat it was made for. I shuddered, trying not to think of Carlson's plans for me, and shoved the fur-covered pallet aside. The chain was welded to a massive iron ring, drilled and cemented into the cave floor. Crap. I was never going to break that. I'd have to work on the collar instead.

I twisted my ring. Ascalon should cut through the collar with ease. But before I started sawing at my neck with a two-foot-plus-long and razor sharp sword, I needed to take care of at least one biological necessity. Dehydrated I might be, but still, nature calls. I chose a spot facing the back of the cave and sighed with relief.

My relief was short-lived as I realised even with the collar off, I'd still be trapped in the circle. And Carlson might be (with any luck) dead and gone, but Marc and the other grey and black stripy cat-shifter, Steve, could turn up at any time.

Damn. How long had I been here? Since yesterday, seeing as I still needed to relieve myself and hadn't had any involuntary accidents. Which meant this was the Summer Solstice. The Forum Mirabilis auction was tonight. And something told me that, no matter what plans Hugh had in place to rescue the kidnap victims, if I didn't get back for the auction, then any chance of the Emperor answering my question about releasing the fae's trapped fertility would be lost.

Crap. What if I didn't get free in time?

'No,' I said, the sound of my voice loud in the quiet cave. 'No. This is *Between*. Like the Fair Lands time runs differently here – faster or slower – if you can make it so.' And I could. The magic liked me. All I had to do was decide 'slower' and it would be so. I clenched my fists, determined. 'Slower, definitely slower.' Hell, I could be here a week or more, not that I was planning to, and still return the same afternoon I'd left.

But first to escape. And find Finn. No way was I going anywhere without him.

I eyed my backpack. As well as water, some handy wipes and other useful stuff, it contained salt. Salt would break the circle, and while I couldn't cross the ashes, it didn't mean things couldn't get in. After all, Carlson had planned to do *whatever* with me in the circle. I frowned at the gold cat. I was pretty sure it was a shifter, and while it didn't seem able to talk to me in its cat shape, it still had ears and presumably a human brain between them.

'Hey,' I called.

The gold cat cracked one copper-coloured eye open.

I pointed. 'Any chance you could bring me my bag?'

It opened the other eye and lifted its head. Finally, after

what seemed an age, it rose with a lazy grace and nosed the bag before snagging it in its sabre-teeth. I held my breath as it padded over and then let it out in relief as it tossed the bag over the ashes, to thud at my feet.

'Thanks,' I said.

It huffed, almost like a laugh, then went back to lie at the cave's entrance. Guarding it from outsiders? Or keeping me in? Whatever, I had my bag.

Ten minutes later I was watered, wiped and had one of Sylvia's always-there BLT sandwiches filling my empty stomach. Thankfully, either by luck or design, her sandwich-replenishing spell on my backpack still worked here. I'd offered the cat water and half the sandwich, which it disdainfully declined by totally ignoring me. I wished I'd thought to ask Sylvia to do the same replenishment trick with the salt too; the plastic shaker was only half full. I started sprinkling it carefully onto the ash circle. As I made it about half way around, a strong breeze ruffled the gold cat's fur, blew my hair back, and jasmine-scented magic tingled like electricity over my skin.

A girl appeared, sitting with her legs tucked under her to one side, in the middle of the cave.

I froze, half bent over, fingers gripping the salt. Gold Cat flattened her ears but otherwise didn't stir. The girl was about my own age, raven-black hair curling extravagantly to her hips, dressed in a mediaeval-style dress in claret red that pooled around her like a puddle of blood. Her eyes matched the claret colour of the dress, and her cat-like pupils matched Gold Cat's. And my own.

She was sidhe.

She was also a ghost.

I clamped my mouth shut on a scream as my stupid phobia hit, panic speeding my pulse. I swallowed the panic back. The ghost sidhe couldn't hurt me, hell, she couldn't even speak to me, since I can see ghosts but not hear them. Well, not unless it's All Hallows' Eve. Which this wasn't—

She was sidhe.

Sidhe don't leave ghosts. If we die, our bodies fade, dissipating back into the ether as our spirits dissipate back into the magic. Damn. Stupid phobia had zapped my brain cells. She wasn't dead, she was some sort of spirit. I straightened, shooting the girl a narrow-eyed look.

She smiled, showing fangs every bit as sharp, white and pointed as Gold Cat's, but way more dainty.

'Nice gnashers,' I muttered, wondering why she'd chosen to Glamour herself with them, then added louder, 'so are you anything to do with the cat?'

She laughed. 'Me, dearie? Oh no, that … cat is not known to me. I am Viviane.'

She announced her name as if I should know it. I didn't. I did know her voice, even if the last time I'd heard it, it had sounded older, deeper and more crotchety. 'You're the spirit of the tarot cards.'

She snapped her fingers and a fan of translucent, blank white cards appeared in her hand. 'I am, indeed, bean sidhe.'

Good to have it confirmed, even if her showing up in person added a whole slew of questions to the suspicions already in my mind. Nor was I thrilled about having Viviane's now much larger and no doubt sharper teeth near my flesh. But now I'd get the last and final tarot card. Looking on the bright side, it was bound to be way more enlightening that the previous four.

I held out my hand. 'I offer my blood solely in exchange for the answer to my questions. No harm to me or mine.'

'Pfft!' She shot me a disgusted look. 'I'm not here for that.'

Disappointment and surprise washed through me. 'Then what are you here for?'

'Oh, just a little chat,' she said airily. 'Nothing more.'

413

Yeah, and I wasn't a sitting duck in a circle of ashes with a magical collar fastened round my neck. Gold Cat seemed to agree with me, if its low growl was anything to go by. Maybe it was on my side after all. 'Start chatting then,' I said flatly.

'Direct. Good.' She nodded. 'I like that.'

She didn't, or she'd have told me what she wanted. No, she'd probably much rather string me along until she got me in a position that she thought I'd agree to whatever it was, without her giving too much in exchange. Well, two could play that game.

I went back to sprinkling salt on the ash circle. Viviane gave me an arch look for a moment then started laying her cards out in what, from the corner of my eye, looked ironically like Patience. Once she was done, she moved a couple, then said to no one in particular. 'That cat is not a cat, nor is it a true shifter. It is an *ùmaidh*.'

An *ùmaidh*. A temporary changeling.

My hand shook and I only just managed not to dump the rest of the salt. It took flesh and a sliver of soul forged to living matter to animate an *ùmaidh*. The living matter had to be Carlson's body; I wasn't entirely clear where the flesh had come from, unless it was the flesh Carlson had fed me (ugh), and then somehow I'd managed to sunder part of my own soul. Did that mean Gold Cat was made from both of us? Was it gold because it was more me than him? And what had happened to Carlson's soul? Or souls, since shifters had two souls. Maybe Gold Cat had two and a bit souls now? Or maybe there was nothing left of Carlson at all. I didn't know. And I didn't know how I'd created an *ùmaidh* either. Unless the magic had helped? It had done that before, made impossible-for-me-to-do things happen because it decided I needed them.

Viviane moved another couple of cards. 'Now you're

thinking that cat is your *ùmaidh*, and you're right, bean sidhe. But you're also wrong.'

Hmm. I kept sprinkling salt; Viviane wasn't done with the free information.

'Shifters have two souls, one human and one animal,' she said.

C'mon, Viv, tell me something I don't know.

'The human soul is the usual reincarnated one, but the animal soul isn't.It's an animus.'

Now she was getting interesting.

She placed a finger on one card. 'Animus are primal spirits who long ago decided to embody themselves in animals, predators mostly, instead of the magical flesh The Mother chose to clothe herself in.'

I wasn't entirely sure what a primal spirit was, but The Mother is our creator, and the first to shape herself out of the magic way back when. A shiver of fear pricked goosebumps over my skin. Bad enough when gods or goddesses take an interest in you, even more so when it's The Mother. If primal spirits were anything like even a minor god or goddess, the last thing I wanted was to have one set its sights on me. I squinted at Gold Cat dozing in the sulphurous sunshine. It didn't look like an überpowerful primal spirit, but hey, looks are deceiving.

Viviane flicked a card into the air and gave a sharp nod as it vanished. 'Unfortunately, the animus shortly discovered the downsides of chaining their spirits to their animal hosts. One was that animals die too quickly. And by embodying themselves in actual flesh, the animus only keep their immortality so long as their spirit lives on in their host, or its descendants. Should all their descendants die, the animus dies too.' She vanished another card. 'But there was an even greater threat to the animus's immortality: their animal hosts were not the most efficient predator in the humans' world. So the animus sought primacy by bonding their animals' bodies and souls with those of humans. In doing so, they succeeded in using the humans' shapes, along with their animal shapes, as they willed, thus creating the first shifters.'

Which hadn't panned out too well for them, since shifters had still ended up being hunted almost to extinction. But it did tell me how Carlson's ritual was supposed to have worked. It should've bonded my soul with whatever part or parts of the animus' soul that Carlson carried and turned me into a shifter. Only it hadn't worked quite right, for whatever reason.

'When the shifters die,' Viviane carried on, 'their human and animal souls move on, but the part of the animus's spirit rejoins with itself by travelling into another shifter, a direct descendant of the human who is dead.'

I stopped sprinkling salt and stared at the back of the cave, hearing Carlson's voice saying, 'Our pride is dying. Adults ain't living once the kits all gone. Only thing keeps us all living is if we's mated an' having kits.' Which sort of made sense if the shifters' pride were all sharing one or two primal spirits. With no more children being born, and the human and animal parts of them dying, the primal spirit had fewer bodies to inhabit. Until it had no body left at all, and died.

No doubt why Carlson had advertised on the Forum Mirabilis for a female weretiger, and when that hadn't worked he'd got hold of a copy of the ritual and used me as his experimental guinea pig. He didn't have any direct descendants. With Carlson dead, the animus was finally dead too.

Except it wasn't. I'd somehow made an *ùmaidh*, and the animus had bonded to the part of my soul in the *ùmaidh*, instead of me. Or maybe I (or more likely, the friendly magic) had severed the part of my soul the animus had bonded to, so I didn't end up a big-cat-shifter.

Whatever.

The ritual hadn't worked. I wasn't a shifter. The animus was stuck in a temporary changeling's body. One that was going to die in a couple of weeks.

My relief came with a thread of pity for Gold Cat. No way did I agree with its methods (or Carlson's methods? I wasn't sure who'd actually been in charge), but it just wanted to survive, like the rest of us. Of course, Gold Cat wasn't the only spirit in the cave; Viviane was another. And she'd been quiet long enough that her info-freebies had evidently come to an end. I turned and gave her and the Gold Cat an enquiring look.

'So have the two of you been chatting' – *and no doubt plotting too* – 'about all things primal while I've been sleeping?'

Viviane shook her head. 'Oh no, that cat isn't interested in talking to *me*.'

Did that mean Gold Cat wanted to talk to me? So far it hadn't been very communicative, other than the odd growl or disdainful look, much like any cat really. But if they hadn't been chatting/plotting, where was Viv getting her info from? Since if all that stuff about shifters was known, if not by me, then by the fae, I was pretty sure Tavish would have mentioned it at some point. And he hadn't.

I asked her.

'Knowledge is easy to come by, bean sidhe, if you know where to research.' Viviane grinned like a Cheshire cat, but unlike the cat she didn't disappear only stretched her head and neck out like a cartoon character across the cave to where Carlson's backpack and its contents were strewn on the floor. She stuck her head into the cloth-wrapped package. 'Let us see.' Her voice was slightly muffled. 'Ah yes, pages thirty-two to thirty-eight talk about shifter creation'– she lifted her head and gave me a smug look – 'with a note from a Witch Whitneyi to say that "animus" as pertaining to shifters bears no relation to Jungian theory, and not to confuse the two. The witch archives contain an amazing collection of knowledge, so vast that even they do not know what insights are to be found within. But I use it often enough that I have become quite proficient in discovering any answer I want.'

Did she expect me to applaud, or something? 'Anything in there about why the ritual didn't work?'

Viviane stuck her head back in, then after a moment she snapped back to her previous sitting position next to her cards. She gave me a sly smile.

Right. No more free info. And no way could I get hold of Carlson's papers on my own— 'Hey, Gold Cat. Any chance of you getting those papers for me?'

Gold Cat lifted its head, gave me another copper-eyed stare, then rose gracefully and padded out of the cave without a backward look.

'I'll take that as a no, then,' I muttered.

Viviane let out a pleased sound and moved three cards.

I went back to my salt sprinkling … and learned that even closing the circle with salt didn't negate its magic. Frustrated, I chucked the empty salt container at the back of the cave, sighed, sat down, and arranged the chain so it didn't touch me. I looked at Viviane. 'What's the deal, then?'

Chapter Fifty-Two

'Let us see, bean sidhe.' Viviane tapped another card. 'You want to be released from that circle. You want to help your troll friend with his rescue of the victims. You want the satyr safe.' She gave me another sharp-toothed smile. 'And you want the last card in the tarot reading so you know how to release the fae's fertility from the pendant. That card, however, is not part of this agreement, since it is already under contract.'

Left unsaid was that she could fudge the timing of the card's appearance, to make it less helpful than it might be. But as for the rest, she'd got it spot on.

Viviane shifted a card from the top of one line to the bottom of another. 'I also get a touch of precognition with the cards. For instance, when it comes to your negotiations with the Emperor, I might be able to help you.'

Help me, or you? 'What sort of help?'

She frowned, moved another card. 'I'm not able to say exactly. It seems I might have a conflict of interest.'

'What does that mean?'

She shrugged. 'Exactly what I said. Some things I can help you with. Others would negate another bargain I have already made.'

'Who with?'

'You know I can't tell you that,' she said chidingly.

It was an easy out. Though that probably didn't make it any less true. And my suspicious antennae said her bargain was with Bastien. The tarot cards had tied in too closely to

419

Bastien's plans for it to be anyone else. Only Viv's mention of bargains had my stomach clenching, but if that was what I had to do … 'So you want to make a sidhe bargain—'

'No,' she shouted, throwing her hands up in horror, her cards flying round the cave like a flight of panicked garden fairies. 'Just a small agreement to help each other out the best we can, nothing more, bean sidhe. I do not want the magic involved in this. That is how I ended up enslaved to the cards in the first place.'

I blinked, surprised at her words, and that she'd admitted it. But it also made me happier to go along with her small agreement; it meant no unpredictable consequences for either of us. Of course, it also left a greater chance of loopholes to wiggle out of.

'So what *do* you want?'

She clasped her hands in front of her. 'I want you to get the kelpie to give you the tarot cards as a gift then, at a time and place of my choosing, I want you to burn the cards to ash and transfer ownership of the ashes to the person of my choice.'

She wanted her freedom. With the chain and collar round my neck, I could relate. 'If I agree, you'll help release me, help save Finn, help me rescue the victims, and get my answer from the Emperor with no harm to me or mine?'

'With no harm to you or yours from me, yes. I can't guarantee what others will or will not do.'

Hmm. Nice qualification for a small agreement. But then loopholes could work both ways. Transferring ownership of the tarot cards was one thing, but she hadn't said it was to be an unrestricted transfer.

'Then we have ourselves a small agreement,' I said. We both held our breath in case the magic decided to chime in of its own accord. Sometimes it can be tricky like that. After a long, thankfully, chime-free minute, we both relaxed. 'So what happens now?'

Viviane gave me a pleasant smile. 'We wait.'

'For what?'

'Your white knight to appear, of course.'

'Who the hell is that?'

'Someone who can release you.'

Crap. She wasn't going to tell me. I narrowed my eyes. 'Thought you were going to help?'

'Incorporeal.' She waggled her hands. 'I can look, but not touch. That collar needs someone with opposable thumbs and magic.' She flashed me her sharp-toothed smile again. 'But I've got it all organised, no need to worry.'

She'd got it all organised? Figured. But then she'd already known I was likely to end up chained in the ash circle. After all, she'd shown me that big grey and black cat on the Moon tarot card, and warned that the beasts were coming for me. Just enough information that I couldn't call her on it. I was the fool for thinking she'd meant the Emperor's werewolves. Shame on me.

Forty-odd minutes later, during which I impatiently (and ironically) watched Viviane play Patience, I was pacing the ash circle and rattling my chain like a trapped animal, or the recently condemned.

I stopped as a bellowing noise came, followed by two more. Swamp-dragons on the hunt. And not too far away, judging by the pitch. Viviane lifted her head, focused warily on the cave entrance.

More bellowing. Eager and excited. The swampies had sighted prey.

A loud, angry roar rolled through the air, sounding like the cat roaring on the Moon tarot card. The roar came from right outside the cave.

Gold Cat? Or some other shifter?

I clenched my fists, pacing the circle and listening to the

cacophony of noise: growls of warning, the swampies' excited bellows … a sharp yelp of pain followed by a long, breath-holding silence … then Gold Cat was backing through the entrance of the cave dragging a body behind it—

Finn.

He was scarily still.

Heart thudding with fear, I slapped my hands against the circle's invisible wall, shouting at Gold Cat to bring him near. Gold Cat hauled him right to the edge of the ash circle and, sides heaving, let him drop. He fell on his front, face towards me. His shirt and trousers were ripped and mud-splattered, with a distinct whiff of swampie sulphur. His hooves were rough, his hair matted, his long curving horns bloody, and cuts and bruises marked his cheek, jaw and what I could see of his back. He'd been in a fight; the purple colour of the bruises suggesting it had happened hours ago. There was a deep scratch on his forehead, more recent judging by the fresh blood still trickling. I slapped the circle wall again, but still couldn't breach the ashes.

'Viviane,' I shouted. 'Do something. He's hurt.'

She held up her hands and shook her head. 'Sorry. Incorporeal, remember.'

Fuck. I kicked the circle, straining to grab its magic, then stopped as Gold Cat snarled and spat at me as if to say, 'Get back!' Hope springing in my heart, I watched as it swiped its tongue over Finn's bloody face then pushed at him with its head. His body rolled over, landing on the ashes, his arm dropping inside the circle.

I dropped to my knees, reaching out to grab him, but as my fingers closed over his wrist, Gold Cat leaped over him and the ashes and vanished in a cascade of golden stars.

Magic exploded inside me, desperate heat spreading through my veins, throbbing between my legs. I tightened my hold on Finn and pulled him fully into the circle, not caring for anything other than needing him in here with me. He moaned, lids fluttering open, eyes a muddy-green with pain. They lit with relief when he saw me.

'Gen?' he murmured. 'Thank the Gods. I thought ... killed ... worse.'

I wanted to tell him how ecstatic and relieved I was to see him alive, wanted to find out how hurt he was, wanted to ask him what had happened, wanted to tell him I was fine, wanted to get him to take the damn collar off, wanted us to escape. Wanted to tell him about the magic driving me. Wanted to warn him. Wanted to stop it. Instead, I took his face in my hands and thrust my magic into him, exalting as the muddy-green in his eyes flickered emerald and he reached up to grip my arms.

His eyes turned solid gold with my Glamour. I lowered my lips to his in a searing kiss.

The steady beat of Finn's heart woke me. My face was pressed into the curve of his throat, my body sprawled atop his where we lay on the furs, and despite Finn's sleeping breath warming my hair and the languorous wellbeing leaving my muscles yielding and pliant, I could feel where a certain part of him was nowhere near so soft. Could feel it so intimately that there was no way I could deny we'd had sex, and we'd evidently fallen asleep still joined.

Only I couldn't remember any of it.

Stunned, I prodded the blankness in my mind. I could recall the swampies bellowing, Gold Cat dragging Finn into the cave, Viviane lifting her hands and shrugging ... then a fuzzy memory of pulling Finn into the circle, the magic and need driving me as I kissed him. But nothing more. Shocked disbelief washed over me, fracturing my sleepy aftermath.

I couldn't remember what we'd done.

Was this some sort of cosmic joke? Had someone stolen

my memory? Or hexed us, or maybe just me— Crap. The Morpheus Memory Aid. One of its side-effects was memory loss. Why the hell did it have to hit now? Then something more horrifying hit me. I'd Glamoured Finn.

Fuck. I'd forced him. Disgust whirled through me. It didn't matter that he might have said yes if the circumstances were normal; he hadn't had the chance. I was as bad as his ex, the Witch-bitch Helen.

I started to move then found myself flipped over and a very awake-looking Finn gazing down at me, horns curving at full length, eyes shining gold. Part of me was selfishly grateful he was still caught in my Glamour, so I had a few more minutes before I got to see his revulsion at how I'd trapped him. And if I was truthful, even sickened with myself as I was, I wanted a few more minutes to enjoy the position I'd woken up in … and was still in. Finn flipping me over hadn't dislodged anything, and what hadn't been exactly soft before was becoming less that way even as we lay here, much to my body's obvious delight. It reacted happily, tightening around him with desire.

'Sorry,' I muttered, ashamed heat burning my face. 'I didn't mean that.'

'Hey.' He grinned, did something that made me gasp beneath him. 'Nothing to be sorry for, Gen. I am a sex god, after all' – he winked – 'and us sex gods love it when we're appreciated. It does wonders for our poor battered egos.'

'Yeah, about that—'

He silenced me with a long lingering kiss, one that made my toes curl and made me want nothing more than to take this where he thought it was headed. As he started moving, my heart cracked a little and I broke the kiss, turning my face away.

He stilled above me. 'Gen?'

'I'm sorry,' I said, staring at the back of the cave, noticing the leather collar and its broken padlock. Finn must've removed it at some point. 'We can't— I can't do this.' Tears stung my eyes.

He gently turned my face to his, brushing his thumb across my wet cheek. 'Gods, Gen, what's wrong?'

'Finn,' I said softly. 'I'm not sure if you'll understand me, but I've trapped you in my Glamour. I'm sorry, I didn't mean to. Whatever we did last night, it's my fault. But we can't do this now. And I can't release you unless we're not touching.'

'You've Glamoured me?' He gave me a perplexed look as he shifted back slightly.

'Yeah,' I said, feeling strangely reluctant to lose my connection to him. 'I'm sorry. You need to move so I can free you.'

'Gen,' he said earnestly, 'we talked about all this last night at length. I've told you before, and I explained then, you can't trap me. See?' He closed his eyes, took a breath and when he opened them again, they were his normal moss-green. 'It's just more fun sharing magic.' He gave me a brief half-smile. 'I know you were knocked sideways with the effects of that stupid cambion's magic coming on top of the fertility spell and all the ambush stuff, but we didn't do anything either of us didn't want to last night, or at least—' His expression turned troubled. 'Are you saying something different, Gen?'

'I don't know,' I said. 'I can't remember. I've used two of those Morpheus Memory Aids in the last few days. I think their magic's—'

'Morpheus Memory Aids usually cause spotty memory loss, like forgetting if you've locked the door, or where you left your keys. It doesn't strip away a whole night.'

'Well, it has.'

Distress crossed his face. 'Gen, we didn't just have sex, we talked about stuff. A lot of stuff. Nicky, Helen … *us*. Don't you remember any of it?'

'Seriously, Finn. Nothing after I kissed you, no.'

His expression turned horrified, and he was gone so fast I

felt a breeze. A fur landed on top of me and I hugged it as I sat up. He had his back to me. Sleek sable hair coated his hips and thighs, and a black tuft nestled at the base of his spine: his tail. The fact that he was too upset to hide it sent my pulse spiking with anxiety. It sped faster as I saw he was tearing Carlson's backpack apart, ripping off all the smaller pockets. He tossed it aside then scanned the cave as if searching for something. Suddenly his eyes lit on Marc's clothes by the cold fire. He snatched them up, shoved his hand in the jeans pockets, but came up empty. He threw them down in disgust.

'What are you looking for?' I asked, hating that my voice shook.

'Something that would explain why you've lost your memory.' His gaze fixed on the fire. He grabbed a stick and poked the ashes. 'Nothing.' He rushed back, his jeans appearing as he did, and crouched down next to me. 'What's the exact last thing you remember, Gen?'

I looked into his worried face, tamped down my own panic. 'The swampies were outside the cave, I could hear them, and something like a fight, then Gold Cat dragged you in, pushed you into the circle.' I frowned. 'I remember wanting to talk to you, but instead I kissed you. Then nothing until I woke up.'

Finn took my hands, an odd look on his face. 'You said a gold cat dragged me in. What cat, Gen?'

'Gold Cat. It's a primal spirit, an animus,' I said slowly, unease clutching my gut. 'The ritual went wrong and I somehow made an *ùmaidh* and the animus bonded to it.'

'I don't know anything about primal spirits, Gen,' he said worriedly. 'But you have to sever part of your soul to make an *ùmaidh*. It's not something you can do without the right knowledge. What's this cat look like?'

'Same size as the shifters' cats. but not as chunky, and it's gold with black stripes, not dark grey. It brought you here.'

Finn shook his head. 'I don't remember any gold-coloured

426

cat, Gen. Just the gnome and the big cats that ambushed us.'

'You were unconscious when it brought you in,' I said, trying to stay calm, but hearing my anxiety in my voice.

'Yeah.' His eyes flickered down at my arms, at the fading needle-marks there. 'Gen, we talked about this last night, how you couldn't remember much about what happened after the ritual went wrong. But you were sure you were okay. Maybe I was a bit hasty believing you. I think—'

'You think what? That Gold Cat isn't real? That I was hallucinating it or something? Finn, think about it. Hugh was waiting for us to turn up at Old Scotland Yard. We'd been kidnapped. Why would we stay the night here and talk and everything?'

He frowned. 'I said that to you, but you reminded me this is *Between*. Said we could spend a week here and make it just an hour in the humans' world if we wanted. That we shouldn't waste the opportunity. You wanted us to get rid of the fertility magic, and to sort things out between us, before we went back. You never mentioned any gold cat, Gen. And we talked about ...'

I stopped listening as Gold Cat padded silently through the cave entrance. I grabbed Finn's arm. 'There! Look!' As he turned, the cat huffed in exasperation, crouched and leaped. As it flew towards us I shoved Finn out of the way and braced for impact. It didn't come. Instead, the big cat seemed to merge into me in a brush of soft fur, sharp claws and alien magic. As it did, my skin felt stretched tight enough to split, the colours in the cave muted to grey and the taste of fresh meat filled my mouth. I looked at Finn's shocked expression and a cascade of memories poured over me; our voices mingling in laughter and tears, our limbs tangling in passionate pleasure, and the deep satisfaction of knowing he was mine.

My mate.

And I/it was his.

Mated.

No! I tried to shout, to push it out, but it raked claws through me, slicing me into smaller and smaller bloody pieces and casting them down into the darkness.

As I fell it reached out to Finn and as my lips met his, I felt it find the memories of it returning as the Gold Cat to the cave, of his and my waking minutes, of my telling him about it, and steal them from him.

The memories rained down on me, burning like acid tears.

Chapter Fifty-Three

I woke with a raging thirst, a hammering in my head that rivalled a dwarves' workshop, and a nauseous roiling in my belly. I groaned, rolled groggily away from the sunlight sending knives into my eyes, and got a face full of fur. I groaned again, belatedly realising my Hot.D/Reviver double-postponed hangover had sucker-punched me. As had Gold Cat.

Fucking animus had mated me and Finn. Or it and him. Or all of us. Or— Fuck if I knew. But whatever Gold Cat had done, it was going to undo it as soon as I got my hands around its funky furry neck.

I scrambled up, dizzy with the hangover, to find Finn and Gold Cat were gone.

But Viviane was back, sitting with her game of Patience.

Shit. I should've known better than to trust her small agreement. I should've negotiated a cast-iron bargain with her and damned the consequences.

'You and Gold Cat planned that, didn't you?' I accused, grabbing my clothes and yanking them on.

She calmly moved a card. 'Not so much planned as, once I knew what the animus wanted, I agreed not to interfere.'

'Why?'

'Why isn't important right now, bean sidhe. Not if you want me to help you save the satyr, as we agreed.'

I snorted then wished I hadn't as the dwarves in my head hammered another couple of nails in. 'No thanks, Viv. After your last bit of *help*, in which you, oh so *helpfully* fucked Finn

429

and me up, you can stick it. And the agreement's off; you've broken our no-harm-to-me-or-mine deal.'

Her cards jerked up on end, quivering with umbrage. 'I agreed to help release you from that circle. In order to do that without your dying, the ritual had to be completed. As stated on page thirty-nine of the notes taken from the witch archives.'

My hands stilled on my shirt buttons as the ramifications hit me. If I hadn't had sex with Finn, I'd be dead … except I'm sidhe, and hard to kill. And I trusted Viviane about as far as I could throw her, which seeing as she was incorporeal was not at all. But I didn't need to trust her, I could check for myself. I lurched over to Carlson's ripped backpack, only to find the cloth-wrapped bundle containing the details of the ritual was missing.

I rounded on Viviane. 'Where is it?'

She shrugged. 'I do not know. But I can tell you that what happened between you and Finn was for the best. If it had not happened, then when the Emperor's *lupus centurions* appeared, they would have killed the satyr and one of them would have completed the ritual instead. I do not think you would enjoy being mated to one of the Emperor's werewolves.'

I stared at her, horrified at the worse-than-having-sex-with-Finn-and-whatever-Gold-Cat-had-done fate Finn and I had averted. 'The Emperor's werewolves were here?'

She tossed her black hair back in irritation and her cards flew up into a line in front of my face. Like a slide show they showed seven huge wolves at the cave entrance. Then three black-haired, olive-skinned males, dressed only in short centurion-style leather kilts with thick hair furring their muscled chests, alike enough to be brothers, if not triplets, and all of them resembling the Latin Lover werewolf guy from Trafalgar Square. Next card showed Finn, his head bleeding, eyes closed, half-bundled into a net. The last card showed the swish of Gold Cat's tail as it chased after them.

A vice squeezed my heart. The Emperor's werewolves had taken Finn. I had to get him back. Rage and fear ignited in my veins. I *would* get him back, no matter what it took. The Emperor wanted something from me—

'I was here,' I said, my voice flat. 'Why didn't they take me?'

'No doubt they had a reason.' Viviane flicked her fingers and the cards returned to a tidy stack in front of her. 'But if you want my help to save the satyr along with all the other victims of the Forum Mirabilis we should get moving.'

'Told you,' I snapped. 'Your help is no longer required.'

She gave me an arch smile. 'Then I wish you luck finding your way back to the humans' world.'

Crap. Like I'd ever find it. *Between* didn't go in for handy signposts and I'd been unconscious on the way here. Even if I struck lucky and found an entrance, right one or not, opening it would take another miracle. Being magically challenged sucks. Big time.

'Fine,' I snapped. 'Let's move.'

The way back felt like I was climbing-through Dante's nine circles of hell. My Hot.D postponed hangover, which even the painkillers in my backpack couldn't nix, didn't help. Neither did the cave being so far off any regular paths, so not only did I have fucking garden fairies screaming in my ears and sulphurous-smelling swampies to dodge but all the other magical beasties and half-formed spirits that plague *Between* decided to come out and party too. Most of them decided retreat was the best option as soon as they got a look at Ascalon, but enough wanted a piece of me that by the time we reached the double oak tree with its bramble- and weed-tangled and impossible-for-me-to-pass exit back to London's Primrose Hill, I already looked like I'd been pulled through a hundred hedges backwards.

I glowered at the bespelled tangle, cursing my lack of magical ability, the Emperor and anyone else who'd had a meddling hand in my life. Slicing and dicing my way through the half-formed hadn't done much to take the edge off my rage and fear for Finn; instead the fighting had solidified it into a gutful of determination. But at least the long trek in between the fights *had* given me time to put more of the 'Viviane jigsaw' together.

I turned to where she hovered silently. Once we'd left the cave she'd changed her outfit to a lavender-coloured Victorian dress, complete with beribboned bustle, feathered bonnet and lacy parasol, and had entertained herself by making small-talk about all the famous artists she'd got it together with, or by critiquing my sword-handling skills, demonstrating with her parasol, after each of my tussles. Of course, none of the half-formed had attacked her; she'd been safe behind a personal Ward. She'd shut up, though, after my frustrated rage had exploded and I'd threatened to slice and dice her wretched parasol.

I reached out and grabbed her wrist.

Her mouth dropped open in shock. 'You can't do that. I'm a spirit! Incorporeal!'

Except I could. As I'd discovered during my skirmishes with the half-formed. It hadn't just been Ascalon that had chased them off; my fists and feet had too. The first time had been by accident; two seven-foot cyclops-types with orange exoskeletons and snapping lobster claws got me in a pincer movement (bad pun aside). Ascalon declawed one (a minor injury, if not for the fact it was caused by the blessed, bespelled sword), blasting the cyclops-lobster back into the magic, and my automatic elbow to the gut got the one behind me. Its surprised look as its carapace cracked had mirrored my own, then, as it gathered its leaking magic back to re-form and at-tack again, I instinctively *called* it and *absorbed* it. Horrified about what nasty side-effects might arise from ingesting a half-formed, I spat it straight back out. Or rather I spat out an orange amorphous mass. It floated off, drifting gradually apart until it *faded* away into the ether.

It took me a few more fights, and absorptions, to put my new ability together with the sorcerer's soul I'd consumed during the demon attack last Hallowe'en, and realised that I could do more with souls and spirits than just chomp on them and regurgitate the magical remains. Like spells, I could grab them and, once they realised my touch controlled them, let them go (at which point most of them beat a hasty retreat) or I could *absorb* them and spit them back out whole. Well, I could after my ninth attempt. Of course, those spirits had found the whole experience a tad traumatic, but then they hadn't exactly wanted to be *absorbed*.

Unlike Viviane, who'd obviously been popping in and out of me as if I'd installed a revolving door.

I bared my teeth in a smile at her. 'Your tarot cards neglect to tell you I was a soul-eater?'

She snapped her mouth shut and a sullen look darkened her red eyes to almost black.

'Thought not,' I said, letting her go as she tugged on her arm. 'So when exactly did you jump ship from the tarot cards to me?'

She made a show of shaking the sulphur dust off the hem of her dress. 'I'm not sure what you mean.'

Yeah, you keep prevaricating like that, Viv. 'C'mon, you're supposed to be bound to the tarot cards. I'm pretty sure Tavish has still got the cards with him, in the humans' world, yet you're swanning around in *Between*. The only way you could've got here was by hitchhiking a ride. With me.' I tipped her chin up. 'Truth time. I wasn't the one who made the *ùmaidh*, you were. And the Emperor's werewolves didn't leave me when they took Finn, you prevented them from taking me.' Both acts seemed to suggest she was protecting me, though, which begged the question why she hadn't stopped the big-cat-shifters abducting me in the first place. I asked her.

'We have an agreement, bean sidhe. No harm to you or yours. Until the cat-shifters threatened you with irreparable harm there was no need for me to intervene. And you should recall,' she finished, like she expected a medal, 'I did warn you about them.'

Right. 'Your warning wasn't exactly clear.'

She lifted one shoulder in a shrug. 'That is how the cards work sometimes.'

How *she* made them work. Still, it made sense of her 'intervention'; her warning had been iffy, so if some 'irreparable harm' had happened to me as a result, she'd have been responsible. The magic wouldn't look lightly on it. In fact, she could still be in for a world of trouble. 'Our agreement was no harm to me or mine.' I stressed the mine. 'So you should've stopped the werewolves from taking Finn, too. Not to mention stopping Gold Cat from getting its claws in him. He's mine.'

She tilted her head with a sly look. 'Is he? Or did you relinquish your claim to the satyr?'

'What the hell does that mean?'

'If you had truly considered the satyr yours, bean sidhe, I would have been able to protect him, and it is possible the animus spirit embodied in the gold cat would not have been able to take him as a mate. The magic listens, you know that.'

I stared at her, aghast. Finn's fate was my fault? Because I'd rejected him when I'd chosen Malik? Fuck. Whether it was or not, Finn wasn't going to suffer for something I'd done. And neither was anyone else.

Viviane was a loose cannon. One I needed to get under control. Not to mention she was in league with Bastien ... Of course, there was always Ascalon. But the sword was an empty threat, and she knew it. If I killed her, I'd never get the last tarot card. Without that card, I'd lose any chance of finding how to release the fae's fertility from the pendant. But she did want something. And wanted it badly enough to show herself to me.

'Right, Viv, this is the way we're going to play it. I'm claiming Finn as mine from here on in—' We both jumped as a small chime split the air. I shot her a satisfied smile. 'See, even the magic agrees. And next time someone's in trouble because of me and your cards, you assume that person is "mine" and allow no harm to come to them either.' I paused, but this time the magic was quiet; probably the 'ask' was too vague. Well, I still had something Viv wanted. I fixed her with a stern look. 'Plus, if you want me to get your tarot cards then you're going to have to help me properly; no more iffy warnings, no more cryptic stuff'– I jabbed her in the chest – 'and no more plotting with Bastien.'

She sighed and gave me a resigned look. 'As I told you, bean sidhe, I will assist as I can, where my assistance does not negate another bargain I have already made.'

It wasn't quite a confession, but it would do. 'Fine. But only if you're going to play it straight with me?' She nodded. 'Good,' I said. 'So, is there anything, that you can tell, that's going to cause us problems in the next short while?'

She frowned at the distant swampies for a long moment, then pursed her lips. 'Not as far as I can *see*.'

'Okay.' I held out my hand. 'Now jump on board or whatever it is you do and get us out of here.'

'At your service, bean sidhe,' she said, placing her lavender-gloved hand in mine then vanishing, leaving a faint trail of jasmine-scented magic behind which the sulphurous reek of swampies quickly obliterated. This time instead of hiding I felt her lodge under my diaphragm as if I'd eaten a heavy meal. Looked like she planned on giving me indigestion. Perfect.

I closed my eyes for a moment and concentrated. After a

bit of huffing and puffing on her part, and a minor struggle of wills, we came to a compromise and I got her settled. An image formed in my mind of Viviane sitting on a grassy bank next to a canal. The hot yellow sun in the bright blue sky overhead reflected a golden ball on the canal's glassy surface, and a few feet from Viviane a willow tree trailed its long curtain of sword-like green leaves into the water.

It is rather naïve, bean sidhe, Viviane grumbled, her voice sounding tinny in my head. *And I do not mean that in a good way. You could always soften the edges a touch, adopt a more impressionistic approach and add so much more depth and interest into the colours. It is a tad bright as it is.* She sighed. *Monet did it so much better. I knew him, you know.*

'Yeah, I do. You've just told me for the umpteenth time, and this is the first time I've done this,' I muttered. 'But if you don't like it you can always lurk in the dark like you did before.'

She sniffed, opened her parasol and positioned it to block out the sun's glare.

'Right,' I said, pointing at the entrance tangled with weeds and brambles. 'C'mon, Viv, do your stuff. And remember to get the date and time right; we're aiming for the afternoon of the Summer Solstice.'

I will try to get us as close as possible, she sniped, then dipped her hand into the canal and pulled out a sparkling glyph; it glistened against her fingers for a second, then my own fingers tingled as the glyph appeared and launched itself at the exit. The brambles parted like the legendary Red Sea, and I walked out of *Between* and into the humans' world.

To find Gold Cat waiting for us.

Chapter Fifty-Four

Gold Cat looked like it had been pulled through a hedge backwards too. Or a war. Its funky metallic coat was dull and stuck up in dried-tinsel clumps. One ear was ripped, one eye swollen closed. Its ribs showed. And a long bloody gash scored its left flank.

'What the hell do you want?' I muttered.

Need help. The words were a low growl in my head.

I gave it a narrowed look. 'It speaks?'

She, corrected Viviane.

'She?'

Your ùmaidh, your gender, Viv said cheerfully. *How else would she mate with the satyr?*

Fury boiled through me and Ascalon appeared in my hand with a burst of green dragonfire. 'Once she's dead, that'll put an end to her mating with Finn.'

Gold Cat opened her mouth and dropped a gold coin. It was one of the Emperor's. *Need me. Save mate.*

She means you can't kill her because she's got the gold coin the Emperor's werewolves gave her for the satyr, Viviane said. *It's her invitation into the Forum Mirabilis to barter for him.*

I scooped the coin up. 'I don't need the cat. Only the coin.'

Viviane twirled her parasol. *The coin only works as an invitation into the Forum for the one it was given to, or their nominated proxy. I doubt she will give you her proxy, if you intend to kill her.*

Frustration had me briefly closing my eyes. I took a calming breath and let Ascalon slide back into my ring. 'If the coin only works for her, or her proxy, what's she doing here? Why isn't she off to the Forum?'

Gold Cat's ears flattened. *Need you speak.*

She wanted me as her mouthpiece. Figured. Except she still didn't need me. Or she hadn't when she'd decided to make Finn her mate. 'Why isn't she just jumping in and doing her possession bit like she did before?'

Her whiskers quivered in disgust. *Not strong.*

I took a closer *look* at Gold Cat. Beneath her 'been in the wars' look, her body was faded, almost transparent. She was my *ùmaidh*. A temporary changeling. They usually had a couple of weeks, sometimes even a month. But Gold Cat didn't look so lucky. My guess was she had a couple of days at most.

She means she's too weak because she is dying—

'I managed to work it out for myself, thanks, Viv,' I said flatly, despite the anxious pounding of my heart. Carlson had been dying too because his mate had died, so he said. So if Gold Cat was dying and she was mated to Finn— I squatted next to Gold Cat, grabbed her by the scruff, demanded, 'If you die what happens to Finn?'

Mated you too.

I blinked. 'Thought you said he wasn't mine, Viv?'

Was not, Gold Cat said sourly. *Is now.*

She means the mate bond jumped to you too, Viviane supplied with a touch of smugness, *when you reclaimed the satyr just now.*

Relief streamed through me. So Finn wasn't going to die when Gold Cat did. That was the good news. And of course the magic would take its pound of flesh for that little bargain. Still, it could've been worse. But that didn't mean I was just going to accept being mated to Finn; not when it wasn't what I'd chosen. And for all Finn saying he wanted us to be together he hadn't chosen to be mated either. If it wasn't what he truly

438

desired, then sooner or later he'd feel trapped, never mind whatever magic the mate bond was supposed to do to make us like each other. I gave Gold Cat a shake. 'Can you undo the mating without killing either of us?'

Not possible. Her copper-coloured eyes slowly blinked and my heart sank. *For me.*

Tentative hope flared in me. *Specific questions, Gen.* 'Is there someone that can undo the mating without killing either Finn or me?'

Her pink tongue swiped her muzzle thoughtfully. *Yes.*

'Who?'

Shrewdness flickered over her furry face. *Save mate first.*

I sighed, not even surprised. Standard negotiation tactics. Next she'd be asking me to find a way to keep her alive before she'd tell me who could break the mate bond. After all, she wanted to survive. But saving Finn was more important right now. In that we were of one mind, so we might as well be of one body. I tightened my hold on Gold Cat's neck and lifted her. For something that looked the size of a chunky tiger, she was as limp and light as a kitten, but then the physical part of her was virtually non-existent.

'Say hello to your fellow passenger, Viv,' I said, as I absorbed Gold Cat in a brush of tickling fur. She landed on the grassy bank next to Viviane in a tumble of tail and paws. Viviane sniffed and brushed a couple of loose cat hairs off her dress. Gold Cat staggered to her feet, shook herself then curled up on the grass, tucked her nose under her paws and went to sleep as if she hadn't a care in the world.

Nice for some. I rolled my shoulders, feeling the muscle ache of swordplay setting in. At least with Gold Cat and her coin on board I could waltz right into the Forum; a way better plan than the original one of letting Mad Max walk me into his 'trap'. But I still needed backup. And I needed to know what else had happened while I'd been stuck in *Between*.

I dug my phone out – *surprisingly, it was working!* – and called Hugh.

'Genny, thank the peaks. Are you all right?' His frantic rumble calmed as I told him I *was* okay and where I was: Primrose Hill.

'I'll send a van to pick you up. What happened.'

I gave him the highlights: we'd been kidnapped by the gnome and the cat-shifters. They'd disappeared, and Finn had been taken by the Emperor's werewolves.

'Finn's safe, Genny,' Hugh said. 'Half the herd were searching for you two in *Between*. They ran across him with the werewolves.'

My legs gave way with relief and I sat abruptly on the rough ground. 'Is he okay?'

'He's been injured. There was quite a battle between the satyrs and the werewolves from what I understand, but he's in a healing trance and should be fine.'

A bubble of joy expanded inside me and I felt a grin spread across my face. 'That's wonderful, Hugh.' I jumped up, punching my arm into the air. Finn was safe. Everything else, like the mate problem and my lost memory, could be sorted out. I told Hugh I had another coin. 'So now we've got three invitations to the Forum auction, which should up the odds of saving the kidnap victims.'

'Sorry, Genny, but Finn's coin isn't going to help,' Hugh said, then filled me in.

The police had already tried to gain entrance to the Forum auction using the coins. Mary (as the police's main undercover girl due to her ability to mind-speak with her mother over any distance and so relay info back) had gone along with the Bangladeshi ambassador (who'd refused to let anyone else use his coin). But as soon as the pair had crossed into the Carnival Fantastique (the ambassador had been told the Forum Mirabilis was at its 'heart', wherever that was), the ambassador had vanished, as had Mad Max's coin, leaving Mary and the police backup team with nothing.

'So we think the coins contain some sort of dormant Translocation spell,' Hugh finished, 'but it only activates if the corresponding lot they'd been given in payment for is actually in the Forum. So now you're back I'd like to put your cousin Maxim's plan into action. If you think you're okay to?'

'Just try and stop me!'

Ten minutes later I reached the park entrance. The gnome's house opposite was sporting crime-scene tape. I jumped into the police van waiting for me and Constable Taegrin told me that the cambion had confessed to buying (unlicensed) dried garden fairy and various other illegal aphrodisiacs from the horrid little gnome. The cambion was under arrest but, annoyingly, the gnome had slipped the police net, obviously by disappearing into *Between*.

'Well,' I said, 'if there's any justice a swampie or one of the other nasties in there will eat him.'

'A fitting end, Genny,' Taegrin agreed with a grin, giving me a glimpse of shiny gold teeth, 'but the boss would rather we had him in custody. He was going nuts with you missing. We were all worried, so glad you're okay.'

'So am I,' I said. 'So we're back to the zoo again?'

'Yes. Back to see the tigers.'

I gave a quiet huff. Gold Cat was gonna love them.

I was right. Gold Cat's hackles went up the minute I'd entered the covered corridor of the tiger exhibit, and she'd circled restlessly around Viviane until Viv poked Gold Cat with her parasol. Gold Cat then slunk off behind the curtain of willows on the canal bank and I hadn't seen her since. Not that her disappearing had made the zoo's tigers happy. Through the corridor's U-shaped viewing windows I could still see them crouched low to the ground, ears flat, their own hackles raised, eyeing me like I was an interloper in their territory and they weren't sure whether to attack or run away.

Much like the two males before me.

I narrowed my gaze at Mad Max. His long platinum pony-tail was tied at his nape with black ribbon, and his diamond dog-tags glinted in the V of his unbuttoned-to-the-waist black silk shirt, which was tucked into black satin dress trousers. He looked like a naff Legolas crossed with an eighties Medallion Man. 'Look, Maxim,' I said, tapping my boot on the blue plastic of my portable circle which I'd laid out in the centre of the corridor. 'Stop being a wimp and get in the circle.'

Mad Max shot me a fang-filled grin and drawled, 'Sorry, love, no can do. Not till the old kelpie here says you're not going to chew my face off.'

'I've told you I won't,' I snapped. 'I gave you my word.'

'Aye, doll, but you're nae the one in control,' Tavish said, the beads on his dreads flashing from black to warning amber and back again, as they had since he'd first clapped eyes on me and seen not only my own golden soul but the red glow of Viviane's too. Damn kelpie. If he'd keep his eyes on everyone's shells instead of their souls, this would be so much easier. So far, for whatever reason, he'd missed Gold Cat. And no way was I planning on mentioning her after his kneejerk reaction to Viviane.

I threw my hands in the air and looked appealingly at Hugh. 'Can't you do something?'

Hugh shook his head silently. He'd bowed to Tavish's greater experience about my so-called possession, though he didn't look too happy about it; his ruddy face was creased with concerned crevices, and anxious red dust sprinkled his straight-up black hair and the broad shoulders of his pressed white shirt. Neither did Mary, standing to attention next to Hugh, her face watchful, her police-issue stun baton extended ready at her side. Backing them up were Dessa, Constable

Taegrin, Lamber and the rest of the WPCs and trolls from the Met's Magic and Murder Squad. If sheer numbers counted in rescuing the kidnap victims, they'd be safe already. As they weren't, we were putting Mad Max's 'trap' plan into action.

Once Mad Max had popped out of his doggy shape he'd told Hugh the details of the 'trap' to get me into the Forum. He was to send me through a replica of the Portal spell the Emperor's werewolves had used to kidnap the victims from here at the zoo. Hugh was hoping that once the replica portal was open all his girls and boys in blue would follow me through but, in case that part of the plan didn't pan out, Mary and the witches were aiming to recast the replica Portal spell once they'd seen it. The preparations had been going swimmingly right up till Tavish appeared and declared me possessed by Viviane.

I gritted my teeth, turned back to Tavish. 'I'm the one in control, not Viviane.'

His lacy gills snapped shut against his throat. 'Aye, well she'll be letting you think that, but with Viviane in occupation, you cannae be.'

And whose fault it that? I wanted to yell at him. *Yours! You should've said I was only supposed to give the tarot cards my blood* once *instead of taking off in a kelpie hissy fit.* Instead, I stuck my hands on my hips. 'Time's running out. Max, you need to get in the circle and, Tavish, I want those cards. Now.'

In answer Tavish crouched, *called* a flick-knife, sliced his finger and flung blood on to the circle marked on my blue plastic. The circle rose, sealing me in, its dome rippling turquoise like the Caribbean Sea in a stiff wind. Tavish straightened, threw his arms wide and started muttering. His eyes swirled the same turquoise colour, and power beaded like water on the green-black skin of his bare chest, trickling down to be soaked up by his black silk harem pants.

The frown on Hugh's face deepened. 'What are you doing, *àrd-cheann*?'

Trying to exorcise me, Viviane said cheerfully. *You should tell him that only works when the spirit is in full possession. Something only a demon can truly achieve for more than a few hours.*

'I'm not interested in telling him anything he already knows,' I muttered, slicing my index finger on my own knife, then jabbing my bloody finger at the watery dome. It popped, as I expected, like a kid's balloon, thanks to the safety feature I'd built into it. And even as I glimpsed shock on Tavish's face, I *called* the Stun spell from Mary's baton and flicked it towards him. He jerked at the last minute and it glanced off his shoulder. It was still enough to take him to the floor in a flash of green lightning and a burst of burned mint.

'Maxim Fyodor Zakharin,' I shouted. 'You are tasked to put my needs above all others, including yourself. I need you to get in this circle now.'

Mad Max's jaw dropped as his legs moved of their own accord and marched him into the circle. As soon as he was in, I bent and touched my blood to the circle. This time the dome rose up with a shimmer of reddish-gold. I gave Tavish a suck-on-that smile.

Mad Max shook as if shedding water. 'It seems it is truly you, Cousin.' He sketched a bow. 'As I am apparently at your command.'

Well, that pretty much confirmed my other suspicion. The text Malik had sent telling me I was dumped, and that I should talk to Mad Max if I needed anything, hadn't come from Malik. But psycho Bastien. Malik hadn't dumped me, though he had still cut me out of the loop when he'd 'sent' me home from the boating lake island, so we still had stuff to sort out. But hell, if the psycho prick was using Malik's phone, it meant the beautiful vamp was in trouble.

I jabbed Mad Max in the chest. 'What's the sadistic bastard

444

done with Malik? And don't try to pretend you don't know what I mean.'

He heaved a theatrical sigh. 'Dogs are given commands, not information, cousin dearest.'

'Dogs also have ears,' I said.

'Doesn't mean they hear anything of interest.'

'Bastien told me you would lead me to Malik,' I snapped.

'Me lead you to the Turk?' Mad Max shrugged then tapped his head. 'Sorry, don't have that order in here, love.'

I glared at him, desperately wanting him to tell me where Malik was, to pound the information out of him. And knowing it would be a waste of my energy. 'Well, that's just crap,' I muttered, frustrated.

He grinned jovially, then wrinkled his nose and sniffed. 'Talking about the Turk, he's not going to be a happy bunny that you stink of sex, satyr and fetid feline, Cousin. Whatever have you been up to?'

Damn vamp supersenses. 'Nothing you need to know about,' I said flatly, trying not to squirm and wishing I'd had time for a longer shower in the zoo's staff facilities. At least Mary had a clean T-shirt and jeans ready for me. I poked Mad Max. 'All you need to do is follow my orders.'

'Then follow them I shall, love. I've always had a yen for woman with power.' He raised a sardonic brow as he leaned forward and whispered, 'Oh, what fun we could have, if not for the Turk and his Royal Brattiness.'

'And the fact that I'd castrate you quicker than you could say "Poodle Power",' I snapped back.

'Ouch.' He shuddered dramatically and leaned away.

'Okay, so now I need the tarot cards.' I looked at Tavish, who was holding his no doubt numb arm and glowering at my circle. 'You can see I'm myself, so you ready to give them to me yet?'

His beads turned murky grey with refusal. 'Doll, I cannae

give you the cards. You cannae trust yourself with Viviane. She'll lead you astray afore you ken what she's doing. She's a leannán sidhe.'

'Leannán sidhe!' Mad Max's eyes almost popped out of his head as he backed up until he hit my circle.

Viviane was one of the dark muses? Well, that explained her obsession with all things arty. And Mad Max's panic and Tavish's alarm. A leannán sidhe's inspiration comes at a high cost: possible madness and early death, though usually nothing that could be pinned on the muse herself. Van Gogh, Marilyn Monroe and Alexander McQueen were all suspected victims of the leannán sidhe. Still, Viviane wasn't likely to drive a non-human to a quick, iffy demise through an overload of inspiration so she could suck down their creative energies, but if she got her metaphorical claws in deep enough, she could probably send a vamp crazy. Not that it would make much difference in Mad Max's case.

Which made me wonder what exactly she'd done to Tavish for him to trap her in a set of tarot cards for near enough quarter of a century. I asked.

His beads turned a cagey purple. 'Ah, she was an apprentice of sorts.'

Pfft! Apprentice! I was his artist's model! His inspiration. The Love of his Life! Viviane's shouting reverberated round my head. *Until he took up with Turner. Don't ever go swimming with him, bean sidhe,* she warned. *He'll whip your soul out of your body faster than you can scream.*

Briefly I closed my eyes. A lover's tiff. Could my night get any better? 'Tavish, give me the cards.'

His dreads writhed in refusal.

But Hugh had obviously decided I was truly me too, as he reached down, hooked a large hand under Tavish's arm and pulled him onto his feet. 'Think it's best if you give Genny the cards, *àrd-cheann*,' he rumbled warningly. 'Otherwise I will have to arrest you for obstruction.'

A frustrated 'on your own head be it' look settled on Tavish's face. He flicked his fingers and the tarot cards appeared in his palm and he said sullenly, 'I make a gift of the tarot cards containing the leannán sidhe spirit, Viviane, to you, Genevieve.'

The cards streamed from his hand to hover in a neat upright stack in front of my face. The top card showed Viviane sitting by her canalbank in her lavender dress and bonnet, twirling her parasol. She was smirking.

'I am in your debt, bean sidhe.' She dipped her head, then, without turning, flipped her middle finger in Tavish's direction. 'Two hundred and forty-one years he has kept me enslaved to those cards. And he did not even allow me to do regular readings. Te-di-ous!'

Tavish flinched. Mad Max gave an appreciative, albeit nervous barking laugh.

'Save your crowing, Viv,' I said, and stuffed the cards into my jeans pocket, ignoring her muffled protests. 'Right, Maxim, time to do your stuff.'

Chapter Fifty-Five

'Time for the blood-letting, Cousin,' Mad Max said, after he'd explained the mechanics of the spell.

One of which involved him sinking his fangs into me, the prospect of which had him grinning at me like a dog who'd found a stash of meaty bones. I shoved my sleeve up, stiff-armed him back, but left my hand on his chest. That was as close as he was getting.

He grinned wider, took my hand and executed an exaggerated bow as if to bestow a kiss, his platinum ponytail falling over his left shoulder as he did. He raised suggestive blue eyes to mine. 'You know, Cousin, necks are much more fun than wrists?'

'Get on with it,' I said, 'otherwise I'll be ringing that vet when this is over.' I scissored my fingers together under his nose. 'I hear he does a good deal on doggy snips.'

'You're all bitch, love,' he drawled, then closed his eyes. The hair on my nape rose like hackles as he drew his magic up. A faint silvery-red glow surrounded him like a thin aura. My own magic answered, turning my skin gold, and a distant part of me noted, thankfully, that I wasn't feeling even the tiniest bit lustful towards Mad Max. Whatever consequences my lost night with Finn in the cave might have, at least the unwanted and embarrassing effects of shacking up with the leaking Fertility pendant were gone.

Mad Max muttered a string of unintelligible-to-me words under his breath, in a language with the same cadence as

Gaelic, and I had my usual moment's envy that a vamp, even one that started out as a wizard, obviously knew and could do more magic than me. I shoved the feeling aside, then braced myself as his grip on my wrist tightened, his lips peeled back from his fangs, and he struck.

Pain, sharp and hot, sliced through me, then was gone. Silver light wound with sapphire blue reeled out from Mad Max like a spool of film unravelling, then vanished, plunging us into darkness. Faint noise, like the distant roll of drums, grew closer and louder and more insistent, and gradually the darkness lightened like dawn colouring the sky—

And then we were in the circle again, Mad Max bowing over my wrist, looking up at me with a lascivious leer, everyone gathered about us, waiting for him to start the spell. The words 'Get on with it' came out of my mouth ...

The air rippled and rolled through the zoo corridor, turning the images around me into watercolours, stretching and streaking and running them together so they flowed counter-clockwise around me, only to disappear downwards as if there were a drain at my feet.

The images streamed faster and faster until I stood in a whirlpool of silvery blue.

The drumming reached a crescendo.

It cut out.

The last of the whirlpool drained away, leaving me bathed in morning light, as the kidnap scene took shape. It was slightly out of focus, as if I were looking through a greasy lens.

Two dark-skinned males – the bodyguards – in their green and gold embroidered kurtas and mirrored aviators stood in the centre of the corridor watching a small black-haired boy who had climbed into one of the U-shaped windows and had his nose pressed against the glass: Dakkhin Jangali, the kidnapped child. On the other side of the window, the zoo's two tigers were rubbing the sides of their faces against the glass as if they could touch him. Behind the boy stood a tall, lithely muscled woman in an orange sari, an indulgent smile on her face: Mrs Bandevi Jangali, the boy's mother and wife to the ambassador. Next to her was a stylish twenty-something male wearing a dark business suit: the zoo's publicity director, Jonathan Weir. He had his phone out, snapping shots of the boy and the tigers.

Look around, love, Mad Max whispered. *Find the beacon. And remember, keep schtum, you can't interact with the spell until I give the word.* I *looked.* But other than the usual patches of wild untamed magic there was nothing to see.

'There's nothing—'

A high *krick krick* noise filled the corridor and the eagle – the changeling – swooped in. It opened its beak and vomited a ribbon of green magic, as it had in Trafalgar Square. The ribbon twisted, morphing into a verdant green serpent that hung suspended in the air.

The beacon!

The eagle dived to land a few feet in front of the group. As the bird's feet touched the ground it shimmered into a pale-skinned woman, her dark hair piled atop her head, dressed in a floor-length Roman tunic. Her pupils were hard black ovals, her irises the same blood-red as molten sulphur, similar in all but colour to any other sidhe changeling's eyes, or mine.

Shock winged through me – not at her eyes, I'd expected them – but that I recognised her, not even needing the black ink marking her bare arms or the tiny black crescent kissing the corner of her lush mouth to confirm her identity.

The changeling was the Empress from the tarot cards, and Bastien's mother from Malik's dream/memory of the harem— *Malik's wife?*

Only she couldn't be. Changelings only lived a mortal lifespan once they left the Fair Lands. The only way a mortal could live longer was through dealing with demons …

or being blood-bonded to a vamp. Then they lived and died on the vamp's ticket. The Empress was blood-bonded to the Emperor. Hard on that shock was what the hell would Malik think that his wife was blood-bound to another vamp, and the Emperor at that; the vamp who'd sicced the revenant curse on him. Except Malik knew the Emperor, so he had to know who and what the Empress was, didn't he? Unless he'd thought her dead all this time? No way could I imagine Malik knowing his wife was alive and not going after her. Whether he loved her or not …

Not that it mattered who Malik loved.

What mattered was rescuing the victims she'd kidnapped.

The Empress smiled pleasantly at the group, all of whom stared back as if stunned, then she lifted her arms outwards as if she were entreating the heavens. The black ink marking her skin slithered into hard-edged glyphs that shot like Cupid's arrows into the walls, throwing a Veil over the corridor. More glyphs shot out and struck the suspended snake. As they hit, the space behind her split open like the wide yawning maw of a swamp-dragon. The portal. Beyond the portal was a shadowed stone tunnel lit by flickering fire torches.

Seven dark shapes loped along the tunnel and leaped through the portal into the zoo corridor— wolves. As they hit the ground the first three wolves morphed into the three black-haired, olive-skinned centurions who'd taken Finn. In the seconds it took for them to shift, the other four wolves had circled the two bodyguards, each snagged the tail of the wolf in front and were now racing round them like they were playing the wolf equivalent of ring-a-ring o' roses. It had to be how they'd stopped the bodyguards from protecting or even knowing what happened to their charges; but whatever magic it was, I couldn't *see* it.

Nets appeared in the hands of the three centurions as they quickly spread out and advanced on Mrs Jangali. She called something that sounded like an order to her son, who crouched down on the windowsill. Then she snarled and crumpled to the ground, her sari disappearing as she shifted into an orange and black tiger indistinguishable from the zoo's tigers behind the glass. She lunged at the nearest centurion. He dodged out of her way, leaping and rolling in an acrobatic-type move, but not before her claws raked across his chest sending an arc of blood droplets through the air to stain the bodyguard's green kurta. As the tiger landed and whirled, tail whipping out, the other two centurions flung out their nets and trapped her. Stun magic sparked green, and she dropped like she'd been shot. The two centurions efficiently scooped up the netted tiger as if she were nothing more than a skinned rug, and raced away with her into the portal.

As the third centurion rolled to his feet and sped after the others, the small boy growled and jumped off the windowsill, chasing after them. His action snapped Jonathan, the zoo employee, out of his frozen shock and he grabbed the boy round the waist, only to find he'd seized a wriggling tiger cub. The cub turned on Jonathan and the two fell in a tangled heap of snarls and surprised yells almost at the feet of the Empress.

She shouted a sharp command and the centurion in the portal ran back, threw his net over the struggling pair, then heaved them both up and carried them into the portal. The four wolves circling the bodyguards broke away and loped after him. The Empress gave another pleasant, satisfied smile then gracefully brought her arms down and together in a sweeping motion. The green snake shuddered, ejecting the glyphs as it plunged down to wrap around her throat. She turned and strolled into the portal, the rest of the glyphs springing from the walls and zooming after her as if she were a magical Pied Piper.

Now, Cousin! Mad Max shouted, jerking me into action.

I reached out and *called* the magic.

The snake and the glyphs flew to me, alighting like insubstantial sparrows on my hands and arms, the birds' tiny talons piercing my flesh with the sharp, hot pain of a vamp's fangs—

And I found myself staring down at Mad Max's head, his platinum ponytail dangling over his shoulder, where he was sucking like a blood-starved vamp on my wrist.

My magically ink-stained wrist. The glyphs were writhing over my skin like a fading memory. For a moment I understood what every single glyph meant, as if the knowledge had rushed up into me like a hot spring from deep within the earth. I knew how they'd been drawn. What they would do. I blinked, amazed and full of wonder.

Reverse the magic, Viviane urged.

Almost in a trance I took Mad Max's ponytail and pulled him from my wrist then swept my foot behind his legs and watched in glee as he sprawled on his arse. He collapsed on to his back, eyes glazed, giggling like he was sloshed, and absently I wondered just how much of my blood he'd drunk. I plucked the black ribbon from his hair. It morphed into a twisting obsidian snake. I flung it out, lifted my arms and *cast* the glyphs after it. They speared the suspended snake and, as it had for the Empress, the air beneath it split, the portal yawning open on to the torch-lit stone corridor.

Run, quick, before it closes, Viviane yelled.

I ran. And jumped through the portal.

Chapter Fifty-Six

I landed, not in the torchlit stone corridor as I'd expected but in a large open area of sun-browned grass, floodlit by halogen lights on metal pylons. Inside a glyph-etched silver and copper chain circle, which rose over me in a shimmer of red in my *sight*. The Portal spell was a trap. But then I'd always known that.

I tightened my hold on my ring. I had a weapon. I had a See-Me-Not, along with Locators – magical and more mundane albeit high-tech electronic ones – and Transportation beacons woven into the long-sleeved T-shirt and jeans Mary had given me to wear. And the plan was for me to sit tight, find out everything I could and, if necessary, stall until the cavalry followed me through the portal. The now non-existent portal. Still Hugh and the witches had monitored the spell, and they had Mad Max and another pint of my blood. With luck they'd be along soon.

I scanned my surroundings. Nearby, the tall minaret of London's Central Mosque cut into the twilit sky. It told me I was in the middle of Regent's Park, at the Carnival Fantastique, in the large area left empty for the shows and formal ceremonies. It was the Summer Solstice, the closing night of the Carnival, and a Party in the Park was scheduled with a concert that was a who's who of British pop, with the ubiquitous celebratory fireworks to end the night. I was about five feet away from the covered stage rising in front of me, prime position if this had been the pop concert. Only, either the party had finished or a lot of folk nearby were unknowingly experiencing an expertly crafted illusion, since no music show bore any resemblance to the stage's occupants.

Well, not unless the show's set featured a backdrop of scaffold and plank bleachers, crammed with a crowd of shadowy indistinct figures.

'Quiet lot? aren't they,' I muttered, scowling at the eerie crowd.

Modified Privacy spells, Viviane helpfully informed me from her sunny canalbank inside me. *They are here to bid in the auction.*

'Thanks,' I said drily. 'I'd never've guessed.'

Front and centre stage were two ornate golden thrones, one larger than the other, pinned in place by overlapping spotlights. Both were empty. The stars of the show had yet to turn up.

Spread out behind me were more chain circles, their silver and copper glinting in the bright halogens. Nearly all of the circles held shadowy figures.

They are those who have accepted the invitation to barter their gold coin, Viviane said, twirling her parasol.

'Nice that the anonymity extends to the innocent too,' I said sarcastically. Still, at least it meant that no one could see me in my own circle.

Around the outer edge of the open space and behind the stage, a twenty-foot wall of pale green magic shimmered with multi-coloured bubbles that drifted slowly upwards, only to sink back again as if the space were enclosed by a huge lava lamp; the magic was obviously keeping folk away, and possibly fuelling any illusions. Standing to attention at intervals around the green wall were vamps, all dressed up as Roman centurions. A lot of vamps. Crap. Were they going to be a problem for Hugh and his witches and trolls in blue? I shook the worry away for later.

Following the curve of the green wall was a semi-circle of exhibition tents facing the stage. They weren't the standard Carnival ones (which were square or oblong to make the most of the space) but were round, suggesting they covered more magic circles. That didn't bode well for whatever, or whoever, was probably trapped inside the tents.

The tents contain the speciality lots.

'Can you ID anyone who's in the circles or the tents?' I murmured.

No. But now you have ownership of my tarot cards, bean sidhe. Viviane smiled, showing her dainty little fangs. *I should be able to give you some information that will help you.*

'Fine. But remember our agreement; no cryptic stuff.'

Of course. If you would remove two cards, please, the foretelling will be easier.

As I dug the tarot cards out, Gold Cat padded from behind the willow curtain and flopped down on the grass next to Viviane.

Oh, and once the foretelling is finished, Viviane warned. *I'll be trapped in the cards until I'm called again.*

'Fine, just remember; no harm to me or mine.'

None from me, Viviane agreed.

I picked two cards out and she vanished from the canalbank inside me. The cards flew from my fingers to hover before me. Viviane reappeared on the left card, while the right showed an image of the Emperor lounging on the larger of the two thrones on the stage. He held up one of his gold coins.

'The Forum Miribilis has its own magic,' Viviane said in a brisk tone. 'As such, the Emperor has to give you a coin so that you may barter. But as you are already here, the coin is not tied to any specific lot, though the Emperor will not tell you that. You will be able to choose which lot to barter for, and you must barter his coin. If you do not then you will not

456

have the opportunity to speak to him until the auction is over. That will be too late.'

'Too late for what?'

'To save those you wish to save, of course.'

'Right. So I choose a lot, hand over my coin, then I get to ask the Emperor how to release the fae's trapped fertility and he tells me what price he wants me to pay.'

'Not quite, bean sidhe.'

I eyed her suspiciously. 'Your cards said: he knows. He will tell you. For a price.'

She twirled her parasol, eyeing me steadily from under her lashes. 'That is correct. But first the Forum's magic must be adhered to or else, like all magical bargains thwarted, it will rebound negatively.'

Crap. 'So what does that involve?'

'You must agree the payment in addition to bartering the coin for the lot you choose. Then you can ask your question about the fae's fertility.'

'Perfect. So I've got to pay something for whatever lot I choose, then I have to pay again to get the info I need. Talk about having your ransom cake and eating it.'

'Ahh,' Viviane said, a 'you're *so* not going to like this' expression on her face.

I sighed. 'What?'

'Well, there is also the Forum's public deterrent that each coinholder has to pay.'

Unease pricked my gut. 'Explain.'

The picture of the Emperor changed to show an unhappy-looking brown-haired man dressed in the green T-shirt and trousers that was the zoo's uniform. 'This is David O'Reilly, the partner of Jonathan Weir. David is a performer on the cusp of fame and fortune. When he barters his coin for Jonathan's return, the extra payment demanded by the Forum will be David's singing voice. Giving up his voice will change his current destiny, but his partner Jonathan will be free and he will survive the bite to become a weretiger.'

David on the card looked even more miserable. 'Okay,' I said, 'so he loses out on future fame and fortune but it's not like he's going to know for sure, or that it's going to be public knowledge, so I take it there's a nasty punchline to the story.'

Viviane nodded. 'Losing his hope in a bright future, David becomes depressed and forgets to pay attention in his job at the zoo. As he deals with dangerous animals this will result in a fatal accident. His partner Jonathan will be distraught.'

Mist swirled on the card and David vanished.

'Ouch, that's definitely not a happy outcome,' I said, feeling bad for David and Jonathan. 'So what? You think I should choose Jonathan as my lot?'

Viviane shook her head. 'It is not for me to tell you which lot to choose, bean sidhe. Any coinholder presenting their coin will trigger a public deterrent. I only described David's future as it was the clearest one I could see.'

Crap. If I didn't choose Jonathan to barter for then, sooner or later, his partner, David, would end up dead. But David wasn't the only one here with a coin, nearly all the circles behind me held a shadowy figure— they were all going to end up paying *something*. As I would. 'So any idea what my deterrent will be?'

'Your future has many threads, bean sidhe. It is impossible to pick out any one. But I will warn you that there is more at stake here than the answer you seek, or even the kidnap victims that you are determined to rescue. For you and your feline friend.'

Gold Cat pricked her ears inside me as I said, 'What the fuck does that mean?'

Viviane brushed a few coppery cat hairs off her dress. 'You care for many people, bean sidhe. It makes you vulnerable.'

Chill fingers scraped down my spine. She was sworn to bring no harm to me. Or mine. 'Who?'

'I'm sorry, I cannot say, bean sidhe.' She snapped her parasol closed and her cards vanished.

Fuck*fuckfuck*. She was right. I did care about a lot of people. I didn't even want to guess who it might be. I dug my fingers into the scorched summer grass, needing something to hold on to. Whoever it was I had to save them. But hell, if I was going to save them, rescue the rest of the Emperor's victims, save their coinholders from triggering the Forum's deterrent magic, and get the answer to my question about the fae's fertility, I needed a plan.

Ten minutes later, as I was still frantically trying to come up with one, the sound of drums thundered through the open space and a burst of magic pricked goosebumps over my flesh.

Lightning flashed, its aftermath plunging the place into darkness.

The lights gradually came back, focusing on the stage.

Five huge werewolves, in their wolf forms, sat on their haunches like guard dogs by the two thrones.

And the thrones themselves were no longer empty.

Chapter Fifty-Seven

Lounging on the larger throne was the Emperor.

Robed in a purple toga, with a golden laurel wreath crowning his head of dark curls, he gazed down his long hawk-like nose at me with an impersonal, idle regard, like I was a bug he might squash with his sandalled foot. There was no emotion, no humanity, nothing to connect to in his green eyes, only a deep sense of alienness. He even made psycho Bastien seem more human. I shuddered. And wasn't that a scary thought?

But hey, for all he was the Scary Emperor, he wasn't as interesting as the woman sitting on the throne next to him. Pulse fluttering with nerves (and no way did I want to examine too closely why) I took a deep breath and checked her out. She looked as young and beautiful as she had in Malik's memory, though she was wearing the same Roman tunic as when she and her werewolves had played magical kidnappers. Her black curls were still piled atop her head, the black inked crescent still graced the corner of her lush mouth, but now she sported a crown of gold stars as she had in the tarot card picture. The Empress, the changeling— *Malik's wife?* In the flesh.

She was staring at me, curiosity and some other emotion – sympathy or speculation – in her crimson sidhe eyes.

I lifted my chin and stared back, wondering why she'd chosen to side with Bastien in whatever showdown he and the Emperor had going on. Okay, so Bastien was her son, but being blood-bonded to the Emperor wasn't something to throw away lightly, not when that blood-bond had given her five centuries of extended life, and not when breaking that bond would mean her death. Unless she hoped to transfer it to another vamp? A vamp who'd been her husband? Malik.

Would he want that? Pain squeezed my heart that he might. I shaved the pain away.

I had to come up with a plan; one that saved everyone and got me the answer to my question about the fae's trapped fertility.

And since offence is the best defence, I bared my teeth in a smile and waved at the imperial pair. 'Nice party, guys,' I called. 'Thanks for the invite.'

'Genevieve Nataliya Zakharinova,' the Emperor said in a soft voice that sent shivers skittering down my spine. 'You are due this.' He leaned forwards and tossed something at me. It skimmed through the air and landed in the circle at my feet.

A gold coin.

I looked up. 'You're not exactly going for subtle, are you?'

'I have no need to,' he said, and sat back.

The tent nearest to the stage vanished. In its place was a giant circular birdcage.

Inside the cage was Katie.

She was sitting, hugging her knees to her chest, long blonde hair scraped back in a messy, high ponytail. A vamp centurion crouched behind her, his grasp on her ponytail holding her head up so her grubby, tear-stained face was easily seen, as was the thick leather collar with its iron chain around her throat. She was inside a circle of ashes.

Rage and fear slammed into me, my vision blurred and somewhere nearby I could hear a low, menacing growl. It wasn't until another centurion loomed in front of me brandishing his fangs and snapping his fingers an inch from my face, as he demanded I be quiet, that I realised I was the one growling.

I clenched my fists and swallowed the growl back. I took a deep breath, concentrating on calming my frenzied heart. I needed my wits if I was going to save Katie.

Save kits. A snarl in my head agreed. *Save both kits.*

Both kits? I swiped a hand over my eyes to clear my vision, vaguely surprised as it came away wet, and saw the cage's other occupant. He was lying just outside the circle Katie was in, a similar leather collar and iron chain around his throat, dark hair matted where he'd obviously been bludgeoned, and pale face smeared with dried blood. Marc. Big-cat-shifter and Katie's *treacherous* so-called-boyfriend—

Want help break mate bond, Finn. Gold Cat snarled again. *No hurt kit. Promise.*

'*Fine. I won't hurt him,*' I snapped back. Then promptly forgot about him and anything else but Katie.

I jumped up and down, waving and shouting at her, wanting to let her know I was here. That I'd get her out whatever it took. She didn't react. I shouted again.

'Merchandise can't communicate with bidders, Ms Taylor,' a familiar mike-enhanced voice boomed out. 'It's against the Forum's ethics.'

Ethics? I whirled round.

A single spot, trained stage right, illuminated an auctioneer's lectern. Standing on a step-stool behind the lectern, holding a golden gavel, was Mr Lampy the gnome. He treated me to a denture-filled leer. 'Cages are bespelled,' he said. 'One-way viewing for bidders and barterers only.'

I slapped my hands on the invisible wall of the circle, desperate to escape it, release Ascalon and skewer the disgusting little gnome, the smug Emperor and the heartless Empress. Instead, I snatched up the gold coin with a shaking hand and forced myself to sit. There had to be a way to fix this.

A loud gong sounded, reverberating through the air and the ground beneath me.

'Romulus Augustus,' the gnome shouted, with a flourish of his golden gavel, 'the last Emperor of the Western Roman Empire, and his lady, the Empress Shpresa, welcome you to the Forum Mirabilis. The Forum where anything can be bought or bartered for, if you are prepared to pay the price.' Another more ominous (to me, anyway) gong sounded. 'Ladies, gentleman and Others, please prepare to view our very rare and very special merchandise, gathered exclusively for your delectation on this glorious Summer Solstice night.' The gnome swept his gavel out towards the semi-circle of tents. 'Full details and 360-degree live videos are available on the electronic tablets located in front of your seat.'

A sensation of movement came from the shadowed bleachers on the stage.

The gnome pointed at Katie's cage. 'Immediately to my left is lot number one: an extremely rare, pre-mated pair of ailuranthropes – shifter subspecies: sabre-tooth cat *cinereus* – long thought extinct. As you will see from the details, I have personally performed all the necessary checks on the female, so survival is guaranteed post ritual, as is breeding, if the pair are mated within the specified period of time.'

Fury rolled through me. I wanted to rip the gavel from the pervert gnome's hold and use it to perform every unnecessary check possible on him, before beating him to gnome puree. Instead, I yelled a curse at him, beat my fists against the circle's invisible wall, then yanked my boots off and threw them. One narrowly missed the gnome's nasty lichen-covered skull. The other hit the vamp centurion. He flashed fang and threw it back. It hit my stomach with enough force I doubled over gasping as I slumped to the ground. The other boot smacked my head a second later.

'Next is lot number two: another extremely rare and hard to come by item' – I peered out between my fingers – 'a pre-change ailuranthrope – shifter subspecies: Royal Bengal tiger

– with no bonds of loyalty in place.' As the gnome spoke, the tent next to Katie's disappeared to reveal a man curled in a foetal position, collared and chained much as Katie was. Jonathan Weir, the zoo employee. 'Bidders note that no refunds will be offered if he does not survive the shift.'

He'd survive. Viviane said so, but only to lose his partner later. Sadness flickered through my rage at the Emperor. He'd only given me one coin. And I had to use it to save Katie. But I wasn't going to let David die, I vowed, yanking my boots back on. I'd find some way to stop the Forum's future deterrent. Then I caught sight of the Emperor. A suggestion of a smile wreathed his mouth. He *knew* what was going to happen to David. And that I knew it too. Bastard ... I was going to make *him* pay. Somehow.

I ripped at the dried grass as the gnome continued to extol the Forum's 'merchandise' cage by cage. Number three held a selkie. The one who'd been squatting on the *Golden Hind* – the replica warship – moored on the Thames at Southwark? I decided I didn't want to know. Cage four held a small black Labrador-like puppy. He was listed as a Black Dog, untrained, so his howl could not be guaranteed to bring about immediate death.

There were five swan maidens, evidently numerically appropriate in someone's mind, in cage five. Cage six: a centaur; cage seven: Mini the Minotaur; and cage eight: a hairless cat in a blue sweater. Looked like the Forum's procurers had raided the Carnival's shows to up their auction specials.

I felt bad for them all and, if I could, I'd help them.

Cage nine was another ailuranthrope – shifter subspecies: sabre-tooth cat *cinereus* beta – which apparently meant he'd been Bitten, not Changed by Ritual or Born, so was infertile according to the gnome's candid description, and was bound by loyalty, so was ideally suited for the epicurean markets. Gold Cat stirred inside me, and at her prodding I lifted my head to check: the man in the cage was the third of the grey and black big-cat-shifters. *Steve Dean*, she murmured, her sorrow filtering through my own thought that *Steve* was more baddie than goodie, so while the idea that he was going to end up as some sick fuck's 'Special of the Day' turned my stomach, he really didn't register that high on my 'Person Who Needs Saving' scale.

The kidnapped woman and her son – listed as ailuranthrope shifter subspecies: Royal Bengal tiger – were in cage ten, to be sold either as one lot or separately, dependent on bids. I raked my hands through my hair. Katie was my main concern, but neither she nor I could turn our backs on a little kid and his mother. Fuck. This was so going from bad to evil. It was almost a guilty relief to hear that cage eleven and twelve held a giant squid in a huge glass tank and an Arabian phoenix respectively, and neither were anyone I knew.

'And last we come to lot thirteen, a number of much import I'm sure you'll all agree,' the gnome's excited voice boomed out. 'Thirteen is The Star Of Our Show. A Once In A Lifetime, Never To Be Repeated Offering here at the Forum Mirabilis, or anywhere else, for your delectation. Thirteen is a Creature of Such Rare Heritage that a name is yet to be coined for it, and all of its abilities have yet to be discovered. Ladies, gentleman and Others, please check the catalogue details for lot thirteen's full history, and please ensure you make your bids with care. Payment will, as for all lots, be due in full immediately bidding is closed.'

Again I had the sensation of movement, of anticipation and eagerness, from the shadowed crowd on the stage.

I looked up, vaguely curious despite myself. And was surprised to see even the Emperor was leaning forwards, an expectant expression on his face—

He was watching me. Not the tent where all was about to be revealed.

Fear cramped my stomach.

I jerked my head towards tent thirteen.

The tent vanished.

My heart stuttered.

Inside the cage was a small dog – a Norwegian elkhound – sitting bolt upright, ears pricked, fur a fluffy mix of silver and grey tipped with lime green—

My niece, Freya.

Chapter Fifty-Eight

A booming voice was wittering on about lots, how to bid, how to pay and complimentary refreshments. I wasn't listening. I hugged myself, almost paralysed with panic. And pain. So much pain. Part of me knew the pain radiating through my body wasn't physical, but that didn't matter, I still hurt. Still felt as though my heart had been ripped out. As if it had been chopped in half with a blunt axe, the two halves pierced with silver nails and then shoved burning and broken back in my chest.

Freya. Or Katie.

No way could I choose.

Katie. Or Freya.

No way did I *want* to choose.

Freya.

I slowly opened my hand. Stared at the gold coin in my palm.

Katie.

Blood smeared the coin where I'd clutched it so hard my nails had split my flesh.

Freya was blood of my blood, flesh of my flesh. An eight-year-old child.

The booming voice was saying something about barterers getting the chance to tender their coins for their corresponding 'lot' before open bidding could commence.

Katie wasn't my blood, wasn't my flesh, and was a young adult of seventeen. She'd never agree to my saving her over

467

a child, if she was asked. But that didn't mean I was going to leave her to the wolves.

Rage and determination pushed back the horrified panic and indecision swirling through me.

I was damned if I was going to choose between Katie and Freya. Or anyone else.

I lifted my head, scrubbed my face and took a few deep breaths to clear my mind. I fixed the Emperor, the Empress, the gnome and the anonymous gathering on the stage with a calculating look. No, the only choice I was going to make was who I was going to kill first. And to do that I needed my, so far elusive, plan.

As the gnome sold some smaller, less sought-after lots, the various items held up for viewing by the centurion vamps, while more centurions wandered among the shadowy bidders with platters and jugs, I counted the chain circles behind me. Including the one I was in, there were thirteen, same as the cages. But only twelve of the circles had shadowy figures in them: someone hadn't turned up. I fisted my hand around the gold coin; I couldn't imagine any of Freya's or Katie's relatives not turning up, so whoever's coin I held, there should be someone here for the other girl.

Like Paula, Katie's mum and my friend. Or Ana, Freya's pregnant mother and my niece; we might not get on, but that meant nothing as it was down to Ana's fear for herself and her child. And, same as with Katie and Freya, no way could I live with myself if anything happened to their mothers.

Not to mention there was still the price to be paid for bartering the coins, and the Forum's future deterrent.

No. If anyone was going to be bartering, it had to be me … I eyed my boots, then glanced down at the gold coin in my hand, a plan finally forming in my mind. If I could make it work.

'Hey, Gold Cat, help me save the kits?'

Save kits, she growled low. *Yes.*

She might be my *ùmaidh*, and house a supposedly powerful primal spirit, but her conversational skills were definitely on the basic side.

'Okay, here's what I want you to do,' I said, and pictured a series of images in my mind. When I finished, I stripped my bra off from under my T-shirt, refastened it and held it in front of me. Gold Cat leaped out of my body with a tickling brush of fur, sticking her head through the circle of the bra so it hung round her neck like a wacky-looking collar. I took a moment to check her out. She was virtually transparent, fading fast enough that I doubted she'd last the night. An odd sadness settled in me. I shook it off and released my hold on the bra. Now I wasn't touching it, the Unseen veil I'd taken from my T-shirt and *tagged* to the bra activated, and Gold Cat totally vanished.

'Good luck,' I whispered, then slumped in relief as a barely audible chuff told me she'd crossed the circle. I'd been right; the circle didn't stop things like my boots, the gold coin and the centurion's arm, so it had been *cast* to hold me specifically. Just as when Gold Cat had crossed the circle in the cat-shifters' cave, she registered as 'not me'; she didn't have enough of my soul in her to keep her trapped.

Now I just had to pray she managed to do what I needed. In time.

Another loud gong reverberated through the Forum, signalling the end of what seemed to be a break. I raised my head from the dried grass I'd been plaiting – to take my mind off worrying about how Gold Cat was doing – and saw the gnome adjusting his mike behind the lectern. The Emperor and Empress had also returned. The Empress was carefully tracing glyphs over a black wooden box on her knees, while two of the centurions were washing the Emperor's hands in a wide gold bowl, like the vamp was some sort of decadent despot. Which I guessed he was. In his world. Never in mine.

He waved the two centurions away. The one carrying the bowl knelt at the edge of the stage, deliberately caught my eye, then tipped the bowl on to the grass below. The water was bloody. Nice. Then the faint scent of dark spice, copper and liquorice hit me. Malik's blood. Malik was here. Some part of me had known he was, but his blood confirmed it. And he was hurt. My chest constricted – I glared at the Emperor, but he was listening to another centurion. The Empress, however, was looking at me, her expression tense.

A bright spotlight blinded me.

Looked like my cue.

I rubbed the glare out of my eyes, calming my desperate pulse, and cleared my mind. Malik was a centuries-old immortal vamp, and could heal anything. I had to believe that and not agonise about him. I had to put my plan into action, but Gold Cat hadn't returned. I had to stall—

'Genevieve Nataliya Zakharinova,' the gnome intoned, the mustard-coloured lichen on his head puffing up with importance. 'The time has come for you to barter the Emperor's coin given to you in exchange for that which has been taken by the Forum. For this barter an additional payment is demanded. Your payment will require you to perform a task, here and now, at the Emperor's direction. Should you refuse to barter, or refuse the task, that which the Forum has taken becomes the Forum's property to do with as it will.'

Nothing new there. Good. 'What's the task?'

He looked down at me smugly. 'If you agree you will be told.'

I've got to go in blind? Could it get any better? *C'mon, Gold Cat, hurry up.* I shaded my eyes, squinting up at the gnome. 'What happens if I fail the task?'

'Failure carries the same outcome as refusal.'

Figured. 'What if I am not capable of the task, let's say if I am asked to *stir* and *cast* a simple spell, which is impossible for me to do' – *and wouldn't my life be* so *much easier if that wasn't true* – 'would that be classed as failure?'

'The task is one you are known to be capable of.'

Which sort of narrowed it down to *absorbing*, *cracking*, or *seeing* when it came to magic. Or ripping the gnome's heart out and stomping on it. Only I didn't think I was going to get that lucky. 'What happens to me, and that which the Forum has taken, if I succeed?'

The gnome opened his mouth, then closed it and glanced over at the Emperor. Obviously I wasn't expected to worry about succeeding. I doubted many did. But I'd got Viviane's heads up about the Forum's nasty punchlines.

The Emperor lifted one finger then leaned forwards, raking me with his alien look. I suppressed a shudder. 'If you succeed, Genevieve Nataliya Zakharinova,' he said softly, 'the lot corresponding to my coin tendered will be returned to you.'

Way too unspecific. 'Will the lot be returned in the same physical, psychic, emotional, mental and magical health as when the lot was taken?'

His left eyelid twitched; almost a flicker of impatience. 'I cannot give you an absolute answer to your question.'

Fuck. What had they already done to Katie and Freya? *Don't think about that now. Keep stalling.* 'Will the lot be returned in the same physical, psychic, emotional, mental and magical health as the lot is now, with a guarantee of no harmful ramifications arising in the future to the lot, the lot's nearest and dearest, or to me?'

He stared at me unblinking for a long minute then mild interest sparked in his flat green eyes. It turned my gut liquid with terror and made me want to run away and hide. The only time I'd seen something scarier was the demon last Hallowe'en. I forced myself to keep meeting his gaze.

'I would be a fool to guarantee a lot's emotional health,' he said in his soft voice. 'But I will guarantee that the Forum, which includes all who are a permanent part of it, but not those who are peripheral, will not intentionally change the physical, psychic, mental and magical health of the lot, from the point of your surrendering my coin until that time when your task is completed. If you succeed, I will further guarantee that no harmful ramifications will arise in the future to the lot, the lot's nearest and dearest, or to you from the Forum.'

As he finished speaking, I made a pretence of studying the dead grass in my circle. His guarantee was about as good as I was going to get. Better than usual really, since it appeared to nix the Forum's future deterrent. Though the fact he was prepared to give it was scary in itself. He really wanted me to do his 'task'. It also meant I couldn't stall any longer. Except—

'One last thing,' I said. 'I want you to tell me how to find that which is lost, and how to join that which is sundered, to release the fae's fertility from the pendant and restore it back to them as it was before it was taken.'

The Empress stiffened. The Emperor made a choking sound. It took me a moment to realise he was laughing. 'If you believe I have the answer you require, Genevieve Nataliya Zakharinova, you have been misinformed.'

I froze. He didn't know? But he had to. He was the Emperor. The tarot cards— I hadn't been misinformed. I'd been played for a fool. As had Tavish. Viviane had somehow lied, despite the cards being sidhe-made. Fuck. If she thought I'd burn her cards and set her free now—

Unseen fur brushed against my cheek telling me Gold Cat was finally back, reminding me Viviane's fate could wait. After all, I'd got her cards in my back pocket; she wasn't going anywhere.

An Unseen head nudged my shoulder; Gold Cat had been successful. Relief washed over me, making me dizzy. I swallowed back the fear closing my throat and stood, hands cupped behind my back, feeling her whiskers tickle my palms as she carefully spat out what she carried.

I composed my words, sent another prayer to the gods and held out my fisted left hand to the Emperor.

'I return to you your coin. I agree to perform your task. And when I succeed, you will return that which the coin is payment for under the guarantee you have offered.'

The Emperor treated me to his alien stare, then nodded. 'Agreed.'

A small chime sounded, startling me. I hadn't intended making a sidhe bargain, but looked like the magic was taking an interest in proceedings. Well, I'd just have to suffer whatever the consequences turned out to be; then, as a perplexed line appeared above the Emperor's hawk-like nose, I felt a grim satisfaction. Whatever happened, he'd suffer some sort of consequence from our bargain too, and, if there was any justice, by my hand.

'A sidhe bargain. It will suffice.' The Emperor lifted his finger again. 'Come, Genevieve Nataliya Zakharinova. Give me my coin. Then we shall begin.'

The etched silver and copper chain was swallowed by the earth, and the circle broke with an audible pop.

I strode forward, lifted my hand up and slapped it on the shoulder-height stage, quickly spreading the gold coins (slimy from the Gold Cat's mouth and my sweat) into a ragged line.

Ten gold coins.

Dismay filled me. She'd missed two, or their owners hadn't wanted to give them up.

I took a breath. With the empty chain circle, three lots weren't included in my deal. Fuck.

'You said coin.' It was the Empress who spoke.

I looked up. She was frowning, and the gnome was watching avidly. I hadn't a clue what the shadowy bidders could see, but the blankness of the Emperor's face told me he understood what I'd done. But hey, his problem if he didn't bother to clarify the semantics of the deal.

'Yep, coin,' I agreed, pushing the ten gold coins back into a heap. 'What's the task?'

Chapter Fifty-Nine

It took a few minutes for the imperial pair to vacate the stage, along with a guard of vamp centurions and three tongue-lolling wolves. Then, with the Empress holding the black wooden box like it was about to explode, we all trooped to a large tent half-hidden in the lee of the stage. The tent's sign said: 'Green Room – authorised personnel only'. At the entrance, the imperial pair turned and barred the way, and I had an errant idea that maybe I wasn't 'authorised personnel'. But the churning in my gut told me I wasn't going to be that lucky.

The Emperor held a hand up, one finger pointing towards the sky. Did anyone else have the urge chop his damn finger off, or was it just me? I swallowed back a hysterical snort and told myself to get a grip. As on cue, the Empress adjusted her white-knuckled hold on the black wooden box, opened it and held it so I could see the contents. A knife lay in the black velvet interior; shiny silver blade, twisting horn handle with a teardrop of amber embedded in its end. The hair on my nape stood up as I recognised it.

'Genevieve Nataliya Zakharinova.' The Emperor fixed me with his alien gaze. 'This is Janan, Beloved of Maluk al-Maut, the Bonder of Souls. Forged by the northern dwarves from cold iron and silver, tempered in dragon's breath, with a handle carved from a unicorn's horn and set with a dragon's tear.'

'Yeah,' I said flatly. 'I know what it is.' *Though not how you got it out of hell . . .* unless it hadn't gone there with the demon at Hallowe'en. Which meant someone had snagged it then and kept it until now. I had a choice of someones, but as most were dead, or wouldn't have known what Janan was, only two counted. One was Tavish, but it wasn't him; no way would he let Janan fall into the vamps' clutches. The other was Malik. I didn't like where that thought was taking me, so I didn't follow it.

The Emperor lifted Janan cautiously by his thumb and forefinger, then the Empress bowed her head and stepped back. I gritted my teeth, wanting to grab the knife dangling so temptingly close and plunge it into his heart. But I'd made a sidhe bargain. I couldn't try to kill him until I'd finished his task.

His lips curved down as if he knew what I was thinking. 'Janan can only be wielded by those who have the power to command souls. Deities, demons, angels or their chosen avatars.' He offered me the knife. As he did, the teardrop of amber – the dragon's tear – in its handle seemed to wink at me.

I held my hands up, sensing an out. 'Okay, well, if that's the case, you've got the wrong girl. None of that applies to me, so the task is a bust. I win.'

He ignored me. 'Or by one whose soul has already been removed.'

'Um, I'm pretty sure I still have mine.'

'Or by an *Anima Devoro*; one who can consume souls.'

I opened my mouth to say, nope really not me either— except I couldn't. I could consume souls; I'd got two parked happily inside me right now. Not to mention all those half-formed spirits I'd chomped and spat back out in *Between*, and then there was the first soul I'd eaten; the sorcerer's soul last Hallowe'en. Damn it. It all kept coming back to then.

I scowled at the Emperor. 'I don't know how to use Janan the Soul Bonder,' I said, looking for another way out. No way did I want to start experimenting with anyone's soul, not when

I'd seen what I'd done to the half-formed. They, at least, could reform. Anyone else would just be dead.

'Janan will speak to you at the appropriate time.'

Great. I took the knife, hefted it in my hand and closed my palm round the handle, only slightly disappointed when it did nothing. 'What now?'

He did his finger thing again and one of the centurions pulled back the tent entrance. The Emperor strode through, obviously expecting me to trail after him like a good little soul-bonding sidhe. I took a deep breath and started to follow—

The Empress stopped me with a touch to my arm. 'I pray for your success, Genevieve,' she said, giving me the same pleasant smile as when she'd played kidnapper, her crimson eyes blank.

Success at what? I shrugged away from her hold, and headed into the tent.

And slammed to a halt a couple of feet inside as my mind tried to make sense of what I was seeing.

Whatever contents the Green Room might once have held, were gone. Instead, the fabric sides of the oblong tent were covered in glyphs, the blood used to draw them still shining wetly in the flickering light of the hundreds of fat red pillar candles that guarded the tent's four sides and choked the air with their waxy scent. Marching down the length of the tent were three huge circular sandstone slabs. Each slab had a groove and hand-sized glyphs carved around the outside, and each was large enough that a body could be positioned on them *à la* Leonardo da Vinci's 'Vitruvian Man'.

Like the bodies already spread-eagled on top of the slabs.

The first body was Bastien's. My eyes skipped quickly past him, noting with disappointment that he didn't seem injured, to the second – empty – stone circle and on to the last circle and the body there.

Malik.

Heart thudding desperately, I gazed down at him, hardly realising I'd moved to stand by his slab. His hair had been shaved off, his black eyes were open, staring blankly up, his body still enough to be truly dead. Or immobilised by a spell. Blood-drawn glyphs, similar to the ones on the tent's walls and carved into the stone circles, painted his shaved scalp, bare chest, hands and feet. His skin was pale and almost translucent ... but then all the glyphs on him and in the tent had been drawn using his blood; underneath the choking smell of the candles the air was layered with his dark spice and liquorice scent. The bastards had drained him dry.

Can you hear me? I asked in his head.

Silence.

Do you know I'm here? If you can't speak, then blink ...

Nothing. Not even a twitch.

Fuck. Either he was totally out of it, or he was gagged by the magic.

'Genevieve Nataliya Zakharinova.' The Emperor's measured voice pulled at me.

I raised my eyes to his. We were alone and, but for the bargain, I'd have taken the chance to end him now, before he made me do whatever terrible thing he wanted done to Malik's soul.

The Emperor pointed his finger at Bastien. 'Your task is to remove the two souls bound to that body, separate them, then return the soul that belongs to that body to it without harm.'

Bastien had two souls? His and ... my gaze flicked back down ... Malik's? Bastien's cryptic comment about why Malik wouldn't kill him came back to me: *Because I have long been that part of him that he cares for above all else.* Yeah, so of course, Malik wouldn't kill Bastien, at least not while Malik's own soul was bound to the psycho. It had nothing to do with whether Bastien was Malik's son. Not that my putting two and two together explained why Malik's soul was bound inside Bastien's body in the first place.

The Emperor lifted his finger for my attention. 'The other soul you will bind to me.'

My hand tightened around the knife. 'You want me to bind Malik's soul to your body?'

'Yes.'

'Why?'

'Your task is to do as I direct, not to ask questions.'

'Fine.' I jabbed at him with the knife. 'But remember I'm new to all this, so don't come crying to me if I get it wrong because there's something you haven't told me.'

His left eyelid twitched with impatience. 'Malik al-Khan is a true immortal. He cannot be killed. Whomsoever bears his soul also bears his immortality.'

I rocked back on my heels. Wow! No wonder Malik's soul was the hot ticket item. Vamps might not die of old age or natural causes but they could still be killed. Of course, the older a vamp is the harder it is to bring them true death; it usually takes the complete destruction of their physical bodies with their ashes scattered over running water before their souls are forced to move on to wherever (the general belief is hell). But once a vamp's soul is gone, that's it, they've had it; no chance of reincarnation, unlike humans, or rejoining the magic, unlike fae. So despite the Emperor being a millennium-and-a-half-years old (if he was the original Roman Emperor Romulus Augustus) and probably being harder to kill than most vamps, I could see the attraction of Malik's true immortality.

Only why had the Emperor waited till now to choose to steal Malik's soul? It was a stupid question the moment I thought it. He'd waited because he needed someone who could do the soul transfer: an *Anima Devoro*, in other words— me.

And no one, least of all me, had known I could consume souls until last Hallowe'en.

Maybe I should be surprised it had taken him eight months to get here?

Then again, maybe I should stop thinking everything was about me. No way was I the sole person who could play with souls (because – bad pun aside – someone had obviously transferred Malik's soul to Bastien, at some point) so maybe I should be more surprised, astonished even, not that the Emperor had taken eight months to get here, but that it had taken him five centuries. The Emperor was the one who'd made Malik and despite siccing him with the revenant curse he evidently hadn't known about the immortalising effects of bearing Malik's soul. Which meant someone – Malik, or more likely Bastien – must have let the Emperor in on that little secret.

My hand clenched around the knife as things suddenly clicked into place.

I'd thought that Bastien was running scared of the Emperor, that the Emperor was muscling up to depose Bastien as the Autarch. When in fact Bastien was the one plotting in the corner of his sticky web to trap the Emperor. He'd used Malik's soul, an *Anima Devoro*, a.k.a. me, and Janan, the soul-bonding knife, as his bait. And he'd teamed up with Viviane and her tarot cards to get me here. Not so I could make a choice to save him, but so I could do his dirty work. And kill the Emperor.

So the real question was: what did Bastien gain from the Emperor's death?

More pertinent, if I did choose to kill the Emperor on Bastien's behalf, how the hell was I supposed to do it?

I narrowed my eyes at the imperial vamp. Despite his impatience he'd seemed happy to let me think things through, but then maybe he thought I was communing with Janan or something. Whatever.

Another question struck me. If I was to shift Malik's soul from Bastien to the Emperor then, apart from donating blood which might or might not be specific to the swapping souls bit, what the hell was Malik doing here?

I asked.

'That answer is not relevant.'

I shrugged. 'Told you, on your head be it, if this soul transfer thing doesn't work.'

The Emperor's mouth thinned in irritation. 'Once the current Autarch is vulnerable I will dispose of him publicly. I will become the new Autarch. The Oligarch has agreed to give me his Oath of Fealty. Once I have his Oath, the other blood families will accept me without any needless Challenges and bloodshed, which could raise irritating questions among the human authorities.'

Malik was a willing part of Bastien's plot. Or hey, since Malik was the Machiavellian one, this was Malik's plot all along ... which meant Malik was the one who'd set me up ... *nope, not going there*. But there was one good thing in all this: the Emperor was going to kill Bastien. And Bastien dead was what I'd wanted since I was fourteen. All I had to do was choose to let this whole thing play out and the psycho would be out of my life for ever. I should be delirious with joy ... except his replacement was treating me to his scary alien stare. And hell, the grass wasn't looking any greener or more inviting on the Emperor's side of the blood-fence.

Letting Bastien live was a high price to pay to gain Katie's, Freya's and the rest of the coins' victims' freedom.

Chapter Sixty

'**O**kay, question time's over.' I tapped the knife against my thigh, mind processing everything. 'So you want me to take two souls out of that body, separate them, put one back in, and bind the other to yours.' I jutted my chin at the empty stone circle. 'If you want to make yourself comfortable, we can get on with it.'

The Emperor lifted his finger. 'Genevieve Nataliya Zakharinova. Your task is not successful unless you bind Bastien's soul back into his body, before binding Malik al-Khan's soul to mine. Do not think to confuse the issue by being less than specific, else I will consider your task a failure.'

I grimaced. It was worth a try. Not that I thought he'd fall for it twice. 'Fine. Bastien's soul bound back to his body, and Malik's soul bound to yours. Once that's done, my task and our bargain are complete, yes?'

'Yes.' He nodded, and two of the silent centurions rushed in through the tent entrance and started undressing him. As they finished and were dismissed, and I sincerely didn't want to see him naked any more than I had to, I turned away and knelt down next to Bastien, wondering exactly how Janan the soul-bonding knife was supposed to work. After all, the only time I could see souls was when they were disembodied, like Viviane and Gold Cat.

Turned out soul-bonding is instinctive and easy.

You grip the hilt in your right hand, blade pointing down, lean over and stab it straight into the heart. It goes in like the proverbial hot knife through butter; little things like cutting flesh, cracking ribs and spurting blood don't seem to happen at all. Which was a total tragedy when it came to stabbing Bastien.

I narrowed my eyes at Janan, hilt deep in Bastien's chest, waiting for the blow back, since magic is never that easy without a price, but all that happened was the knife's handle warmed and the dragon's tear on the end glowed with a soft amber light. Then silvery smoke, scented with cloves, spiralled up into a humanoid shape and a recognisable translucent figure formed within it, as if I'd uncorked a bottle and released a djinn. Bastien. He looked down at me, doe-brown eyes calm as if having his soul removed was an everyday occurrence. But then he'd been expecting this. Expecting me to 'save' him.

I cut him a flat look. He was so dead if I had my way.

He blinked, startled, his expression rapidly changing to an almost comical one of anger as he started patting himself as if to check he was actually there, his mouth spitting words I couldn't hear. Evidently, unlike Gold Cat and Viviane, his soul couldn't mind-talk to me. A minor upside to go with my impatience for Malik's soul to put in an appearance.

A few seconds later the heat from the handle began travelling up my arm. As the heat reached my elbow, burning pain flared over my hand and wrist, red blisters bubbling on my skin as if I'd stuck my hand in flame, the dragon's tear turning bright amber, flashing like a warning light. Crap. I knew the knife went in too easy. There had to be some sort of time limit on using it. But there was still no sign of Malik's soul—

I shot a look up at Bastien, suddenly realising what his patting and silent words meant. He was wrapped in shimmering silvery smoke, like an aura. Had to be Malik's soul. Only the dragon's tear was a fiery ember and the knife's handle was scorching hot. Holding it wasn't going to be an option much longer. My gut told me I wouldn't get another chance at this.

Fuck. I didn't know how to separate them. But I couldn't fail. Not with everyone's lives and Malik's soul on the line. Heart pounding with panic, I did the one thing I knew I could. I *focused* on the cool silver aura, and *absorbed* it. It peeled away from Bastien like a banana skin, burning briefly as it sank through my skin and pooled inside me like a ball of moonlight. Bastien sagged, swaying as if blown by a strong wind, horror flashing in his eyes. I reached out and grabbed him, forcing him down through the knife and back into his body. As the last wisp of him disappeared, I yanked the knife out and let it fall.

My palm was seared down to bone, the skin black and cauterised like I'd gripped a red-hot poker; my stomach heaved at the roast flesh smell.

I hugged my arm close, jaw clenched to block the pain, and picked the knife up with my other hand.

I swivelled on my knees, turning to face the Emperor now lying on the second stone circle, his skinny body nude apart from the golden laurel wreath still crowning his head.

He smiled at me. A wide, fang-filled, eager beam. I froze. It was the most human thing he'd done, and it scared me more than any of his flat alien stares. He was a vamp. He was going to be the Autarch. Head Fang over all of Britain's suckers. Malik was going to give him his Oath. And I was acknowledged as Malik's blood-property. He would own Malik, and through him me, and none of those I loved would be safe.

And he would be unkillable.

I had to put Malik's soul in him. That was my task. I'd made a bargain. I couldn't not do it. But no way could I leave it in him. Bastien was a psycho, I still wanted him dead, but at least through whatever dysfunctional relationship they had, Malik could control him. I looked over at Malik trapped by magic on the third stone circle. Did his plan include a way to kill the Emperor once Bastien was dead? But then how could Malik kill the Emperor, if he still bore Malik's soul? And hell, even if he didn't, Malik had a ton of power, but the Emperor still had a good thousand years on him. Not to mention the Emperor had made Malik a vamp.

Fuck. I had to stop this, but I couldn't see how ...

I frowned back at the Emperor and the stone circle he lay on. I couldn't *see* any magic.

Of course—

'Ready or not,' I muttered grimly, then leaned over and plunged the knife into the Emperor's chest. His eyes widened fractionally but he didn't flinch. The dragon's tear flashed to life and the handle heated. Smoke spiralled, bringing the Emperor's soul with it. I gritted my teeth, *called* Malik's soul from inside me and slapped it around the Emperor's. He did flinch at that, face contorting with pain. Good. I grabbed both souls and forced them down the knife and into the Emperor's body, then yanked the knife out, dropping it safely between my knees, shaking my hand to dispel the scalding pain.

Nothing happened. The Emperor's body was still and life-less. Shit, had I done it too fast? Panic choked my throat—

His eyes flickered open and he touched a tentative hand to his chest.

Relief washed the panic away. *Now for the next bit ...* 'I've done all you directed,' I said, surprised my voice came out calm. 'So my task is complete. Agreed?'

He squinted at me, deep lines bracketing his mouth, almost as if he were in agony.

I leaned over, got right in his face. 'Romulus Augustus, I have bonded Malik al-Khan's soul to yours. Are we agreed that I have completed the task to your satisfaction?'

My heart stuttered desperately as his frown deepened. *C'mon, say it!*

'Agreed.' His voice was faint and there was a thread of ques-tion in the word ...

A chime sounded.

… but not enough to stop the magic.

Bargain executed.

I collapsed back on my arse, head bowed, hardly believing it had worked—

It had fucking worked.

Yes! Katie, Freya and the rest were almost safe. One more thing…

Pulse pounding in my ears, I snatched the spells from the glyphs on Malik's stone circle and slammed them into the glyphs carved around the outside of the stone where the Emperor lay. Hoisting him with his own magical petard.

Grabbing up the knife I stabbed it back into his chest again— *C'mon, c'mon…*

His soul appeared, face contorted with rage, mouth flapping silently like a landed fish.

'Do not think to confuse the issue by being less than specific about exactly what you want me to do,' I muttered, then smiled grimly, ripped Malik's soul from around the Emperor's, bundled it tight back inside me, then shoved the Emperor's soul back, jerking the hot knife out with a pain-filled grunt, cradling my hand as I gagged on the reek of my own scorched flesh.

I shot a glance at Bastien still trapped on his circle. *Kill him before or after giving Malik his soul back?* 'Hell, you're not going anywhere,' I muttered, then trembling from adrenalin and expectant exhilaration, I half scrambled, half ran the few feet round to where Malik lay, and dropped to my knees next to him.

Even without the magic holding him, he still showed no signs of reviving from whatever the bastards had done to him. But he was immortal. They could hurt him, but they couldn't kill him. Not ever. Right?

'I have your soul safe here,' I murmured, taking his icy hand

and pressing it to my chest. His soul moved inside me, enfolding my heart within its cool embrace, and a curious peace settled in me. I gently laid his hand down, touched my fingers to my lips then placed them over his own heart. 'Now I give you back your soul, Malik al-Khan.'

I gripped Janan, sent a prayer to any gods listening and sucked in a calming breath – *need to do this right* – then carefully leaned over and positioned the knife above Malik's unbeating heart—

A hand seized my wrist, jerking me up.

A steel-hard arm pinioned me against a hard body.

And a familiar voice said, 'You really do not want to do that, my lovely sidhe princess.'

Chapter Sixty-One

I froze as my old panic and fear flashed through me. Then fury scoured it away. I was done being scared of him, done letting my teenage memories of him rule my life, done letting him play with me like I was some sort of sidhe doll to prod and poke and push around whenever he felt like it. The sadistic psycho was a vamp and without Malik's soul he was mortal.

He could die.

Of course, the psycho would be easier to kill if he wasn't hugging me like a slobbering bear.

I released the knife as he wanted, then grabbed his arms where they banded beneath my breasts to stop him getting me in a choke-hold. Flexing my knees I dropped my body weight, shifting our joint centre of gravity forwards. Jerking my left leg up, I stomped hard on the bridge of his foot, hammering the heel of my boot down like a pile-driver, hearing his foot break with a happy crunching sound. The human foot has twenty-six bones – a quarter of all the bones in the body – thirty-three joints and more than a hundred muscles, tendons and ligaments. And even if the foot is no longer human but vamp, all those bones, joints and other things are still just as easily damaged. Stomping on anyone's foot *hurts*.

A surprised yell blasted my ear and his hold loosened.

In one smooth move, I tightened my left hand on his arm, stepped into a spread-leg sumo-style stance, and double-hammered my elbow back into his groin, grim delight sparking as he let out a high-pitched squeal and started to double over.

Sweeping my right leg behind him, I shoved it into the back of his thigh, further unbalancing him as I hooked my right hand under his leg, heaved him up, and threw him around my hips and down on to his back. He landed with a gratifyingly heavy thud, a startled pain-filled scream whooshing out of his mouth. I backed away, sucking in deep breaths to calm the adrenalin-shakes, working out my options.

Bastien was huddled on the ground in front of the Emperor's slab, hands cupping his Mr Very Unhappy and moaning for England. Vulnerable, if not totally defenceless. The Empress must've released him from his stone. Nice for the Big Girl's Blouse to have his mother watching over him. At least the Emperor was still lying on his stone circle, trapped by his own magic. Totally defenceless. Two vamps with one sword came to mind.

Time for Ascalon.

The ball of green dragonfire engulfed my hand, and grunting through the searing pain from Janan's burns on my palm, I gripped the blessed sword.

I started towards them both.

Mr Moany Bastien stopped his over-the-top whimpering and rose to his feet as if a puppet master had pulled his strings. Creepy.

'Well, well, princess,' he said, backing around the stone slab. 'I see you have your sword again. I take it you intend to dispatch Romulus Augustus with it before he calls any of his minions to the scene. He is a much more dangerous threat than I, is he not?'

I shot Supercilious Smiling Bastien a narrowed look. Killing the Emperor first was playing right into the pyscho's hands. But, much as it irritated me, it was the way to go. 'You're right,' I said coolly. 'The Emperor needs dispatching. First.'

Smiley Bastien inclined his head in acknowledgement. 'I am glad we agree, princess. On that, at least.'

Mentally I flipped him the bird and moved to the Emperor, positioning myself at the top of the stone circle. I looked into his flat alien eyes, then raised Ascalon two-handed over my head and brought the sword down. The blessed blade sliced through the Emperor's neck with absolutely no resistance until it hit the sandstone. But unlike Janan, the sword cleaved cleanly through flesh, muscle, ligaments, tendons, blood vessels and bone, separating the Emperor's laurel-wreathed head from his nude body. His eyes blinked, then his head slowly rolled to the side, stopping to glower at my feet as his crown lodged on the stone. Viscous claret-coloured blood seeped out of his severed neck and pooled beneath his head. I poked the head with the sword, moving it out of reach of the blood – better safe than sorry – then quickly changed my grip on the sword so the blade pointed downwards.

'The heart, my bride,' Eager Bastien urged. 'Do not forget the heart.'

'I know,' I snapped back, thinking *you're next, buddy*. I moved sideways, lining myself up with the Emperor's chest, then stabbed down into his heart; again the blessed steel cut cleanly, resisting only as it bit into the stone beneath. The Emperor's body stiffened, limbs going rigid, then it sunk in on itself like a pricked balloon until all that was left was withered, wrinkled skin over jutting bone.

I poked at the Emperor's remains with the sword. I'd sort of expected something more to happen when ending a millennium-and-a-half-year-old vamp. Not that I'd wanted him to put up a fight, or even thought he could, trapped as he was. Nor was I particularly bothered about killing him while he was defenceless. He was a baddie. And I was pragmatic, not stupid. I'd never have won in a fair fight. If any fight I had with a vamp could ever be called fair.

Of course, his remains would still have to burn, and his ashes scattered to be sure he really wasn't going to pop back up at some point in the future. But still, deflating like that was a pretty anti-climactic end.

Bastien clapped, flashing fang. 'Felicitations, princess. I applaud your swordsmanship.'

I bared my own teeth at him in a smile. 'If you liked that wait till you see what I've got for an Encore.'

'Encores are all well and good, my lovely sidhe, but I do believe we have only seen the Prelude.'

'What the hell does that mean?'

'Behold! Act One!' He threw something at the Emperor— Gold flashed through the air: one of the Emperor's coins.

The Emperor's body twitched and lit itself on fire, the flames burning the cool blue of an ice-dragon's breath. I stumbled back in shock as the blaze licked the tent roof, then spread out and rained down the tent sides, trapping me – and trapping Malik in the roaring inferno. A panicked scream twisted inside me. Even if he was immortal, no way did I want to see him crispy-crittered and endure the pain of healing. If I could get to his stone I could protect us both. All it needed was my blood in the circle's outer groove, and hey presto, one Blood Ward. Only, a curtain of flames burned furiously between us. I'd have to jump and roll to smother—

Bastien lunged forwards and snatched something from the Emperor's stone. The fire snuffed out as if it had never been. All that remained on the slab was a body-shaped pile of ashes. I sagged in relief then scowled at Bastien.

Somehow he'd managed to dress himself in the Emperor's purple toga. He stood with his arms held out like he was offering benediction. In one hand he held the Emperor's gold laurel-wreath crown, and dangling from the other by its dark hair was a small shrunken head the size of a crab apple.

'Here we have Act Two, my sweet sidhe.' He brought the shrunken head to his lips, kissed it, then popped it into his mouth and munched down.

'Nice illusion,' I said drily, trying not to heave.

'Ah, but is it?' He held his finger up much like the Emperor had done. I shuddered, the sight weirding me out. 'Act Three comes, my princess.'

The hair on my nape rose as a low keening wind rushed through the tent's entrance and the Emperor's ashes spiralled up in a small tornado. An unseen hand briefly cupped my cheek with a gentle feeling of gratitude, startling me. Then the wind-gathered ashes exploded outwards and dissipated into the ether, leaving the candles still burning.

Bastien held the golden laurel wreath out before him. 'Now for the Grande Finale.' He placed the gold crown on his head and intoned. 'The Emperor is dead. Long live the Emperor.'

I narrowed my eyes at him as the final piece clicked into place.

Bastien wanted the Emperor dead so he could steal his power. But the real kicker in all of this wasn't that the psycho had set me up to do his dirty work, but that now his (or Malik's?) plotting had made Bastien the Emperor, there was no way I could kill the sadistic sack of shit.

At least, not until he'd told me how to save the fae's trapped fertility.

I gripped Ascalon, battened my frustration down and said flatly, 'Tell me how to find that which is lost, and how to join that which is sundered, to release the fae's fertility from the pendant and restore it back to them as it was before it was taken. And the price you want me to pay.'

Chapter Sixty-Two

'**A**h! And now we come to the Encore.' He raised a mock-ing brow. 'To have something you want, my sweet sidhe, fills me with such glorious anticipation.'

I glowered at him. Sadistic prick was obviously going to spin this out, whereas I wanted it done so I could kill him. 'What's the deal, Bastien?'

'Patience, my princess.' Slyness glinted in Bastien's brown eyes as he moved to squat by Malik. He brushed a hand over Malik's shorn scalp, smudging the glyphs painted there. 'Does my loyal commander, my shadow, my kingmaker not deserve some care first?' He bit into his own arm and held his wrist over Malik's mouth so drops of dark crimson blood splashed on to Malik's parted lips. 'Were it not for his perfect plan none of this would have been possible.' He smiled gleefully.

Fuck. Malik *had* planned it all. He'd used me, put those I'd cared about in danger and all to help Bastien gain power. It felt like his soul turned to ice around my heart and shattered into sharp icicles. Leaving me bleeding. How the hell could I have been so stupid to think that Malik cared for me? That we could have something together? We couldn't. Not if he was prepared to put innocents like Katie and Freya in danger to get what he wanted. Furious and heart-sore, I wanted to shout at Malik, tell him there'd been no need to involve them. Hadn't the Machiavellian vamp understood that if he'd told me his plan, I'd have gone along with it willingly? After all, he'd known I needed to see the Emperor, and I'd told him I'd help. And even if I'd ended up hurt or dead as I had in the past with a couple of his plots, it wasn't as if I'd held it against him—

Malik wasn't the type to put innocents in danger for his own ends.

But Bastien was. Bastien was also the sort to slither like a poisonous snake into my head and sic his mind-mojo on me. Sadistic prick was playing me. And, as an amber glint near Malik's slab caught my eye – the dragon's tear in Janan's handle – I realised Bastien's gameplaying wasn't only for his own amusement. He wanted me angry with Malik because he wanted something from me. Malik's soul.

'You want me to give you his soul back, is that it?' I snapped.

'Actually, my bride' – he lifted one shoulder in a dismissive shrug – 'I do not. It is liberating to be without its depressing weight.'

Depressing? I blinked 'What about its immortality?'

'Ah. It appears that while my loyal shadow and his soul are truly immortal, that immortality is not bestowed on the bearer.'

I frowned. 'But then why—'

'Greed, envy and the lust for power are eternal motivators, my princess. In that the Emperor and my beloved mother, the beautiful Shpresa, were very much alike.' As he spoke a centurion marched into the tent like an automaton. He carried a woman's lifeless body. He laid her down on the stone circle recently vacated by the original Emperor, then saluted Bastien and left.

The Empress.

Bastien looked at her like she was something he'd scraped off his shoe. 'She was the favoured *Ikbal* of Suleiman the Magnificent, Sultan of the Ottoman Empire, powerful, rich, vaunted, her children destined for greatness. But it was not enough. She lusted after eternal youth and beauty and so absconded with

Romulus Augustus willingly. He did not, as some imagined at the time' – he sneered down at Malik – 'force, or persuade her in any way.' He squeezed his arm to reopen his bite wound, so more drops of blood splashed on to Malik's mouth as if he were performing some sort of vamp Chinese water torture. 'Shpresa, as the blood-bound consort to a vampire, gained the immortality the sidhe denied her as a changeling. The Emperor lusted after a sidhe to bond to his blood. It was a match made in mutual delusion and betrayal. He discovered too late she was not the solid gold he sought, but only polished brass. *She* paid for her duplicity with her freedom and the enslavement of her children. But in spite of his Empress' predilection for perfidy' – Bastien squeezed the wound on his arm with a slight grimace – 'the Emperor did not heed the lesson history should have taught him. Once again he let his lust for something he wanted override his good sense, and found the sting in the tail. As we are all wont to do at times, my lovely princess.'

I rolled my eyes, so not appreciating his spouting off about how clever he thought he was. 'I get it,' I said. 'You and Mommie Dearest pulled a fast one on the Emperor. Bully for you. What I was asking, before you so rudely interrupted, was, if Malik's soul doesn't bestow immortality, why the hell did you have it?'

He gave me a smug smile that told me I wasn't going to get an answer.

'Fine. Don't tell me,' I snapped, irritated, 'I'll ask Malik myself when he wakes up. So how about you forget your final curtain speech and let's cut to the deal.' Then I can kill you.

He flashed fang at me. 'I would not think you were so eager for my loyal shadow to wake, my bride. Not when your … situation will dishearten him so.'

'What the hell does that mean?'

He gave me a sideways look. 'My loyal commander might not be recovered for some time, even with my blood' – he lifted

495

his chin and sniffed – 'so it may be that the stink of the satyr will have faded somewhat by then. Your *secret* is safe with me.'

Fucking vamp supersenses.

I cast a concerned look at Malik, wondering if he could hear. It didn't matter that I thought Malik would understand how it had happened; it would still hurt. If it had been the other way round … *damn it*, I'd be hurt too, devastated, even. In fact, I *was* devastated about Finn, Gold Cat and the whole mating thing: it was a heartrending muddle of epic proportions. But it wasn't something I'd planned keeping secret from anyone, let alone Malik. It would turn what happened from a muddle that could be sorted into a nasty festering sore that would come back and bite me and everyone else. But I had hoped to pick my moment, not have Malik hear it from Bastien, especially not with the spiteful spin the sadistic prick was bound to add.

'That.' I jabbed Ascalon at Bastien. 'Is none of your business.'

'I quite agree, my lovely sidhe.' He stood, keeping his gaze on me as he licked the wound on his arm with obvious enjoyment. I frowned at Malik. He looked as pale and lifeless as before; Bastien's meagre donation didn't seem to done anything. Still Bastien wasn't the only one with blood. If Malik didn't wake up after I gave him his soul back, I'd feed him myself. And if Bastien was finished—

'Look,' I said, forcing a conciliatory tone. 'You want something from me. I want my question answered. So let's get things sorted.'

'I will be delighted to, my bride.' He lifted a creepy finger. 'When the time is right.'

'Which is when?'

'When the last tarot card appears, of course. Or have you forgotten that part of the proceedings?' I hadn't, but since he and Viv were in league with each other, I doubted the last card was going to tell me anything Bastien didn't already know. 'Now I must leave you and greet my new subjects. Until anon.' He turned on his heel, marching away, toga flapping around his knees. The previous Emperor had been about a foot shorter, and, I noted bitchily, Bastien had the legs of a scrawny chicken.

'You told me you didn't know,' I shouted after him. 'And the Emperor told me the same.'

He swung back, anger twisting his face. Accusing a vamp as old as he was of lying, even if only by suggestion, was a huge insult. Not that I cared if it got me the answer I needed.

'Knowledge is one side of the equation, bean sidhe, application is the other. Two plus two do not become four until one understands how they should be tallied. A tally, in this instance, that will not be complete until the last tarot card has been read.'

He turned and left, leaving me scowling after him.

In other words, Bastien had known part of the answer but not the whole of it until he'd munched on the Emperor, and now he had to confer with his scheming spirit sidekick. Crap. I wanted to run after him, lop his scrawny legs off at the knees, skewer Ascalon through his sadistic heart and turn him into a magical bonfire. Reluctantly, I let Ascalon slide back into the ring, wondering how long the sadistic psycho was going to make me sweat. And what price he wanted.

'As if I can't guess,' I muttered, glowering at the dead Empress. After all, I couldn't count the number of times he'd called me 'my princess', 'my bride', or 'my sidhe'. Still, he wouldn't be the first vamp to get my blood-bond and, like the last one, I'd be happy to make sure the psycho's ashes ended up feeding the fish in the River Thames.

Frustrated and angry, I sighed and took stock. I needed to go and 'claim' Katie, Freya and the rest of my bartered auction lots and get them to safety. But first, Malik needed his soul back.

Gingerly, I scooped Janan up, glad my hands had started healing—

A shimmering, transparent figure padded into the tent carrying something in her mouth.

Gold Cat.

Chapter Sixty-Three

Gold Cat padded over and dropped what she was carrying in front of me. It squirmed around then scrambled to its feet. Mr Lampy, the gnome, though how she'd managed to haul him round in her fading state was anyone's guess.

'Ms Taylor,' the gnome spluttered, smoothing the ruffled lichen on his head. 'I really must object to this animal's treatment of me.'

Gold Cat coughed. My mind translated the cough as *Hungry?*

I frowned. 'Hungry?'

'Ms Taylor,' the gnome objected. 'You can't—'

Gold Cat batted the gnome off his feet and coughed again. *You. Hungry?*

Oh, she'd brought me a present, like a cat bringing a mouse. Which was sort of … gross. 'Um, no thanks.'

Mine.

I wrinkled my nose at her, not sure if she was kidding. 'Are you sure? A juicy steak might be better. He doesn't look very appetising.'

'Ms Taylor—'

Gold Cat snarled in his face, baring huge sabre-tooth sharp canines, then when he started squealing like a stuck pig, shut him up with a large paw on his mouth.

Hurt kits.

Ah. She wasn't joking, and she wasn't hungry for food as much as revenge. 'Rather you than me,' I said, nudging the disgusting gnome with my toe. 'But if you want him, have him.' I let Ascalon free. 'Do you need him skewered first?'

The gnome gave a muffled squeak.

No.

Fair enough. Though really even eaten alive was way too good a fate for him, but … I grinned at her. *Bon appétit.*

Police troll here.

Hugh was here? Heart in my mouth, I rushed to the tent entrance. Sure enough the place was swarming with trolls and witches wearing the Met's Magic and Murder Squads' hi-vis yellow waistcoats. The cavalry had arrived.

My knees almost buckled with relief.

And right in the centre of the yellow-waistcoated mass was the solid, ruddy-coloured bulk of a black-haired troll in a pristine white shirt and black trousers, organising the rescue. (Acting) Detective Inspector Hugh Munro. Hugh would take care of everyone. I trusted him with my life. More, I trusted him with the lives of those I loved. I shouted, jumping up and down, waving my arms to catch his attention, then when he saw me I gave him a double thumbs-up to say I was okay, and held my hands up, fingers splayed. 'Ten mins,' I mouthed.

As he nodded, Gold Cat padded past me carrying the protesting gnome.

I grabbed her by her scruff. 'Don't forget our deal. I save both kits, you tell me how to undo the mating with Finn.'

Her lip curled, copper-coloured whiskers stiffening. *Take stronger mate. Break mate-bond with satyr.*

I rocked back on my heels, stunned. I had to mate with someone stronger to stop being mated to Finn? That wasn't exactly a winning solution for me. Damn it. I'd imagined an invocation to the gods, or some sort of spell or ritual—

'How do I take a stronger mate?'

Circle. Share flesh. His seed in you. Gold Cat's tone suggested

I was stupid not to know that. She tugged out of my hold and padded away to disappear into the darkness beneath the stage with the struggling gnome. I stared after her, thoughtful.

If all I needed was a bit of mutual cannibalism (ugh) and sex with someone more powerful than Finn, well, that probably gave me the option of a good ten per cent of London's fae as a starter. Not that I had any intention of going down the 'another mate' route. But at least the answer wasn't one of those Herculean tasks. In fact, if I ignored the whole ick factor, it actually seemed way too easy an out.

Something to investigate later, once everyone was safe. And Malik had his soul back.

I rolled my shoulders and turned back to where he lay on the stone circle.

Dropping to my knees, I placed my palm on his chest. Despite his heart not beating, and his skin hard and cold like stone, not living flesh, he didn't seem like a vamp who'd been drained dry, but more as if he were in his daylight sleep. But the tent was painted in his blood. So never mind what he looked like, or the stingy couple of mouthfuls Bastien had dripped into him, which even with his Autarch's power would no more quench a vamp's thirst than two drops of rain in a drought, it was always possible Malik would wake to full bloodlust. Not a particularly reassuring thought, but I wanted him to have his soul back.

Though really, it wasn't like I didn't have plenty of blood to spare. Thanks to my time in *Between*, I hadn't donated for two nights. Nor had I sated my body's need for vamp venom with blood-fruit. With my sidhe metabolism, that was like a week to a human and the 3V addiction rioting in my cells was near enough at its ideal. My venom levels not so low for the craving to be vital, and my blood levels high enough that losing two or three pints wasn't going to do anything more than treat both of us to a good time.

Anticipation speeding my pulse, I positioned Janan's silver point over his heart—

Malik's eyes flew open, power flamed hot in his pupils, and his hand clamped round my wrist. 'No.'

Malik's order snapped around my mind like a net. I resisted automatically. The net tightened, then broke and shredded to nothing. I jolted in surprise and the blade's point pierced his flesh.

He groaned as if in agony, then too fast for me to counter, I was on my back, arms pinned above my head, his legs straddling my thighs, his body atop mine, all four of his fangs fully out, his eyes black and opaque with no hint of recognition in them.

My childhood training kicked in and I forced myself to lie still, concentrating on slowing my thudding heart; struggling with a vamp gets them too excited, makes them more likely to rip your throat out by mistake.

After a long perilous moment, he gave a slow blink. 'Genevieve?'

I frowned at the question in his voice. If he was lucid enough to ask, he shouldn't need to. 'Yes.'

His nostrils flared and the reason clicked in my mind. Damn vamp supersenses. As Mad Max and Bastien had both *oh, so helpfully* pointed out, I smelled of more than just me. And damn Bastien. I had a sudden inkling the sadistic prick had deliberately given Malik just enough blood to get him up and reacting instead of thinking. Malik either sensed I wasn't totally me, thanks to Gold Cat's recent residence, or Finn's scent on me had triggered his territorial instincts. Neither of which was good.

'It's okay,' I said, keeping my voice calm, despite the anxious knot in my gut. 'I'm not possessed or anything.' I released my bracelet, hearing the quiet chink of charms. 'See, I'm still wearing the cross.'

He gave another slow blink, nostrils flaring again. 'The scent of fae and blackberries clings to you.' A mix of accusation and anger lit fire in his pupils.

'I can explain,' I said quickly, not that I particularly wanted to right now, nor was I sure an explanation would work … hungry/territorial vamps aren't too big on listening. I held my breath, flinching as a sudden gust of wind buffeted the tent, flapping the entrance wide for a moment then, as it ruffled my hair and cooled the sweat prickling my skin, Malik visibly reached for control. His needle-sharp venom fangs retracted, the tension in his muscles relaxed and the flames in his pupils flickered out, leaving behind a sea of anguish and concern.

'Explain?' A concerned line furrowed his brows. 'Are you hurt, Genevieve?'

I frowned. 'No. I'm fine.'

The furrow deepened. 'Have you been forced against your wishes?'

'What? No, of course not.' Surely he knew Finn would never do that.

Desolation flickered in his eyes, spearing an odd grief through my heart. 'You were willing, then,' he murmured, his face blanking to his usual enigmatic mask. He glanced at where he pinned my wrists and his grip loosened as he suddenly seemed to realise he'd been holding me captive. 'My apologies.' His tone was as remote as if we were strangers. And then vamp-quick he was gone, leaving me scowling in disbelief up at the peaked roof of the tent.

Did he think I'd had sex with Finn deliberately? After what had happened between us on the island? Was this some sort of jealous snit? Or was his blood hunger screwing with his mind? The only one way to find out, as Hugh would tell me, was to ask.

I scrambled up, ready to demand what he was playing at, only to find him staring at the Empress.

My heart went out to him. 'I'm sorry,' I said, and I was. I didn't know her, and didn't particularly want to. But even if he hadn't seen her for centuries, and even if Bastien's story about her hitching up with the Emperor was true, Malik must have cared for her at some point. Losing someone hurts.

After another long moment, he raised his gaze to mine; beneath his carefully blank look, he seemed relieved, not sad or angry. 'The Emperor is dead.'

'Yes,' I said, even though it was a statement, not a question. Obviously he was aware that his wife, though ex-wife was probably more appropriate, only got to live as long as she did thanks to her blood-bond with the Emperor. If she'd expected a new blood-bond with a vamp as reward for her part in the plotting, then she'd pretty much lost that gamble.

He scanned around the tent as if searching, spied Janan and scooped the knife up, then attacked a pile of clothes in one corner. As I watched, feeling oddly redundant, he efficiently turned out pockets and patted the clothes down, then pulled on jeans and a shirt, both black. They fit, so had to be his. He slipped Janan into the back of the jeans in a practised move, then strode back to contemplate the Empress again and demanded, 'Where are the Emperor's ashes?'

Of course, he'd know the Emperor would go up in flames once he was dead. As Bastien had gleefully informed me, the whole 'fool-the-Emperor-into-thinking-he-was-getting-Malik's-immortality-sting' had been Malik's plan.

I frowned, not happy he was virtually ignoring me. 'A wind blew them into the ether.'

'All of them?' he queried, still not looking at me.

'No. His head sort of shrank and Bastien ate it before the ashes dissipated.'

Malik's shoulders slumped as if in defeat.

'I take it that's bad?' I asked, more for something to get him talking. Because no way in hell was it good.

'It was not meant to happen this way,' Malik murmured, almost to himself. 'I was to be the one to wield Janan, not you. No one but I knew that you could also use the Bonder of Souls.'

Yeah, not even me. 'So how did Bastien find out? Because I take it he was the one who decided to add me in as an extra to your plan?'

Malik gave a sharp shake of his head. 'I do not know how he discovered it. It was only after your mention of Janan at the lake that I realised something was amiss. After our time together—'

'When you decided to send me home without consulting me,' I interrupted flatly.

'I hoped to keep you safe, Genevieve,' he said, voice toneless.

I settled for a loud huff – he knew my thoughts about that – and said, 'So, what happened after you sent me home?'

'I learned Bastien had deviated from the plan we had agreed.' A puzzled frown drew his mouth down. 'He has not done that in centuries.'

Right. Well, my bet was that a certain leannán sidhe had a hand in inspiring Bastien's deviation, but I didn't say it. I also didn't say that maybe if Malik hadn't kept me out of the loop, I might have had a chance to destroy the Emperor's head along with the rest of him. As it was, the psycho had taken me by surprise. And he'd chomped the Emperor now, so recriminations were sort of meaningless. But there was one thing I needed Malik to tell me.

'Bastien says now he's the Emperor he can put two and two together and tell me how to release the fae's trapped fertility.' Or in other words: *did you know that the sadistic prick knew? And if so, why the hell didn't you tell me?*

'My apologies, Genevieve,' he said, still staring at the side of tent. 'Bastien gave me his word not to harm, or even speak to you in person so long as I did not divulge to another that he knew of the original spell to trap the fae's fertility. Since you recovered the pendant I have been negotiating with Bastien for the information you and the fae require.'

So Bastien had him over a barrel because of me. Damn exasperating, over-protective vamp. 'Thanks, but now I know I can do my own negotiating. And I plan to as soon as I've double-checked everyone is safe.'

'Speaking to Bastien will put you in danger—'

'Malik.' I threw my hands up. 'I've told you, you can't protect me from everything. And I don't want you to. You need to tell me what's going on, let me make my own decisions about what to do, or not do, and then at least if I end up in danger, I'll know how and why I got there. And I'm not stupid; if I need help, you can bet I'll ask for it.' *Unlike you, you stubborn idiot*, I added silently, balling my hands in frustration. 'Same way I told you to ask me if you needed help. And okay if it was just your business and you didn't want my help, fair enough. But it wasn't. This was my business too. Hell, maybe if I'd been part of the plan from the beginning, or got to talk to Bastien, then he and the spirit of the tarot cards wouldn't have got together, I might have got decent warnings from her and prevented Katie and Freya ending up here in the Forum.' All right so maybe I wasn't above getting on the recrimination bandwagon.

Malik's jaw went rigid, bone jutting sharp against his pale skin. 'I did not intend for any innocents to be put at risk.'

'Of course you didn't,' I agreed with a sigh, despite the fact he *still* wasn't looking at me. 'It's not your style. I'm just saying you shouldn't keep me in the dark, and you don't have to do everything alone.'

He smoothed a hand over his shaved head, brushing off the dried blood from the smudged glyphs there. He stared down at the rust-coloured flakes sticking to his palm as if they were able to predict his future then clenched his fist. 'My apologies, Genevieve, you are right. If you would allow me, I would assist you in your negotiations with Bastien. In order to expedite matters, I would request some of the power your blood holds. I would not ask, were it not of importance to you.'

Chapter Sixty-Four

He wanted to assist me, did he? Well, no way was I going to refuse an offer like that, but first he could damn well stop acting like talking to me was akin to sucking garlic. 'On one condition,' I said flatly.

'Which is?'

'You listen to my explanation about what happened with Finn.'

He turned, fixing his gaze somewhere near my left ear. 'I do not require you to explain. It is your choice alone who you decide to bed. You have said you were willing—'

'No,' I said, gritting my teeth at his *oh so polite* tone. '*You* said I was willing. *I* told you Finn didn't force me. There's a whole lot of story in between that.'

'I do not need to be told a story, Genevieve.' His eyes met mine for a moment, his black and pitiless. 'In truth, I would prefer not to listen to one.'

'Listen, buddy.' I thumped him in the chest. 'Things happened between Finn and me. Things which were not entirely of either our choice. So stop assuming you know what's going on.'

He slowly met my eyes again, anger flickering. 'You are saying I am an ass?'

'Yep. But hey' – I grinned, though it was more a baring of teeth – 'I won't hold it against you; we all assume things at times.' Like I had. Good thing he hadn't seen the blackmail threat I'd sent him. Yet. I suppressed a shudder. 'I've just had more time to think my assumptions through.'

He was silent for a long moment then raised an elegant, not quite mocking brow. 'Then I will, of course, listen, Genevieve.'

'Great,' I said drily. 'Only it's a long story, so maybe we should leave it until later? Say, when you're less volatile?'

Tension sang through his body, then he inclined his head in acknowledgement. 'It might be wise, yes.'

'Though there was one thing' – I pursed my lips, waved at the Empress and took the plunge – 'was she your wife?'

An odd, startled look crossed his face, followed by a longer, more pensive one. 'You believed Shpresa was my wife?'

Did that mean she wasn't? Hope lit in me. I tamped it down, keeping my voice dust dry. 'I believe I might have made that assumption at certain points during the last day or so, yes.'

'I see.'

The two small words were bland, giving nothing away, but underneath I sensed he was pleased at the 'assumption' I'd jumped to, and was now ... *stretching the answer out* ... I crossed my arms and gave him a narrowed look. 'Well?'

The last of the tension between us dissipated as his mouth softened into a barely there smile. 'I have never had a wife, Genevieve.' He cast a look at the Empress, his smile fading. 'Shpresa was my mother.'

His mother? I reached out, touched his arm. 'I'm sorry.'

'Thank you,' he said softly. 'But she was aware this would happen. It was her choice.'

Which didn't make it any less sad for him. Though if Shpresa was his mother ... 'So,' I said tentatively, 'Bastien's your brother?'

He nodded. 'Half-bother, yes. His father was Suleiman.'

Half-brother? Still not wonderful, but way better than son. And the Empress on the tarot card telling me to save her children made even more sense now. She wasn't just talking about Bastien and his vamps, but Malik too. 'Ah. Right. So who was your father?'

'As with your story, that is one for another time.' His enigmatic mask reappeared as if a switch had been flipped. Looked like I'd hit a sore point. Still we'd have plenty of time for talking about all sorts of things, later. 'Now, Genevieve, I would drink, please. If you are agreeable?'

I glanced at the dead Empress, uncomfortable. 'Here?'

'No. Not here.' He held his hand out.

I placed my hand in his and he led me to the far side of the tent. The heavy material sliced open with a touch from Janan. We stepped outside into a small shadowed area enclosed by high, dense bushes, the only light from the stars studding the night sky above us.

We stood, my hand in his as anticipation stretched a taut line between us. 'Do you wish me to drink from the wrist?' His question was neutral, but a dark intensity glittered in the black depths of his eyes.

'Hmm,' I murmured. 'It seems practical, unless you have a better idea.' I let a smile ghost my lips.

'I believe I may.' He inclined his head, the glitter taking on a heart-fluttering promise as his gaze turned dark with need and possession. Pulling me into his embrace as if leading me into a dance, he moulded my back against the firm planes of his chest. 'Genevieve.' His murmur grazed my hair, causing my heart to race. His tongue traced the sensitive whorl of my ear and I gave a small, surprised yelp as he nipped the tender lobe, then sucked it hard into his mouth, making my knees weak. Dark spice and honeysuckle entwined in the air; our scents mingling. My breathing quickened as lust coiled inside me, and a blood-flush electrified my body in readiness for his bite. I let my head fall back to his shoulder, offering him my throat, the pulse there jumping beneath my skin as desperate need and joyous desire collided inside me. His hold about me strengthened and I felt the thick hard length of him press against me, ready and eager.

He cupped my cheek, his thumb gently circling the vulnerable spot beneath my jaw. 'How long, Genevieve?' His murmured question glided over my collarbone like a summer breeze.

'Two nights.' My own whisper was breathless. Two nights since I'd satisfied my body's craving for vamp venom.

A low growl vibrated through him as his lips marked a heated trail from my ear to my pulse. His mouth closed over it, the teasing press of fangs drawing a whimper of need from me. For an achingly long, heart-thudding moment he held me, his arms wrapped about me, his mouth at my throat, only the thin barrier of my skin separating us. Then he pierced my flesh.

Pleasure, sharp and exquisite, sliced through me as his venom shot into my veins. But even as my body reacted in fierce delight to the demanding draw of his mouth, the feeling morphed, twisting into excruciating, torturous agony. I screamed, throwing myself away from him, only to have my legs give way as I collapsed on the grass, shaking with pain-filled aftershocks.

I slapped a hand over my bleeding neck and gaped up at him. 'What the—?' My croaked demand stuttered. He was staring with enough horror that an errant part of me wondered if I'd suddenly grown three heads, half-a-dozen assorted limbs and shifted into some sort of monster.

'What the hell was that?' I croaked again.

He crouched before me, with none of his usual elegance, his body radiating panic, whispered, 'You bear my soul, Genevieve.'

'Yeah,' I said, shivering as I realised it wasn't only Malik who was panicked; his soul was too. The ball of silvery light felt like it had stuck claws into my body; the source of all the pain. 'How else was I going to give it back to you?'

He pulled Janan from behind him. 'You will allow me to transfer it to this.'

511

I frowned, then remembered him telling me Malak al-Maut, whose knife Janan was, had used the knife to carry those souls he'd collected. 'Sure—'

He stabbed me in the chest, the stench of burning flesh hit me and Malik gave an agonised yell, his hand spasaming open.

I stared in shock at the blade buried to the hilt between my breasts, its amber dragon's tear flashing like a warning beacon, instinctively thinking it should hurt, and that there should be blood. Only, of course, it was a soul-bonding knife; there was no blood, and if there was any pain the claws piercing my body eclipsed it. I swallowed then looked at him. 'Give a girl some notice next time ...' I trailed off. Pink-tinged sweat beaded his forehead, his stare fixed on the knife in dismayed disbelief. 'What's wrong?'

'It refused!'

'What did?'

'My soul.' He grabbed my wrist, yanking me to my feet. 'Come. We must find Bastien. You must bond my soul back to him.'

I bit back a scream as the claws gripped harder at Bastien's name. No way did Malik's soul like that idea. 'Why can't you have it back?' I said, then yelped as the claws shrank back and tried to burrow inside my heart; his soul obviously wasn't on board with that suggestion either.

A shudder rippled through Malik. 'It does not like the revenant.'

I opened my mouth. Then shut it again. We were heading back into weird possession/alter-ID territory again and I didn't feel up to debating it, not with his soul chiming sharply in on the discussion too.

'Bastien said he didn't want your soul back,' I told him.

'He will.' Resolve crossed Malik's face. 'You should not have bonded my soul to yours, Genevieve.'

'I didn't bond them,' I said. 'I'm an *Anima Devoro*, remember?'

Shock flashed in his eyes. 'You *ate* my soul.'

'No, of course not. I *absorbed* it. It was happy about it so it's not hurt. That only happens when the soul or spirit objects.'

He released me, horror filling his eyes. 'How many souls have you eaten, Genevieve?'

'Stop looking like that,' I said, annoyed. 'It was only some of the half-formed in *Between* and I spat the pieces back out again. They'll stick themselves back together soon enough; maybe even manage better shapes next time. Oh, and the two that didn't fight' – Viviane and Gold Cat – 'are fine. Same as your soul' – I placed a hand over my heart – 'it was here, quiet as a mouse, until you bit me, so why not leave it—'

He shook his head, eyes blazing. 'My soul is damaged, Genevieve. It will cause you harm. You have seen how Bastien is.'

I blinked. 'Bastien is a crazy psycho because he had your soul?'

'Yes.'

I frowned, recalling Malik's harem memory and the child Bastien ripping his sister's doll apart. He'd seemed pretty much fully-fledged as a psychopath back then. 'Did Bastien have your soul as a child?'

Malik swiped an anxious hand over his head. 'No, he did not. He took it some years after I was cursed with the revenant. Come, we must find him.' He took my wrist again.

'Wait!' I pulled out of his hold. 'I can't wander around with a knife-hilt sticking out of my chest. People will freak out.' I carefully wrapped my hand around the flashing dragon's tear, hesitated, then, under Malik's worried gaze, yanked it out. As far as I could tell, my own soul stayed in place, seeing as I didn't drop down dead or float off with the breeze, as did Malik's; its claws still had their death-grip on my heart.

I tucked Janan safely in the back of my jeans. 'Right,' I said, pleased my voice only shook slightly. 'Let's go and find Bastien, but remember, the priority here is to get the info about the fae's trapped fertility out of him. We can worry about your soul later, okay?'

'I do not think—' He stopped, stared up at the heavens as if entreating some god, then just as I was about to push the point, he took a breath he didn't need. 'We will do that, Genevieve.'

'Right.' I rubbed my breastbone as the pain there vanished. Malik's soul had sheathed its claws the second he'd agreed and was now back to being a soft ball of silvery light. Damn. It was determined to become a permanent resident. *Later*.

'So,' I said, 'did you get enough of my blood for whatever it was you were planning to do?' Not that I thought either of us were up to him trying to bite me again.

'It is possible, but we shall see.' His mouth twisted and he offered his hand, wary. I took it just as cautiously, braced for the claws. Nothing. We both sighed in relief.

He held the slashed tent open and we stepped back in together.

Waiting for us was Bastien.

Chapter Sixty-Five

Bastien flashed fangs. 'Well, well, my loyal shadow and my lovely sidhe princess.'

Malik stepped smoothly between me and Bastien. 'Our agreement was that you should cause Genevieve no harm, Emir.' His voice was soft with threat. 'You will take my soul back now; else I will consider it broken.'

'You know I have not broken any agreements, Abd al-Malik. The sidhe took your soul of her own volition.'

'Genevieve would not have been in a position to do so, had you not altered the plan. This is—'

Malik fell silent as Bastien held up one finger then treated me to a gleeful smile. Dread crawled down my spine as I leaned forward to look at Malik. He was frozen, his beautiful face etched with anger and determination.

Crap. Looked like Malik didn't get enough of the power in my blood. And going by Bastien's expression, he hadn't had the juice to trap Malik before. Damn. I so didn't want to find out what other little extras chomping the Emperor's head had given the psycho.

He waggled his finger at me. 'I find my elevation to Emperor is proving to be immensely enjoyable, my sweet bride.' He gave the statue-like Malik a delighted poke.

'You mean the power you stole,' I said flatly.

'Stealing? Ah, yes, it appears thieves abound. For instance, did you know there is another who looks exactly as you do? I believe she may have stolen your identity.'

Confusion winged through me. 'What the hell are you talking about?'

Bastien whirled away, his toga flaring about him, calling, 'Come and I will show you.'

Heart pounding, I raced after him, barely noticing the four werewolves who had taken up sphinx-like positions around the Empress on her stone, to a spot outside in the lee of the stage.

Bastien waved a hand at the open space with its chain circles and cages. 'Behold!'

I looked. And stared in horror, my eyes refusing to believe what they were seeing.

The place was a hive of movement. Hugh's boys and girls in blue had corralled the vamp centurions and a crowd of folk dressed in their designer best, who had to be the auction bidders, into some of the cages. And now they were taking statements from the huddle of Others who were obviously the 'lots' from the cages and their 'coin-holders' from the chain circles. But despite all the activity under the fierce glare of the halogen spotlights, my eyes fixed on the small group gathered at the heart of it all.

I, or someone who looked enough like me, right down to my black jeans and T-shirt, that *I* couldn't tell the difference, was standing talking to Hugh, Tavish and Finn. Bastien said something, but his words didn't register past the pulse thundering in my ears. Finn had his hand protectively on the imposter's shoulder, his horns curving up in full threat mode. Tavish had a nimbus of watery power surrounding him like an aura – a personal Ward – and, held securely in his arms, was a bundle of brown fluff that I recognised as Freya, my niece in her doggy form. The imposter had her arm round Katie, hugging her close. And loitering a few feet away from Katie, his shoulders hunched over, was Katie's treacherous 'boyfriend', Marc, the big-cat-shifter.

It was his gaze, fixed unerringly on the imposter, which tipped me off.

She was Gold Cat. Somehow she'd got herself enough power to make herself solid and then Glamour herself up to look like me, then she'd pulled a fast one and taken my place. And none of my friends appeared to know the difference ...

Gold Cat

Gold Cat hugged the trembling girl as she sank into the sliver of 'Genny' inside her, searching for— *ah, the trembling girl was called Katie, and was much loved.* She hugged *Katie* closer, in spite of the acrid stink of fear, sweat, werewolf and the faint remnants of some disgusting perfume that clung to her. But beneath the stink were the cleaner scents of will and strength and courage. *Katie* was a good choice to breed the next generation of their pride. Gold Cat looked over at the young male, *Marc*, nodding her approval. He jutted his chin, angry and frightened for the girl – *protective. He'd make her a good mate* – and confused for himself, but not enough to tell the rest gathered around them here, on this, the Summer Solstice, that Gold Cat was not who they thought. Not their 'Genny'.

How's it going? The voice of the leannán sidhe came in Gold Cat's head. *You finding your paws okay?*

Yes. But not every "lot" is here. There are three missing. The gnome continued with the auction in the Emperor's absence. The part of me that is Genny is worried about the missing, as is her police friend, the mountain troll. Do you know what has become of them?

'Hmm, let me see … Ah, yes, here's one. Lot number eight, the hairless cat in the blue jumper.'

Everyone froze as a tarot card appeared in front of Gold Cat. The card showed a tall, shimmering gold female, with shapely devil's horns and a magnificent peacock tail, standing in one of the silver and copper chain circles. As soon as the gnome released her from the circle, the female smacked him on the head with her coin, then ran over, yanked open the cage and scooped the cat up, raining kisses on his hairless head before the pair vanished with a pop.

'I wonder what misfortune will befall them from the gold coins,' Gold Cat said, as the smiling image of the leannán sidhe, twirling her lavender parasol, took the pair's place on the card.

'Oh, I would not worry about them. I hear she has connections in low places. Very hot, low places. Like one of the lowest levels of H.E.L.L.'

'Hell is a place I have never visited,' Gold Cat said.

The leannán sidhe laughed. 'You should work on your delivery. You don't sound like the bean sidhe at all. You need to add some attitude. Oh, and your breasts are too big. The bean sidhe's are smaller.'

Gold Cat scrutinised her generous proportions. Were they too large? The sliver of Genny thought so, though something else seemed to be encouraging Gold Cat to add to Genny's slender curves. But she couldn't afford to draw attention to her Glamour. Reluctantly, she adjusted her shape and size down. 'I appreciate the advice,' she told the leannán sidhe. 'What befell— happened to the other two lots?'

The leannán sidhe tilted her head. 'Now, who else didn't give you their coin? Oh, yes, the selkie. His ex-wife kept it. She didn't want to lose her shot at revenge after he abandoned her and their kids to go back to sea. But she didn't barter for him. A man from the *Golden Hind* bought him.'

'I am confused. Has the selkie not been ... squatting in the *Golden Hind* for the last few months?'

'The ship on the River Thames, yes. He's been quite the tourist draw. But his purchaser owns another replica, one in Devon. He wants the selkie so he can use him to drum up trade down there. Which is where the selkie's family lives anyway.'

'Why is … what's the catch in that?'

'Well done! That sounded more like the bean sidhe,' Viviane nodded approval. 'The catch is the selkie's wife will keep his skin, and all his wages as alimony. Wrong decision, really, she should have let him go. This way neither of them will be happy.'

'That is unfortunate.'

'Oh, he's got a better outcome than lot number nine. One of your pride's ailuranthropes, I believe. No coin-holder turned up for him.'

'Yes. Steve Dean. My pride memories tell me he was a human turned accidently by a Bite. He was given a position as one of the pride protectors.'

'Well, Mr Kaito, International Purveyor of Rare Epicurean Delicacies, bid the highest at the auction for Steve Dean, so Steve is now on his way to the next Tōhoku Fukushima Annual Charity Banquet. He is to be the main course.'

Gold Cat frowned. 'Can he be rescued?'

'He's already on ice.'

'Ice? Does that mean he is dead?'

'Yep.'

'This makes me sad,' Gold Cat said. 'It also makes me glad I consumed the gnome.'

'How was he?' the leannán sidhe enquired.

Gold Cat hawked and spat. 'Ancient, big power, but bad taste.'

'What about the satyr?'

A satisfied smile spread across Gold Cat's face and she purred before she could stop herself. 'The satyr is a good mate.'

'Glad it worked out for you,' the leannán sidhe said, her tone envious. 'Well, I shall return to my cards now. I have one last reading to do for the bean sidhe then I shall gain my freedom. I wish you good luck.'

The world around Gold Cat unfroze and she plucked the tarot card from the air before it dropped. 'Good luck to you too, leannán sidhe' she murmured. *I owe you one, as Genny would say.*

'Everything okay, Gen?' The satyr's concerned voice was warm against her ear.

She smiled at him. 'Soon will be.' She waved at the hive of activity in front of her. 'Once we sort things out with Hugh and this is all over. Then we can go home.' Which would be the second test.

She'd already passed the first test when the kelpie – *Tavish* – the one who could taste souls, had shown himself as the coin-holder for the small fluffy dog – *Freya, niece, sort of,* the sliver of Genny reminded her – though that sliver had been surprised and intrigued that Tavish was the one who'd come for the little shapeshifting faeling. Gold Cat hadn't been interested enough to ask why. An oversight, she realised now, and something she'd need to rectify. Soon. Consuming the ancient gnome had given her power and living flesh. Shaping that flesh to replicate Genny had been easy, coating her spirit with the sliver of Genny's soul not much harder, but the true test, as the leannán sidhe had pointed out, lay in aping Genny's personality.

A human male approached – *Bangladeshi ambassador* – and Finn gave her shoulder a reassuring squeeze before leading Katie away.

'Ambassador,' Gold Cat said, injecting her tone with interest and sympathy; two things she did not feel, but the sliver of Genny did. 'How can I help?'

The ambassador, his grey suit crumpled, orange and black striped tie loose about his neck, bowed in front of her, relief plain on his lined face and offered 'Genny' his gratitude for his part in rescuing his wife and their son. As Gold Cat listened, she shaded her eyes against the glare from the bright mechanical candles on metal sticks – *halogen lights* – the sliver of Carlson's soul that she'd retained informed her. The world had moved on since last she'd walked it in human skin rather than fur, and with her own spirit almost intact. She had a lot to learn from the slivers inside her.

'… we would be delighted to grant you a boon, Lady Genevieve,' the ambassador finished quietly, 'should you require one in the future.'

'That's very kind,' Gold Cat said, echoing his deep bow, then felt a prickle of irritation as Genny's sliver noted she wouldn't have bowed; too archaic. 'Thank you, Ambassador.' Gold Cat forced her mouth to smile. 'And thank your wife too.'

'My wife and I wish to extend our gratitude to Mr Jonathan Weir, the zoo's employee, for his heroic attempt to save our son, Dakkhin. We would not want Mr Weir to suffer for his actions. Unfortunately, the magic in the Bite cannot be taken back. However, Dakkhin is a godling; the grandson of Byaghradevi, the guardian of the Sundarbans, the beautiful jungle. Dakkin wishes to repay Mr Weir's sacrifice by offering him his blessing. It will ensure Mr Weir will survive the shift. My wife would also offer to care for Mr Weir during this difficult time.'

Byaghradevi, the guardian of the Sundarbans. One of the minor Indian goddesses. A part of Gold Cat remembered meeting her once, millennia ago. Inwardly, she licked her lips; they'd feasted well together on the jungle's two-legged inhabitants. She searched Genny's sliver for the appropriate answer to the ambassador.

'Fine by me, Ambassador,' she said. 'But maybe you should check with Jonathan Weir and his partner, who gave up his gold coin. It should be their decision, really.'

The ambassador gave his agreement to do so and moved away, his place taken by the five swan maidens dancing gracefully up to her with their thanks. The three dwarves who had been their collective coin-holder milled anxiously around the scantily feathered girls, getting affectionate, if somewhat sharp pecks on their bald pates for their fussing. The two centaurs came next and offered their own gruff gratitude, then after a mildly suggestive twirl of their 'taches, cantered off towards the Carnival where a spontaneous celebratory party appeared to be getting under way.

Mini the Minotaur stomped up and proffered her thanks by way of a free chase in her labyrinth to the pot of gold, then swung her coin-holder, the leprechaun, up on to her shoulder. The leprechaun gave a long-suffering sigh and grabbed one of Mini's horns, and they too strolled off in the direction of the party, with a saucy flip of Mini's tail.

The Arabian phoenix flew past with a grateful dip of its wings then joined her coin-holder, the chipped concrete troll with his fast-food cart. The bird landed on the cart's burner, scoffed down a fireproof bun as the troll turned the flames up, and, whistling off-tune, pushed the cart towards the rest of the Others.

A fae male in a strange pirate outfit approached. He'd been hanging around the giant squid's tank. Gold Cat licked her lips at the enticing scent of fish drifting from him then gave a small growl of disappointment. The male – *Ricou, dressed in his Captain Jack Sparrow Glamour* – lived with Genny as a ... *flatmate? – Ah, part of her pride* – It disappointed Gold Cat that she wouldn't be able to eat Ricou either in this guise or the male's true naiad form. He smelled like he'd taste delicious.

'Hello, luv, how's tricks?' the pirate said cheerfully. 'Hear you've had a busy time of it.'

'Hey, Ricou.' She twisted her mouth in a grin. 'Didn't expect to see you here.'

Ricou pointed at the giant squid madly waving three of its tentacles. 'That's Gustaf, he's Bertha's pal.'

The name Bertha produced an image of a huge angry eel

in Gold Cat's mind. An angry eel with very sharp teeth that delighted in terrorising Genny. 'Bertha's got a pal?'

Ricou twirled his beard. 'Bertha got a bit upset when old Gustaf didn't turn up the other night, so I've been out looking for him. Wasn't till she spat out a gold coin that it clicked what had gone on. She couldn't come herself, obviously, so I did the honours. Thanks for saving him, luv.'

'No worries,' she replied. 'Maybe Bertha will stop trying to take chunks out of me now.' And if not, the eel would make a tasty meal in place of the naiad.

He made a high clicking sound: *laughter*. 'She might, luv, you never know. I'll get him home and see you later. Sylvia's looking forward to catching up on the gossip.'

'Sure,' Gold Cat agreed, thinking gossip was not something she was accustomed to. Or overly interested in. Nor was she interested in talking to Sylvia, the other flatmate. Dryads were only useful when it came to sharpening one's claws.

The kelpie sauntered towards her, the small faeling dog nipping playfully at his heels. Trailing after them was a small black Labrador-like puppy. As they neared, the Black Dog puppy lifted its head and fixed Gold Cat with its red eyes. Fear slammed into her and she almost shifted and killed it before she remembered she wasn't herself; she'd deal with the Black Dog later. It was still a puppy so there was time to reverse its Prophecy of Death.

The kelpie indicated the tarot card Gold Cat held. 'I'm thinking that card holds our answer, doll,' he said, the beads on his dreads flashing an eager green.

Gold Cat forced her attention away from the Black Dog and looked down at the card. Against a blue velvet background it showed two images. The top image was of a Fabergé egg encrusted with sapphires and diamonds. The image below showed the same egg, but open, and nestled inside it was the sapphire pendant that contained the fae's trapped fertility. The sliver of Genny recognised it as the Fabergé egg the sorcerer had used to trap souls last Hallowe'en, and was surprised and frustrated that she'd let it slip through her fingers more than once.

'Yep, this is what we're looking for.' Gold Cat held the card up to show the kelpie, twisting her face with worry. 'But it was lost in the demon attack. It's in the River Thames somewhere.'

The kelpie's eyes swirled black with satisfaction. 'If 'tis in the river then 'tis as good as found.'

'Good to know.' Gold Cat handed him the card. And the problem. The only fertility she was interested in was that of her pride.

As if on cue, Finn wrapped an arm around her shoulders. 'That's everyone safe and sound, Gen. And Hugh says he'll catch up with us tomorrow. Ready to go to the party and celebrate with the rest?'

Gold Cat smiled. She had a lot to celebrate, not least the satyr. 'How about we have our own party at home?'

He dropped a butterfly-light kiss on her mouth. 'If you're sure that's what you want, Gen?'

Gold Cat glanced over her shoulder to where the real Genny stared from the lee of the stage, anger and the urge to kill radiating from her. Gold Cat stiffened subtly, her hackles rising as the Death she'd seen in the Black Dog's eyes flashed before her. She readied to defend herself, then as Genny slowly stepped back into the shadows, Gold Cat relaxed and turned to the satyr.

She smiled and cupped Finn's cheek. 'Oh, I'm very sure that us together is what I want.' *Mate.*

Genny

The evil, life-stealing cat had her hands on Finn!

Rage and fear exploded in me, Ascalon leaped into my hand, and I ran—

Straight into an invisible wall. I bounced off, landing painfully on my tailbone, and belatedly *looked*. The blue curtain of a Ward shimmered like a heatwave, the grey drops of a Look-away veil distorting it like sheeting rain.

I *focused*, ready to *crack* the Ward and Look-away, then froze as Bastien spoke. 'Before you go racing off to demand satisfaction, my lovely sidhe, there is one small matter we need to discuss.'

I turned to find him with a gleeful smile on his sadistic teenage face. 'What?'

'I believe you have a set of tarot cards. Now would be an excellent time to consult them.'

I stared at him for a long moment, wanting nothing more than to plunge Ascalon into his heart as I'd done in the Dreamscape, then do the same to Gold Cat. Instead, I forced myself to stay calm, to play this out to the end. I let Ascalon slip back into the ring, slowly got up, and fished the cards from my back pocket. A gust of jasmine-scented wind blasted my hair back as one card flew to hover in front of my face.

The last tarot card.

The last tarot card didn't need my blood, it already depicted an image. A male and female stood side by side, a plump cherub floating on a sunny cloud above and the Rod of Asclepius with its entwined serpent between them. The female figure was Sylvia, hands protectively spread over her pregnant belly and the sapphire fertility pendant nestled between her 'Hello Boys' breasts. The male figure was Bastien, crowned with his new imperial laurel wreath and (thankfully, since he was naked too) holding a misty grey disc about the size of a dinner plate strategically in front of him.

Of course, the last card would be The Lovers. The sadistic prick would revel in the irony of it. Especially as this was no doubt where the smarmy smiling psycho asked for my blood-bond and my body in exchange for telling me the answer to my question. Trouble was, I hadn't a clue how I was going to get out of saying yes.

I curled my lip in disgust, hiding the dread icing my spine and flicked the card. 'Hurry it up.'

Sylvia on the card gave me a tremulous smile I'd never seen on her in person. 'You have a choice to make, Genny. It has to be made now, and if you make the wrong decision, then what has gone before will not matter; the fae's fertility will never be recovered, it will be lost for ever and the fae will die.' Her hands clutched at her bump.

I glared at Real Life Bastien. 'Do you really think I'm going to believe that bullshit? When I know you and Viv have been in league since the beginning?'

He shrugged and tapped the card. Sylvia vanished to be replaced by Viviane, twirling her parasol with an affronted expression on her face. 'The cards are sidhe-made, bean sidhe, so speak the truth. I can influence them to show less, but I cannot make them lie. You would do well to listen to them.'

Right. 'What's the choice?'

She reached over and touched the shoulder of Bastien in the card. A ripple ran through the picture and he blinked, then looked out of the card at me and flashed fang.

'Ask your original question and he must answer truthfully,' Viviane said.

I snorted. 'Tell me how to find that which is lost, and how to join that which is sundered, to release the fae's fertility from the pendant and restore it back to them as it was before it was taken.'

'That which is lost is already found,' Card Bastien said, and from behind the misty disc-thing he produced a Fabergé egg encrusted with sapphires. My heart stuttered as I recognised it as the one lost in the demon attack at Hallowe'en. Shit. I'd had the answer to the fae's problem in my hands (or rather the bank) until the sorcerer had stolen the egg, and I'd never fucking known it. And now Smugly Smiling Bastien had it. I wanted to scream in frustration.

Real Life Bastien's smile widened. 'I know who has the Fabergé egg and on my word they have agreed to give it to you.'

'Who's got it?' I demanded. 'And when will you tell them to give it to me?'

Both Bastiens shook their heads, not that I'd expected anything else, then Card Bastien said, 'To join that which is sundered and release the fae's fertility from the pendant and restore it back to them as it was before it was taken, you will need this.' He held up the misty grey disc and flashed something else. Thankfully, the tarot card was small, and everything else smaller, making it easy to ignore. 'You will obtain it and bring it back to me.'

I gritted my teeth. 'What is it, who has it and where is it?'

'First you must agree the price.'

'What's the price?'

Both Bastiens closed their eyes, Card Bastien rubbing his fingers over the disc in a show of deep thought.

I clenched my fists as impatience warred with anxiety. The sadist knew exactly what he wanted; he was only drawing this out to make me sweat. While I needed this over with. Needed to do the bargain. Then I could kill Gold Cat and make sure my friends were all safe. Hug Katie and Freya. Talk things through with Finn. Tell Tavish how to restore the fae's fertility. Get back to Spellcrackers and my life, away from all this craziness. And find out what happened next between me and Malik. Only, the roiling in my gut told me some, maybe even all, of that probably wasn't going to happen.

Finally, Card Bastien nodded as if he'd come to a decision. 'You are to keep Malik al-Khan's soul.'

Surprise washed through me. Okay, that was unexpected and not necessarily a deal breaker—

'No, Genevieve. You will not.'

—for me anyway. I winced as Malik's shouted order clamped my mind, and his soul speared its claws into my heart. Then Malik's order cracked and melted like ice caught in fire. I shot an astonished look over my shoulder to see him striding towards us, flames burning in his pupils, black shadows writhing about him in fury.

Real Life Bastien gave a grunt of disgust and, out the corner of my eye, I saw him lift his finger again and Malik and his shadows froze. I turned back to scowl at the psycho unease shivering over me. Bastien was determined to be rid of Malik's soul, Malik was just as determined I shouldn't have it, while his soul looked like it was clinging – literally – to my heart. And I was the one stuck in the middle. I didn't need any of Viv's predictions to tell me this wasn't going to end well.

Bastien waggled his finger. 'You will notice, my princess, that while you bear my loyal shadow's soul you are no longer under his sway. He can no longer order you to do his bidding. Am I correct?'

Ah, well, that explained why Malik's order didn't take. Not that I was going to tell the psycho he was right. 'Get on with it.'

'You will also find you no longer carry his marks on your

flesh.' He waved a dismissive hand at me and I resisted the urge to check the bruises on my wrist and my chest, refusing to give him a milligram of satisfaction. 'I believe that is what you wanted; to be the one in control of your life. To not have other people making decisions for you. To make your own choices, on your own terms. Well, now you can, my lovely sidhe.'

He was repeating – almost word for word – what I'd told Tavish at the gnome's house right before the first tarot card reading. Fucking Viviane, earwigging on private conversations. And never mind what Bastien said, stripping Malik of the power to order me around didn't instantly grant me control of my life. Or stop self-satisfied sacks of shit like Bastien from blackmailing me.

'Fine!' I snapped. 'Your price for giving me the information I need to be able to sort out the fae's fertility is to keep Malik's soul. I—'

'Not so fast, princess,' he interrupted, angry colour staining his cheeks. Inwardly, I cursed. I'd known he'd want more, but I'd nearly had him. 'There are two parts to your question,' he said, 'so there are two parts to my price. The first is that you are to keep Malik's soul until either he agrees to take it back, or I agree its transfer to myself or another.'

Now we were getting to it. 'What's the second?'

'When you attain that' – he pointed at the misty disc Card Bastien was holding – 'I am to have first use of it before any other.'

I clamped down on my shock. He didn't want my blood-bond? Was this a trick? I narrowed my eyes. 'Will your first use in any way negate or destroy the disc's power, or stop it from having the ability to join that which is sundered and release the fae's fertility from the pendant, so that their fertility is restored to all as it was before it was taken, in an acceptable time frame – which I would nominate as no longer than three human-world days – or in any way deny the fae the use of the disc immediately after you?'

'No.'

Nice unequivocal answer, so no deal-breaker there. Something which had suspicion twitching over my skin. Really, if I ignored Malik's agitation about keeping his soul, it was way too easy. 'What's the disc?'

'An item of great power,' Bastien said, an ecstatic expression lighting his face.

Figured. 'Does it have a name?'

'The Hidden Rune of Iron.'

Well, at least it wasn't the Holy Grail or a Golden Fleece. 'What's it do?'

He gave me a look as if it were a stupid question. 'One of its other names is the Restorer.'

I cut him a look. 'What do you want to restore?'

He smiled.

I shrugged. 'So where is it?'

'The Hidden Rune of Iron is also thus named due to its ephemeral nature which makes it difficult to locate.'

Damn. Easy just got hard.

A sly look crossed his face. 'But I have it on good authority that it has been seen recently at The Court of Love and Beauty in the Fair Lands.'

Crap. Hard just hit dangerous. An impossible to find magical item, and— 'The queen of that Court is Clíona, my grandmother.'

He inclined his head. 'Then maybe she can be of assistance to you, my princess, and your quest will be concluded quickly.'

Concluded and quick it would be, but not because I'd find the Rune. 'My grandmother wants me dead.'

'Well, well, not everything in life is convenient.'

He'd got that right.

On the card, Viviane twirled her parasol. 'The time has

come for you to choose, bean sidhe. Do you accept Bastien's price, or not?'

'So I keep Malik's soul and attain this Hidden Rune of Iron under the exact conditions specified, and at that point you will ensure that the person who has the Fabergé egg will give the egg to me, or to any of London's fae, with all knowledge that they have about the item, in its undamaged condition.'

A frown lined his brows. 'The egg will be undamaged from their possession, as for anything else, I cannot say.'

I grunted in acknowledgement. 'Fair enough. So that's it? There's nothing else?' Like wanting my blood-bond?

Bastien smiled. 'There is one other condition.'

Of course there was. 'What?'

'Time is of the essence,' Card Bastien said. 'You must leave now. No stopping to converse with your friends or anyone else. Otherwise the opportunity to attain the rune will be lost.'

I rocked back on my heels. 'You're kidding me?'

'He cannot lie, bean sidhe,' Viviane said softly. 'His spirit is guided by the cards.'

I looked away from the card to the open space, at those I loved gathered around Gold Cat the imposter. If I left now, with her there, they might never know I was gone ...

An ache closed my throat; my eyes stung. I took a deep breath, swallowed the threatening tears back. No way would I give Bastien the satisfaction of seeing how much leaving would hurt. Then panic overwhelmed that hurt as something way more crucial hit me. Gold Cat was out for survival, her own and her pride, and ruthless with it. If I left now, who knew what she'd do to Katie, and to Finn. And Bastien's price meant I couldn't even warn them, let alone protect them—

I had Ascalon. I could kill her.

It would take no more than a minute.

Or ten.

Or she'd fight back, and even with Ascalon I might not be a match for a primal spirit. Then what if I killed her? There'd still be the fallout. Ten minutes could end up an hour or more ...

But no way did I trust Bastien or Viviane's tarot cards not to skew things in their favour. For all I knew I could have days, weeks even, before the chance to locate the Rune was lost. But could I take that risk when the fae's fertility was at stake, and ultimately their lives too?

In a weird déjà vu moment, I realised I'd been here before, not this exact spot, and not this exact choice, but I was still making a decision that would affect them all. But as Tavish had told me, it was my blood on both my fae and vamp sides that had started this. I was the key. If I screwed up and chose wrong it wasn't only Katie and Finn in peril, but Tavish and Ana and Freya and Sylvia and Ricou and Baby Grace and all the rest. They were all fae. They would all die.

My heart hurting as if it were being ripped in two, I turned back at Bastien.

'Well, what choice do you make, my sweet sidhe?'

I pointed at Malik a get-out-of-the-deal idea sparking. 'Unfreeze him, or there's no deal.'

One eyebrow rose, then Bastien smiled. My stomach sank – he looked way too pleased with himself – as Malik's hand closed on my arm. I turned and gave him a short and not-so-sweet update, then asked, 'Do you know who holds the Fabergé egg?'

Malik's eyes emptied, turning opaque as black glass as he flicked a look towards Bastien. 'No, I do not.'

Damn. Bastien's reaction had told me that would be Malik's answer, but I'd still hoped. I clenched my fist around Ascalon's ring. Maybe I should just kill the psycho vamp and take the chance that, with Malik's help, I could find the egg.

Bastien laughed, the sound grating on my ears. 'Oh, yes,

one more point. If I die, then the one who holds the Fabergé egg will destroy it.'

Fuck. He was right. I couldn't kill him. Not yet. Not till I had the egg in my hands. And no way was he going to give me that before I got the rune.

'Genevieve.' Malik took my hand in his and drew me aside. 'You do not have to do this. I will fetch this rune you need. Give my soul back to Bastien, stay here and help your friends, and live your life. Let me do this for you.'

My heart filled with warmth, and more, that he would offer.

But I had to do this. I knew it in my gut.

I had to make this journey.

I kept my gaze on Malik, but spoke to Bastien and the magic. 'I agree the terms.'

A chime split the air. The sound reverberated inside me. Bargain made.

I took a shaky breath. Then another stronger one, and gave Malik a grim smile. 'Looks like I'm leaving for the Fair Lands.'

Malik's hand tightened around mine, my own resolve reflecting in the black depths of his eyes. 'Then, Genevieve, we shall go together.'

**Read more about Genny's
adventures in**

THE HIDDEN RUNE OF IRON

Coming soon from Gollancz

Acknowledgements

Writing a book is a solitary endeavour but getting it from first draft to publication takes a lot of hard work, encouragement and support from a wonderful and generous group of people. My deepest thanks and appreciation to everyone whose help has made this book a thousand times better, any errors are my own.

As with all my books, the characters in this one are a product of my imagination and bear no relation to any real people, living, dead or otherwise ... except for where they do!

So grateful thanks to Steve Dean for his generous support in the Genre for Japan auction and for agreeing to be a baddie and suffering a suitably horrible fate! I hope you like your tuckerisation! And to Jonathan Weir, publicist extraordinaire at Gollancz, for allowing me to take his and David O'Reilly's names in vain, and for being eminently bribeable, err, kindly arranging for me to meet one of my all-time writerly heros – the fabulous Charlaine Harris.

Thanks to John Jarrold, my agent, for his belief in me; thanks to all the Gollancz crew for their support, commitment and the gorgeous new covers; and especially to Gillian Redfearn, editor magnifique, for her patience, her words of editorial wisdom, and her enthusiasm for Genny & Co.

Thanks to the Thursday Writers, a truly inspiring bunch: Malcolm Angel, Alison Aquilina, Judy Monckton, and Doreen Cory, who have travelled this amazing journey with me from the start.

Thanks to my wonderful intrepid beta readers: Caroline Allard, Hasna Saadani, Reece Notley, Lisa Wynn, Calie Voorhis, Ailsa Floyd, Marc Mullinex, and Jen Neil, you all rock, bigtime!

Thanks to Jaye Wells, my always awesome crit partner (look out for the Giguhl Easter eggs!), and to the amazing Ann Aguirre for their superb writerly back-up and advice.

Special thanks to Che Gilson for her endless encouragement.

To Norman, my love, my best friend, and the light in my life, without you the dreams would not be possible, or mean as much – thank you, now and always.

And last, but not least, a massive thank you to all you readers who have taken my books into your hearts – I truly hope you enjoy this latest adventure of Genny & Co's!

Suzanne McLeod
Dorset